Prais…
Mark Chisnell

The Defector

'An excellent drug-smuggling thriller.'
The Bookseller

'This is a remarkable thriller – chillingly violent, full of tension and with a very original ending.'
Publishing News

'New British fiction writer Mark Chisnell will have to go a long way to top his debut.'
Bristol Observer

'A fabulous and brilliantly written story.'
Peterborough Evening Telegraph

'What an impressive debut it makes … Compelling, hard to put down.'
City Mix Auckland

'A taut thriller... *The Defector* allowed Chisnell to create Janac, a truly memorable anti-hero.'
The Press, Christchurch

'An evil storyline, with little relief and with great tension created.'
Hawke's Bay Today

'This thriller has pace and immediacy.'
Wairarapa Times-Age

'Throw in a love triangle, the microcosm of a boat at sea and some good sailing and you've got a fine yarn... Chisnell has managed to create a smart and articulate villain, always the best kind.'
Sailing Magazine, USA

'The culmination of the game will astound you.'
Trade-a-Boat, NZ

'Never, never, never would I read a psychological thriller ... Just as well, then, that I didn't read the description on the back cover until after I'd finished the book, and by then was too breathless, terrified and awed to care.... The book's strength is the author's confident, original, at times tawdry, writing style.'
Boating New Zealand

The Wrecking Crew

'It's a great escapist yarn with Janac a really nasty villain who gives Hamnet untold grief. I enjoyed this one.'
Hawkes Bay Today

'I found it impossible to put down.'
Boating New Zealand

'A real ripping yarn... begging to be made into an all-action film.'
Qantas in-flight magazine

'Perfect for summer reading.'
CityMix Auckland

To Jeremy

The Fulcrum Files

Very Best Wishes

Mark Chisnell

ISBN-13: 978-1470197780
ISBN-10: 1470197782

This first paperback edition was printed by CreateSpace.

www.markchisnell.com

Also by
Mark Chisnell

Fiction

The Defector
The Wrecking Crew

Non-fiction

Risk to Gain
Spanish Castle to White Night
Pressure Falling – Short Stories of Stormy Seas
Sailing Gold

For Tina

The Fulcrum Files

Fulcrum

1. The point or support on which a lever pivots
2. An agent through which vital powers are exercised

Prologue

Saturday, 26 September 1922

Ben Clayton sagged onto the stool in the corner of the ring. His legs were shaking and his arms were heavy, the gloves hanging off them like lead weights. He sucked the air back in quick, harsh gulps, but it was thick and smoky and provided little relief. He tugged at the vest, slabbed to his skin with sweat, the blood rushing through his ears so hard he could barely hear Mr Daly's words.

'He may be bigger and stronger, but you are quicker and smarter – now use your head and stick to the plan,' said Daly.

Ben was only vaguely aware of the faces peering up at him, eyes ablaze under a sea of flat caps. The bodies, smelling of beer, horses and engine oil, were pressed hard up against the canvas all around the ring. The crowd faded quickly back into the darkness, the clamour of the conversations ebbing and flowing around him. Daly's deft movements with the sponge wiped the sweat out of his eyes, and Ben could see clearly across the ring. Slater was staring at him.

'Go in low. His hands are always too bloody high. When you get in under him he drops 'em for a while. It puts him off balance, that's when you try to take his bloody 'ead off.'

Ben nodded, coughed and spat. He didn't take his eyes off Slater.

'One more round, and I reckon you're only a couple of points behind. This is not over by a long way,' hissed Daly.

Ben nodded again. The water from the sponge was ice-cold on his chest. The rushing in his ears receded. The bell rang.

'All right, lad, off you go, and remember the bloody plan,' finished Daly.

Ben stood. Daly ducked out of the ring, taking the stool with him. The referee waved them forward. Ben took three quick steps and then went up onto his toes. This had to be quick. He only had a couple of good punches left in him. Slater went for an early right as Ben came onto him. Ben slid under it and managed to get in a double to his ribcage. He felt the second blow connect all the way back down to his toes. Slater stepped back. Ben kept going forward. Slater twitched and dropped his hands as Ben ducked in towards him with a feinted right-cross to the body. If Slater saw the left coming for his head he didn't move fast enough to do anything about it.

Ben's blow crunched home on the other boy's chin. Slater went down as if he'd melted. Ben stepped back, too tired to raise his arms, but anyone could see that Slater wouldn't be getting up any time soon. Suddenly, there were people everywhere. They pushed past him and crowded around Slater. He heard the words in snatches, the meaning lodging in his gut like ice from Daly's bucket.

'He's out cold. ...'

'Is he breathing? ...'

'Bloody hell, get a doctor. ...'

'No, get a car, we'll take him straight down to Dr Finnegan. ...'

'The hospital's not much further. ...'

Then Mr Daly was in front of him, holding his shoulders, his hot beery breath in Ben's face. 'It doesn't look good, lad, I better go with them. Are you all right to get home on your own? Your dad's not here tonight, is he?'

Ben locked onto Daly's worried eyes, and heard himself say, 'I'm not going home, I want go to the hospital with him.'

Chapter 1

Friday, 28 February 1936

Ben Clayton first saw her as she moved onto the covered aft deck of the MV *May*, a thousand tons of resplendent luxury motor yacht, moored a few dozen yards away. She was a young woman of about his age, pushing tresses of jet-black hair off her face with one hand as she lit a cigarette with the other. And she was quite something, he thought, as she strolled to meet a glistening Riva launch at the *May*'s boarding platform. The exotic, unfashionably long hair tumbled onto a mink stole thrown casually over her shoulders, her slim frame outlined by the pencil-thin, camel-hair coat. She held the cigarette in a long holder. A thread of smoke drifted from her lips. He couldn't have been more intrigued if it had been Greta Garbo playing Mata Hari – *who was she?*

The Riva's engine revs built, throbbing out across the oily waters of Portsmouth Harbour as soon as she was seated. The white-uniformed helmsman turned the boat towards where Ben stood aboard the *Windflower*, 130 feet of just-launched, flush-rivet-plated racing yacht, still moored at her builder's quay. Camper and Nicholsons was the oldest yacht-building yard in the world, and right now it was also the most prolific. Almost everything of any size that raced at Cowes Week came from the board of their brilliant designer, Charles Nicholson. Never mind all the big, fancy motor yachts that would watch the racing, boats like the MV *May*, luxurious floating homes for the smart set. They too were all designed and built in this Gosport yard, right opposite the Portsmouth Royal Navy base.

Ben pushed himself up from the winch that he was sitting on to meet her at the gangway. She disembarked from the Riva with the same easy grace, hesitating only to finish her cigarette before stepping aboard. 'Can I help you, Miss ...' he asked, taking a quick glance at her feet, but the elegant court shoes had no heels to damage the brand-new yellow-pine planking.

'Anna,' she said in a husky, warm, Home Counties English with the faintest trace of something more exotic, a tiny foreign inflection.

There was no clue in the reply as to what she was doing there, and why she felt sufficiently emboldened to come aboard the *Windflower* without so much as a by-your-leave. If there was an answer, it was in her presence aboard the *May* – both vessels were owned by Harold Dunwood, along with much else besides.

'So, where is everyone?' she asked. 'Harold seemed to think that there was an absolutely *frantic* amount to do today.' She waved up at the crane that had just lifted the mast into the yacht, still attached, as it would be until they had all the rigging in place.

'The crew are having a cup of tea, getting warmed up after a soaking in that last downpour. We don't need them for a while, not until Stanley Arbethwaite comes back. He's down below, talking to Mr Dunwood,' he replied.

'Ah, I was wondering where Harold had got to,' she noted. Then she added, 'Mr Arbethwaite is obviously very important.'

'Yes ... he designed the mast; it's unique, revolutionary, and he's the only one who can really set up the rigging. In fact, I think he'd probably strangle anyone that tried to do it for him,' Ben replied, with a slight smile.

'I don't suppose you could spare a cigarette?' he added, lifting the soaking arms of his reefer jacket. 'Mine got a little wet.'

She flipped open her quilted Chanel handbag and pulled out a slim silver case. He took the offered cigarette, and then discovered by tapping his pockets that he didn't have either matches or a lighter. She fixed her big brown eyes on him as she lit his Park Drive – her gloved hand steady, a faint hint of perfume from her wrist as he bent forward to the flame. It was a seductive, unsettling gaze – with a slightly quizzical lift of the eyebrows.

'The weather doesn't seem terribly good for all this work,' she said, frowning, as he pulled away, inhaling gratefully.

He followed her gaze, and saw for the first time the banked-up storm clouds gathered – a jagged heap of ugly, mottled cumulonimbi. Where the hell had that come from? Even from this distance he could see the wall of rain traversing the South Downs as the storm closed in on them.

'Bloody hell,' he swore, then remembered himself. 'I'm sorry ...' he started.

'No matter,' she replied, and smiled sweetly.

He glanced hopefully towards the stern again, and this time was rewarded with the slight figure of Stanley Arbethwaite hurrying towards him. Ben nipped out the cigarette between his fingers, pushed the remainder behind his ear and then stuck his little fingers between his lips and whistled, loud and piercing. A head poked out of the tea-room window, and he beckoned urgently. Bodies started to file out of the door, headed for the gangplank, onto the deck and down below.

'Quick smart,' he urged a couple of stragglers.

'Just saw this weather coming in,' said Stanley, as Ben turned back to him. 'Where's that chair?' he continued, flicking his cigarette butt over the side as he spoke.

Ben bent and grabbed the chair from the coil of rope. Stanley stepped in between the wooden seat and the harness, and began to attach the wire rope that would haul him up the mast. Ben started picking up tools and placing them in the bag tied to the side of the chair. He caught Stanley's eye. For a moment, the older man maintained his serious expression, but he couldn't keep it up and smiled.

'Happens we have us new jobs,' he said, dipping his head to look in the bag, revealing the bald patch on his crown. 'I'll need the other spanner, too ...' he added.

'And?' asked Ben, ignoring the request for the spanner.

'Quarter more money again than what we're getting at Supermarine,' replied Stanley.

'Ruddy hell!' said Ben.

'The spanner, my boy, the spanner,' prompted Stanley, and Ben stooped for the tool, all his attention still on his friend. 'Dunwood will take us on the payroll for his factory, but we'll stay with the *Windflower* this summer, finish the mast properly –'

'You're going to America with him?' interrupted Ben, as Stanley pulled the spanner from his motionless hand.

'Ready below,' yelled Stanley. A second later the rope started to go tight and he eased his weight into the chair. He turned back to Ben. '*We*, Ben! *We* are going to America with the *Windflower*!'

'We?' Ben strangled the word.

Stanley Arbethwaite started to rise off the deck, lifted by the men below on the winch. A broad grin pushed up the deep worry lines around his eyes. 'Yes, both of us – he says you can help on the *May* when there's no work to do on the mast.'

Ben felt the breath gasp out of him; he clenched both fists hard in triumph – it had been his dream for as long as he could remember. The thought of working on the *May* reminded him of Anna, and he glanced around. But she had disappeared – doubtless beating a retreat at the arrival of so many of the great unwashed. Then a fat solitary raindrop landed at his feet on the wooden deck, and the first gust of wind tugged at his jacket. He glanced upwards, and in that instant, everything changed.

'Bloody hell,' he said, his voice rising to a frantic yell. 'Stop! Stop on that winch!' But even as he watched there was a fearful shout, and Stanley started to accelerate away from him.

Ben was aware of nothing but the inexorable combination of scientific law and fate that pulled his friend upwards. Stanley was turning, twisting in the chair, fending himself off the mast as he bounced upwards ever faster. Ben saw the impending impact coming – a spin of the chair, an unknowing, fateful push from Stanley's right foot, then there was a sickening crack as his head connected with the jib of the crane. A curious whining noise resonated down the hollow Duralumin mast as the spinning pulley reached its peak just before the entire weight of the wire rope slammed the chair and Stanley's inert body into the top of the rig.

But Ben was already heading for the crane. Only he and Stanley knew that in the frenzy to get the mast ready for the boat they'd just had time to fit that single wire rope into place on its pulleys. And now the only way to reach Stanley to bring him back down was to climb the crane and then the mast. He raced up the ladder to the cabin and, under the gaze of an astonished driver, climbed out through the maintenance access port and onto the jib. Beneath him there were cries and shouts, but he heard nothing as his mind narrowed to the task. He crawled out onto the square beam of latticed metalwork. It was wet and slippery beneath his fingers, but he could grip the narrower cross-struts and his plimsolls found some purchase on broken bubbles of rough rust. He glanced down – he was out over the deck of the yacht now and it was a long way down already.

A rogue gust of wind snatched at him and he tensed to regain his balance. Looking up, it seemed as if someone had tipped the sky and poured it towards him, dark and angry. Urgency pushed him on faster, more recklessly, snatching at the struts. Then the rain hit hard. Ben wobbled, prone on the end of the jib. *Bloody madness*, he thought, but there was no other way. The hook of the crane was attached to a harness round the mast, about eight feet below his position. Rising straight up from there, the mast passed less than a couple of feet in front of him. He tried to look up into the deluge, but couldn't keep his eyes open. But he knew what was there; he had been over every inch of that mast so many times he could see it clearly in his mind.

He lurched into a crouch and then half fell, half lunged outwards. He got both arms as far round the mast as he could in a desperate bear hug and then started to slip. His feet scrabbled and kicked for something, anything ... and found a grip; he couldn't see what and didn't care. His downward slide had halted and that was all that mattered. He tried again to look up, and again the rain pummelled his eyes shut. The wind plucked at his trousers, battering the canvas against his goose-bumped skin. He pressed his forehead to the cold metal, water streaming through his hair and washing into his eyes, rain dripping from his nose. He pulled away from the mast a little and saw the solid rigging rods strapped in place beside it. He carefully eased his grip and shifted to get hold of a couple of them with his hands. Then he reached up and pulled, feet scrabbling until they too found purchase.

It was desperately slow – but he found enough traction on all the rigging to make steady progress. Eventually, the mast section narrowed to the extent that he could get a grip around it with his legs. But as he rose higher above the shaky security of the mast's attachment to the crane, it started to move under him in the wind, shifting his weight unnervingly. In one of his sporadic punishing attempts to look up, he glimpsed a shape. The knowledge spurred him on, and the next thing he knew there was something soft against the skin of his scalp. It was Stanley's hand.

Unconscious, Stanley had flopped back in the chair

and harness, arms dangling loosely towards the deck. His left leg was trapped between the chair and the mast, and that was all that was stopping him from sliding backwards off the wooden seat to his death. As Ben assessed the situation, a trickle of blood dripped from Stanley's fingers above him. There was no time to lose. Ben was perhaps three feet from the chair itself. He had to add his weight to Stanley's and at the same time stop him sliding out, so the crew could lower them both back down to the deck. He shuffled carefully up the last few feet. Then he lunged through the chair's harness and grabbed Stanley's belt with his left hand, swinging his right to hang on to the top of his friend's old woollen jumper. The only thing holding Ben to the mast now was the vice-like grip he had with his legs. He started to let his weight come onto the chair; the harness creaked, but they didn't move.

Then his legs were torn free and his heart leapt up his throat. An instant later, he realised they weren't falling – someone had control of the wire rope below decks. Momentary relief swept through him as they bumped and shuddered down the mast. But hanging off the chair by one arm crooked around the harness, the other holding Stanley in place, he was at the limit of his stamina. It seemed impossible that he could hold on long enough, but they were being lowered a lot faster than he realised. The brakes came on a few feet off the deck, and the shock broke his fragile hold. He fell – so exhausted and drained that he barely registered the fact before he hit the deck in a heap.

After that it was a blur. There was a stabbing pain in his hip. The crew gathered round him and he was helped to his feet – feeling woozy, head spinning, almost in a dead faint – but he insisted that he was fine and that they should tend to Stanley. There were plenty of men for that too, and in moments Stanley was rushed up the gangplank by using a canvas sail bag as a makeshift stretcher. Ben stumbled behind him. Stanley Arbethwaite was eased into Harold Dunwood's Bentley and a woman from the office climbed in the back seat with him, trying desperately to stop the flow of blood from his head wound. Ben was bundled into the front.

'Go, go!' he urged the driver as soon as the door slammed shut behind him.

'Mr Clayton?'

'Hmm?' Ben Clayton turned back to the policeman. 'Sorry ...' Miller he'd said his name was, Detective Sergeant Miller. 'Sorry, Sergeant Miller ... I ... I just ...' He waved at the door of the hospital room in which Stanley Arbethwaite was fighting for his life.

'It's all right, sir, but if you could perhaps just explain that a little more.' Miller's tone was not unkind, his eyes were steady above a bulbous nose and large moustache. 'You're saying that the weight of this wire rope pulled him up the mast? It wasn't the lads pulling on it?' A nurse swept past, the starched white wings of her headdress tapping her shoulders, her heels clicking on the spotless parquet floor. Hot water throbbed and gurgled through the pipes and radiators; the electric lights hummed. An uncrowned Edward VIII peered down on a scene of calm and order from a picture on the far wall. Then the weight of an influenza campaign poster finally overcame the limited resistance of a single drawing pin, and fell to earth with a flutter. Miller stood up from the bench where he sat beside Ben, and walked over to replace it on the wall. There was a squeak of boots on wax polish. He sat back down. 'So, this er, wire rope, sir?'

Ben shrugged a little deeper into the dressing gown they had provided when they took his clothes away to be dried. 'Think of it like a set of scales,' he started. 'The pulley at the top of the mast that the halyard turns around is the fulcrum ...'

'The fulcrum?'

'Sorry ... I mean the pivot ... or balance point.'

'Ah, all right, sir, I've got it, carry on.'

'Stanley was hoisted up the mast by men working on a winch, pulling down on the wire rope on one side of the pulley. As Stanley rose up the mast on the other side, the combined weight of him and the wire on his side of the pulley was reducing. The mast is so tall that it got to a point where the weight of the wire rope on the other side of the pulley was greater, so it took over and started dragging him up the mast. It was nothing to do with the lads pulling him up there. He wasn't moving fast at all until the weight of the wire rope itself took over.'

'And how tall is the mast, sir?'

'Just over one hundred and fifty feet.' Ben shifted as he spoke to take the weight off his bruised hip and ease the pain.

'I see, so was it Mr Arbethwaite hitting the top of the mast that injured him?'

'No. He was desperately unlucky. He hit his head on the crane on the way past. Otherwise he would probably have got away with bruises or a broken limb.' He looked back to the door, willing it to open with a flood of good news. But nothing had happened since Vivian Arbethwaite, Stanley's distraught wife, had arrived pale-faced, and disappeared inside without a word. The waiting was awful. He hated hospitals and with good reason – the smells of antiseptic and wax polish, the fading flowers and over-ripe grapes – and this time was worse, much, much worse.

Miller bent his head to scribble in his notebook. 'What do you normally do to prevent this happening?' he asked.

'It's the practice to tie another rope to the bottom of the chair that the man is sitting in. This second rope – it's called the downhaul – rises with the chair, adding weight as it goes up. It also gives you something to pull on if it threatens to get out of control. Anyone under seventeen stone needs the downhaul – and Stanley Arbethwaite is five foot six and no weight at all,' replied Ben. He looked the policeman in the eye. 'I was with Stanley before he went up there. It was my responsibility to check that the downhaul was attached.'

DS Miller held his gaze for a moment before asking, 'And what was your job on this yacht, sir?'

'I helped Stanley to design the mast.'

'And what would be your experience for doing such a thing?'

'We're both engineers at Supermarine.'

'Oh, the aircraft company?'

'Yes, in Woolston, although what we were doing for Mr Dunwood was nothing to do with Supermarine. It was more of a favour.'

'A favour?' said the policeman, a little incredulously.

'Yes,' Ben hesitated, 'I'd seen pictures of a mast like this being used on one of the American boats, and I knew Mr Dunwood wouldn't stand a chance racing against them if he goes over there with a wooden one. So ... we offered to help, to design the mast and ... sort of manage the construction. I er ...' Ben swallowed, his mouth dry. 'I wanted to do it, sailing's my thing. I needed Stanley's help, but he was keen, that's what Stanley was like – he'd help anyone he could. But if I hadn't got him involved, then he wouldn't even have been there yesterday. It's all my fault, the whole thing.'

Miller's head dropped; there was just the sound of his pencil scribbling. 'So you've known each other for a while have you, you and Mr Arbethwaite?' he asked, eventually.

Ben coughed to clear his throat before he replied. 'I lodge with Stanley and his wife, at their home in Hamble. I've been living there for a couple of years, but I've known him since I started at Supermarine in '31, when I came down from Cambridge. Everyone at Supermarine knows Stanley; he's their top structural man.'

'So how did you meet Mr Arbethwaite?'

Now Ben looked at Miller. 'I don't see what this has got to do with the accident.'

'I have to fill out a report, sir, and they'll expect to see some background. Any accident involving someone who worked for Supermarine is going to attract attention. All those Schneider trophies, the world speed records, that plane going over four hundred miles an hour and all that – that's important stuff that is, especially if there's going to be another war. Any nasty happenings to anyone at Supermarine, no matter how innocent-looking, is going to attract the attention of my Inspector. So if you don't mind, sir.'

Ben stared at him. 'There's not going to be another war.'

Miller held his gaze for a moment, then made another note. When he looked back up, he had a puzzled frown. He rubbed his forehead with the back of his hand, and said, 'If you don't mind me saying, sir, you look familiar ... you didn't by any chance do some boxing when you were younger?'

'A little.' Now Ben was frowning.

'I knew it, I saw you fight ten, twelve years ago now. Fast hands, very fast hands, everyone said you were the next Ted Lewis. Wasn't there talk of a deal to fight at Premierland and then ... well, I always wondered what happened.'

Ben shook his head. 'I stopped.' He clasped his hands. 'Lost the taste for it.'

The door opened. The doctor came out first and gave a faint shake of his head. Then Mrs Arbethwaite appeared, her face completely white, the steadying grip of a nurse at her elbow. Ben lurched off the bench towards her and took her hands, which were clenched into tight fists.

'I want to go to Elsie's,' she said, rocking slightly, her eyes fixed on Ben, tears welling. Then the puffy, dark lids closed and she moaned, a most terrible keening.

It cut Ben to the core, and his mind froze in a blank, horrified panic. Then he remembered – Elsie was her sister, in Winchester. He latched on to the need for action. 'Do you have a telephone?' he asked the doctor. 'I'll get us a car.'

'In my office,' the man replied, indicating up the

corridor. Then he added, 'The nurse will stay with Mrs Arbethwaite.'

Ben nodded, squeezed her hands one more time and then followed the doctor.

Chapter 2

Ben Clayton had been awake all night. Faintly, he heard a knock on the front door, two flights of stairs down from his attic room. He knew instantly who it was, and his eyes flicked to the bedside table. The pencilled note, in a neat cursive hand, was typically short and to the point – *Came to check you were all right, Lucy*. He tried to take a deep breath, but his chest felt tight, as though there was something wrapped around it that stopped him filling his lungs. He didn't want to move. He wanted nothing to do with the world. The warmth of the sheets and blankets huddled round him provided the only shred of comfort – but it was Lucy at the door. She'd helped him through some bad times, and while there had been nothing like this, she was still the only one that would understand.

He pushed himself out of bed, almost falling onto his hands and knees. The movement sparked a shot of pain into his hip, and he gritted his teeth and clenched his fists until it subsided. He heard the knock again, more insistent. He struggled to his feet, the cold adding urgency to his movements, finding his clothes in a pile on the floor. He shrugged into the chilly, faintly damp shirt and trousers, and then clattered down the narrow attic stairs, the pain grinding in his hip. Into the hall, he bumped against the old shell case that had been pressed into service as an umbrella stand, opening the door just as Lucy was about to knock for the third time. She was wearing her battered red cloche hat, drooping down at the sides. She peered out solemnly from under the brim before tucking her blond hair – styled into a Louise Brooks bob – behind her ears in a familiar gesture. Even at that moment, he thought how lovely she was. He tried to force a smile.

'Ben, I'm so sorry.'

He shrugged helplessly. The action released an emotion that had been held deep inside him. He could feel it welling up from his guts, through his chest, a choking, trembling, uncontrollable wave. He stepped back, half turned from her, raised a hand to his face. He would not cry in front of her. And then she was in his arms, her face pressed to his chest. He took a sharp breath and managed to release it slowly, almost steadily, with just a single short juddering shake. He concentrated on the feeling of her, so strong and alive, so close to him, her ribs against the muscles of his arms, and a sudden wave of desire washed through him. Then he felt her ease a couple of inches away. His breathing was steady now, he opened his eyes, sniffed a couple of times. Everything inside his face seemed to have loosened. Lucy was examining him, her gaze as intent as ever.

'I was worried about you,' she said.

He wiped his sleeve across his nose.

'How's your hip? Dad told me about what you did, climbing the mast like that to get him down ...'

'It's just a bit stiff.'

She reached a hand up to his shirt collar, her expression concerned. 'You've got the buttons out of order.' She pushed herself out to arm's length and looked him up and down.

He could see a familiar light in her eyes, then tiny twitches at the corners of her mouth. He knew she was teasing him, trying to cheer him up. Normally he would smile, and they would laugh together. But nothing came. There was just this endless blank blackness.

'It's just terrible what happened to Mr Arbethwaite,' she said.

He nodded.

'I'll make you a cup of tea.'

He led the way down the hall and sagged into a chair at the big oak kitchen table. Dropping his head into his hands and shutting his eyes, he listened as she moved about – putting the kettle on the electric hob, gathering the teapot, the tea, cups, saucers. When he finally looked back up, she was sitting beside him. 'This will help,' she said, pouring milk from a blue jug.

He pressed his fingers into his forehead and massaged, in an effort to clear the fog from his mind.

'What time did you get home?' she asked.

'I'm not really sure.'

'It must've been late. I came up to the house about nine.' Lucy picked up the pot and started to pour, then spooned in two sugars and put the cup in front of him. 'Poor Mr Arbethwaite – but you did everything you could,' she said.

'Except tie the bloody downhaul on,' he replied.

'Don't be ridiculous, the downhaul wasn't your responsibility.' Lucy laid a hand on his forearm as she spoke.

'Then whose was it?' he asked, meeting her gaze.

'My father's,' she said, so softly he barely heard her.

Joe Kirk, the first mate on *Windflower* and a man Ben couldn't help but respect. Pugnacious, always faintly disapproving and with a bitter streak that ran close to the surface, but one hell of a seaman. Ben shook his head, sipped and then gulped the tea. It was the first thing that had passed his lips for almost twenty-four hours. He had missed lunch in the rush to get the mast ready, and missed dinner in the hospital. He put the cup down, empty. She took his hand, stroking the fingers with her thumb, and he wrapped his hand around hers. Finally, he said, 'He was organising the men on the winch below – did he say anything to you about it?'

'Only that you did an amazing job getting Mr Arbethwaite down. Normally he'd tell me all about any sort of ... accident, but not last night.' She hesitated. 'He was a bit more his normal self this morning – then the police came round.'

'What did they want?' he asked. He could hear the concern in her voice.

'They talked outside – when I asked him afterwards, he just told me it was nothing to worry about, although ...'

'What?' he prompted.

'He looked worried ...' Lucy pushed a second cup of tea over to him.

'The police came to interview me at the hospital.'

'Do you think there'll be any trouble?'

'If there is, it'll be me they'll be after – I was the one with him when he was getting in the chair. I should have checked that the downhaul was attached. That's what I told the policeman.'

Lucy leaned forward. 'I told you already, the downhaul is not your job. And anyway, Dad always has it spliced on, so it's permanently attached to the chair. He told me a story about this same accident on one of the American boats. And Dad always makes sure the downhaul is spliced to the chair now, so no one could forget. *Always.*'

He stared unfocused into the cup, feeling the hot liquid already inside him, his heart beating a little faster. It hadn't helped that neither he nor Stanley had set a mast into a big yacht like *Windflower* before. There had been a lot to think about, especially with that squall coming in so fast, the news of the job ... and the woman appearing, Anna. But if only he'd just glanced up at Stanley a moment earlier, before the balance shifted and the weight of the wire rope took over, it would still never have happened. 'I guess there wasn't time to do the splice, everything was so rushed,' he said, shaking his head again. 'But I still should have checked, and anyway, Stanley wouldn't even have been there if it wasn't for me,' he added.

'Oh Ben, that's ridiculous. You two worked on everything together, he would never have let you do it on your own.'

'And that's the point, if I'd never ...' he started.

'Ben! That is completely silly, that mast meant everything to you, it would have been the best chance you've ever had ...'

He looked up and Lucy put her hand to her mouth.

'Would have been? Had?' he asked.

'It's damaged.'

'It's damaged? The mast is damaged?'

'I thought you knew.'

His head dropped again.

'I'm so sorry. Dad said it happened in that squall, while you were trying to get Stanley down, what with the rigging not being set up.' She touched his arm again.

'Hardly matters now anyway ...' he tailed off, shivering, as if to emphasise his words.

'It's freezing in here,' she said, 'you need a sweater.'

'I could put the fire on.'

Lucy followed his gaze to a shiny four-bar electric fire. 'When did they get that?'

'A couple of months ago.'

Lucy examined the kitchen. 'Electric cooker, a Hoover even ... look at the wireless – I bet she didn't choose that.'

He didn't reply.

'When did you last eat?' asked Lucy.

He shook his head. 'A while ago,' he said.

'Come to our house. I've got leftovers from tea last night. And the range is on, it'll be warm.' She stood, moved closer to him, her eyes on his.

He rose and slid his hand tenderly through her hair – so soft – and then pulled her tight to him. They stood like that for a long while, before he whispered, 'Is your father at home? I'm not sure I want to talk about ...'

'He's gone to work.'

'They're working today?' he replied, leaning back to look at her.

'I know. How could they? It doesn't seem right,' said Lucy.

'They offered us jobs,' he said, after a pause. 'Stanley told me just before ... we were going to America with the *Windflower* together ...'

Lucy put a finger to his lips and he fell silent. She squeezed closer to him and he held her, until eventually she said, 'Let's go and get some hot food inside you, that'll make you feel better.'

Ben Clayton glanced at his watch, just before five o'clock. He sipped his beer at a lonely table, the warm amber liquid glowing in the firelight. Lucy had filled him up with lamb, potatoes and dumplings, and then taken her ten-year-old brother, Tom, to a Sea Scout football game. It would be another hour before they would get back home on the bus.

A couple of men sat at the bar of the King and Queen, each nursing a pint – he recognised them as shipwrights from Luke's yard, they must have knocked off early. Otherwise the place was empty; there was just the occasional rustle as the publican turned a page of his paper, the low murmur of the sporadic conversation at the bar and the background crackle from the fire. He moved in his seat – the pain in his hip was steady, nagging. Then the door to the pub clicked open, admitting a blast of cold air. And the Honourable Charles Lerup walked in with it. He stepped into the centre of the bar and swept a haughty gaze around him, the neat moustache twitching – slumming it, not happy about it, and wanting everyone to know.

Out of instinct Ben stood; Lerup with his Eton education, then Oxford University and a Blue, scraping a third in something classical. Perhaps a few innings for the county cricket team when he wasn't at the club in London – the usual certainty of loyalties to the land, to God, King and to Country. And then Anna followed him into the bar. Ben didn't think he had ever seen a woman in the public bar before – they just knew better than to come in there, it was a male domain. If you took a girl out for a drink, then it was to the lounge bars in Southampton, not here in the village, not the King and Queen, definitely *not* a girl like her. But there she was, jet-black hair washing in slow motion around her shoulders as she moved into the room, her long arctic fox coat rippling in the weak light.

'Ah.' Lerup's cool gaze settled on him. 'I thought I might find you in here; where the devil were you today?'

Ben snapped out of his staring – *where the hell did Lerup think he'd been?*

'Mr Dunwood wants to talk to you,' Lerup continued, giving him no chance to respond, 'you'll be on the lorry to go to the yard tomorrow with the others.'

A meeting with Harold Dunwood, owner of the *Windflower – a reckoning*, thought Ben.

Lerup flipped open a cigarette case, picked one out and tapped it on the polished silver lid. He bent his head to his lighter, the first puff of smoke pointedly exhaled in Ben's direction. 'It's Sunday, but we've lost a couple of days already. Early start, six o'clock sharp,' he said, before spinning on an immaculate handcrafted Perugia heel and sweeping out through the door.

But Ben's gaze had already returned to Anna – motionless as Lerup moved past. She was staring into the fire, expression quite blank, watching the flames. Then she looked at him and big, gentle brown eyes rested on his face. A blink of long, straight lashes, the faintest flicker of a smile playing around the corners of the red lips, and for a moment he thought that she was going to speak to him.

'Anna.' It was Lerup's voice from beyond the open door.

Her gaze stayed on him for a moment, before she turned and followed Lerup outside. The door clanked shut. They were gone.

'Boy,' came a growl from the bar, 'she be so far above you, you shouldn't even be able to see her from there.' A hoarse laugh quickly turned into a phlegm-ridden cough, which hindered further comment from the shipwright. Ben turned to the man, needing to reply, something sharp, something about Lucy – but still there was only the blackness. He downed the rest of his pint of Fielder's, picked up his overcoat and hat, put the empty glass on the bar with a nod to the publican and headed for the door. He needed to walk; he had to do something, anything.

Once outside he hesitated, before finally turning right, slowly heading up towards the Square with no clear idea of a destination. The shipwright was correct, of course – even if he hadn't got Lucy, Anna was way above him, whatever she might have revealed in that look. He'd met her type at Cambridge. They'd loved him – the unthreatening scholarship boy, playing in a game several leagues below them. A handful of them had made that latter fact very clear, and then taken him to their beds – expensive fragrant beds, with down pillows, soft mattresses and silk sheets. It was no surprise to find one like that with Lerup.

In all the time he had been working on the mast, the *Honourable* Charles Lerup had only spoken to him to give him an order. And this was despite the fact that, like Lerup, Ben was an amateur sailing enthusiast – *and* a damn sight more skilled than Lerup. They even had mutual friends, but it wasn't nearly enough. Lerup had learned his sailing in crisp white ducks on the aft deck of yachts like *Windflower*, while Ben had learned aboard the fishing boats and barges of the Mersea and the Thames – boats that had been his refuge, the end of a journey, an escape that had started with Slater's collapse in the boxing ring.

Teddy Slater had fared better than Stanley and walked out of hospital – but he hadn't been the same; noticeably slower in thought and action, Slater had never boxed again. When his vengeful older brothers had put the word around that they were coming up from the East End to look for Ben, his father had quickly moved the family out of Ilford. He'd left a middle-management job at Plessey to take a post as the administrator of a small but expensive public school in Colchester. Ben's education was supposed to be a perk of the job, but he was never left in any doubt about his status as an outsider – and once he was seen wearing the school uniform there had been little welcome from the local town lads either.

Isolated, it was a book that had provided the inspiration for a different direction. *Riddle of the Sands* was a pre-war spy story, a tale of great daring and seamanship set amongst the rivers and tidal flats of Germany's North Sea coast. Ben soon found his way to the river and tidal flats outside his window, and then downstream to Wivenhoe. There he met the men who sailed the great yachts for the king, Sir Thomas Lipton and others like them – and he found new dreams and new goals. The school helped to get him the scholarship to Cambridge, and once there his sailing skills got him into boats with the University's top men, winning national prizes.

But he was still the outsider, admired and desired for his skill, but never quite as welcome as the others to the parties and dinners, those bonding rituals that cemented them all together. And so it was with Lerup – things had got off to a poor start the first time that Lerup had turned up at the boatyard. He'd arrived with a capuchin monkey that he had won in a card game. It had chewed his car seats, so he had ordered one of the men to dump it in the harbour for him. Mrs Dunwood had stepped in and rescued the poor creature, and somehow Ben had ended up with the task of finding it a cage so that it couldn't do the same to the Dunwoods' Bentley. In the process, the animal had bitten his index finger damn near through to the bone – he still had the scar. No, he had to admit, he didn't like Lerup. He wanted to believe that the feeling was mutual, but he had a suspicion that Lerup was not sufficiently interested in his existence to have developed a feeling about him one way or the other.

'Ben Clayton?'

Ben stopped with a jolt and looked up to find Detective Sergeant Miller ambling across the Square towards him.

'I just saw the other gentleman from the *Windflower* before he drove off,' said Miller, 'and he mentioned that you were in the pub. We didn't really finish our conversation at the hospital, and I wondered if you might answer a couple of questions. Won't take but a moment.'

Ben stared at him.

'The sooner we do this, the sooner I can write my report up and we can put it all behind us. Won't take but a moment.'

After several more seconds Ben replied, 'Let's walk down to the river. We can find a quiet spot to talk.'

Miller nodded and fell in beside Ben as he turned back down the High Street. Hamble was a biggish village, a few hundred houses, mostly clustered around the Square, the High Street and the fishing and marine businesses that lined The Hard along the river's edge. And it was getting bigger quickly, as more aviation companies set up on the outskirts by the new airfield, looking to take advantage of local construction skills. The heart of the place was still the High Street though; the road ran from the Square down the hill to the river, past the pubs and shops that made the place tick. They covered the hundred yards to the water in silence. The High Street emptied out onto a muddy beach, close to the bottom of the tide. Ben found them a seat on the upturned hull of one of several rowing boats. Seagulls strutted along the shore, but otherwise, there was no one about.

Miller pulled out his notebook. 'I thank you for taking the time to do this, won't –'

'Take but a moment,' Ben finished it for him, snugging his hat down and pulling his coat a little tighter around him. They were out of the wind, but it was still cold.

Miller licked his pencil. 'So, you were going to tell me about you and Mr Arbethwaite?'

Ben drew a breath and let it back out slowly. 'There's not a great deal to tell. He was a very good friend to me, right back to when I first started at Supermarine. Originally, when they gave me the job they thought I'd be working on the Schneider Trophy planes. But then that summer of '31 they won the trophy for the third time, and so they kept it outright. They'd done it all, and when it finally became clear that there was no more government money for those planes, management shut the project down. I arrived and there was no work to do – it looked very iffy for a while. It was Stanley that rescued me. He took me under his wing. I started working with him on a flying boat called the Scapa and never really looked back. I suppose we had a fair bit in common too – scholarship boys, him at Imperial College, me at Cambridge.'

Miller looked up, then nodded, licked his pencil again and wrote for another ten seconds before he said, 'And when did you move in with him?'

'It was probably late June ... no, maybe early July of 1934. My lodgings in Woolston fell through and the Arbethwaites had a spare room in the attic. Everyone was looking for a little extra money back then. It worked for all of us.'

'Everything all right between you after that – Mr Arbethwaite being your landlord didn't change things at all?'

Ben hesitated. 'No. Everything was fine,' he said, warily.

'It was just that I heard you had some problems over that fighter plane that Supermarine is building.'

'You know about the plane?'

'I understand it'll be general knowledge pretty soon, sir.'

'Yes, I suppose, but still ...'

'Anyway, you had a bit of a falling out over it, as I believe.'

'Not really a falling out. When management moved

Stanley across to work on the fighter, he wanted me to go with him. And I didn't want to work on that plane.'

'Seems a bit surprising, isn't that where the excitement is, the fast planes?' Miller's thick greying eyebrows arched over his misty blue eyes.

'Look, I know what you're getting at – I didn't want to work on it because it was a fighter. I was comfortable with reconnaissance, and the search-and-rescue aircraft, like the Scapa and then the Walrus. But I didn't want to work on a real warplane.'

'That some sort of a conscientious objection, is it?' The scorn was just audible in Miller's tone.

'Yes,' replied Ben.

'And I have you down as a member of the ...' Miller flipped a couple of pages of his notebook. 'No More War Movement?'

'That's correct.'

'And I understand that Mr Arbethwaite accompanied you to a couple of meetings back in 1933?'

'You have been busy.'

Miller didn't reply.

'Stanley came with me, yes, but it wasn't his cup of tea. I'm sure your extensive research has told you that the Movement has socialist sympathies, and that wasn't to Stanley's taste. He rather liked the good things in life.'

'And Supermarine has no problem with your membership, what with them building warplanes for the RAF?'

'An Englishman's politics are none of his employer's business,' retorted Ben.

Miller nodded, made another note. 'Still, it must have come as a disappointment to you that Stanley would work on the fighter.'

'It did, and that's why we had a bit of a falling out.' Ben stood, suddenly more animated. 'That's why this whole thing is my fault. I read about this American yacht and a special Duralumin riveted mast in *Yachting World* magazine. Building that kind of structure was Stanley's speciality, and I knew we could come up with a better one. So I showed it to Stanley and he encouraged me to go to Dunwood, who snapped at the opportunity. But I manipulated the whole thing; I knew Stanley would push me to go to Dunwood. He knew how much I wanted to sail on those big yachts, and he knew he'd let me down over the fighter. And I knew he wanted to make amends. So you see, none of this would have happened if it wasn't for me. The whole bloody accident is all my fault – now is that not enough for you?'

'You're quite convinced it was an accident.'

'Of course it was – ask anyone at the yard, anyone on the crew. It was an accident that should never have happened, but an accident nevertheless.'

'And Stanley Arbethwaite had nothing to do with the anti-war or pacifist movements?'

'No. And if he had, then he'd still be alive, because he'd never have worked on the fighter and I'd never have dragged him into this ...' Ben stuffed his hands into his coat pockets.

Miller made a final note. Then he tucked his pencil into the binding, and the notebook into his jacket pocket. 'I think that'll be all, sir.'

Ben just nodded, still frowning.

Miller got up and walked back towards the High Street and the Square. Ben turned and went the other way, and was soon outside the Kirks' darkened cottage. Lucy still hadn't returned, and after a moment's hesitation he decided to walk across the Common, out towards the Fairey aircraft factory at the mouth of the river. He stepped up the pace, pounding at his unhappiness and the stiffness in his hip. A thick screen of trees loomed on his right, killing much of the light filtering through the glowering cloud. He emerged out into the low sun at the Common; the only sound was the tramp of his feet along a road washed clear of the rotting leaves of winter by February rain. The cold north-east wind blustered across the old salterns, torturing trees and tugging at his hat. He pulled up just short of the sombre Fairey buildings. The mudflats stretched away from him, and the grey sky pressed down and sealed itself against the horizon. He tried to get a full breath, but he still had the tightness across his chest that he had woken with.

When Harold Dunwood decided to spend some of his fortune on the *Windflower*, he had presented Ben with the most wondrous opportunity. But now that Stanley was gone, so was the chance of realising his dream of racing in the big yachts, the trip to Rhode Island to take on the best the Yankees could muster in the America's Cup. He shuddered; the wind was cold again now that he had stopped. But he deserved whatever he got. The whole thing was his fault, right from the first idea of the Duralumin mast. Now it had brought them to this – he was responsible for Stanley's death, and he would never see his friend again.

Chapter 3

Matthew Faden sat slumped in the saddle, the reins slack as the bay mare turned in through the yard gate. Immediately, he heard Fleming White's voice booming above the throng of busy grooms and chattering riders, the clip of hooves on cobbles and the rich smell of horse sweat. They had all beaten him back.

'Ah, there he is!' Fleming White and Harold Dunwood were standing together just inside the entrance to the yard. 'Thought we'd lost you, old man,' went on White, starting towards him as a uniformed groom grabbed the bridle and Faden sank weakly out of the saddle. White pulled a hip flask out of his pocket. 'Looks like you could do with a nip,' he said.

Faden managed a wry smile and accepted the proffered drink. It was whisky. He pulled a face and handed the flask back. 'More of a cocktail man, myself,' he replied. He should never have come, but there had been little choice with Fleming White. White was a friend of his father's, from the days when they had served together in the Second Boer War. His lean, tall figure – with its distinctive and unconventional mane of almost albino-blond hair – had hovered in the background of Faden's early years: godfather, there to pat his head at birthdays, weddings, christenings and funerals. But White's invitation to go hunting had come from nowhere. Faden had not seen the man since his early teens, more than a decade ago. He would never have accepted if it hadn't been for his father, who had demanded he go along – *because he's your godfather, but also because he heads up a section at MI5, and it would be unwise to turn down an invitation from the Security Service.* The Security Service – thinking about it led to lots of uncomfortable possibilities for Matthew Faden.

'My God, what have you been up to?' said Harold Dunwood, pulling up beside White.

'I had a fall, got separated, and then couldn't find my way home. Good job the horse knew what she was doing ...' Faden waved at where the borrowed bay mare was being led towards the stable block.

'Ah, good old Nessie, she can find her way back here from anywhere within twenty miles,' replied Dunwood.

'So it seems,' offered Faden, looking at Dunwood rather resentfully – the man must be twenty years older than him, but apart from a little flush to the plump weathered cheeks, he appeared ready to do the whole day's sport again, while Faden had mud in places that soap would barely reach. He rubbed his stiff neck, fingers lingering habitually on the raised skin of the half-inch-long birthmark that poked out from under his hairline, all but hidden by his auburn hair.

'Just the animal for young Matthew then,' said White, smiling. 'Harold, you've done us proud,' he continued, offering the flask once again.

Dunwood took it. 'Thank you, just what a fellow needs – so you're not staying for dinner?' He slugged back a nip.

'No, my apologies, but I have a prior engagement back in town,' replied White.

'That's a pity, we've not had much chance to talk.' Dunwood returned the flask.

'No ... and I wanted to hear about this fantastic yacht you're building,' said White, replacing the flask and pulling a pipe and a tobacco pouch from his pocket.

Faden shifted a step closer. He didn't want to miss

anything. Dunwood wasn't the only one building a fine new racing boat – the legendary sportsman and industrialist Sir Thomas Sopwith had his own yacht under construction in the same Gosport yard. It had sparked a rivalry between the two men that had set the gossips chattering.

But Dunwood frowned as he replied, 'Unfortunate business yesterday, had a fellow hurt in an accident while we were putting the mast in her for the first time.'

There was a moment's hesitation before White asked, 'Was it serious?'

'Very – got him up to the hospital, but they lost him last night. He'd done a wonderful job for us too, built this extraordinary mast – Duralumin panels put together with a hundred thousand rivets. It's less than two thirds the weight of a wooden mast, but the bloody thing got bent in yesterday's fiasco ...'

White was tamping tobacco down into the bowl of the pipe with a gloved thumb. 'Anyone we might know?'

Dunwood shook his head. 'I doubt it – Stanley Arbethwaite was his name. He and another structural-engineering wallah from Supermarine approached me with the idea for the mast at the end of last summer. In fact, it was Clayton that did such a tremendous job of rescuing Arbethwaite ...'

'Not Ben Clayton?' asked Faden.

'Yes, actually,' replied Dunwood.

'Faden sails a bit – don't you?' interjected White, pushing the pipe between thin lips and tapping his jacket pockets for his lighter.

Faden's gaze flickered over towards him – was this the reason he was here? But the man's expression had not changed by as much as a creased eyelid.

'So you sail, do you, Faden?' Dunwood was saying. 'And you know this fellow Clayton?'

'Yes, we sailed together for a couple of years at Cambridge. He's an exceptional talent in a small boat, and a brilliant engineer – he got a double first, I believe.' *And he's over six foot of lean muscle with the kind of blue eyes a man could lose himself in*, thought Faden. Unfortunately – *most damnably unfortunately* – Clayton wasn't queer.

'You should come sailing with us, Faden,' Dunwood was suggesting.

'I'd love to, but I've only really sailed small boats,' he replied.

'Don't be so modest, man, sounds like a marvellous opportunity,' White added encouragingly, between vigorous puffs at the pipe, now streaming clouds of smoke into the cold winter air.

'Well, small boats are a different game to the bloody great pantechnicon I'm building – but give my office a call in a month or so when we get things back on track and we'll sort something out,' said Dunwood, smiling at him.

'Thank you,' replied Faden. 'And what are you going to call the new boat?' he asked.

'*Windflower* – my wife's choice,' replied Dunwood, slipping a hand between the buttons of his tattersall-check waistcoat as he spoke. 'Now, we should be getting up to the house, sun's way below the yardarm, hot toddies all round, I think – most of the others are ahead of us ...'

'My car's that way. I'll walk with you,' said White.

The three of them headed out of the yard and up the immaculate gravel drive lined with expensive motor cars. Faden trailed behind, wondering about the older men. They had clearly met before, but not often – perhaps some encounter contrived by White to get them this invitation. Faden pulled off his hunting cap for a moment and swept his hair back, musing. He was sure that White was up to something, this wasn't just about a day's hunting with his godson. The old blighter had positively egged him on to accept the invitation to go sailing. But what possible interest could MI5 have in getting him to sail on the *Windflower*? Perhaps it was something to do with Dunwood.

Everyone knew about Harold Dunwood. An ace fighter pilot in the Great War, he'd chalked up fifteen kills over the

Western Front in Tommy Sopwith's Camel fighter – not bad for a man who had started the war digging trenches in the mud and blood of Ypres. Then later there was May, a great beauty and pick of the debutantes of 1920. Dunwood had whisked the much younger woman out from under the noses of several wealthier, better-connected or -titled suitors. And the match was a legendary success. Dunwood had combined his father's pre-war bike shop and his own renown as a fighter pilot, mixed it with a successful motor-racing career, May's charisma and connections, and come up with a chain of Midlands factories, churning out parts for everything from prams to planes.

'Quite ironic,' White was saying, 'you and Sopwith both building one of these damn great yachts – the two of you must own a good piece of Britain's aviation-manufacturing capacity between you.'

'Don't forget Richard Fairey, with the Swordfish – he's sailing *Shamrock V* at the moment as well,' put in Faden.

'Indeed,' said White, 'the Swordfish – that's a reconnaissance and torpedo plane, isn't it?'

'Bloody thing's a biplane,' retorted Dunwood, 'I don't know what the hell use the Air Ministry think that's going to be to the RAF.' His hands were plunged deep into the pockets of his jacket, his chin jutting forward.

'I heard that you have land in Hamble and a new factory under construction,' added White, bending his head to relight the pipe.

Dunwood looked up sharply. 'You heard that, did you?' he asked, with a faint trace of sarcasm. 'Well, it won't be building planes for the RAF, I can tell you that. I didn't fight that bloody awful war so we could start another one not even twenty years later.' His tone was sharp enough for White to look up from his pipe.

'It may not be us that start it.' White's voice was languid and even. His long strides comfortably covered the ground. And for a moment, there was just the sharp crunch of footfalls on gravel. Then Dunwood snorted, but he made no other response.

'I don't understand sailing, I've always been a rugby man myself,' said White, smoothly.

'It's new to me too,' replied Dunwood, eventually.

'So how on earth does a fellow prepare himself for getting involved in a game like that?'

'Get the best advice,' said Dunwood. 'I got the top fellow a few months ago – Charles Lerup, a very experienced man.'

'Ah,' murmured White.

'Damn fine shot, too,' noted Dunwood.

Faden turned away to hide his smile at the note of arriviste pride that had crept into Dunwood's voice. These chaps, all that money and power, but they could still be complete fatheads when it came to a title: the Honourable Charles Lerup would become Lord Maybridge when his father died. The family had arrived with William, and helped to dispatch poor Harold at Hastings. Theirs was blood as blue as the oceans – but Dunwood was wrong about Lerup's abilities as a sailor.

They were passing the cars now, and Faden watched a chauffeur stub out his cigarette and set about starting his vehicle. Dunwood drew up at the steps. 'Sorry you're leaving us, White,' he said.

White waved the pipe apologetically amongst a cloud of exhaled smoke. 'I'm the one that's sorry, but duty calls. Faden is staying, aren't you, old boy?'

Faden looked at them both, hoping his dismay did not show on his face. He had hoped for a chance to make his excuses, but that was no longer an available choice. 'Of course,' he replied.

'Goodbye then, White.' Dunwood held out a hand, and White stepped forward to take it.

'I'll see you inside, young man,' Dunwood said, with a nod to Faden.

White's expression remained blank as Dunwood's boots clipped up the steps, yet Faden had the feeling that things had not gone as hoped. He found the thought curiously satisfying. Then White turned to him. 'I was talking to Bill Derry about you the other day. He works for me, you know.'

And Faden felt a chill settle on him, a heaviness lodge in his gut.

'I understand you were ... what should I say ... *good friends*?' Each word, even the pause, was carefully measured.

Faden didn't move, didn't twitch. The world sank away, and then gently started to spin around him. How could he be so stupid? But he had always known it was possible – there were always risks. Bill Derry had been so obviously interested, so quick with the signals, the tiny gestures, the coded declarations of intent – too quick. He felt himself start to flush at the memory of the scene in the Garrick's toilets. What had he been thinking? He'd not been thinking – that was the trouble. He'd had far too many gin slings.

'Don't worry,' said White. 'I won't tell your father. But we should catch up more often. I've been neglecting my role as godfather. Make sure you get in touch during the week,' he continued, his voice relaxed, reassuring.

Faden closed his eyes to stop the world spinning. Then he felt the pressure of a hand on his upper arm. Something was slipped into his coat pocket.

'That's my card,' said White. 'Now, I really must be off.'

Faden opened his eyes. He watched as the royal-blue Daimler Light Straight Eight rumbled up beside them, and Fleming White stepped into his motor car. Now Faden knew why he had been invited. And it was worse than he could possibly have imagined.

Chapter 4

Lucy waited a couple of minutes after her father had left before she followed him out of the house. She shut the door quietly behind her. It had frozen hard overnight, and she made her way cautiously down to The Hard – he was just turning up into the High Street as she got to the water. She kept her distance and he didn't look back, preoccupied no doubt with the piece of German steel still in his knee. It was always worse on cold days.

The black-and-red-bricked houses on the High Street were hunkered down against the predawn chill. Just the occasional flicker of light came from behind the drawn curtains. Empty milk bottles stood outside all the front doors, and smoke curled from a handful of chimneys before being teased away by the northeaster. The sky had cleared, and she picked her way past the icy puddles under the light of a new quarter moon. The crew lorry hadn't arrived when he got to the Square, and she watched him join the edge of the gang without a word. Everyone was numbed into silence by the cold and the hour.

She waited a little longer, and eventually he drifted into the group and was hidden from view. Footsteps coming up the High Street behind her were the final nudge. She stepped out into the open and, trying not to hurry, made her way towards the crew. No one paid any attention to her as she approached. She was muffled in a thick coat, scarf and hat that only her father would recognise. If she could just stay out of his sight until they were all on the lorry, she'd be fine.

'Lucy?'

She jumped at Ben's voice behind her, pulled the scarf from her face and raised a finger. 'Shhh!'

Ben moved a little closer. 'What are you doing here?'

'I was going to ask you the same question!'

'I asked first.'

She wiped at her runny nose with the back of her worn woollen mitten. 'Dad was saying last night how desperate they are for more hands. And Tom has another Sea Scout trip today and left early with Michael and his mum. So I thought if I could get on the lorry and get to the yard without Dad knowing, once I get there the Captain will just be glad of the help.'

A momentary flicker of a smile came and went on Ben's face. 'I'll try and keep myself between you and your dad. We'll wait till he gets on, then you follow me onto the lorry.' He glanced over his shoulder at the crew as he finished.

She nodded. 'Thanks, and how are you feeling?' she asked, reaching out and squeezing his arm. 'I didn't expect to see you here today,' she added.

'Dunwood wants to talk to me,' he replied.

'Oh,' she said, 'about the accident?'

'I suppose. I hardly think it's going to be good news. That policeman was around last night again too, asking questions about Stanley and the No More War Movement.' His face was set in a tired grimace, his voice flat.

'But that's ridiculous, what's that got to do with anything?'

Ben shook his head. 'Nothing, but he says he has to check it all because Stanley worked at Supermarine. It's an important place apparently, because of the Schneider Trophy.'

'That's a bit ... Damn! Behind you!' In her concern for

him, she'd missed her father separating from the group. He had started towards Ben.

'Mr Kirk,' said Ben, as he turned round.

'Ben,' said Joe Kirk. He thrust his hands into the pockets of his blue seaman's coat as he spoke. He had his shoulders hunched forward, his chin tucked in, the tidy grey beard buried in the scarf round his neck. There was always a faint tension between the two of them. Lucy noticed the nudges and nods amongst the crew, all now watching in the background.

'What's she doing here?' Joe Kirk asked Ben.

'We thought she might come and give a hand today, need all the help we can get.'

Joe leaned forward and spat on the ground, then shook his head as he spoke. 'I should have had you out scallop dredging in Caen Bay all winter. See how you like that,' he said to Lucy.

'It can't do any harm, Mr Kirk, and she'd be a great help.'

'Save that till you've married her,' replied Joe Kirk. 'Till then, she's my concern. Now bugger off back home, Lucy.'

'No,' replied Lucy. 'You can't stop me working.'

'Yes I can, this is man's work, no place for a woman.'

Joe started to move around Ben to get closer to his daughter, but Ben edged back into his path. 'Mr Kirk,' he said softly, leaning forward, 'considering all that's happened, this is not going to be an easy day for any of us. I'd be thankful if you'd allow Lucy to come to the yard and work.'

Joe Kirk opened his mouth as if to speak, then hesitated, frowned and spat off to one side again. The silence extended for a moment or two longer, before Joe tried again. 'You did well the other day. I'm, er ... right sorry about Mr Arbethwaite. I know ... he was a good friend to you. It weren't your fault, the downhaul, you know that.' He stopped. The air between them tightened further, as Joe stared at his feet, cleared his throat, spat one more time. The lorry rescued them, a gear crashing loudly from the Hamble Lane direction. 'All right,' said Joe. 'Just for today, I'll find her something proper to do.'

Ben nodded his acknowledgement. Kirk moved away to join the line already forming to board the lorry.

'Oh, thank you,' said Lucy when he was gone. 'I thought he was going to make a scene.'

Ben grimaced. 'If he's any trouble tonight, you will tell me, won't you?'

'It's all right. It's not the first time we've had this argument.'

'You can say that again. Come on, let's get on the lorry.'

Lucy followed her man to the back of the queue, and waited patiently. She had always loved the ocean. And it had always got her into trouble, right from the time when, aged ten, she'd stowed away aboard a yacht her father had been working on. The boat had not been able to return her home for a week, and even her frantic mother's thrashing couldn't wipe the grin off her face when it did. They had made it hard for her to repeat her adventure after that, but fortunately, new inspiration had come a year later when another Lucy, a swimmer called Lucy Morton, had won an Olympic gold medal at the 1924 Games in Paris. The teachers had told her all about Morton, even showed her the pictures in the magazines. One of them had offered to teach her, and soon Lucy was swimming every day in the river. No one could stop her doing that. Two years later she was winning club and county races, and starting to get her name in the papers.

Then one day the headmaster had come to her class to find her. She would never forget the moment. She had been staring out of the window, across the field towards the church. It had been early autumn, the trees a riot of gold, yellow and brown. She had turned round at the sound of her name, and knew instantly from the man's face that winter had come, that every last flicker of colour was about to be extinguished from her life.

Her mother had died giving birth to Tom. And just when school and teachers were revealing people, places and lives of infinite variety and ambition, everything had narrowed to a suffocating cottage kitchen and a screaming baby. She'd had help, of sorts – the village had rallied round for a while. But she had lost her father to work. He took anything that was going – crab boats, scallop dredgers, racing yachts – and distant had become simply absent. In the end it was just her and Tom, left alone to find their way in the world. She'd had to stop competing, but had never completely given up the swimming, going out in the river when she could. And she was so glad that she did – after all, it had brought her together with Ben. They'd met on the river, him rowing, her swimming. The memory made her smile, but it quickly evaporated – her father had a point about marriage. She'd been with Ben for eighteen months now, and people were starting to talk about it. But Ben had never even so much as mentioned it in passing.

The lorry took forty minutes to cover the sixteen miles to Gosport. It bumped into the yard, a faint whiff of roasting chestnuts coming from a glowing brazier at the gates. They stopped on the quay beside *Windflower*. Ben climbed down with Lucy and watched the crew trickle away in twos and threes, most of them still arguing about Southampton's Second Division loss to Bradford on the previous afternoon. Joe Kirk directed a couple of hands to the jobs he had on his list. Then he came over to them.

'I've got something for you, Lucy, it'll keep you out of Lerup's way,' he said.

'All right,' agreed Lucy.

Then Joe drew closer to Ben. 'Something I wanted to ask you,' he said.

Ben glanced at Lucy.

'Before we pulled Mr Arbethwaite up the rig, the chair

was sitting on some rope, three strand, about half-inch, wasn't it?' asked Kirk. His tanned forehead and eyebrows were deeply furrowed.

Ben tried to remember, but everything immediately before the accident was vague. He could recall Stanley getting into the chair, telling him the news of the job offer ... Had he picked the chair up off a pile of rope prior to that? 'I think so, Mr Kirk, I don't remember all that well.' He frowned. 'Why do you ask?'

'Oh,' Kirk eased back a bit. 'No reason, but don't you be worrying about it. I told the bogey it was just one of them things, Arbethwaite being so light and everything so rushed.' He began to walk away. 'Come on, Lucy, work to do if you want to get paid, you can clean the saloon cushions that have been stored in the shed, dust all over them.'

Lucy's expression folded into disappointment, and Ben intercepted her hands as they headed towards her hips. A familiar gesture – he knew what was coming next. 'It'll be all right, Lucy, I'll get you working on the boat later.'

'You will?'

He nodded. 'But what was that about, the stuff about the rope?'

Lucy looked towards her father's departing back, shook her head. 'Not sure,' she said. 'Something's bothering him about the accident, but he won't talk about it, keeps saying it doesn't matter.' She hesitated. 'I hope there isn't going to be any trouble. It hasn't been a good winter for other work.'

'I suppose I'll find out when I see Dunwood ...'

'Come on, Lucy,' shouted Joe.

'Cleaning bloody cushions in the shed ...' she muttered. Then she squeezed his hands and hurried after her father.

Ben huddled deeper into his coat at a cold blast from the north-easterly. He glanced around – the yard seemed unnaturally quiet, but the sun was barely up. A seagull wheeled into a turn on another gust, dipping towards the water with a squawk, chasing the ripples towards him.

What did it matter if the chair had been on a pile of rope or a pile of wood? He ran his tongue across dry lips.

'Morning, Clayton.'

He turned to see Captain Emerton, *Windflower*'s professional skipper.

'I just wanted to say,' continued Emerton, in an accent that hadn't changed since he grew up a couple of hundred yards downstream of the Itchen Ferry, 'that I'm very sorry about what happened to Mr Arbethwaite. And I wanted to thank you for your efforts to save him. I've never lost a man before.'

Ben stared at him. He had always been singularly impressed with Emerton. If the old skipper had been born at the right time, he would surely have been a fighting captain in Nelson's navy. But the days of bloodletting under sail were thankfully past, and Emerton had been left to rise peacefully to the top of an elite cadre of racing men. He had a reputation as completely unflappable. He was a man who never raised his voice unless it was absolutely necessary and, in Ben's limited experience, only spoke when he was absolutely sure he had something worth saying. His words were high praise.

'Do you want to have a look at the mast with me while you're waiting for Mr Dunwood?' asked Emerton.

Ben nodded, mouth dry, and followed the Captain – a polio survivor with a heavy limp in his right leg – slowly across the yard. They reached the shed where *Windflower* had been built. Wooden scaffolding and ladders were stacked against the wall. The spare timber was shelved up, and offcuts of wood and steel were neatly heaped. Piles of sawdust and rubbish dotted the floor, waiting for someone with a brush and pan. The mast lay on trestles, rigging stripped off, and he walked slowly along it. Emerton watched his progress, pulling a battered tobacco tin from his pocket. It didn't take Ben long to find the damage. Several of the panels were deflected inwards, bent beyond the design limits by the storm and his and Stanley's weight hanging from the unsupported top. Luckily, it was nowhere near as bad as he'd imagined, and it was clear enough what had to be done. He ran his hand back and forth over the spot, feeling the tortured rivets.

'I think we can repair this,' said Emerton, 'but Lerup's trying to *buy* one of the spare masts lying around.'

Ben's hand stopped, the metal cold under his fingers.

'What do you think?' probed Emerton, cigarette in the corner of his mouth, match set against the box side, ready to light.

He took his hand off the mast. 'Stanley Arbethwaite did the design, I just helped him,' he said. Stanley had been a structural genius. It was what made him so valuable to Supermarine and to their brilliant designer, RJ Mitchell, and the new fighter plane, with its state-of-the-art metal frame and shaped skin. Ben was unwilling to presume to take his place.

'You're a good, modest lad,' said Emerton, as the match flared. 'But Stanley always spoke very highly of you. I believe you know what needs doing. And I know he would want you to finish what you *both* started.' He took the first drag on the roll-up and waved out the match, all the time watching Ben carefully. 'It can be fixed, can't it?'

'Yes,' he said, after a moment's thought, 'it can be fixed.' Emerton was right – Stanley wouldn't have wanted Lerup to throw away all the work they had done.

'Good, that's what I thought.' The skipper nodded. 'What do you need, lad?'

'I beg your pardon?' The question startled him.

'What do you need to do the repair? I'll put you in charge. What men and materials do you want?'

He looked at the Captain for a moment; Ben could feel his lips twitch towards a smile. He pushed his hand through his hair and scratched his scalp. 'I, er ... think a couple of men ... the best would probably be Fitzhardy and Class. As for materials ... I'd need to do some measurements, calculations ... a slide rule and some paper and a pencil would be enough to be going on with ...'

'All right,' said Emerton. 'Let's go and see what we can rustle up.'

The sun was inching into the shed as it rose, lighting up the whorls of dust that drifted on an air rich with the boatyard smells of warm glue, wood and burning metal. Ben sat at a table that he had put together from a couple of trestles and some spare timber. Albert Fitzhardy was bent over the mast, his stubby fingers carefully marking out the section that Ben had indicated should be cut away, while Frank Class had gone to the store to see if the Duralumin they needed for the repair was available. Captain Emerton had wielded some impressive influence with the boatyard, but that was the only thing that hadn't surprised Ben. Sitting at his makeshift desk, he couldn't believe the speed with which things had turned around.

He cocked his head. Absorbed as he was, he couldn't miss the distinctive tearing roar of *that* engine. A sunbeam-yellow, boat-tailed Bugatti slowed as it crossed in front of the entrance, and then turned and drove into the shed towards them. Ben watched, lips pursed in a low involuntary whistle – it was a Type 35A straight-eight. But he frowned as the driver pulled off his old leather flying helmet and scarf, and eased himself out of the seat. It was Lerup.

'What the devil's going on here?' said Lerup, tossing the helmet and scarf into the car and approaching the mast, leather coat flapping around his legs, a hand smoothing his moustache.

Ben stood, pencil in hand – *it wasn't right, grooming facial hair to that level of perfection ...*

'Talk to me, dammit,' barked Lerup.

Anger rose through Ben like bile. *Calm down, don't let the buggers get to you* – that's what Stanley would tell him – *use them, don't fight them.* 'Well, obviously we're repairing the mast,' he said, making no effort to hold back the sarcasm.

'I gave no instructions for that,' snapped Lerup.

'I wasn't aware that you had to ...' replied Ben.

'I gave the instructions for them to start work on the mast,' boomed Emerton's deep voice, as he approached from the entrance to the shed.

Lerup spun round.

'Mr Clayton has a plan for repairing this, and if it goes well for us, we won't be needing to buy a replacement,' continued Emerton. He stopped beside Fitzhardy, and leaned on the spar. 'How's it coming along, Mr Clayton?' he added, glancing at the damage.

'The men can have it ready by next weekend,' said Ben.

Emerton looked back up at Lerup. 'One week, that's all. And there's a week's work anyway to get everything else done. The lads all need a day off too ...' He pushed his blue peaked cap back and scratched his forehead.

'Captain Emerton.' Lerup's tone was icy. 'We'll discuss this further in the office. Right now.' He stalked out of the shed.

With a slight smile and a wink to Ben, Emerton followed. The Bugatti clicked and ticked as the metal cooled in the ensuing silence. Ben sat back down, avoiding a look at Fitzhardy. And in a few moments, he heard the man resume his work. Ben fiddled with the calculations and drawings for a couple of minutes, smoked a Woodbine, then another. It was after the monkey incident that Lerup had become Dunwood's representative aboard *Windflower*, wielding all of the owner's authority. His arrival had changed everything. Dunwood had been cut off, isolated from everyone else on the project – all lines of communication ran through Lerup. The familiar almost-family feeling amongst those working on the boat had evaporated. All the schedules had been altered, launch dates had been brought forward and the whole thing had taken on a relentless, frantic atmosphere.

The rumours said that Lerup was desperate to beat Sir Thomas Sopwith because Sopwith had given Lerup the push from his boat last summer. Revenge was driving Lerup and he wanted *Windflower* in the water early, to get a head start in preparing for the season's racing. It was a ridiculous time of year to be launching a big yacht; there was no chance of getting good enough weather to sail – but no one had wanted to tell Lerup that. He was said to have dined with the new king, and people were careful around the man, or at least they had been, until now.

'Excuse me.'

Ben looked up. It was Anna. Her jet-black hair tumbled out from under her beret onto the shoulders of her coat. Her brown eyes flickered around his makeshift desk for a moment, before settling back on his face.

'Good morning,' he responded, recovering from her sudden presence.

'They told me I'd find you and the Bugatti here,' she said.

Find me? he thought.

'Perhaps you can help,' she went on, 'I was hoping for somewhere that I might get breakfast.'

'Ah ... I'm not really a Gosport man,' he replied. 'At least, not beyond the Castle Tavern on the corner there.' He waved in the pub's direction as he spoke, then he added with a rueful smile, 'Not really the kind of place a lady might find breakfast on a Sunday morning. Albert, perhaps you can help?'

'If you head down the High Street, ma'am, there's a turning to the right, North Cross Street, the Bell Hotel's on the corner. If anywhere will do a proper breakfast for a lady in Gosport, that'll be it,' said Albert Fitzhardy.

'Thank you,' said Anna, with a little nod. A smile flickered across her face as she turned back to Ben. 'Mr Dunwood offered his Bentley and driver, but I thought this might be more fun.' She started to walk towards the Bugatti, then hesitated, calling to Ben over her shoulder, 'I almost forgot – Mr Dunwood said he'd like to see you as soon as you can manage. He's borrowed Charles Nicholson's office for the morning.' And with that, she proceeded to the Bugatti, pushed the helmet and scarf off the driver's seat and climbed in. The engine fired in a moment, the tearing roar crashing around the shed. She revved it hard, the tyres bit into the packed dirt and she hauled it round to face the door. The clutch came up the rest of the way a little too fast, and sawdust and grit swirled in her wake as the car disappeared out into the boatyard.

'Bloody 'ell,' said an admiring Fitzhardy, 'what a piece of work!'

Indeed, thought Ben, as he gathered his papers. He made his way up to the office. So had Dunwood heard the arguments presented by Lerup and Emerton? What had he decided? Ben wasn't sure what he felt about Dunwood. He was grateful for the opportunity the *Windflower* had given him. But it was laced with some resentment that the whole thing was poised on the enormous fortune and the whims of one man. Ben hadn't much liked the rich people he'd met – they had ranged from the downright obnoxious to the wilfully self-centred, or perhaps more generously, self-absorbed. But then, as an individual, he had found nothing to object to in Dunwood, and a fair amount to admire – at least, until the running of the *Windflower* had been handed over to Lerup.

The tap of a typewriter echoed down the corridor, mixing with the more distant whine of the circular saw and the pounding of rivets. He pulled himself up to his full height, took a deep breath and strove to order his thoughts. Stanley was dead. All their work was at stake. The thought had a rapid, chilling effect. He knocked twice, and half opened the door. Dunwood was behind Nicholson's desk, Lerup beside him, leaning against the windowsill, arms folded – while Emerton was seated on the other side of the desk, in front of them both. With a couple of waves of his cigar, Dunwood indicated that Ben enter and sit beside

Emerton. The room was tense.

'First things first,' started Dunwood, 'my deepest regrets for the appalling tragedy on Friday. But I commend you for your actions at the time; it was a terrifically brave show you put up, climbing to the top of the mast like that, to get him down.' Dunwood puffed at the cigar, and then continued. 'I understand the police have already spoken to you. Their investigations are almost complete, and they have indicated that their conclusions are as we expected – that no criminal charges will be forthcoming. Their evidence will be passed to the coroner and he will decide if there is any sort of further blame to apportion in this awful affair. But I want you to know that you need have no concerns about this matter, you were in no way at fault for what happened to Mr Arbethwaite. If there is responsibility for that, it lies elsewhere – you came to us in the best of faith, to do a specific task, and you have striven mightily to achieve it. You have only our thanks for your efforts.'

Ben was aware of Emerton making an awkward shift in his seat. Lerup had not moved a muscle, his face set. Was that really it? Had he let Detective Sergeant Miller worry him unnecessarily?

Dunwood continued, 'On a more cheerful note, Captain Emerton tells me you've got a scheme for repairing our broken mast. Is that correct?'

'It is possible to repair the mast, yes sir,' Ben replied, indicating the calculations and drawings he was holding. 'If it all goes well, it should be ready to go back in the yacht by next weekend.'

Dunwood made no move to take the papers. 'Excellent,' he said, 'I don't know if Mr Arbethwaite had the opportunity to make you aware of it, but I had offered you both jobs just before the accident. I want you to know that the offer still stands. I'd like you to work on *Windflower*'s mast for the summer, and come to America with us. Then in the autumn you can join the staff at the Hamble factory to help us with the new airplane we're building for the postal service. The pay is ten pounds a week. I'd like you to start tomorrow.'

America. *Windflower*. Ten pounds – it was a fortune.

'Well, what do you say, young man, will you join us?' asked Dunwood.

Ben realised he was still proffering his drawings like a schoolboy with his homework. He dropped the papers into his lap. 'Yes, yes sir ...' he managed to say.

'That's settled then; now, gentlemen, I really must return to my family.' Dunwood stood, and both Emerton and Ben rose also. Dunwood turned to Lerup. 'The other thing we've got to sort out, old chap, is your trip to Germany to see about these engines for the new motor yacht. I thought you could take Anna with you. My wife says she's bursting to get back there – you're both still having lunch with us, aren't you?'

Lerup nodded, muscles pumping the skin just under his cheek bones. He still hadn't said a word.

'Excellent, we can talk about it then – chance for you to catch up with your monkey, too,' said Dunwood, smiling. 'See if it can bite your fingers. Now, we must find Anna.' Then he addressed Ben. 'Do y'know where she went?'

'The Bell Hotel in the High Street, I believe,' replied Ben, unconsciously rubbing his thumb along the line of his own monkey-bite scar. 'She took the Bugatti,' he added.

'Oh,' said Dunwood, for a moment knocked out of his stride. 'Well, I'm sure we'll track her down, she won't be hard to spot in that motor.' Dunwood came out from behind the desk as he spoke and shook Ben's hand. 'I hear from some friends of mine that you're an accomplished small-boat sailor,' he said, 'Prince of Wales Cup winner, I believe.'

'That's right ...'

'We'd be glad to have you sail on *Windflower* one day, see if you can teach any of the old dogs some new tricks.'

'That would be a great honour, there's nothing I'd love –'

'Excellent, excellent. Well, I'm sure you've got plenty

to do, good luck with the mast. We're all relying on you,' Dunwood emphasised the final point with his cigar, and then indicated the door. It was clear that the interview was over, and Ben was more than happy to leave the room.

Chapter 5

Matthew Faden took the steps two at a time, up to the discreet oak door with its restrained brass plate. It opened at his approach and he slipped inside to the heavy familiar smell of leather and wax polish. Faden handed his trilby to the doorman, and a moment later his Chesterfield overcoat was slipped effortlessly off his shoulders by another attendant. They directed him to the club's smaller dining room. Faden noisily clipped his steel heels along the oak floorboards – anything to shatter the life-sucking Saturday silence in the long corridors.

Faden found Fleming White at a table in the right-hand corner at the back, looking out on the little garden. He picked his way through the otherwise empty tables, neatly laid with linen and silver for lunch, and sat without a greeting. He tried to loosen the tension from his neck – fingers reflexively finding and tracing the outline of the birthmark. 'Ah, Matthew,' said White, the albino mane of hair lifting from the obituaries page of *The Times*, 'good to see you again. Thank you for getting in touch, and how have you been this past week?' The grey eyes hovered on Faden. 'If you behave like a sulky schoolboy, it will only draw attention to us. So order a drink like a gentleman and let's talk – I don't have as much time as I thought. I have to leave for another meeting in half an hour. Have you heard the news?'

'I'll have a gin sling,' said Faden, looking up as a frock-coated waiter arrived at the table.

'And another coffee,' added White with a frown, nodding to end the order. He tapped his pipe out into the ashtray, then covered his mouth with his hand as he stifled a yawn. 'Sorry, I've been up half the night. Hitler moved three battalions across the Rhine and into Aachen, Trier and Saarbrücken first thing this morning. We've been hearing the beat of the jungle drums for a couple of days and knew something was coming, but the Cabinet are, inevitably, still all out of town for the weekend, and it's unclear what response we're going to make.'

'So? The Rhineland's part of Germany, isn't it? Why shouldn't they be in there?' replied Faden, almost involuntarily.

'Because, dear boy, a demilitarised Rhineland is crucial to a European peace, which is why it was central to the Versailles Treaty – if we give it up, Hitler will overrun the continent.'

Faden frowned. 'I hardly think the –'

'The Rhineland is Germany's industrial heartland,' interrupted White. 'The whole point of the Versailles Treaty was to forbid the German army from occupying or fortifying the region, so France could take over German industry any time she liked – you can't wage modern war without factories and machines.'

'But it doesn't automatically follow that Hitler intends to conquer Europe,' retorted Faden – he had a huge urge to puncture White's overweening confidence.

'This isn't my private fantasy, Matthew. An hour ago I saw an article that the *Telegraph* had just received from their Berlin correspondent. Hugh Greene was in the Reichstag this morning, listening to Hitler, and he lays it all out clearly. Once the Rhineland is fortified – and you can be damn sure the Germans are already digging in – France cannot come to the aid of any of her eastern allies without taking on that German line. And since, as we speak, the

French are sitting around smoking Gitanes rather than tackling three battalions in open country, the message is clear – *you're on your own*. Hitler can hear it as loud as everyone else – so, Austria will go first, and that will outflank the Czechoslovakian defences, then he'll move on Danzig and the Polish Corridor.'

Faden shook his head; White's superior tone continued to provoke him into arguing. 'But what if Hitler is just lowering his exposure to a French attack? Why make this conclusion of aggressive intent?'

'Because of his book,' replied White, with a trace of sarcasm. 'You should try reading more than just Marx. *Mein Kampf* explains it all – the German people need more land, more space, *Lebensraum*. And it's to be found in the east, and eventually that means – *Russia*.'

Faden remained silent as the waiter returned. White reached into the pocket of his battered tweed jacket and pulled out a stiff leather pouch. He fingered a wad of tobacco into the bowl of his pipe as the drinks were placed in front of them.

'I shall read the article,' said Faden, neutrally, as the waiter withdrew.

'I wouldn't bank on seeing it in print,' replied White. 'Hitler's representative in London, Herr Ribbentrop, is already halfway to getting it spiked.'

Faden picked up the tumbler, swirled the clear fluid for a couple of turns, and then watched as the rich liquid ran back down the sides.

'Matthew, please understand that I'm no happier than you are about why you're here. But this country is in mortal peril, the future is balanced on a knife-edge – and someone in my position has to use every possible tool at his disposal,' said White, bending his head to light the pipe.

Faden tipped back the gin in one swallow. He slammed the tumbler down and took a quick, hard breath – and every possible tool included the sexual blackmail of a godson. He glanced around; a waiter hovered at the bar. He lifted the empty glass an inch off the table and the man nodded.

White frowned again, chewing on the pipe, puffing volubly, before removing it and saying, 'Your father tells me that you've applied to the RAF this week?'

The alcohol reached Faden's brain in a warm surge, and he stared at White, allowing a faint smile to play across his lips.

'I realise that you've done this to put yourself in a position where you are of no use to me. But things are changing fast – we have common cause, Matthew. A week ago at the hunt, I wanted to speak to you about your friends in the East End, but after these events ...' White leaned forward slightly. 'Germany is the principal threat to what we both believe in. I have no more reason to want to see Russia overrun than you do – can you imagine what resources that would make available to Hitler? That's the reason we went to war in 1914; it's been the basis of British foreign policy for hundreds of years – one country cannot be allowed to dominate mainland Europe or they will become strong enough to threaten us.'

White relaxed back into his chair. 'Churchill thinks we can use the League of Nations as a mechanism for building Russia into a coalition against Germany. Frankly, I don't believe the League of Nations could organise a piss-up in a brewery – it's been completely discredited after the shambles over Abyssinia – but Churchill's right about Russia. It is quite possible that soon, on the principle that my enemy's enemy is my friend, I will find myself allied with your comrades in the East End. We may have to abandon the class war temporarily, Matthew – there is a greater enemy at the gates.'

Faden was silent as this speech ended, and a few seconds later the second drink was placed in front of him. He didn't touch it. He didn't take his eyes off White, who now sipped at his coffee, gaze levelled back at him over the rim. The chink of china was loud as White put the cup back down and said, 'You must understand that this thinking is not yet widespread in government circles. A handful of men – Vansittart at the Foreign Office; Churchill, of course – have been warning about the German danger for some time. The rest are coming round, but this might be our last chance for a cheap victory. Things are finely balanced. This is a critical moment. If we send those German troops back across the Rhine with their tails between their legs, Hitler won't last the week. But instead, we're sitting around talking, the French haven't moved from their barracks and our glorious leaders haven't moved from their grace and favour weekend retreats. I think we can be confident that Hitler's move into the Rhineland is already a fait accompli. In the eyes of the German public and his generals, it's a move of strategic genius. And the more they believe in the man, the more likely they are to let him do anything, and he will. Ergo, there will be war.'

Now Faden shook his head, sat back and folded his arms. The leather creaked under him. 'No, there are too many people against it – even your types haven't the stomach for any more of it. Didn't the Oxford Union vote that *this house will not fight for King and Country*?'

'They are your type too, Matthew,' said White, steepling his hands over the coffee.

'No, not any more.'

'We both know you're here because you're terrified I might tell your father about your sexual proclivities, and so get left out of the will and the money.'

Faden smouldered – but he wouldn't be baited any further.

White smiled, a little more conciliatory. 'Look, only a madman could want a repeat of the last war. But Hitler is a madman, and I don't believe for a moment that the British people will stand by and watch while he rapes Europe. All the pacifist protest votes and peace pledges will count for nothing when the bombers start across the Channel, and an invasion fleet gathers in captured French ports. No, the question is not whether there will be a war, the question is whether ...' White leaned forward again. '... *we will be ready*.'

'Rearmament,' Faden ground out.

'Yes.' White nodded. 'Gutless, dissembling politicians have allowed the situation to develop – like so many in the past and doubtless more in the future – to the point where it is balanced on a knife-edge. And now, once again, they won't act in time and all we can do is prepare for the consequences.'

Faden picked up the tumbler and sipped at the gin. 'So what does this mean for me?' he asked, flatly. He looked out of the window. A sparrow was splashing in a Gothic stone bird bath in the middle of the lawn.

White eased back into his chair and relit the pipe. 'I want you to be aware of the situation, and aware of ways that you might help. We have to look at all the alternatives. The first plodding steps towards rearmament are finally being taken in government, and sentiment in the Tory Party is slowly coming around to what Churchill's been telling them for years. There's talk of a new Minister for Coordination of Defence, and if we can get Winston into that job there's real hope. I've a meeting with him this afternoon to see if there are any other ways of making Baldwin see sense.'

'I cannot imagine that you expect me to help you get government money into rearmament, rather than social programmes?' said Faden, but he continued to gaze out of the window – a regal-looking black cat with white flashes over each ear had emerged from the shrubbery, and was slinking across the lawn towards the sparrow.

'No, I don't.'

'Then what?' asked Faden, turning back to White, unable to keep the surprise out of his voice.

'We need as much concrete intelligence as possible about the German rearmament. The Olympic yachting is in Kiel this summer; we'd like to know more about what's going on in the Germania, Howaldt and Deutsche Werft shipyards – do you know anyone going to the Games who might keep their eyes peeled for us?'

Faden shrugged. 'I haven't done any sailing recently. I'm a bit out of the game ...'

'But you could find out?'

Faden nodded.

'Then there's Dunwood,' said White, 'and the rest of those sailing and aviation millionaires.'

'Last weekend?' Faden smiled. 'He didn't seem much of an enthusiast for your war.'

'Not at the moment, but if we get someone into a position of influence, perhaps someone of value to his sailing, then who knows?' continued White.

'And talk him into building fighters?' Faden laughed incredulously.

'If the state is incapable of action, we must turn to private capital to save us. Plenty of rich men have stayed rich through the Depression. If these fellows can afford their damn great yachts, then they can afford to build some planes.' White leaned forward and tapped his pipe out into the ashtray. 'Now what about this fellow Clayton?'

Faden shook his head. 'A scholarship boy, quite brilliant, but he'll have no influence over someone like Dunwood. Lerup would be your man.'

For the first time White hesitated; he scratched at an ear. 'Lerup has a role to play already,' he said. 'I have to look at other alternatives. Reggie Mitchell and his engineers at Supermarine successfully flew a new fighter for the first time a couple of days ago. Both Vickers and Rolls-Royce have backed this plane with their own money, and we need to keep them going full steam ahead. Jimmy Bird, who runs Supermarine, keeps a yacht on the river out at the front of the factory. At the other end of Southampton Water, you have Dick Fairey's business – and he's developing that Swordfish torpedo bomber. But things are stalled at Hawker Siddeley, where Sopwith has another monoplane fighter – the Hurricane – that's actually ready to go into production. But like Dunwood, he seems more worried about building bloody yachts than planes. Sopwith isn't going to move on the Hurricane without an order from the Air Ministry, and my sources tell me that could still be months away. And every month lost means we could be short another couple of squadrons when the balloon goes up.'

White jabbed a finger at Faden. 'Yachting is your world, Matthew, you know people. Get me some good information on what's happening in Kiel, or find some way to help me exert influence on any of these men – particularly Sopwith and Dunwood. I want people pushing on with fighter or bomber production *without* an Air Ministry order. Help us do that and I'm prepared to forget your little indiscretion.'

'Forget?'

'I'll destroy the file.'

'Doesn't make any difference, a word from you to my father ...'

'I give you my word, as a gentleman.'

Faden repressed a sardonic smile. He swirled the gin a couple of times around the tumbler. 'I'll see what I can do,' he said, and poured the rest of the drink down his throat, glancing out of the window as he did so. The cat was playing on the grass with the broken body of the sparrow.

'Good. Not a word of this to anyone, you understand? If you find someone, you call me and give me a name – leave the approach to us, these things have to be handled in a particular way,' said White.

Faden nodded, dropped the glass on the table, pushed back the chair and walked out.

Chapter 6

Ben Clayton felt it in his guts before he heard it – a throbbing bass growl. The mourners were gathered round the grave in cold, watery sunshine amidst further hints that winter might be over – one or two brave daffodils, a softness to the air – even if spring had not yet begun. It was a beautiful day for Stanley Arbethwaite's funeral. Like Ben, many of the men were resplendent in morning dress, others in full uniform – swords and epaulettes glittering, along with the Great War's legacy of medalled chests and missing limbs. The women were equally splendid in their best black lace, silk and linen, with matching hats. Some held a handkerchief in a spotlessly gloved hand. The remains of Stanley Arbethwaite had arrived in style – the hearse drawn by two magnificent black horses, ostrich-feather plumes on the bridles, the clip of their shoes on the road sharp in the cold air. They had jostled to a nervous halt at the church gates, and Ben had stepped forward to take his place amongst the pall-bearers.

Now the noise got louder and others at the grave started to turn their heads to the sky, and he knew he wasn't imagining it. It was the sound of the V-12 Merlin engine that Rolls-Royce had supplied for the fighter that Stanley had helped to design. The plane had completed its maiden test flight from Eastleigh airfield just two days previously. Now it was approaching from the north, coming down the Hamble Valley, following the river. It broke off and banked into a turn, coming straight towards them, almost brushing the trees over Hamble House as it flattened out. There was a flash from the low sun reflected in the cockpit glass, the distinctive silhouette of the elliptical wing, and that visceral engine note, booming back off the solid Norman walls of St Andrews Church. Then it was gone. He didn't listen after that. Only by disengaging himself from it all was he able to get through it. When the first earth hit the coffin with a sound like death itself, he stepped back from the grave, throat choked, blinking back tears. The crowd started to ease its way towards the road, and he allowed himself to drift along with it. Then Lucy was beside him. She linked her arm round his and took his hand.

'All right?' she asked.

He nodded – he didn't trust himself to speak.

'You'll feel better soon,' she said, softly.

He didn't answer.

'When my mother died,' Lucy spoke slowly, deliberately, 'I thought everything had come to an end. I couldn't see how I could ever feel happy again. But I did, I do. I still miss her terribly, but there is a time when it's not so ... painful ...' She trailed into silence. He squeezed her hand a little tighter.

As they reached the top of the High Street, Dunwood's Bentley passed them, heading out of the village. 'I heard Mr Dunwood helped pay for the funeral and the wake,' said Lucy, more matter-of-factly. 'So Mrs Arbethwaite invited more people. There are a lot of the men here from the yacht.'

He nodded, and coughed to clear his throat, before trying out his voice. 'Plenty of people from Supermarine as well,' he said.

'He was very popular, your friend,' replied Lucy.

'He was a good man.'

They walked on in silence.

'How have you been?' asked Lucy, eventually, as they went past the Victory Inn.

'It's been a tough few days.' He rubbed a hand across his face.

'I was hoping I might have seen you,' said Lucy.

'I'm sorry, Lucy, but all I've done is work.' He could hear the exhaustion in his flat voice, feel it in every bone in his body. 'Supermarine insisted I do my week's notice before I could leave, and the only way I could do that and get the mast finished was by going to Gosport before and after work every day.'

'Is the mast done?'

'Yes.'

'Well, I forgive you,' said Lucy, then after a moment, 'And nothing more from the police?'

'No, Dunwood told me the investigation was over, and it certainly seems that way.'

Lucy nodded her acknowledgement but didn't say any more. The wake was being held at the Hamble River Sailing Club, and when they arrived Ben went to get them both a drink. He returned with two cups of tea to find Lucy alone, looking out of the window at the river. He stood beside her. The marshy foreshore beyond The Hard leaked away from them down to the water, where yachts and fishing boats were lounging indolently in their mud berths. Behind them, someone stifled a too-high-pitched laugh. Lucy took the cup of tea. 'It's a nice do, isn't it,' she observed.

He nodded his agreement. Dunwood's money had been at work; the clubhouse looked uncharacteristically smart. The trestle tables were swathed in white linen and sagged under mountains of food, while frock-coated waiters swirled soundlessly to and fro, through the thick cigarette smoke. It was all rather incongruous against the battered noticeboards with the yellowing 'For Sale' signs and the list of results posted from the previous autumn's racing. He would have been more comfortable with something simpler, but he wasn't sure that Stanley would have agreed. He'd had a taste for the high life.

'Is that Lerup?' said Lucy, nodding towards a figure approaching the club along The Hard.

Ben followed the direction she was looking and snorted, 'Still wearing that linen suit, hardly right for a funeral.'

Lucy shook her head, turning back to the room. 'It is a bit strange, him coming here, don't you think?'

Ben sipped at his tea as he watched Lerup disappear from view down the side of the building. He'd forgotten to put the sugar in. He grimaced, and felt his pockets. He was out of cigarettes.

'There's something going on out there,' said Lucy, suddenly. The open rear door of the club led out onto a scrubby piece of grass, and a knot of men was starting to gather round it. 'Come on, let's go and see what's happening,' she added, putting her cup down. Ben followed Lucy's slight figure through the gaps in the crowd, moving forward in her wake.

Lerup's voice was clear as they approached. 'It's self-evident, Captain Emerton, that you are ultimately responsible for the safety of everyone aboard the yacht.'

Ben arrived at the edge of the open door on Lucy's shoulder. The two men were standing toe-to-toe on the sickly grass. Emerton had his arms folded. Lerup held his leather driving gloves in his right hand, and was tapping them into the palm of the left. The panama hat was set at a particularly jaunty angle.

'I'm not denying the responsibility,' replied Emerton. 'I never have.'

'Well then, you must take your responsibility seriously, and resign.'

The crowd gasped.

Even the unflappable Emerton was momentarily taken aback. 'Resign ...?'

'Of course, the only decent thing a man can do in your position,' said Lerup, in a tone that suggested this should be completely obvious.

'My position? That accident happened because of your ridiculous schedule. I've been warning for months that the men couldn't keep this up, that there would be trouble,' replied Emerton.

'I'm sorry, Captain, we agreed you were responsible. A man has died, most tragically' – Lerup waved his gloves at the wake – 'and you are at fault. You will resign.'

'No,' replied Emerton, shaking his head.

'Then I'm afraid I shall have to fire you. Consider yourself removed from all your duties aboard the *Windflower* forthwith. Mr Dunwood has generously offered to pay you two more weeks' wages. I'll have the money sent round. Don't come anywhere near the yacht. Good day to you, Captain.'

Emerton didn't protest. He just watched, his face bemused, disbelieving, as Lerup turned on his heel and strode back the way he had come. As he disappeared around the corner, Emerton glanced at the silent crowd. He gave a momentary puzzled shake of his head, before turning and limping up the hill away from the river. Everyone watched him go, but no one followed. Anxious chatter started to bubble up all around.

'That ain't bloody right,' growled an unfamiliar voice.

'Who's that?' asked Ben, indicating the source – a big bearded man in a too-tight lounge suit, now bumping through the crowd.

'Jim Rails,' Lucy whispered in his ear. 'Got a nasty temper and beats his wife, poor love. The Captain just hired him because there's so much still to do – but you shouldn't have anything to do with him.'

Ben watched Rails head straight to the bar, and then turned back to Lucy. 'Where's your father?' he asked.

'I don't know,' replied Lucy. 'I haven't seen Dad since breakfast. When he left this morning, he said he had some work to finish and might be late. He didn't come back on the lorry. I haven't seen him here.'

'Someone should go and talk to the Captain.'

'I'll get Dad to go round and see him, as soon as he gets here. Where on earth is he?'

'I don't know, it must be something important, or he'd be here for certain.'

'The Captain's not been fired because of the accident, has he?' said Lucy, looking at Ben.

'No, it's because he stood up to Lerup, when he got me to repair the mast,' he replied. 'Lerup won't stand for anyone interfering with the way he runs the boat. He just wants the Captain to shut up and do as he's told.' He glanced around again; the *Windflower* men were gathering unhappily, the biggest group had formed around Rails at the bar. 'But I can't believe that Dunwood agreed to this,' he said.

'Maybe that's why he didn't come to the wake,' replied Lucy. 'Do you think if Lerup gave him an ultimatum – me or him – Dunwood would back the Captain?'

Ben shook his head. 'No ... but ... this is just awful; if anything, Lerup is more responsible than the Captain. He was the one rushing everything. We shouldn't just have to accept this ...'

'There's nothing we can do,' said Lucy. 'Bosses don't change their minds on things like this. It'd make Lerup look foolish. Never forget it's a game for rich and powerful men, and little people sometimes get crushed. So you watch yourself, because the Captain helped get you the job and Lerup will have it in for you now. And it won't help if he thinks you're a gentleman in competition for Dunwood's ear either. So be careful for the time being. Let things calm down again.'

He looked at her circumspectly for a moment, and then sighed with frustration, pushing the hair back out of his eyes as he did so. 'You're right,' he replied, grudgingly, 'but I just hate feeling so bloody powerless.'

'Something you're going to have to get used to if you want to race the big yachts,' replied Lucy.

'Maybe,' he muttered in half-hearted agreement. 'I need something stronger than tea; I'll get us a proper drink,' he added.

Matthew Faden walked briskly east along Commercial Road, watching a powerful chestnut dray horse clip past in the opposite direction, towing a vast wagon of barrels. He waited till it was gone, then stopped abruptly to look in the window of a haberdashery. A quick glance told him once again that there was no one behind him. He'd checked every few minutes to see if White's men had been following him from Piccadilly, drifting north via glittering Regent Street shops and then east by smoky Soho cafes. Finally, convinced that he was in the clear, he'd headed to Embankment and rattled his way out towards the docks on the District Line. White's reference to his 'friends in the East End' was pretty loose. Faden could only guess at how much the spymaster knew, but however much it was, it was critical that the slippery old bastard didn't learn any more.

Faden had talked through this possibility with the most important of those friends a couple of times. They had a plan, although he'd never really thought that it would come to this – that's why he'd left it till now. He should have made this drop last week, as soon as White had made his approach and his intent was clear. But right up to the meeting in the club this morning, he'd hoped that there might be some other way. Not any more. Faden fingered the thinly folded paper message in his coat pocket. He'd coded it on the one-time pad, just as they had showed him. Now he had to deliver it.

The cry of a rag-and-bone man reached him on the cold east wind. Realising that he needed to take advantage of the quiet streets, Faden set off again, turning at the next left. He made the small chalk star on the brick as he went past, walking slowly up into Settles Street. There was a crack carved out of the cement in the terrace wall just twenty yards further. He glanced around one more time, but could see no one. He stopped to light a cigarette, slipping the message into the crack as he did so, and then walked on. It was done.

Ben drained his glass of Fielder's, then took Lucy's empty sherry glass from her and returned them both to the bar. Mrs Arbethwaite was seeing the last guests out of the door.

'Is she walking back to the house with you?' asked Lucy, as he returned to her side.

'Yes, I think so.'

'Would you like me to come with you?'

He looked at her. 'Would you, really?'

Lucy nodded; she smiled encouragingly.

'What about your father?'

'I can't believe he'd get back to the village and not come here first. I'll see him later, when he gets home. Don't worry, I'll get him to go and talk to the Captain after tea.'

'All right.'

'You'd better go and talk to her.'

He walked over. 'Mrs Arbethwaite,' he began, uncertainly, he hadn't seen her since the night Stanley died.

'Oh, Ben,' she sighed. 'What a terrible, terrible thing. I wish you had never gone to work on that yacht.'

Ben swallowed back a hot flush of guilt. 'I know, Mrs Arbethwaite, I'm so sorry ... I should never ...'

'No.' She shook her head. 'It was something you both wanted to do. Stanley was always happy when he was working with you.' The hazel, slightly beady eyes regarded him circumspectly from over dark bags in the fleshy cheeks. She fiddled with the black-and-silver celluloid-and-diamante brooch on her lapel.

He could think of no way to respond.

After a couple of seconds, she took a deep breath and sighed again. 'It was a good sending off though, Stanley would have been so proud to see all these people here for him.'

'Yes, yes, he would,' he replied. She was still wearing

her hat and veil, and as he was almost a foot taller, he could see where the silk tulle had been attached to the felt with an uneven series of hat pins and a single safety pin. The imperfection was not like Mrs Arbethwaite.

'Generally,' she went on, 'as you know, I wouldn't trouble with a big to-do like this, all these people. I can't believe who turned up.' She laid an anxious hand on his arm. 'Did you see Mr Dunwood? I must have missed him, but so kind and generous. And that Mr Lerup, the one people have taken against? He was here. People say he's dined with the King. Can you imagine, at Stanley's funeral?'

Once again, he could think of no reply; at least the day seemed to have temporarily eased the pain of Stanley's passing.

'It's nice to be home ...' Mrs Arbethwaite hesitated. 'You'll come with me up to the house? Only I ...'

'Of course,' he replied; he indicated Lucy, still standing some distance away, watching. 'We thought ...'

Vivian Arbethwaite straightened her back. She had compressed her generous figure into a slightly too-small black dress. Now she smoothed the wrinkles from over her hips, folded her arms and leaned towards him. 'You know what I think about that girl. You can do better than that, and I won't have her at the house.'

He hesitated. Several seconds passed agonisingly. And then he returned to Lucy.

'She doesn't want you to come,' he told her.

'Oh,' said Lucy, surprised. 'I thought that today ...'

'So did I.' Ben shrugged.

'Silly woman, thinking her shit don't stink and her tea's a dinner.'

'Shhh ...'

'What did you say to her?'

'I didn't. Lucy, for God's sake, it's Stanley's funeral. I can't argue with her today.'

Lucy looked at him, her mouth setting in a firm line.

'You know I don't think like her,' he said. 'I've never given you any reason to believe that I think like her. Men like your father taught me to sail. They were my only real family when I was in my teenage years. How could I have anything but proper respect for you?'

Lucy bit down on her lower lip. 'But then, why ...?' She tailed off, an imploring note to her voice.

He knew what she was thinking after that tactless remark from her father a week ago. And he knew that this was not the moment to try to explain that for them to wed, he'd have to talk to his parents. Something he'd not done for over eight years. 'Lucy, please. Not now.' He reached out and touched her forearm. 'I'm really sorry, but let's just get through this day.'

She gazed into his eyes for a moment, seemed to be reassured by what she saw there and nodded. 'All right, of course.'

'The mast goes in *Windflower* tomorrow; I'll come and see you when it's done.'

She nodded again, blew him a discreet kiss, turned and left.

It was late afternoon and the low sun cast dark shadows over the cold cobbles as they headed up the hill towards the Square, Ben lugging the suitcase that Mrs Arbethwaite had brought back from Winchester. It was heavy and he was grateful when she turned the key in the lock and he could dump it in the hall. Mrs Arbethwaite hung her coat up and then led the way to the kitchen. She hesitated for a moment in the doorway, and surveyed the scene. Not much had changed since she'd left it. Lucy's and Ben's teacups from the previous weekend still stood on the draining board, there was a big pile of mail in the middle of the kitchen table and things were a little dustier.

'Perhaps you'll take that suitcase up to our ...' She hesitated, a catch in her voice. 'Up to my room, and I'll put the kettle on and make some tea while I open this post.'

He did as she asked, and continued up to his attic room to change out of the rented morning suit and into some slacks. When he returned downstairs he found her in tears, surrounded by the opened post. She looked up at him, her flushed heavy cheeks gleaming wetly, and indicated the letters.

'What's all this, Ben? I don't understand,' she said.

He moved to switch off the furiously gurgling kettle and then sat beside her. There were some letters of condolence, but the vast majority appeared to be bills. He picked one up – electricity, six months in arrears, a threat to disconnect. Another – hire purchase for the electric heater, two months overdue, nothing paid since they had bought it. Then a letter from Supermarine, about the mortgage on the house. He knew that the company was generous with loans for staff to buy their own homes. The letter was addressed to Mrs Arbethwaite – condolences for the loss of her husband, didn't want to bring her attention to this under the circumstances, but ... the payments were six months overdue. The letter requested a meeting at her earliest convenience to discuss the matter, and gave the phone number of a Mr Cavendish in accounts. Ben let the paper slide out of his fingers back onto the table and took a deep, slow breath. She passed him a hire purchase from a furniture store with red all over it. There were the rates – unpaid. It was all debt – hundreds of pounds of debt.

'I don't understand,' she said, through heaving sobs. 'Stanley was always so careful with his money, where's it all gone?'

He was as astonished as she was; from this evidence, eight months ago the Arbethwaites' bills had started to spiral out of control. Drink didn't seem likely; he felt sure that he'd have noticed that, either at home or at work. No, Stanley had been working perfectly normally, with all his faculties. Tired and harassed, yes – but who wasn't? So, the money must have gone into some kind of investment that had failed – or he'd spent it on girls or gambling, or both,

God forbid.

Ben made the tea, tidied the bills up and did some sums, trying to relieve her misery. But since there was nothing practical that either of them could do about it that night, he eventually cleared it all away – out of sight, out of mind. He told Mrs Arbethwaite not to worry, that there had to be some kind of mistake, that Stanley couldn't have left her in this mess. He would make some phone calls on Monday from work and try to sort it out. But he didn't have any confidence in the comforting words; from what he could see there was every danger that she could lose it all – house, furniture and car. He could feel his guilt at Stanley's death being supplanted by a sense of responsibility for his friend's wife.

Finally, she declared that she was going to bed, and he too made his way up to his room. Without thinking, he flicked the switch and dropped the gramophone needle into the opening groove of Duke Ellington's 'East St Louis Toodle-Oo'. But as the mournful refrain from Bubber Miley's trumpet crackled into life, he realised Mrs Arbethwaite wouldn't appreciate it quite as much. He turned it off again and slumped onto the bed, feeling his pockets for cigarettes, and then remembering that he had none. A smoke and the Duke – that was what he needed, and he could have neither. Christ, what a day. He lay back, fully dressed, and stared up through the skylight at the stars, listening to the creaks, groans and gurgles of the house as Vivian Arbethwaite made her way from kitchen to bathroom to bedroom. He wondered about Stanley, and the money. And he wondered what Lucy was doing, what she was thinking. He always missed her at this time of day. He knew about the whispers behind their backs in the High Street, the chattering over village fences. *That Ben Clayton fellow, bit above her, he is, don't think he'll ever pop the question, poor Lucy, hanging on, not getting any younger ...* Damn, he needed a smoke.

Chapter 7

Although Ben had the alarm set early, he woke before it sounded. He switched it off, rolled out of the bed and realised he had fallen asleep fully dressed. He thought he should change, but Mrs Arbethwaite hadn't been there to do the washing, nor had he had time to take it out to anyone. He had no clean shirts or underwear, so he didn't bother. He stumbled to the washstand, threw cold water on his face, rubbed hard with a towel to wake himself and then crept down the attic staircase, dodging the loose floorboards. He had a sense, as he tiptoed past Vivian Arbethwaite's door, that she was awake – but perhaps she was also unable to face company over the bacon and eggs.

He found his coat, goggles, helmet and gloves by the back door, then pushed his motorbike down to the road in the half-light, just a scrunch of gravel to mark his passing. It took him a full minute to kick the bike warm. But once the twin-cylinder engine of the Scott was going, he sank into the saddle with relief and lost himself in the ride to Gosport. He gunned the bike hard, snapping down through the gears into the corners, hunched low to the distinctive petrol tank as he accelerated out of them, the wind flapping the ear covers on his old flying helmet, blasting past the dark meadows and shadowy farms of the Hampshire countryside.

Once through the gate of the boatyard, Ben angled

over to where the mast had been positioned on the dock, lying on trestles beside the *Windflower*, and turned off the engine. He kicked the stand down and eased himself out of the saddle, still sore on the hip from more than a week ago. He unbuttoned his leather topcoat, rolling his tight shoulders and rubbing his stiff neck, then pulled off his goggles, helmet and gloves. He was already scanning the mast to check that everything was as they had left it. It had rained overnight and there were puddles around the yard, but at the moment they, like the surface of the harbour, were pristine, unruffled. Not a breath of wind, and although it was warmer than it had been, it didn't look like there was going to be any imminent change in the weather. He just had time for that final tweak to the spinnaker sheave block while the mast was still on the ground.

He was tidying the tools away an hour later when he heard footsteps. He looked up to see Dunwood and Lerup approaching. He felt hostility rising. He dropped a screwdriver into the tray, and told himself to calm down. However he felt about Lerup and to a lesser extent Dunwood, he needed them both. He badly wanted to keep the job and go to America. He tried a smile.

'Good morning,' he said.

'Where the bloody hell is everyone?' asked Lerup.

Ben straightened, checked his watch. It was past eight; the Hamble lorry should have arrived by now. 'I don't know. I came on the bike.' He waved at the Scott.

'A Scott, huh?' said Dunwood, pausing to spit out a stray piece of tobacco from his cigar. 'I had one of those back in the early twenties. May forced me to give it up after we had Edward. Too bloody dangerous by half she reckoned. All right for you youngsters, eh?'

Ben picked up a rag off the mast and wiped his hands. 'She rides like a dream,' he said. 'They've done a nice job getting the centre of gravity low and the balance right.' He loved his bike, but it wasn't a Bugatti Type 35A, and he could see by the sardonic half smile that Lerup knew it.

Dunwood nodded thoughtfully. 'I might get you to help out the design team at the factory for a day or two when you can spare the time. We could do with a fresh mind working on the new plane just at the moment.'

'I'd be happy to do whatever I can, sir,' he said, rolling the rag into a ball.

'And any other ideas you've got for the *Windflower* are welcome,' continued Dunwood, 'don't feel restricted to just the mast; we're going to need everyone to pull their weight if we're to beat Sopwith. I know you're a clever chap, so don't hold back.'

Lerup had wandered off along the length of the mast and was now ten yards away, tapping a cigarette languidly on the back of his silver case and apparently inspecting the repair work. But before Ben could reply, the *Windflower* lorry drove through the gate. It parked just inside the entrance, and Joe Kirk got down from the cab carrying a coil of rope, then walked round to the back and opened the tailgate. The crew streamed out of the lorry and gathered around him. This was not, Ben noticed, the normal procedure. The two men with him also seemed to sense that something was different. Lerup moved to stand beside Dunwood, as the crew formed themselves up behind Joe Kirk and started towards them. Ben was aware of the sense of injustice, of perpetual conflict, of the iron-hard vein of seriousness that ran through Lucy's father – but he had never seen such intensity grip the man's body. And when they all pulled up a couple of yards away from Dunwood and Lerup, Ben was not unhappy to be on the other side of the mast. It left him slightly detached from the scene. He leaned on the spar to watch.

'Morning, Mr Dunwood,' said Kirk. 'Sir, me and the crew got a few words to say, if you please.'

'Go ahead,' said Dunwood.

'This is the missing downhaul.' Kirk presented the rope in his hand. 'I spliced it to the bosun's chair the night before we put the mast in. It was by the mast, all ready to go. But when I checked the morning after the accident, there was an identical coil of this same rope, in the same place as I left the original, but with perfect factory finished ends.' Kirk held up one end of the downhaul, showing roughly severed strands. 'And *this* one's been cut away from the chair.'

Ben felt his heart thump.

'I found it yesterday afternoon,' continued Kirk, 'dumped at the bottom of a bin round the back of the rigging shed.' There was a pause. 'Mr Lerup sacked the Captain over an accident, but it looks more like murder to me.'

Ben felt a connection click in his brain even through the flash of astonished scepticism.

Then Lerup laughed. 'You must be mad, Kirk. That is the most fantastic tale I've ever heard. You want us to believe it was *murder*?'

Kirk's forehead furrowed, eyebrows darkly set. 'There's no other way these things could have happened. No one on my crew would cut the downhaul off the chair the morning before the mast was going in, and no one on my crew would replace it with a new one and not do the splice. Someone wanted to hurt whoever went up that rig. And we all knew Mr Arbethwaite would be first in that chair.' Kirk glanced at the crew either side of him. 'So we want the bogeys back and we want Captain Emerton back. He can't be held responsible for something done by a murderer.'

Lerup tossed the cigarette to one side. He stepped forward and snatched the downhaul out of Kirk's hands, waved it in his face. 'This proves nothing, you idiot. You could have got this anywhere, you could have cut the end off yourself, for God's sake. The whole thing's just a fabrication to get Emerton back. It's utter rubbish from beginning to end.'

Joe Kirk hunched his shoulders and folded his arms. 'There won't be any more work done on this boat until the Captain gets his job back, and the bogeys are brought in to investigate,' he said.

The rope sagged to Lerup's side. 'A strike?' he said, in a voice tight with fury. 'I don't believe it. Put this back wherever you found it, and get some work done.' Lerup tossed the rope in the dirt at Kirk's feet. He looked around the crowd. 'You hear me? The lot of you get to work and stop this nonsense.'

'We've got a right to strike, Mr Lerup,' said Kirk, 'and you can be damn sure you won't find no one else'll sail on this boat, not who knows his port from his starboard anyways.' He bent and picked up the downhaul, and then turned to the crew, who made a path through so he could lead them back towards the lorry.

'If you think you can take that lorry back to Hamble, then you've got another think coming,' yelled Lerup. 'You touch that vehicle and I'll have you all up for the robbery.'

The men changed direction and marched towards the gate.

'And the same goes for that rope, it doesn't belong to you and it doesn't leave the premises,' shouted Lerup.

'I'm taking this to the police for the evidence,' Kirk yelled back over his shoulder, shaking the downhaul. 'So if you want to call 'em down here you'll save me the trouble of the journey.'

'How utterly bloody,' said Lerup, as the strikers disappeared out of the gate. 'The nerve of the fellow.' He reached for the cigarette case and lighter inside his jacket.

'What if he's right?' said Dunwood, hand around his chin, working the loose flesh, huffing out volumes of smoke.

'People like Joe Kirk aren't right, they just have a ruddy great chip on their shoulder.' Lerup pushed a cigarette between his lips as he finished.

'So you're convinced that there's nothing in this?'

'Of course not, he's made the whole thing up to get Emerton back. What did that detective fellow tell us a couple of days ago? An unfortunate accident, no one to blame.' Lerup twitched his thumb impatiently at the lighter's ignition wheel.

Dunwood had taken off his homburg and was poking and prodding at the brim. 'Well, I have to say,' he began, 'things haven't gone that well for us recently. The boat's late, then Arbethwaite gets killed ...'

'All the more reason why we should push on,' said Lerup, finally filling his lungs with smoke, thrusting the lighter and cigarette case back into his jacket pocket. 'We didn't win an empire by giving up at the first sign of trouble,' he continued. 'We can't let ourselves be derailed by a man like Kirk – he's red through and through, a pinko commie bastard. We need tough leadership and now's the time to show it, Harold.'

Dunwood's jowls set as he clenched his cigar. 'Kirk's a communist, you say?'

'I know it,' replied Lerup.

Dunwood's face tightened; he placed his hat back on his head, adjusted it till it was just right and then squared his shoulders. 'I don't like being pushed around by the bloody commies; I've had this problem at the factories. Only way to deal with it is to sack the lot of them. No question – problem is, where the hell do we find another crew? Kirk's right about that – it won't be easy finding professionals who will work for us now.' Dunwood stabbed the hot end of the cigar in Lerup's direction. 'Come on, Lerup, it was you who insisted on sacking Emerton; if you hadn't we wouldn't be in this situation – can't you come up with men that will sail the boat for us? All these years in these damn yachts – you must know people that will break a strike?'

Then Dunwood spun on his heel, snapped his fingers and pointed at Ben. 'Of course! Of course! Amateurs! Just like Sopwith in '34, we'll get an amateur crew! When those damned Essex fishermen went on strike for more pay in '34, Sopwith sacked the lot of them and got amateurs in.' He turned back to Lerup. 'And he got one of those university chaps to organise it, that fellow who sailed on *Shamrock* with Dick Fairey.'

Lerup frowned. 'Are you sure that's going to work? No one thought that crew did Tommy Sopwith's chances any favours. And while I'm damned sure that man for man the amateur is better than the professional, we still don't have much time to get a crew trained up from scratch. Isn't there another solution?' Lerup took a final deep drag on his cigarette and then flicked the butt into the water.

'Like what?' Dunwood's gaze bored into Lerup, who looked down and ground a stone under the sole of his shoe in silence.

'Exactly,' continued Dunwood, 'it's just like breaking the General Strike, we'll get the students in – Clayton, you must know people, the top amateurs?' The cigar was stabbing urgently in his direction.

Ben nodded.

'Excellent, excellent. Well, first thing tomorrow morning we'll get you into the Hamble factory, give you a desk and a telephone and you can rustle up a crew for us. What d'you say? You'll be the first aboard, of course.'

Ben gazed at the gate through which the crew had disappeared.

'Well, come on, man, what's wrong, for God's sake? Don't you want to sail aboard the *Windflower*? Don't you want to go to America?'

'Of course I do, Mr Dunwood,' murmured Ben.

'Then that's settled, nine o'clock sharp at the factory in Hamble tomorrow morning and we'll get you started.' Dunwood glanced back to Lerup. 'And what I want you to do right now, Charles, is tell Kirk and his cronies that they're fired.'

Lerup looked up, a faint smile on his lips. 'Ah, now that I can do for you with pleasure, Harold.'

Chapter 8

Lucy ran along The Hard, dodging the baker's van as she flew into Back Street, turning down towards the Luke Brothers boatyard. She held her skirt clear of her legs with one hand, and clamped her hat firmly onto her head with the other. Yes! The gates were open. She tore down the passage beside the main shed, a corrugated iron wall stacked with offcuts, scaffolding poles and shoring timbers.

'Morning, Bob,' she gasped, slowing as she rounded the corner onto the muddy foreshore.

Bob Allet, the yard's bosun, was on the waterfront, bent over a little pram dinghy, painting. He straightened slowly, brush held carefully to avoid a drip, rheumy eyes blinking. 'You'll be late for your own funeral, Lucy,' he said. 'What is it this time?'

'Late for work,' she gasped, breathing hard, 'please can I borrow one of the dinghies? My bike's got a flat tyre.'

'Well, I think that'd be all right,' said Bob, with a serious tone. 'But I need to have a quick word with you about something first, that thing we talked about the other day.'

She looked at him blankly.

'The *Silver Crescent*?' he prompted.

'Oh, yes,' she said. The *Silver Crescent* was Captain Emerton's boat.

'You were right,' he said. 'I had a bit of a poke around,

and Jim Rails has put that repair onto some rot and painted right over it.'

Lucy frowned at the recollection. She had been doing daywork in the yard when Rails had done the job on the stern of the *Silver Crescent*, and a shocking botch he had made of it too. But Lucy wasn't sure she wanted to be the one responsible for catching him at some shoddy work, so she'd told the bosun, hoping he might report it.

'Have you told anyone else?' he asked. He rested the brush in the pot as he spoke, taking the cigarette out of his mouth between thumb and forefinger, carefully blowing the ash off it, fingers already yellow with the nicotine.

She shook her head.

'See here, Jim Rails caught me having a look at it, and he made it pretty clear that he wasn't going to be happy if Captain Emerton found out. He said he'd be blaming me for that ...' He let the idea hang in the air.

Her expression darkened. The bosun was sixty-five years old, and he'd lost a foot to the Boer War. He'd then lost his only son to a German sniper on the Somme in 1916, and his wife and the two grandchildren to the influenza epidemic of 1918. He didn't need any more trouble, not with a man like Rails.

'The boat's back in the water now anyways,' went on Bob, finally, 'so not much could be done about it till the autumn. It won't come to no harm, the bad patch being high up on the stern like that, and next winter when she comes in, I'll make sure one of the other lads just finds it accidental-like, and we'll redo it proper ... I don't think it'll make no trouble for anyone then.'

She hesitated. It was wrong to say nothing; they really should tell Captain Emerton – even if it did mean trouble with Rails. But on the other hand, as Bob had said, the rotten patch was well above the waterline, and what could happen between now and the autumn?

'Perhaps you're right,' she said, conscious that time was slipping away and she badly needed the loan of the dinghy.

'Best not to mention it again; we'll wait till the boat comes back in here in November. You won't say anything to your father?' he added.

'No, all right.' She managed a quick, tight, little smile, feeling both guilty and relieved.

'So you take *Greta,*' he replied, 'no one else is going to be using her, it being a Sunday and all.'

'Oh, thank you.' Lucy grinned with relief.

'You young 'uns should be out having some fun on a Sunday,' replied Bob, dipping the brush back in the paint.

'Ben's putting the mast in *Windflower*. And I promised I'd go in and help Miss Ritchie with the books for a few hours, she's got behind while she was off sick.'

He nodded at the dinghy. '*Greta*'s right there, the oars are in her.'

'Thank you,' she said, then leaned over and pecked him on the cheek. Bob smiled at her. She ran over to *Greta* and started untying the tether. Now she was really late. She didn't notice the motorbike engine until the bike itself rounded the corner. She looked round, rope in her hand, to see Ben come to a halt in a little hail of mud and gravel ten feet away. He kicked the stand down and pulled off his helmet and goggles, hooking them on the handlebars as he climbed off the bike.

'What on earth are you doing here?' she asked.

'We need to have a talk,' he said.

'Talk? Now? What about? I'm late for work,' she replied, already turning away and tugging at the rope tether. The little rowing boat bobbed towards her obediently.

Then he was beside her, his hand on hers, taking the rope. 'I'll row. We can talk on the way up the river.'

'How will you get back? I need the boat to come home at lunchtime,' she said.

'I'll wait, or walk back. Come on, you said you were late.'

'All right,' she replied, and hopped across the two thwarts in a couple of steps, treading lightly, the boat barely rocking as she planted each foot neatly on the centreline. Ben followed, rather more heavily. He pushed off and the boat slid backwards out into the river as he readied the oars. He spun the boat around and set it heading up towards Bursledon. The water was calm, the sun hovering over the tree-lined eastern bank, with a faint smell of woodsmoke hanging in the air. It reminded her of the day they had met, although that had been late summer, warmer and earlier in the morning.

She had borrowed one of the yard's dinghies that day too, rowing upstream to find a quiet, secluded spot to go swimming. Ben had been sailing downriver, taking a boat to Luke Brothers for a friend. He'd slowed when he saw her and asked if she needed help. She'd told him no, that the water was beautiful, and that she did this for fun. He'd suggested that he might join her. She'd agreed that that was a fine idea. He hadn't realised that she was naked until he was in the water. She smiled at the memory. They'd been going together since that first day. She'd only seen him around the village a couple of times before that and didn't know much about him, only that he worked in town and wasn't local. It might have been intimidating if they'd met in a different way, and worse if she'd known then about university and his degree and everything. And ever since then he hadn't just made her feel loved but ... his equal. And now, well ... eighteen months together was a long time.

A small Bermuda-rigged yacht – no more than thirty-five feet on her dark blue waterline – was motoring up behind them, and the light *phut-phut* of the engine attracted Lucy's attention as it drew level. The boat appeared to have completed a long passage. The mainsail was loosely gathered on the boom, the headsail still lay in a heap of canvas on the foredeck. A tattered German ensign hung limply over the stern, and a man sat slumped at the tiller in dirty yellow oilskins. He raised a tired hand, and

Lucy waved back. The boat was well down on its waterline, maybe they'd had some trouble, taken on water.

'Have you talked to your father since he left for the boatyard?' asked Ben.

She looked at him, her head cocked slightly, puzzled. 'No, how could I, he's at work ...'

'What about the downhaul your father found, did he tell you about that?'

'Yes, he told me last night – is it possible that someone could do that to Stanley? But Dad said he was going to show it to Dunwood and set things straight, get Captain Emerton his job back. Why, what's happened?' She shifted impatiently, suddenly concerned.

'He did just that,' started Ben, 'but it didn't go well.' He stopped at the top of a stroke, pausing before he started into the next, the boat beginning to slow. 'Lerup dismissed the idea that Stanley was murdered as ridiculous, and your father called the men out on strike.'

'What! Oh my God!' exclaimed Lucy.

Ben told her the whole story, and as he did so, she felt anger growing through her shock. 'My father,' she fumed, the moment Ben finished. 'It's all those books on communism that he reads, and the *Daily Worker*, getting him excited about the strikes – it's gone to his head. This isn't a Welsh mine, it's not even a bloody London bus depot, it's the River Hamble. Who does he think he is – Bert Papworth? It's Dunwood's sport, not his business. What does Dad think Dunwood's going to do? He'll do the same as Sopwith did two years ago – sack them all!'

'Lucy, I –'

'It's all very good to try to get the Captain his job back' – she wasn't even aware that she had trampled right over Ben's attempt to speak – 'and if he's right about Mr Arbethwaite, then someone needs to do something about it – but to call a strike? It's madness! Families need to eat. You wait till he gets home, I'll tell him. What are they all doing, did they come back on the lorry?'

Ben had stopped rowing now, oars in his lap, boat drifting to a halt. 'No, the lorry belongs to Dunwood, and Lerup wouldn't let them use it to come home – but you're right about Dunwood, he's already sent Lerup to sack everyone.'

Lucy stared at him, mouth open. 'Oh' was all that escaped as she slumped against the tiny backrest.

'Your father and the crew were going to the police station in Gosport to hand over the downhaul and report what they'd found. Dunwood sent Lerup after them to tell them they'd all got the sack. I ... came straight back here to tell you ...' Leather creaked as Ben twisted the oars in the rowlocks, one way, then the other, back again. 'There's more, Lucy. I probably shouldn't tell you this, but Mrs Arbethwaite's in terrible trouble. Stanley's left her with huge debts, we found out about them last night.'

Lucy didn't reply. After a moment, Ben looked over his shoulder. The boat had spun gently; it was sideways to the stream. It wasn't far off mid-tide on the flood, and the current was still carrying them upriver. He pulled a couple of strokes with the left oar to straighten them up, and then began rowing again.

'The thing is,' he said, 'Stanley could've got himself mixed up in some kind of a racket, and that's how he ran up all this debt. And it could have got him killed. If we can show that your father's right, then we can get everything worked out. I was thinking about it on the way over here. If we can prove that Stanley really was murdered, then Dunwood will have to give everyone their job back – including Captain Emerton. And Lerup might even end up getting his marching orders.' The oar jumped a little in the rowlock as he finished, the lapse followed by two precise strokes.

Lucy sat up a little straighter as this idea sank in. 'Why don't you go and talk to that policeman and tell him all that ... what was his name?' she asked.

'Detective Sergeant Miller, but I don't think that'll

help.'

'Why not?'

'They've obviously decided that it was just an accident, and shut the investigation down. We'll need some good evidence to get them to reopen it.'

'What about the downhaul and these debts?' she replied.

'Unfortunately, on its own the downhaul doesn't prove anything,' he said. 'Your father could have just cut it off a reel of new rope. That's what Lerup thinks has happened – that your father has done this to try to get Captain Emerton his job back. And who do you think the police will believe, Lerup or your father?'

'But you believe my dad, and the police might believe you,' she insisted.

'They aren't going to take my word over Lerup's any more than your father's. If he hadn't gone and demanded that the Captain be reinstated, then there would have been a better chance that people would have listened to his theory and maybe looked into it. But he has, and now it's pitched Lerup against the idea and that's that. We need more evidence.'

She frowned. 'What about the debts?'

Ben shook his head. 'Mrs Arbethwaite is frightfully upset about the debts. We can't tell anyone until we know why Stanley owed all that money. It isn't fair to her. No, we need to work out what's going on and make a really strong case before we go to the police. If we can convince them, they will convince Dunwood and he'll have to get rid of Lerup. And I have to be careful too – if Lerup finds out I'm on your father's side, he'll have me out of my job in a heartbeat, you said so yourself.'

Lucy stared at him. 'So ... you didn't go on strike and get fired with the others?'

Ben stopped rowing. The trickle of noise from the bow wave eased. 'Umm, actually, no,' he said.

'I don't understand.'

'I was already at the yard when your father and the others arrived,' he spoke softly. 'So I wasn't part of the plan for the walkout, and then Dunwood came up with the idea of replacing your dad and the others with an amateur crew like Sopwith did in '34, and he wants me to organise it.'

She closed her eyes. It was incredible enough that Mr Arbethwaite might have been murdered, and dreadful that her father had got the crew fired for striking because of it. But to hear that Ben was responsible for replacing that crew with *amateurs* was something else all together.

'Lucy, let's think about this,' said Ben. The drip of water off the oars was slowing gently, like the tick of a clock winding down. 'I can sort this thing out if I can prove your father is right, but I'm the only one who can do it. I'm the only one that Mrs Arbethwaite trusts. I need to keep that trust. I need access to Stanley's paperwork to investigate what was going on. If I lose the job now, I'll lose all that because I won't be able to afford to stay at the Arbethwaites', and I'll have to waste time looking for work. It all just becomes impossible ...' He leaned forward and touched her gently on the knee. 'I know what it looks like, but this is the best chance of sorting everything out – get rid of that beggar Lerup, get the Captain back, and maybe even help out Mrs Arbethwaite if we can find out where all their money went. Your father will understand, once we put things right.'

After a while, she opened her eyes and looked into his. 'And in the meantime, what the hell am I going to tell him?'

'Well ...' Ben pushed the oars back out. He checked which way they were facing. A single stroke straightened the boat, and he started to row. 'We can't tell him about the investigation, no one must know about it until we have some answers. But we could tell him that I need to keep the job for her. Mrs Arbethwaite has no one else to turn to; she has no income at all now, apart from my rent.'

Lucy watched the vortices swirl off the blades as the strokes dragged them through the water.

'What can *he* do for Mrs Arbethwaite?' Ben continued. 'Who else is going to look after her? As far as your dad is concerned, she's just as much a victim as Stanley.'

Lucy didn't reply. She let her hand slip over the stern, the cold water swirling around her fingers as they flowed through the river. She watched him row with a smooth, rhythmic grace, long arms reaching forward until they almost touched her knees. She could see his thigh muscles tense under the cotton trousers as he braced for the stroke, forcing the blades through the water without hurry, hands crossing neatly in the middle. Then she pulled her hand out of the water and said, 'All right. Dad might accept that – I can't think of anything else to tell him, anyway.'

'Thanks, Lucy, I knew you'd understand.' He stopped rowing for a moment, shipped one oar and reached out, took her hand and squeezed it. 'If we can get rid of Lerup, you know what it might mean?'

She nodded. Ben could replace him.

'So, did your father say anything else about the downhaul?' He returned to the rowing.

'Well ... I think he's been worried about it ever since the accident,' she replied. 'I told you he likes to have the downhaul permanently spliced to the chair. But last night, he told me that he's certain he did the splice the day before the rig went in. Then, after the accident, when he had a look, he found the downhaul rope on deck but not attached to the chair. He thought he was going mad. He started to think that maybe he just *thought* he'd done it – but didn't actually do it. It seemed the only explanation; I mean, splices don't come untied.

'Dad didn't say anything to anyone because he was worried that if it came out that he was supposed to have done the splice and hadn't, the bogeys might blame him for it. But the more he thought about it, the more certain he was that he'd done it. So, on Saturday, when everyone had gone to the funeral, he went and had a good look around the yard, and he finally found the original downhaul in the bottom of one of the bins at the back of *Windflower*'s shed.'

Now it was Ben's turn to sigh. 'I don't see how it's going to help us prove the case.'

'The debts are a better line of investigation,' she said.

'I think you're right. I'll start by talking to Mrs Arbethwaite, go through the paperwork. Maybe Stanley's left something in the house that will tell us what all this is about.'

They continued in silence, now into Bursledon Pool, a stretch of open water on a bend of the river. Deacon's boatyard had its home on the western bank. The yard was quiet, a couple of people working on their boats. The dark blue German yacht had dropped anchor just off the slip of the neighbouring Elephant yard. The man in yellow oilskins was not to be seen; the only sign of life was a little smoke drifting from a cabin-top chimney.

'Lucy!' said Ben, suddenly.

'Yes?'

'It says *Dulcibella* on the stern of that boat.' He was facing the opposite way to her and pointing in that direction, away from the Elephant yard and towards the eastern bank.

She twisted round. 'It's the one from *Riddle of the Sands* – it's been there for a while, stuck in that mud berth,' she said.

'The actual boat – how extraordinary,' exclaimed Ben.

'If I wasn't so late, you could come into work and talk to Miss Ritchie – she knows all about it.'

Ben gazed in a reverential silence at the boat. 'Wouldn't it be terrific to take her back up to the Frisian Islands?' he said, finally. 'I'd love to see that part of the world.'

'What do you mean, take her back?' replied Lucy. 'She's never been there; the book's just a story.'

'Well, maybe, but who really knows how much is made up and how much really happened? The boat's there, isn't it? I can't believe you didn't tell me. Can you imagine running that route through the sands? I'd love to see if I could do it.

One day, we'll go there and have a crack at it. I'll take you. I'm going to find out who owns her – I wonder what they'd want for her.'

'Ben, I'm late for work.'

'Oh yes, sorry,' he said, and turned to the oars again.

Miss Ritchie was peering through the window of the barge that served as the Deacon's yard office. She waved cheerfully, and Lucy waved back. Things would be all right, she'd soon be at her desk by the window, one of the dogs slumped on her feet, surrounded by the litter of ironmongery, sails, shackles, blocks and goodness knows what else in for repair. The chaos drove her half-mad, but she'd learned to live with it for two and a half days a week.

'I'll ask Miss Ritchie if there's anyone going downriver, see if I can get you a lift back,' she said, as Ben brought the boat neatly alongside a pontoon that was anchored ashore.

'It's all right,' he told her. 'I want to row over to the *Dulcibella* and have a look. I'll tie *Greta* up here for you when I'm done and walk back.' He managed a smile, and rubbed his forehead. 'I could do with stretching my legs.'

'I'll talk to Dad about this amateur crew thing as soon as I can,' she said. 'I think it's best if I try to explain.'

Ben nodded slowly. 'Yes, I'd be grateful.'

'Am I going to see you this week? Why don't you come for dinner one night, or maybe we can go for a walk or to the flickers or something?' she asked.

'Let's see how it goes with your father first,' he replied.

'But I just want to see you ...' she said. Why was everything so *difficult*?

'Soon,' he replied, holding her gaze, 'we should just let things settle a little first.'

She frowned. She reached out and gripped his hand for a moment, then stepped carefully over the gunwale and onto the pontoon. She blew him a sombre kiss, and headed towards the office.

Chapter 9

Lucy's afternoon trip back downriver was assisted by the fast running ebb, with waves steepened and shortened by the southerly breeze that had filled in against the current. She was grateful for some help; she didn't need a long struggle against the wind *and* the tide. She tied up *Greta* where she had found her. *Bette Davis* sat gleaming in her new coat of paint, and Lucy glanced skywards; she hoped Bob was watching out for rain, the breeze had piled clouds up over the village. She hesitated; an aircraft was towing a sky sign along Southampton Water and over the city, but she couldn't read it. She started back to the cottage, glancing up the hill towards the Bugle as she reached the quay. There they all were: her dad, Captain Emerton and the crew.

'Lucy!' yelled Joe Kirk.

Her father sat in the centre of the group, a pint in one hand, the other raised in greeting. Lucy waved back, and then hesitated. She could leave tackling her father till a moment when he was alone ... but she wanted to get it over with, and if she told him now, they would all learn about Ben at the same time. It would force them to react to her face. It was better than word going round later, behind her back. She took a decisive step up the hill.

There must have been fifteen men around the steps leading down from the Bugle to the street, some sitting, others propping up the walls, their wool jackets unbuttoned, flat caps tilted back on their heads. Her father sat three steps from the road, with Captain Emerton a couple above and Bob Allet in between, not too far from *Bette Davis* and her wet paint. Squatting at the bottom of the steps was the bearded heavyset figure of Jim Rails. They all had glasses of beer in their hands, were all still in their work clothes. It seemed to her that no one had been home to tell their wives the news, or to change for the Sunday roast.

'Looks like trouble,' said Lucy, as she approached. There were a couple of wry grins, but that was it, the mood was subdued.

'Already had plenty of trouble for one day,' said her father. He shook his head. 'Don't need any more.'

'I heard, so you're all out of work then?' she said.

'Seems that way,' replied her father. He leaned over and spat down the side of the steps. 'It's that bastard Lerup, but the word's gone out. He'll not find a crew.'

'I wouldn't be so sure about that,' countered Lucy, hands on her hips.

Suddenly, everyone was quiet.

'What do you mean?' asked her father.

She couldn't miss the alcohol-tinged belligerence – *waddayamean*. She wondered how long they'd all been sitting here, drinking. 'What did Sopwith do in '34, when those Essex lads walked off?' she asked, folding her arms.

Joe Kirk shifted on the step, picked his glass up. 'Got an amateur crew in, but they weren't up to it, everyone knows that. Dunwood wouldn't try it.' He raised the glass to his lips.

She waited till he'd taken the slug of beer. 'Oh yes he would,' she said, softly now, face carefully concerned. The silence continued for a moment, then everyone started talking at once.

'Hush. Shut up. SHUT UP.' Joe Kirk's response built in volume, until the crew finally quietened. 'How do you know that?' he asked, leaning forward.

'I heard it from Ben,' she replied.

The crew's silence seemed to expand into the street and swallow her.

'Ben? How does he know?' asked her father, finally.

'Dunwood wants him to help raise the new crew,' she said, unable to keep a trace of defiance out of her voice, expecting fury.

But her father just snorted. 'Hah,' he said, and took a long slug from his glass. There were a couple of uncomfortable coughs. 'And what did Ben say?' he added, the beer almost gone.

'He didn't have a choice,' Lucy replied. 'He had to say yes, he isn't a toff like Lerup with his own money. He needs a job just like the rest of us, and if he loses it, who else is going to look after Mrs Arbethwaite? What's she supposed to do? She's only got Ben's rent now that Stanley's gone.' Her hands were firmly back on her hips, her feet spread. She watched her father run his tongue around his lips, sweeping the foam off his beard, his green eyes hot on her face. 'An amateur crew won't be any good,' she went on. 'Ben knows that, he knows those people even if he isn't one of them – soft hands, no idea. But he's got to do it for Mrs Arbethwaite's sake; it's bad for her at the moment. She needs someone to look after her, and there isn't any of us can take that on. He needs to keep his job with Dunwood.' There was a murmur of agreement from the back of the group. She didn't check who it might have been – her eyes were fixed on her father's.

Then Joe Kirk let out a noisy breath. 'I don't see it makes any odds. Clayton might not be like Lerup, but he isn't one of us neither. It won't do no harm if this lot of amateurs is anything like Sopwith's.' There were a couple of mumbles of assent as Kirk drained the last of his beer. Then he said, 'Give me another pint from that baby,' and passed his glass over his head towards the four-gallon stone jar filled with Fielder's bitter – normally used aboard on race days. Lucy glanced around her, trying to see if there was any real dissent. No one would meet her eye. Slowly the conversation started to pick up again, as her father's glass was filled and passed back down to him.

'Is there a drink for me, then?' she asked, deciding to stay a while.

'I might be able to help,' said Albert Parks.

She looked up to where Parks sat beside Captain Emerton. Parks had sailed with the Captain since he'd left the Hamble school a few years ahead of her.

'And please have my seat, Lucy,' added Parks as he stood, with a shy smile.

'Thank you, Albert, a half of shandy, if you please.' Bob Allet winked at her as she caught his eye on the way up the steps. 'Hello,' she said. 'I put *Greta* back where I found her, and *Bette* looks beautiful with her new coat of paint.'

'So long as the rain holds off,' said Bob, scratching at his stump through his trouser leg. The wooden replacement sat next to him, carefully carved and painted to match the black leather boot on the foot that remained.

Captain Emerton calmly raised his glass in recognition as she sat beside him, and then leaned into her a little and spoke into her ear. 'He's a good man, is your Ben Clayton, I don't wish him no ill, and you're right about Mrs Arbethwaite, after what happened to Stanley. But some of these lads have got the fighting talk about them. They aren't happy with the way they've been treated, and if he picks the other side, then he might need to watch himself a bit around the village.'

She looked at Emerton – his eyes were moist and serious. 'I'll tell him,' she said.

'It's nothing big at the moment, mind,' said Emerton, 'he just needs to keep his self out of sight for a while. I don't think anyone would do anything stupid, but best not to tempt them, especially once they've had a couple of drinks.'

'I'll tell him,' she repeated.

Parks leaned over her shoulder and held her shandy

out to her, the little half-pint glass lost in his huge hand. She thanked him, and he stepped past her to take up a position sprawled on the pavement close to the foot of the steps. 'What are we going to do on Monday, Joe?' he asked her father.

'I think we might try picketing, go down to the yard, make it a little harder for these scabs to get to work,' replied her father. 'We need to let Dunwood know we mean business.'

'Good – bloody strange not having anything to do otherwise,' replied Parks, pushing a hand through his thick dark brown hair.

'For God's sake, don't be so bloody lame, there are blokes up north who've been unemployed for years,' said Kirk.

'Huh,' muttered Parks, 'I've never been out of a job before, don't we get some dole money or something?'

'It's barely worth having,' Kirk replied, 'the bloody Tories cut it to the quick in '31 and it's means-tested now. Believe me, you don't want the government picking through everything you earned, or might have earned, unless you absolutely bloody have to ...'

'Easy for you to say, with just the one kid to support,' muttered Jim Rails.

'We'd better hope Dunwood sees sense then. We won't make anything fishing, there're no bloody fish left, you can barely pull five bobs' worth out and cover the day's diesel,' said Parks, before sipping at his pint.

'I'm not sure we've done the right thing, meself,' said Rails, 'we could end up labouring on New Docks or the ruddy Civic Centre if we're not careful.' He drained his glass and put it at his feet.

'Should we look for another job, Joe, or do you think the boss'll come to his senses?' asked another voice from behind her.

But before her father could answer, Jim Rails stood up. 'I'll be looking for a job,' he muttered. 'I don't see any more work on the *Windflower* for us, not now her fancy man' – he jutted his bearded chin at Lucy – 'is going looking for gentlemen. We won't be getting work on any more yachts if Dunwood puts the curse on us neither. And I'm not digging dirt at the Civic Centre or the Docks.'

'You've got nothing to worry about compared to some, Rails,' said her father, not looking at the man. 'At least you can dig dirt; there are men so broken from that bloody war that all they can do is scavenge for anything they can eat or sell from that New Docks rubble.'

'Yeah, well, that's the ruddy bosses for you, they always betray us; they did it in the war and they're doing it again now,' said Rails, glaring at Kirk.

'Ben doesn't have any choice, Mr Rails,' said Lucy, in a voice that came out at least an octave higher than she'd hoped.

Rails looked at her malevolently, his brow heavy over bloodshot eyes. 'One thing to keep working, another to find the scabs,' he said. Then he turned away and lurched off up the street. Lucy exchanged a glance with Bob Allet, very relieved that they'd agreed not to say anything about the rotten patch that Rails had left unrepaired in Captain Emerton's boat.

Chapter 10

The telephone's jangling demand for attention made Matthew Faden jump. He hesitated for a moment, pen hovering above the paper. Damn. Just when he'd finally managed to drag himself through the thick edge of a hangover, out of bed and to his desk. He cursed the instrument. It hadn't been installed long, but with no butler to answer it, he was finding the thing a demanding taskmaster, impossible to ignore. God forbid that everyone should have one of the infernal things, he thought. He pushed his chair back and stumbled barefoot down to the hall of his Soho flat, still in his pyjamas, toes squishing through the carpet.

'Hello, this is Faden this end,' he said, receiver to his ear, stooping to pick up the shepherd's-check tweed overcoat that he'd dropped on the floor when he'd come home in the early hours of the morning.

'Matthew, it's Clayton, Ben Clayton,' replied the voice on the other end of the line.

'Ben! My God! How marvellous!' Faden straightened as he spoke, and the coat slipped from his fingers – gorgeous Ben Clayton, with his ice-blue eyes and dark hair. 'Such a long time, where have you been, old man?' Faden felt a flood of tenderness as he spoke.

'I've, er ... been working on the *Windflower*, Dunwood's new yacht ...' said Ben.

'Ah, yes, yes, of course, I heard about that, wasn't there ... an accident? Was he a friend of yours?'

'He was ...'

'I'm terribly sorry to hear that, Ben.'

'Well, partly as a result of that there's been a bit of trouble with the crew ...'

'Yes,' he prompted, as Ben hesitated – Faden could hear a tension in the other man's voice, even over the crackle of the telephone line.

'Mr Dunwood has asked me to find some amateur chaps to sail the boat, a bit like Sopwith did a couple of years ago, and I was rather wondering if you might be interested?'

'Of course, I'd love to, old boy,' he said, unable to prevent a smile spreading across his face.

'Is there any chance you can join us for this weekend?' continued Ben.

'I'm sure I can,' Faden answered, without hesitation.

'Be at Camper and Nicholsons boatyard first thing Saturday morning. I'm not sure quite what the plan is yet, but I can tell you more later in the week.'

'I'll be there,' he said, 'and I can bring a couple of chaps down with me if anyone needs a lift.'

'I'll bear that in mind, many thanks, Matthew.'

'Not at all, it'll be marvellous to see you again,' replied Faden.

'Yes, goodbye.'

The line went dead. Faden let the receiver click down into the cradle. Now this was an interesting development. Despite the opinion he'd expressed to White two days earlier, Ben had obviously moved into a position of influence with Dunwood. What had happened to Lerup, was he out of the picture completely? Or had Ben just started to undermine him, to get a foot in the door? Faden found his cigarettes and a box of Swan Vestas from under the chaos of papers on his desk, and then sank into the deep leather armchair by the crackling fire.

He lit the cigarette, and exhaled thoughtfully. His friendship with Ben extended well beyond sailing; Faden had got him involved in the No More War Movement. They had met early in the first term; he'd rescued Ben from a boxing-club recruiting squad. They had him pinned into a corner of the quad late one evening, and were busy pushing him to accept a spot on the team and the Full Blue that went with it. Ben had been far too polite to tell them to go to hell. Faden had spotted those gorgeous blue eyes a few days earlier at a sailing-club shindig, and now he saw his opportunity. He'd waded in on the pretext of reclaiming Ben for the boaties, pulled him out of there and taken him back to his room for a drink.

Matthew Faden would be the first to admit that he'd been driven by less than pure motives. Unfortunately, it quickly became clear that Ben wasn't interested in any of his advances. Nevertheless, he'd found a good friend, and after learning of Ben's background, he'd sought to bridge the inevitable isolation of a scholarship boy. He'd adopted him as a project, trying to draw him into his circle of university sailing friends. It was a rather embarrassing episode in retrospect. It hadn't gone well. Ben Clayton was ... how would he put it? Not quite shy, nor aloof, although he could be read that way ... no, self-contained, that was it – rather a handicap amongst his loud friends.

But Ben had never taken any of Faden's ham-fisted social efforts badly, and away from the crowd they had always got on rather famously. Then late one night, deep into a case of rather fine Beaujolais, the story about the boxing and the injured boy had come out. After that, it had been easy to persuade Ben into a more formal expression of his aversion to violence. He'd joined the No More War Movement the following day. They had both done their time in the trenches for the cause while they were up at Cambridge, and although he was unsure if Ben was still active in the Movement, Faden was damn sure about his friend's principles.

And now Fleming White needed someone close to Harold Dunwood to persuade him to build fighters and bombers – and somehow, implausible though it sounded, Ben had got himself into just such a position. And that made Ben the perfect person to put forward. Faden would get the credit for proposing him, and White's plans would go nowhere thanks to Ben's pacifist principles. He pushed himself out of the chair, went back to the desk and lifted the telephone. After a moment, the operator's voice came on the line and he asked for the number White had given him in Whitehall.

Ben Clayton stared out of the window, tapping his pencil mechanically against the blotter. His new office was small and sparsely furnished, with a down-at-heel walnut desk that looked as though it had just been brought up from a storeroom – there were still finger marks in the dust where it had been carried. There was a metal-framed chair with walnut panels that matched the desk, a green lamp whose bulb turned out to be dead, a pad of paper with damply curling edges, a black pyramid Bakelite telephone and some second-hand pencils. The room smelt of dust and disinfectant and, judging by the noise, he was directly over where they were installing the machine shop. But he had all that he needed – and the window looked out onto Southampton Water.

He tossed the pencil on the desk, got up and walked the couple of steps to his view. He leaned on the windowsill and considered the blue and white cloudscape racing across the chopped-up estuary. A squat black tanker with dirty white-tipped funnels sat at the Atlantic Gulf and West Indies oil refinery over at Fawley, on the other side of the water. He should make another phone call to his list of prospective *Windflower* crew. He was offering a unique opportunity – only a handful of his most gilded sailing friends had ever raced aboard a J Class yacht. But he wondered what response he'd get from some of them – *that*

Clayton fellow, got a bit above himself, he called me the other day asking if I wanted to be a part of his Windflower crew, what a ridiculous notion, who does he think he is ... Pompous idiots.

Still, the calls could hardly be worse than those to Mrs Arbethwaite's creditors – all of them so far had been an unpleasant experience. The debts were real, people wanted payment and they wanted it now. He had sorted the bills into order of urgency and listed all the items with dates and amounts due. The first payments had gone awry eight months ago. It started with things you could get away with for a while, bits and pieces on hire purchase, an electricity bill. Two months later it got more serious; that was when the first payment had been missed on the house. What didn't make any sense was that before that, Stanley appeared to have been a model customer, paying on time, every time. What the hell had gone wrong? And could whatever it was really have led to murder? He dug his hands in his pockets and found the packet of Woodbines he'd bought on the way back to Hamble yesterday. Empty. *Bloody hell ...* He crumpled the pack slowly, catching the last whiff of tobacco odour as it collapsed, before lobbing it into the waste-paper basket.

There was an urgent rap on the door. He stepped back to his desk and quickly hid the lists and bills under the papers detailing his recruitment of new crew members. Just in time – a balding head adorned with tortoiseshell spectacles and a nose that dominated everything else peered into the room.

'Hello, are you Ben Clayton?' said the visitor.

'That's right.'

'I'm Phillip Bartlett, Head of the Performance Section, for the new plane,' said Bartlett, footsteps echoing in the half-empty room as he entered.

'How do you do?' asked Ben, moving round his desk to greet him. Bartlett took his outstretched hand with a ready smile and a warm grip. Ben liked him immediately.

'You're from Supermarine, I hear,' went on Bartlett.

'Yes, I started today.' Ben waved his arm around him. 'They gave me my own office.'

'Oh, there's plenty of room here while we're still in the design-and-prototype phase, things will fill up a bit once all the production wallahs and bean counters arrive.'

'Well, it's nice while it lasts.'

'And Mr Dunwood's got you working on some special project, has he?' Bartlett glanced at the desk, pushing his spectacles back up his nose as he did so.

Ben followed his gaze, relieved that the bills were hidden. 'Yes, I'm trying to find a crew for his yacht; the old crew went on strike and he sacked them.'

Bartlett nodded. 'I heard about that, bit of bother over Stanley Arbethwaite's death?'

Ben nodded, unsure how much he could or should say. It wasn't this man's business, however well intended the enquiry.

Bartlett blazed on, missing Ben's uneasiness. 'I worked with Arbethwaite up at Riley's in Coventry,' he said, 'brilliant engineer, great chap – but I always wondered what he got up to on his weekends, if you catch my drift.' He gave a short knowing laugh.

'I don't follow you,' said Ben, abrupt at the implicit slight on his friend.

Now, finally, Bartlett hesitated. 'Oh, you know, just gossip, he left in a bit of a hurry, it was never really explained, that's all ...'

'From Riley's, you say?' asked Ben, curbing the aggression in his tone.

'That's right, must be four or five years ago now – used to have a reputation as a bit of a player, old Stanley.'

'How do you mean?'

'Umm, liked a bet, trifle fast and loose with the cards is what I heard. But as I say, I'm sure there was nothing much in it. Shop-floor talk – you know how people are, give them a molehill and before you know it you've got a mountain.' He wrinkled his nose, pushing his spectacles back up again. 'Did you know him well?'

'Yes, I lodged with him in Hamble and we were working on the mast for *Windflower* together ...' Ben trailed off.

'Oh ... I'm terribly sorry,' said Bartlett, momentarily dismayed. He pulled a watch out of his waistcoat pocket and then quickly changed the subject. 'Look, old chap, I've got a meeting this afternoon and you might be able to help me. I checked with Mr Dunwood – he says you're a structures specialist, is that correct?'

'Engine mountings and structures, yes.'

'Good-oh, I could do with your advice. Mr Dunwood said it was all right to haul you away from your Herculean labours here for a moment, so perhaps we could go and have some lunch in the canteen and I can explain the problem.'

Ben took a deep breath. 'Of course, I ... of course.'

'Jolly good,' said Bartlett, opening the door. And before Ben could say anything more, Bartlett was out in the corridor and springing up the stairs.

It was almost half past five before Ben escaped from Bartlett. He picked up his knapsack, coat, motorbike gear and the pile of the Arbethwaites' bills from his office and headed home. He parked in the drive and let himself into the kitchen. Mrs Arbethwaite was standing by a boiling kettle, staring through the steam in the near-dark room. He hesitated for a moment – did she know about the accusation of murder? He hadn't seen her since they'd found the bills. He slammed the door loudly with his foot and switched the light on with his elbow.

'Oh, Ben,' she exclaimed, jumping a little and blinking in the glare.

'Evening, Mrs Arbethwaite.'

'How are you?' she asked, as he dropped his knapsack on the floor, and put the helmet, gloves and keys down on the dresser beside a Pools coupon.

'All right, Mrs Arbethwaite, as good as could be expected,' he replied. He looked at the rows of completed predictions – Chelsea to beat Bolton 3–2? How did she come up with that? And she hadn't previously approved of gambling. 'Have you been doing the Pools?' he asked.

'Yes, I thought ... well, it might help,' she said with a frown, before quickly adding, 'Would you like a cup of tea?'

'Yes, please,' he replied, taking off his coat to put it on the hook on the back of the door.

The kettle was still billowing steam. She switched it off and poured the hot water into the prepared pot. 'Ben, you didn't do any cleaning while I was away, did you?' she asked.

Clayton was toying with a letter that she had left out for him on the kitchen table, propped up against a crystal paperweight. It was from his mother. 'Er, no, of course not,' he said.

'That's what I thought ...' She hesitated, touched the black-and-silver brooch on her lapel.

He put the letter back down, his curiosity aroused by the tone of her voice. 'Why?' he asked.

She was leaning back against the cupboard that the kettle stood on. 'Things have been moved,' she said.

He shook his head, confused. 'What do you mean, things have been moved?'

'Everything has been moved, not much, just a little bit, but I know where things should be.'

'Show me,' he said.

Mrs Arbethwaite led the way out of the kitchen and down the corridor into the dining room. It was freezing, damp and musty. They hadn't eaten in here since Stanley died. He turned the light on.

'I wasn't feeling that well this morning,' she said. 'But I thought if I did a bit of cleaning I might feel better. It gave me a funny sensation when I noticed it, but I thought it might have been you. Things are different, little things.

Like the Toby jugs.' She stepped over to the sideboard, which was adorned with the Arbethwaites' three Royal Doulton figurines – the *Night Watchman*, *Parson Brown* and *Dick Turpin*. 'I always line the noses up, and put the handles of the jugs to the right and straight. But they're not straight any more, they're twisted – someone's moved them.' She adjusted *Parson Brown* so he could see the difference. 'Once I realised, I started looking around and it's all like that, the whole house, nothing's quite where it should be.'

He couldn't see the difference – *Parson Brown* had barely moved from straight – but he didn't doubt her judgement. 'Is anything missing?' he asked.

'That was my thought. But I can't see anything that's gone. There's no money to take, and my little jewellery box is still there, that was the first thing I looked at.'

'Is there any sign of a break-in?' he asked.

'No, nothing like that, that's why I thought it was strange and wanted to ask you.'

'Someone's searched the place – perhaps it's to do with Stanley,' he said – this possibility was suddenly obvious, and extremely sinister.

'Searched? Why would anyone want to search the house?' she replied, with a touch of belligerence.

'Because if Lucy's father is right and Stanley was involved in something ...'

Vivian Arbethwaite's face crumpled; she reached for a handkerchief from her dressing-gown pocket, as tears wet her cheeks.

He cursed himself, realising the impact of what he had said. She wasn't being belligerent – she was frightened, and he'd been stupidly thoughtless in that flash of comprehension. 'Mrs Arbethwaite ...' he said. 'Let's sit down and have that cup of tea ...' He gently touched her elbow, but she didn't move, her face buried in the handkerchief, shoulders silently shaking. He stood there for several moments, before retreating to the kitchen.

Ben poured two cups of tea, found the biscuit tin in the larder and set it all out on the kitchen table. He pulled the electric fire closer to her chair. What else could he do? Then he had a thought, and dashed up the stairs to go to check his own room. He surveyed the mess: gramophone records scattered around the player, half of them out of the sleeves; a pile of books in the corner, the engineering manuals and biographies that, along with the Duke, grabbed most of what little time he got to relax; the much bigger, tottering pile of sailing magazines beside them; his toolbox and sailing-gear bag both spilling their contents onto the floor around them. The washstand had a few things on it – his toothbrush, razor and the like – and then there was a faint smell of damp unwashed clothes coming from the garments scattered across the open drawers, wardrobe and floor.

But he didn't think anything had been moved, although it was hard to tell. The Waterbury dress watch his parents had given him for his eighteenth birthday was still in its box. Then he thought of all the times he had looked for an envelope or a stamp and had poked around in drawers and cupboards that weren't strictly his business. Mrs Arbethwaite must have seen the signs of this every time. But then, he thought, she would also know that he'd never found, taken or moved anything he shouldn't have. He came back down the stairs more slowly and, getting to the bottom, turned along the hall towards the kitchen. When he entered the room, Mrs Arbethwaite was in her normal seat at the head of the table, her cup of tea and a couple of custard creams on a plate in front of her.

Ben went through the comforting ritual of selecting some garibaldis from the tin. He sat in his usual seat, on her left, facing the sink and window. The silence was broken only by the clink of a china cup on saucer. He stole the occasional look at Mrs Arbethwaite. Her face was composed, but her normally immaculate make-up was absent; for the first time he noticed the crow's feet around her eyes, skin bruised by sleepless nights and tears. Her hair was unwashed, and tucked up in a net. And even though it was nearly six in the evening, she was still dressed in the thick woollen pink dressing gown that Stanley had bought her for Christmas the previous year. Ben had no idea how to start. But if nothing else, they had to deal with the debts.

'I telephoned some of the people the bills are from today ...' he said, finally. He saw tension narrow her shoulders. She didn't reply. 'Those debts are real. The money is all gone. I've got some accounts ...'

'No.' She shook her head. 'I ... don't know ... Stanley always ...' Her lower lip quivered.

'You need to think about this, Mrs Arbethwaite, things are very serious. I've made an appointment for you with Supermarine tomorrow, you need to decide whether to try to keep the house or ...' But the look in her eyes was so fearful that he stopped again.

She looked down at her tea. 'I don't know anything about these things,' she said.

'Would you like me to try and work out what's best?' he asked.

'Yes.' She snatched at the word, looking at him, her expression one of defeated misery.

'There are some things that can be sold, perhaps the car ...?'

'I can't drive,' she said.

'So we can put that up for sale, and maybe there are some things around the house that you can manage without – like the electric toaster, perhaps we could sell that?'

Her lips pursed doubtfully, but she didn't dispute the suggestion.

'And I'll talk to Supermarine about the mortgage; explain that we need a little time to work things out now that Stanley is gone.'

'Yes, yes, that's what I need, more time.' She lifted the cup a little, perhaps in an effort to appear calm. But it rattled hard against the saucer, and she quickly lowered it back down, eyes fixed on it.

'Of course, and is there anyone that might help – your sister, Elsie, perhaps?'

'No! She mustn't know.' She looked at him, eyes wide. 'You haven't told anyone about this, have you?'

'No, of course not,' he lied.

'Good – I can't believe Stanley was mixed up in any funny business,' she said.

'Neither can I, Mrs Arbethwaite, I'm sure it's all some terrible mix-up, like a mistaken identity in one of those Agatha Christie books.'

'Yes, of course it is, that's what it is – a mistaken identity.' She sat up a little straighter.

He saw his chance. 'But it would really help with the money if we could work out whatever was going on ...'

'I don't want to go to the police just because a few things have been moved,' she interrupted. 'I don't want them poking around here and finding out about ... you know, the debts and everything, it would just be too much, too much to bear,' and she shuddered.

He hesitated. 'But if the house has been searched,' he said, 'it means someone was looking for something ... and it's possible they didn't find it.'

'You mean it's still here?' The tinge of fear was back in her voice. 'Do you think they might come back?'

He strove to make his tone reassuring. 'It's not at all likely. It seems as though they had a very good look,' he said. 'But if *we* can find what they were looking for and take it to the police and sort things out, we might even get the money back.'

She frowned, folding her arms. 'I don't want people poking around in my business; you know what it's like in this village.'

'Just have a really good look through the house,' he coaxed. 'Check for anything unusual, maybe accounting records or other bills or receipts. It might be something like that, or it might be something completely different. But anything you find we'll look at together, and then decide what to do.'

Mrs Arbethwaite tried again to take a sip of tea, and this time managed it with just the merest tremor of her hand. 'I suppose I could do that,' she said. 'The house needs a jolly good spring clean anyway.' She refolded her arms. 'But in the meantime, not a word of this to anyone.'

'Of course,' he replied, 'goes without saying.'

'Right then,' she said, rising to her feet. 'I'd best get us some dinner on.'

He drank his tea, watching as she pulled the chopping board out from behind the taps and fetched some potatoes from the larder. The woman had pride, which might make it difficult to keep her out of the bankruptcy court – that would have to be his final card, the frightener, the way he'd try to get her to agree to the really hard choices. Mrs Arbethwaite started peeling the potatoes under a running tap. He got up to take his teacup to the sink. Then the letter from his mother caught his eye. Normally they went straight in the rubbish. He picked it up, hesitated for a moment and then slid it into his back pocket, thinking of Lucy.

'I might just go down to the King and Queen for a quick pint before dinner,' he said, as he put the cup down by the sink.

Mrs Arbethwaite glanced over her shoulder and said, 'Don't be too long, I'm only grilling a couple of chops.'

'Ten minutes, that's all.' He smiled reassuringly, now wondering if he should leave her alone at this moment. But he couldn't change his mind without appearing overprotective and probably making matters worse. So he grabbed his overcoat from the back of the kitchen door, shivering a little as he stepped outside into the winter air with its smells of mulch and smoke. He couldn't wait for the long hot days of summer – summer on *Windflower*, summer in America – but it was all too hard to believe on a bitter night in Hamble. He pulled the overcoat on as he walked down the drive, patting Stanley's little Morris Eight as he went past. He would be sorry to see it go; they'd had some great days out in that motor.

As he approached the pub he could see it was full for a Monday night. The windows glistened with condensation – smoke, movement and noise behind them. Then he remembered that many of these men wouldn't have been at work today. He pushed the door open. Immediately, the place went quiet. He stopped, one foot inside, his hand on the door handle, feeling every eye in the room on him. There wasn't so much as a cough or a rustle. Slowly, he stepped back and withdrew, pulling the door carefully shut. The silence seeped out into the night, broken suddenly by a single whisper and a *hush.* He retreated across the courtyard, and only when he reached the road did he hear the chatter resume.

Clayton was shaking as he strode back up the High Street. He passed The Victory without even daring to glance up at its windows, but stopped when he got to the Square. He didn't want to return immediately and have to explain what had happened to Mrs Arbethwaite. He turned downhill into the alley that led to Well Lane, back towards the river, coming out by Luke Brothers. The cheerful green and red navigation lights and their calm reflections twinkled back at him from the channel. He flipped his collar up and buried his hands in his pockets, and stood there for a long while, staring out at the water. The coming isolation would be nothing new to him; he just needed to get over the shock. Finally, he walked back up to the Square and on towards the Arbethwaites' house and dinner.

Chapter 11

The next morning, as he approached his office, Ben could see that the light was on inside. The frosted glass dappled shadow onto the opposite wall in the dim corridor. He opened the door to find Bartlett leaning over his desk, looking at a plan spread out in front of him. Smoke curled from a cigarette in his ink-and-nicotine-stained fingers.

'Ah, there you are, old chap,' he said as Ben entered, pushing his spectacles back up his nose. 'This is the detail of what we were talking about yesterday.' He tapped the drawing, then raised the cigarette to his lips, held between thumb and forefinger.

Ben forced a smile. Being thrust into the middle of Bartlett's engine-mount design problem was just what he didn't need. 'You're up and at 'em,' he observed.

'Early bird gets the worm and all that,' replied Bartlett.

'But the second mouse gets the cheese,' he responded automatically, as he dumped his knapsack by the side of his desk. Bartlett chuckled and Ben frowned – he hadn't provoked a laugh from someone since ... since Stanley had died.

The knock at the door surprised both of them, and after a moment's silence it was Bartlett who said, 'Come in.' Ben hadn't quite got used to ownership of his office. It was a further surprise when Dunwood entered.

'They told me this was where I'd find you,' he said, his gaze taking in first Ben and then Bartlett, as he stepped into the room. 'And I see Bartlett hasn't wasted any time getting your hands dirty.'

'No, we're right in the thick of it,' said Ben, as Lerup followed Dunwood into the room. Lerup was impeccable in white ducks and matching jacket, panama in one hand and cigarette in the other. The sartorial rule in the factory was the engineer's uniform: dark grey flannel jacket, unpressed slacks, white shirt, soberly striped tie. Both Ben and Bartlett had adhered to the rule, although Bartlett had marked himself out as an extrovert with the addition of a grey waistcoat. But Lerup appeared to revel in being so hopelessly out of place. He took up station beside the door, leaning against the wall, arms folded.

'I popped in to find out how you're getting along,' said Dunwood.

'Very well, sir,' replied Ben, 'there's a similar problem here to one I tackled at Supermarine' – he waved at the drawing – 'and I think we'll be able to work it out.'

'Excellent, excellent, and how are they doing over in Woolston? A little building work I understand?' replied Dunwood, with a sly smile.

Ben stiffened. He was too soon out of Supermarine to be comfortable with criticism of his old firm. 'It's expansion – Vickers has been investing hugely since they bought the company, so yes, there's plenty happening over there ...' His description didn't get close to the borderline chaos Supermarine had been in for what felt like years, as the site was redeveloped and the business brought under Vickers's control. But he wasn't prepared to admit that to Dunwood.

'And how's that fighter doing? It looked good when I saw it fly over at Arbethwaite's funeral. I understand the first test flight was only a couple of days before that, wasn't it?' continued Dunwood.

Ben's brow furrowed – the fighter had been a confidential project, but the test flight and the plane's dramatic appearance over the Hamble church had made it public knowledge. 'I don't really know, I was working on a flying boat,' he said, with a quick smile to defuse any offence that might be taken from the guarded nature of the reply.

Dunwood beamed and waved a hand in acknowledgement. 'I'm just kidding you, my boy – the *Echo* has a report on it. And anyway, I've got no intention of building any fighters.' Dunwood pushed a Napoleonic hand inside his navy-blue double-breasted Scholte jacket. 'They're all going to lose money on them. We don't need 'em, we're finished with wars – Prime Minister Baldwin will keep us out of trouble. The Germans have some grievances, and you can't really blame them, but Baldwin'll work that out, let them have what's legitimately theirs, and we'll have many more years of peace in Europe. Believe me, I don't pay my taxes and Tory dues for them to go starting a war.' Dunwood glanced at Lerup. 'Am I right?'

'Quite right,' drawled Lerup.

'Which reminds me, Lerup, we really must sort out that trip to Germany so you can go and see M.A.N. about the engines for the new motor yacht,' continued Dunwood.

Lerup nodded. 'Of course.'

'Excellent, excellent.' He turned back to Ben. 'So how's my new crew coming along?'

'It's going all right. I ... er ...' He scrabbled under the drawing for his list. 'I have six confirmed for this weekend *and* the rest of the season. Another four can make this weekend but wanted to see what it was all about before they committed for the rest of the year ...'

Dunwood was looking dubious.

'You've got a way to go then,' said Lerup, dryly.

Ben glanced down, forced a smile into place before he looked back up. 'I've got lots more people to track down,' he said. 'I've made telephone calls, sent telegrams, left messages, written letters, and got a lot of suggestions for fellows I hadn't initially thought of that I still need to contact – I'm sure we'll be all right, even if it's not a full crew for the first weekend,' he finished.

'Rome wasn't built in a day,' said Dunwood, his dark eyes flickering in their deep sockets, from Ben to Bartlett and back. 'And you've got enough time to spare to help Bartlett?'

Ben didn't intend to hesitate. He would have struggled on with the engine problem on top of everything else, rather than cause any trouble. But he wasn't quite quick enough. 'Yes ...' he started.

'Excellent,' said Dunwood, smoothly cutting him off, 'but perhaps until you've got a crew for the weekend, Bartlett can manage without you.'

The order was given so mildly that both men could have mistaken it for a suggestion – but they didn't, and nodded. Ben was careful not to look at Bartlett, who took a long drag on his cigarette, the smoky exhalation suspiciously like a sigh.

'Good, I'll let you get working on it,' continued Dunwood, already moving towards the door. Lerup pushed off the wall and followed him out into the corridor, closing the door rather more loudly than was necessary.

Ben turned to Bartlett. 'I'm sorry about that,' he said.

Bartlett looked rueful as he started to roll up the plan. 'Don't worry, old boy,' he said, cigarette between his lips, ash tumbling onto his jacket as he spoke. 'I knew I was on a sticky wicket, but it was worth a try.'

'Look, I can sketch something out for you pretty quick if you like, might get you going in the right direction.'

'Are you sure? It sounds like you'll be in trouble if you don't get this crew together,' Bartlett replied, stubbing out the cigarette.

'I'm sure.'

'Thanks.' Bartlett flashed his quick smile again and then said, 'So you weren't working on the fighter with Stanley when you were both at Supermarine?'

'No, I was mostly working on the production version of

the Walrus – the flying boat. It's supposed to be finished in the next few weeks,' he replied.

'That must have been hard to leave.'

'Yes ... but I really want to go to America with *Windflower*. And to be honest, it's heavy going at Supermarine at the moment, what with the constant rebuilding.'

'It was like that here six months ago when this lot was still going up.' Bartlett waved the plan around, before turning to the window and the grey morning. 'But now you have a room with a view.'

'And very grateful I am too,' he replied.

Bartlett looked at him speculatively. 'I heard a rumour that Stanley had also agreed to join us, just before he died,' he said.

'That's true, it was right before the accident.'

'Fancy that.' Bartlett frowned. 'I only talked to him a month ago and he was so excited about that fighter at Supermarine.'

Ben shrugged.

Bartlett gave the plan one final tap, then put it on the desk. 'Anyway, I'll leave this with you, and let you get on,' he said, heading for the door.

Matthew Faden tossed a handful of seed into the cooing, fluttering flock of pigeons strutting anxiously in front of him. It landed like a hand grenade; the feathered brigades scattered, quickly returning to peck at the shrapnel. Faden looked up to see a schoolboy in a kilt grinning at him from the edge of the blackened fountain. There was a pigeon on his shoulder. He smiled back, mechanically throwing another handful, his gaze lifting to the mother – bright lipstick, heavy rouge and a camera – and then up again to the thick smoky cloud that had lowered onto the city, swallowing Nelson and the workers on the roof of the National Gallery alike.

'Got your message,' a voice said on his shoulder.

Faden started, but he had no need to look. So, he'd come himself; the voice was Leon's, its Geordie rhythms softened by a university education, courtesy of the munificence of a dead northern coal baron. But he knew that Leon wasn't his real name, and he knew that he had good reason for using the alias.

'What do you think?' Faden replied, using the minimum lip movement. He was confident that no one could hear them over the squawking pigeons, the crowds and buses and the hiss and splash of water from the fountains. But it would be better if no one even thought they were talking.

'I've been enquiring. I've got some friends with people inside the FO, and they've heard nothing about this operation. I think it's something White is running on his own.'

Faden felt a little thrill go through him. He had no idea they had penetrated the Foreign Office. He tossed another handful of seed into the squawking frenzy. This time the pigeons didn't bother to scatter, just kept their heads down, pecking, pecking, pecking. 'What do you want me to do?' he asked.

'String him along, until we learn more.'

'I gave White the name of a friend who's close to Dunwood, but he's a pacifist, so he won't help,' said Faden.

'Can you trust him completely? If White turns him ...'

Leon's voice had taken on an urgency that Faden hadn't heard before, and he felt uneasy. 'Yes, yes, I think so, but I suppose I haven't seen much of him recently.'

'This is desperately important,' insisted Leon.

Faden nodded. 'I understand, I'll see him at the weekend. I'll make sure.'

'Sooner. Whatever happens, White can't get away with this, Sopwith and Dunwood cannot start building those planes.'

'All right.'

'I'll hear from you.' Leon emptied the rest of his bag of

seed on the ground and was gone in a flurry of manic hungry birds.

Ben Clayton stared at his office telephone for a long while after Bartlett had departed, thinking through what he might say, how he would get what he needed. Then, when he was sure he was ready, he picked up the handset and asked to be connected to Riley's, the motor-car people in Coventry. There was a pause and then a clunk, followed by an eerie silence. Then the phone started to ring. His heart thumped faster with each repetition.

'Hello, this is Riley's,' a smooth, clipped female voice echoed down the line from Coventry.

'Excuse me,' he said, clearing his throat. 'I'm looking for a reference for a former employee of yours.'

'One moment, sir, I'll connect you to Personnel.'

There was a series of clicks, and then another phone rang just once, before a deeper male voice with a soft Midlands accent answered. 'Hello, Personnel.'

'Ah, yes, hello,' he said, 'we're interested in a chap by the name of Stanley Arbethwaite. We understand he worked for you some time ago, and thought perhaps that you might be able to provide a reference.'

'And who's that speaking?' said the voice, somewhat imperiously.

'This is Dunwood's, in Hamble.'

'Wait a moment and I'll check the records. Arbethwaite, you say, does it have an *e* on the end?'

'Yes,' he replied.

'Righto,' said the voice, in a slightly friendlier tone. There was a thump as the handset was put on the desk.

He waited. After a while he heard mutterings in the background, then it went quiet again. Out of his knapsack, he pulled the adverts he had composed for the car, the Hoover, the toaster and the electric heater, ready to put into the *Daily Echo*. With them came his Arbethwaite accounts and the bills – he still had more of Stanley's creditors to contact.

'Hello, are you still there?'

The voice jerked him back into the present. 'Yes, yes, of course.'

'Did Arbethwaite suggest you call us for a reference?'

Something in the tone of voice made him wary. 'Er, no, I don't think so; one of our chaps remembers him from up there.'

'I'm not surprised; well, I'm sorry, but we can't give a reference.'

'Not at all?'

'No, and ...' Perhaps something covered the handset, because there was a muffled roaring down the line, as if he was holding a seashell to his ear. Then the voice was back. 'We can't tell you why either.'

'What?' Ben was astonished.

'All I can say is that I'm surprised it's taken Arbethwaite this long before he needed to look for a new job, that's all.'

'But surely ...' he replied, thinking hard, '... we're looking at employing the man ... you have some responsibility here.'

There was just the crackling in his ear. Then the voice returned, soft, urgent. 'We think he had his fingers in the till, but we couldn't prove it. We know he had a lot of gambling debts and we asked him to leave the company. He eventually agreed, but part of the settlement was that our suspicions remained private. So you never heard this from me. Good day to you.'

The line went dead. Ben stared at the handset, disbelieving. He'd thought he'd known Stanley better than anyone on earth, and suddenly, it seemed that he barely knew him at all.

Chapter 12

Ben pushed his papers into his knapsack and stood.

'Can you find your own way out?' asked Mr Cavendish, picking up the manila folder containing Stanley Arbethwaite's mortgage documents, and tucking it between his thin arm and bony ribs.

'Yes, of course,' replied Ben, smiling. 'I used to work here, after all.'

'Of course ... it's just that I've got a big pile of invoices to get through ...'

'Please, go ahead,' said Ben.

'I'll be hearing from you then,' Cavendish replied, as he picked his way through the chairs to the door of the Supermarine tea room. It had been the only private space they could find for their meeting. 'Goodbye.'

The final words reached Ben from the corridor, and he stood silently for a moment, gathering his thoughts now that he was alone. But it had gone well, better than he could have hoped. He'd had the idea on the way over to Supermarine, never thought the Accounts people would agree to it, but Mr Cavendish had been very decent. The missed house payments were being added to the original debt, and as long as everything was in order from now on, nothing more would be said about it. At last he had something positive he could tell Mrs Arbethwaite.

He fastened the straps on the knapsack, pulled it onto

his shoulder, tucked his overcoat across his arm and headed for the door. He turned left to go down the stairs, taking the shortcut through Fanny Penton's Dope Shop. As he approached, the air thickened with the potent, intoxicating cellulose-acetate lacquer that they used to finish and tighten the wing fabric over the frames. Several of Fanny's girls waved and called hello, their hair tied back with scarves, the sleeves of their blue cotton shirts rolled up to their shoulders. He cheerfully acknowledged their greetings – there were a couple of them that had a bit of a reputation – and he realised he was happy for the first time since the accident. The mortgage agreement came on top of the morning's meeting with Dunwood, and a successful string of recruiting conversations that had provided twelve of the crew he needed for the weekend.

Ben hesitated by the curtain of green tarpaulin that kept prying eyes from the restricted area next to the Dope Shop. He pushed the canvas aside and looked in. The fighter sat there, nose up on its wheels, squat and workmanlike, painted in a drab patchy grey primer.

'Oy!'

He turned, startled, to find the slight figure of Ken Scales bearing down on him – one of the four-man team responsible for building this prototype.

'Oh, it's you, Clayton. Sorry – management's been on at us about those Jerry Lufthansa pilots poking their noses around here when they should be clearing their mail through customs.'

'Hello, Ken,' replied Ben, 'but someone told me that there was a report about the fighter in the *Echo*.' He nodded towards the plane.

'I know, and there's a rumour it'll be shown to the press in a month or so anyway. But we still don't want some Hun pilot crawling all over it so he can report back to Willy Messerschmitt and his engineers.'

Ben shrugged. 'Has it got a name yet?'

'Nothing official,' said Scales, with a hand on the

curve of the wing tip. 'I hear the top brass at Vickers want to call it the Spitfire, but RJ doesn't like it much.'

'It sounds like a good name to me,' replied Ben. 'How did the test go?' he added, shifting the overcoat from his left arm to his right.

'Bit disappointing on the top speed, and the undercarriage wouldn't lock up – nothing we can't fix.'

Ben would have liked to ask how, but he couldn't expect any more now that he didn't work here. Still, this was the first time he'd really bothered to examine the fighter, and he had to admit – it looked the part. It had an air about it.

'It looked terrific at Stanley's funeral,' he said.

'It was a tragic shame about Stanley,' replied Scales, looking solemnly at him.

Ben frowned. 'Yes, it was,' he said, feeling his mood shift, the lightness evaporating.

'We miss him around here,' said Scales, 'and we miss you too – I hear you've gone to Dunwood's. Is that right?'

'Yes, I'll be going to the States with the *Windflower*, Dunwood's yacht.'

Scales shook his head. 'We need you here, working with us on this – after Stanley, you were our best structures man.'

'That's very kind of you to say so, but ... you know how I feel about working on the fighter. I couldn't possibly.'

'There won't be no place for those sentiments when those Jerry bombers start coming over the Channel,' retorted Scales. 'You look at what's going on in the Rhineland right now; even if we bust a gut, we'll still be bloody lucky to have enough of these ready to stop 'em – and that's only if the bloody government pull their fingers out of their ears and order them.' He patted the wing. 'This beauty is the best chance we've got against Hitler, we need 'em quick smart, or we'll all be singing bloody "Deutschland über alles" by the end of the decade, you mark my words.'

Ben smiled, but Scales just looked at him seriously, reaching out to grip his shoulder fiercely. 'Think about it, young Ben.'

Ben dropped the smile and nodded, then slipped out of Scales's grip and back through the tarpaulin screen. He made his way out to Hazel Road. Notwithstanding Scales's fanaticism, Stanley had been so excited about that fighter – Bartlett had made the same point that morning. And Stanley's suggestion that they work for Dunwood had come out of the blue. The only possible motive for him to abandon his work on the fighter was for the extra money. Ben got to his bike, pulled on his overcoat, then got the old flying helmet, goggles and gloves out of his knapsack, put them on and slung the bag back across his shoulder. He slid the list he'd made that lunchtime out of his inside jacket pocket, along with a map of Southampton. He'd telephoned six of the town's eleven turf accountants, listed in Kelly's Directory, and none of them had heard of Stanley Arbethwaite. But there were five more that didn't have the infernal instrument.

Two hours later he was back outside the Supermarine office. If Stanley had been gambling, it hadn't been through any of the legal avenues in Southampton. He sat on the motorbike and tried to decide what to do. Illicit gambling was a world that he knew little about. Where would he find Stanley's bookie's runner? He tried to put himself into his friend's shoes. Around him the Supermarine works dominated both sides of the road, the cream walls and blue tile window linings of the office block rose sheer from the pavement, linked by the overhead bridge to the Mould Loft. Behind him was the Royal Oak. A pub that might be the obvious answer – perhaps too obvious, too close to home, and anyway, it was shut. There was just a row of neat houses further down by the Floating Bridge, leading into Woolston – perhaps the answer was amongst the Woolston shops.

He kicked the engine into life at the second attempt

and headed south, turned left, gunned the bike up the hill towards the crossroads and then took the right down Victoria Road. He eased over and pulled in. He clunked the stand down and glanced around, not knowing quite what he was looking for, only hoping that he might recognise it when he saw it. Boots the Chemist, the Midland Bank and Stead and Simpson's definitely weren't it. A couple of kids in ragged jumpers were kicking a tin down the other pavement. A woman scurried towards him with a scarf across her face, her hat pulled down and an empty shopping bag flapping around her legs. The sun had dived into a grey film of cloud above the western horizon and the temperature was dropping with it. He climbed off the bike, pushed his gear back into the knapsack and started to walk down the quiet road.

He passed Lankester and Crook's grocers, Price's Meat Pies, Southampton Co-op, the Prudential, a taxi rank, a row of houses and a fishmonger's – amongst others – without feeling he was getting any warmer. On reaching the junction with Keswick Road the houses stopped – replaced by the huge shipbuilding sheds of Thornycroft's. He glanced down the side street. Three kids were watching him curiously, their backs against a garden wall. They all wore shorts, one had no shoes – his feet were black with dirt. A discarded dustbin lid lay at their side. He looked away, conscious of their stares, flipped up his overcoat collar, then hesitated. He turned to the boys. 'Any of you know where I can find a bookie's runner around here?'

'Why should we tell you, mister?' retorted the biggest, his face a lippy sneer under a dark mass of matted hair.

Ben fished in his pockets and came up with three pennies. He flicked them off his thumbnail – each one was neatly caught.

'Down there,' the boy waved, 'the newsagent on the other side.'

Ben nodded his thanks and crossed Victoria Road. After a quick glance back to where he had left his bike, he carried on down towards Southampton Water. The newsagent was on the corner at the next junction, opposite a small tired-looking park. He took a deep breath. Stepping over the threshold, he flipped an *Echo* out of the hanging rack of papers and approached the counter, one hand fumbling for a penny. The shop was rich with the smell of sugar and newsprint. The newsagent had a ruddy cherubic face, but his expression was blank as he took the money.

'And actually, I'll have a packet of twenty Woodbines and a box of Swans,' said Ben, after a moment's hesitation.

The cigarettes and matches were placed on the counter. 'Anything else, sir?'

Ben examined the wall-to-wall display of sweet jars. 'And a quarter of toffee crunch, please,' he said.

The man took down the jar and shook a generous quarter into the big silver dish on the scales. With a smooth, practised movement he transferred the sweets to a paper bag, twisted it shut and placed it by the Woodbines.

'Is that all, sir?'

As he picked up the toffee crunch and shoved it into his pocket, Ben said, 'I just started work down the road, and a friend of mine, Stanley Arbethwaite, reckoned there was somewhere round here I might put a couple of bob on the gee-gees for the weekend.'

There was a flicker of expression, an eyebrow half-lifted. 'Oh, aye, and there was me thinking the law says that gambling has to take place on the race courses,' said the man, sarcastically.

Ben slit the cigarettes open with his thumbnail, watching the other man's face. Why was the fellow playing dumb? He tapped out a cigarette and bent his head to light it. 'I'm sure he meant a race track or something,' he said, through his first exhalation of smoke, pushing the cigarettes and matches into his overcoat pocket.

'Stanley Arbethwaite's been dead for more than a week,' replied the man, creases forming around his narrowed eyes. 'Are you from the coppers or something?'

'Bloody hell, no,' said Ben, startled, 'what makes you say that?'

'Why else would you be in here telling me some made-up story about Stanley tipping you off about an illegal bookie?'

Ben frowned – *he called him Stanley*. 'You knew him?'

'Maybe – what's it to you?'

'We were friends, I lodged with him. Stanley's wife and I think that Stanley might have left some ... unfinished business around here.' He raised the cigarette in a shrug, took another drag.

The man rubbed his chin. His hazel eyes wavered over Ben. 'Nasty accident the way he died, I read about it in the *Echo*.'

Ben nodded.

There was a clatter from beyond the door at the back of the shop; it sounded like a pan lid hitting the floor. The man rolled his eyes and glanced over his shoulder before he continued. 'The fellow that climbed up to get him down, the papers said he lodged with Stanley – was that you?'

'Yes, that was me,' replied Ben.

'Gutsy,' the man replied, the tone indicating a grudging respect. 'So what did Stanley tell you?'

'Nothing, actually,' he confessed. 'His wife ...' Then he stopped. He didn't want to mention the horrendous debts. 'His wife had her suspicions, she asked me to look into it. I want to sort it out, make sure there are no problems. There's no one else to look after her, she doesn't want any trouble.'

'So why here? Not that I'm saying I know anything about it, mind.'

'I had some free time, would've tried the pubs but they're shut, then some lads told me to try here.'

'Did they now?' The man hesitated, circumspectly. 'Stanley sometimes bought a paper here on his way to work in the morning. If it would help his widow out, I don't mind asking around a bit. Not saying I know anything, but why don't you come back in an hour on the off chance I can find someone who does?'

Ben glanced at the clock on the wall. 'About six?' he asked.

'Little bit after,' came the reply, 'and don't forget about that toffee crunch and them cigarettes.'

Ben paid the man, and then walked back up the road, smoking the last of the cigarette, the paper tucked under his arm. The lights of a café were shining, so he went in. The room was heavy with the warm smell of fried food. A line of empty tables with stained red-check tablecloths stood sentry down either wall, each with a set of sauce bottles and salt and pepper shakers. He undid his coat and found a bell on the counter. When he rang it, a young girl appeared almost immediately. She took his order – a cup of tea and a bacon sandwich – and he paid and sat down. He wanted to find the paper's report on Stanley's fighter plane. The tea and sandwich arrived.

'Watch out, your tea's hot,' said the girl as she put it down.

He tipped on the ketchup. The sandwich was excellent, oozing with butter, the bacon juicy and melting in his mouth. He sipped cautiously at the cooling tea, then returned to the sandwich and opened the paper. The front page was full of news of the German military reoccupation of the Rhineland. It was a year since Hitler had torn up the Versailles Treaty, while simultaneously promising peace. And now here he was, at it again. So far the French army had made no move against the Germans, but could Scales be right and Dunwood wrong? Perhaps there would be another war. It occurred to him for the first time that if there were to be another war, he would be expected to fight. He was old enough to kill for his country. He felt an anxious churning kick into his gut. He already knew that he must be a conscientious objector. It was the only thing to do, but ... he also knew what his father would think. The sandwich dried in his mouth; he put it down and took another sip of tea, quickly flicking on past the grim front page.

He finally found the story he was looking for tucked away on the 'Topics of the Hour' page. It was short and general: *all metal monoplane ... has a high top speed and devices to make relatively slow landings possible ... fitted with a Rolls-Royce Merlin engine ... retractable undercarriage* ... He sighed; Stanley had loved that plane.

Two cigarettes later, at a little before six o'clock, he could no longer restrain himself. Ben left the café and headed back down towards the newsagent. The sun was setting behind the towering frontage of Thornycroft's, and the park beyond the junction was dark. Shadows alerted him as he approached the shop, and his pace quickened – the rack of papers was gone, the door shut, all the lights off. He banged on the window, waited for a couple of moments, banged again. Then he tried the door. It was locked. Dangling on a piece of string in the upper pane of glass, a yellowed sign said 'Shut, come back later for your copy of The Illustrated London News'. He took a step back, looked up. None of the lights were on above the shop either. What was the man playing at?

'Ben Clayton?' said a voice to his right.

He spun round – the man had appeared without a sound. He must have come out of the park. 'Maybe,' said Ben.

'You're asking after Stanley Arbethwaite?'

'Yes.' Ben nodded at the darkened shop. 'The man in there ...'

'Our friend gets a little nervous.'

Ben saw a white smile in the gathering gloom, predatory rather than reassuring. The man wore a long black leather overcoat with the collar turned up, a dark trilby tipped nonchalantly to the right, and had both hands buried in the coat pockets. Ben could see nothing of his face. He would never recognise him again if he saw him, and that was probably the intention. Whatever happened next, there would be no comeback for this fellow.

'I'm just trying to sort things out for Stanley's widow. We don't want any trouble,' he said.

'There's no trouble,' the man replied. 'Let's walk, looks a bit odd, standing here,' and he started down towards the water.

Ben hesitated, but then fell in beside him, to the man's right. Tactically, he'd much prefer to be going the other way, back towards the bike, the café, the lights, rather than into the deep shadows thrown by the park and the factory. He thought of the thin wound and the razor-sharp pain. That's how it would be – but which hand would he use, which side would it come from? He was gambling on it being the right.

'Our newsagent friend holds a few bets for one of my runners to come and pick up,' the man was explaining. 'It's not a big involvement, but he knows what goes on. He introduced Stanley to me, so at the moment he's nervous, seeing what Stanley owes me.' The mild tone didn't disguise the meaning. They weren't discussing the odds on the three thirty.

'I don't normally allow anyone to run an account,' the man continued, 'my mob just pick up the cash with the betting slips from the pubs and around about, people know them, know where to find them. I don't like to get involved with debt and reckonings, it's bad for business taking too much money off people, getting 'em in the poorhouse. But I made an exception for Stanley. He was spending a good bit of money with me, and didn't seem to mind losing. I looked into him. He had a good job with Supermarine, so I was happy. He was earning it. But lately he started to worry me. He hadn't paid anything for more than three months. I told my lads to stop taking bets from him. Then he dies.'

There was nothing but the sound of their footsteps on the pavement. 'How much does he owe you?' asked Ben.

'Thirty-one pounds, fifteen shillings and sixpence.' The man paced evenly forward, gazing directly ahead. 'And it's going up at one per cent a month,' he added.

It was more than three weeks' wages, with an interest rate that was nearly three times that on the house loan; but it still wasn't the source of the financial haemorrhaging that had taken place. 'It'll take a while to get that much money,' he said.

'I don't need it all at once; you pop in to our friend back there once a week with a pound or two and there will be no more said.'

'All right, but it's half a per cent a month,' Ben countered.

The man gave a short laugh. 'You'll put me out of business.'

Ben walked on for a few more strides. 'Are there others?' he asked.

The man glanced at him for the first time. 'What do you mean "others"?'

'I mean did Stanley owe anyone else money, or are you the only one? I need to know the scale of the problem.'

The man did not reply.

The lights were on in Thornycroft's now, mixing strange shadows and patterns of light across the road. Ben realised he was going to have to take a chance with this man. 'Look, I'll be straight with you,' he said. 'I need some help, there's the possibility that Stanley's got himself in a lot deeper with someone not so, ah, scrupulous as you. And there are some concerns about the way he died ...'

The man pulled up short in a darker patch of shadow. 'What are you trying to say?' His left hand came up to scratch at his cheek for a moment, before returning to his pocket.

Ben stopped a couple of paces on, shifting as he did so to get closer to the man's left side. He kept both of his own hands hanging loose. 'There are people in Hamble who think he was murdered,' he said.

'There's no point killing a man who owes you money,' the man replied, evenly.

'No, I understand that – unless you wanted to teach him a lesson for the benefit of others.'

'Not with thirty quid at stake you wouldn't.'

'No, of course not,' said Ben, letting a slight trace of impatience creep into his voice. 'I'm not suggesting for a minute that you were involved, but you might know something, about Stanley, who else he was mixed up with – I need to know what was going on. It's important.'

The man was silent for a few moments. Then he said, 'And if I help you, you'll make sure I get my money?'

'Yes. And you can have three-quarters of a per cent. A pound a week. Till it's done, you have my word.'

It was a long while before the man finally replied, 'Eight-tenths – I'm not taking any less.'

Ben was so close to what he needed to know that he could smell it. 'All right,' he agreed.

'There's only one name, and you didn't hear it from me.'

'Of course,' replied Ben.

'Spink. He runs a high-stakes card game for some posh types, in a big house off The Avenue. It's a few doors down from the 'Blackshirt Club'. I heard Arbethwaite was up there and getting out of his depth – that's when I started to get worried about my money. Spink's not one to mess with, he'll use a razor on a man quick enough – but ... I don't think he'd go as far as murder. Otherwise, there's no one else down here, or I'd have heard about it – but maybe he went up to London and got himself into something up there.' The man glanced at Ben. 'Now, I don't expect I'll be hearing from you again, Mr Clayton, and I'm sure you'll keep the payments regular. Nice doing business with you.' There was a final flash of that rapacious smile, and the man strode off, still going towards the water, the black leather coat flickering through the light and shade thrown out by Thornycroft's until he merged into the darkness. And slowly, Ben relaxed.

Matthew Faden paused at the entrance to South Kensington Tube Station to pick up a copy of the *Evening News*. He tucked it under his arm after a quick glance at the headlines – all about the Rhineland – and then turned right through the crowd, the ermine coats and the perfumed hair, and headed across Onslow Place. What little warmth that the day had generated had disappeared with the sun, but he didn't bother to button up his tweed overcoat as he hit the cold. He had a good walk ahead of him down to Drayton Gardens, and that would keep him warm enough. He waited while an elderly couple went past in an open horse-drawn carriage. A couple of bicycles followed and the clip of hooves had faded before he could cross, the pause giving him time to think about White again. He'd heard nothing, so perhaps giving up Clayton's name had been enough; but if that was so, he had to be sure that Clayton wouldn't help. He stepped out into the street and began to follow the weak pools of lamplight towards the Old Brompton Road.

'Matthew?'

Faden turned at the familiar husky voice. 'Belle! My God, what are you doing here? I thought you were still in Germany.'

Annabelle Venuti emerged from a café doorway, framed in the light, her dark hair tumbling onto her shoulders from under a fashionably angled beret. She was wearing a stunning ankle-length dark blue wool coat that had to be from Coco Chanel.

'I've been home for a while,' she said. 'Daddy's job ended, and I was missing England – so, here I am.' She held out her hand, stepping down to the pavement. 'I saw you passing and dashed out to catch you.'

Faden snapped his heels together and bowed, his lips lightly caressing the back of her leather glove.

She laughed. 'Oh Matthew, you remember?'

'There is only one way to greet the Belle of the ball,' he replied, grinning. He had started the courtly manner and the nickname 'Belle' at a May ball. She'd been there with mutual friends from Oxford. And then she'd disappeared to Germany, trailing the most extraordinary degree and a string of suitors – but still unattached. And now here she was, alone outside a café and more beautiful than ever. A visceral thrill went through him, the power of a potent piece of gossip – *Belle was back!*

She sighed, theatrically. 'But you simply must call me Anna now, everyone does, darling – this Belle thing is just too embarrassing.'

'Not a chance, my sweet, once a Belle, always a Belle.' Faden smiled.

Anna laughed again, 'You're impossible, always were – but how are you? I can't remember the last time I saw you.'

'I daren't even think – probably Cowes Week, after you came down from Somerville.'

'Yes, it was just after that that we all went out to Germany.'

'So how long have you been back?'

'Not quite a year.' She pushed the hair off her shoulder as she spoke.

'All that time!' Faden sighed. 'I can't believe I haven't bumped into you before.'

'I did a lot of the social season – I was at Cowes Week.'

'Yachting, darling?'

'Only when I didn't have to pull any ropes,' she replied.

'Of course.' Faden smiled; he was familiar with Belle's dislike of anything that involved exertion. But she steered a yacht with a better touch than any man he knew, and had won a Fastnet Race aboard her father's ketch.

'So we didn't see you at Cowes,' she said.

'I've rather dropped off the social map I'm afraid, old thing, I've hardly even stepped on a boat since I came down from Cambridge.'

'Oh no, that's a terrible shame – why not?'

Faden hesitated. It was all just too damned elitist to

be bearable, that was the real answer, although Belle was one of the few amongst his old friends who might be sympathetic to his views. He remembered her as quite progressive. But he wasn't much for the soapbox these days. He liked to keep his politics and his sexual inclinations to himself and a tight group of like-minded friends. And besides, the café she had emerged from was the Russian Tea Rooms, owned by a White Russian admiral with links to the far right. Perhaps her politics had changed during that time in Germany. 'Well,' he started, and he was still fumbling for a bland reply when the café door opened.

'Anna?' called a cultured nasal voice.

'Oh darling, have you met Matthew Faden?' she replied.

Faden looked up at the figure on the café steps. 'Lerup, how do you do,' he said, holding out a hand. 'I think we met at a gallery opening, a couple of years ago.'

'Oh yes,' replied Lerup, unconvincingly, and stepped down and shook his hand. 'You know Anna?' he added.

'Forever – our parents are friends. And you two?' asked Faden.

'We met during Cowes Week last summer,' said Anna. 'I was a guest of the Dunwoods, and Charles came sailing with us.'

Faden nodded – May Dunwood's father had been at King's College with Belle's.

'Now he's the owner's representative aboard *Windflower*,' Anna continued, laying a possessive hand on Lerup's forearm. 'Harold Dunwood's new yacht.' She smiled proudly, looking from one man to the other.

'So I heard,' replied Faden. 'Actually an old friend of mine, Ben Clayton, telephoned me yesterday, asking if I wanted to go yachting with you chaps at the weekend.'

'Yes,' drawled Lerup, 'he's getting some fine amateur men together for us – the wretched professionals have gone on strike and we've had to dismiss the lot of them.'

'What's that all about?' asked Faden.

'Oh' – Lerup waved his hand – 'too boring to even worry about, damned untrustworthy workers, that's all.'

Faden pushed his fists deep into his coat pockets out of sight – *reactionary fathead* – but he hadn't seen Belle for so long. He hardly wanted it to be the occasion of a stand-up row with her new beau ...

'But we'll get some proper Corinthian fellows aboard and have it ticking along again in no time, be top notch with you chaps and it'll only improve our chances,' Lerup was saying.

Faden hesitated – and into the pause leapt Anna.

'So will you join us for a drink?' she asked. 'They have the most wonderful vodka.'

Faden glanced in through the windows at the polished wooden furniture, panelled walls and open fireplace, crowned with a thick layer of cigarette smoke, and shook his head. 'I'm late for a meeting, but we simply must get together soon.'

'I shall be down with *Windflower* at the weekend,' exclaimed Anna, smiling.

'We can catch up then, or at the very least make an arrangement for next week, back up in town.'

'Wonderful, Matthew, I have so missed you.' Anna leaned forward and kissed him on the cheek as she spoke.

'You too, Belle,' Faden replied, before rather reluctantly adding, 'See you Saturday, Lerup.'

Lerup nodded, and then ushered Anna in through the café door.

Faden hurried away – *Belle back in England and with Lerup*. It would have been a great piece of gossip, if it hadn't been months out of date. He must be the last to know. And it made more sense that Lerup was Dunwood's man on the *Windflower*. While Ben was a smart chap and a fantastically talented yachtsman, Faden still couldn't see him as an owner's representative. But Fleming White had mentioned that Lerup had a role in his plans – what sort of role? Had MI5 got Lerup to keep an eye on the Russian admiral and his right-wing friends in the tea rooms? If so, then Lerup could hardly be the one to win over Dunwood to the cause of rearming against the Nazis. In which case, White would need Ben Clayton, and would be trying everything to get him to help. Faden rubbed at his neck anxiously; he had to be absolutely sure whose side Clayton was on, and he had to know soon.

Chapter 13

Lucy didn't know what it was that caused her to hesitate and – a page of her *Yachting World* magazine half turned – to sit up and listen. She got up and went to the door, opening it to a curtain of rain running off the lip of the little porch. She could see nothing beyond a few feet of paving stone and mud that held a vague promise of spring grass. Lucy glanced back into the kitchen and saw Tom staring at her, *Comic Cuts* open on his knees. *Perhaps I'm mad*, she thought.

'Ben?' she called into the gloom, just as he stepped into the light thrown by the open door, a stream of water dripping off the brim of his brown fedora.

'Your father's not around, is he?' he asked through the waterfall.

'No, I don't know where he is, come in for goodness' sake.'

Ben stepped inside, pulling off his hat and shaking the loose water out into the night as he did so.

'I've been worried,' she said. 'I heard what happened at the pub yesterday. My goodness, you're soaked,' she added, as water puddled onto the floor from Ben's sodden coat, shoes and trousers.

'Good evening, Tom' he said, as he took off his coat and hung it on the back of the door.

Tom looked up, jabbing a black fingernail onto the

page to mark his place. 'Hello, Mr Clayton,' he said.

'How about going upstairs to your room,' suggested Lucy. 'I bought you the comic, now you can give me and Mr Clayton a bit of peace and quiet.'

'I s'pose.' Then Tom's face lit up. 'I got a new valve for the radio, Dad bought it for me, you said you'd show me how to fit it,' he said to Ben.

'Not tonight, Tom, come on now, Mr Clayton's had a long day, maybe at the weekend?' She looked from Tom to Ben as she spoke.

Ben nodded. 'We could have a look at it at the weekend, if I don't have to work. How about that, Tom, you can bring it round to my house,' he replied.

'Yeah!' Tom jumped out of his seat. 'I like your house.'

'But only if you're in that room of yours and quiet as a mouse in ten seconds,' she told him.

Tom bolted up the stairs, comic in hand. They heard the door of his room shut with a crash, and then peace descended.

'I think he's been listening to that new Radio Luxembourg station,' she said.

'Lots more dance music than the stuffy old BBC,' Ben told her, pushing at the fringe that had flopped into his eyes.

'You need a haircut,' she said, thinking that his face had recovered some of its old animation.

'I know – there just hasn't been time.'

Her eyes found his. 'You're feeling better, aren't you?' she blurted out.

'Some of the time,' replied Ben, his expression draining, flattening. 'Then I remember.' He shivered, and moved a chair beside the range. He sat down, huddling close to the warmth while he pulled his brogues off and propped them up to dry.

Lucy went to her room to fetch a blanket, hesitating at the mirror, quickly brushing her hair. She hurried back out to the kitchen. She was glad now that she had stoked the fire up after she'd finished cooking, although she knew she shouldn't have – they couldn't afford it any more. She gave the blanket to Ben and poured him a cup of tea, putting in a little extra sugar. Then she retrieved hers from the table and drew up another chair.

'Something smells good,' he told her, as she sat close beside him.

'It's only a bit of fish, do you want some? There's a fair bit left over.' The smell still dominated the room, a pleasant warm fug.

'No thanks, I already ate,' he replied. 'Where's your father?'

'He's up at the King and Queen, far as I know. I haven't seen him since this morning. He didn't come back for dinner. But you shouldn't be avoiding him, Ben.'

He had both hands around his mug of tea, face in the steam. 'I just thought it better to keep out of his way – things might be said which can't be unsaid.'

Lucy watched him. It was sensible, she couldn't argue with that. This thing would blow over and in the meantime, the less that was said in bad temper, the better. 'The one you've really got to watch out for is Jim Rails,' she warned. 'He's unhappy with you and Dad. Captain Emerton thinks you should stay out of the pubs for a while, lie low a bit.'

'It seems everyone else agrees with them – not much of a welcome for me in the King and Queen the other night.'

She drew closer to him, and he let go of the edges of the blanket, opened it out and pulled it round her too. 'They'll get over it when they realise what we're trying to do,' she told him. She was content to just sit there with him, listening to the sound of water drumming onto the mud from a leaking gutter. The smell of damp earth rose from Ben's shoes, mingling with the fish.

'You remember that dark blue German yacht that came up the river when you rowed me to work on Sunday?' she said, eventually.

'They anchored off the Elephant yard, didn't they?' he

replied.

'That's the one,' she said. 'There was a couple on board, he's a dentist. They had all his equipment and their belongings below – everything – absolutely jammed it was. I thought it looked low on the waterline.'

'And they're from Germany?'

'Yes, they told Miss Ritchie they've left for good, they want to live here.'

'Why?' he asked.

'Miss Ritchie said they're Jews.'

'Hitler's making things pretty uncomfortable for the Jews.'

'I read about that in the paper, it sounds awful,' she said.

'So what happened to them?' asked Ben.

'I don't know, the Elephant yard telephoned the council and they said they'd send someone down to talk to them. But they're still anchored out in the river at the moment.'

'It's a bloody heroic effort sailing over here with everything they own,' he mused.

'Ben, the papers ... some people think there's going to be another war,' she said, suddenly. 'They talk about the bombers turning cities to dust, and it all seems too horrible for words.'

'Lucy, don't be so silly,' he replied, squeezing her into him. 'I was only talking to Mr Dunwood about it today, and he was saying that there's no chance of that happening. He's sure Mr Baldwin is set on keeping us out of all that. And types like Mr Dunwood should know – he's even a member of the Tory Party. You know how those people are connected; they know what's really going on behind the scenes. I'm sure that if Mr Dunwood thinks it's all right, then nothing like that will happen.'

Lucy smiled; that was the kind of inside information you couldn't read about in the papers. Then it struck her. 'You were talking to Mr Dunwood?'

'Yes, he ... came in to my office to talk about work, and the crew.'

'And you've got an office!' She looked at him, eyes wide.

'With a view of Southampton Water,' he added.

'Oh my goodness – that's wonderful! This will be worth it, all this trouble, I know it will!' she exclaimed. And then he kissed her, and everything melted away in the sensation of his lips on hers.

She froze. There it was again, the creak from upstairs. She pulled away from Ben and for a moment they just looked at each other. 'So,' she said, a little more loudly than she had intended, pointing upstairs, 'Dad and a couple of others were down at the yard yesterday – and today for all I know – picketing the gate. I had a bit of a row with him about the whole thing this morning.'

Ben frowned. Then he said, 'That's a bad show; not much use proving Captain Emerton wasn't at fault if they're going to stir up that sort of trouble ...'

There was a creak from the landing floorboards. She could have pointed out the very one, such was her experience in both sides of the matter. 'What do you want, Tom?' she called, standing.

There was a moment's silence – *he's working out what to do*, she thought. Then a patter of light footsteps down the stairs, and Tom's face appeared. 'Can I have a glass of water, please?' he asked.

She gave him a long hard stare, before she replied, 'Yes. And then that's it. What did we agree?'

'I'm thirsty,' was his plaintive response. She poured the glass of water, and Tom took it from her in silence. She watched him turn and go back upstairs. The last time he'd caught them kissing, he'd blurted it out to Dad and there had been an awful scene.

'Why is your old man being so bolshy about all this?' asked Ben, as Tom's footsteps retreated up the stairs and crossed the dodgy landing floorboard. His bedroom door closed.

'It's his politics,' she replied, sitting beside Ben. He pulled the blanket back round her as she slipped under his arm.

'How do you mean?' he asked.

'He used to be a communist. Didn't you know?'

'So Lerup was right. That's what he told Dunwood.'

'Dad left the party years ago, but it came from the war originally – some posh lieutenant gave him all these books. At least, that's what my mum told me. He came home from the war running on about the proletarian revolution, and has done so ever since. Sometimes I think he's been waiting for something like this strike. He feels he's missed out – the General Strike, hunger marches – he's missed his vocation, leading the workers. It's not really been bad enough for it down here.' She reached into her skirt pocket and pulled out a pouch of tobacco. 'You want one?' she asked.

'I'll have a puff of yours,' he replied.

'Anyway,' she went on, deftly rolling the cigarette, 'I gave Dad what for this morning, for getting us in this mess. He started on me, about you working for Dunwood, but he daren't say it in front of the others.'

'What others?' he asked.

Lucy outlined the events on the steps of the Bugle as they smoked the cigarette, taking it in turns to place it between the other's lips. 'You were right about the downhaul though,' she finished up, leaning over to open the range door to toss the butt inside, 'the bobbies just threw it back in Dad's face. Lerup beat them to the police station, he was waiting for them. Stood on the seat of that fancy car of his and told them they were all fired, then cleared off.'

Ben shook his head. 'I thought as much. We need more evidence, but I'm starting to get somewhere with that,' he said.

'Tell me!' she responded, with an admonitory slap on his knee.

He told his story and she listened in silence until he got to Spink and the illegal card game. 'This Blackshirt

Club,' she interrupted, 'I've heard Dad talk about it. I remember him going on one time about that Lady Verdon Roe –'

'*The* Lady Verdon Roe?' interrupted Ben.

'I suppose so – married to the aircraft gentleman – anyway, she invited Lady Diana Mosley, Sir Oswald's wife, down here to talk at that place. Dad was ranting and raving – *bad as Mussolini and Hitler, shouldn't be down here, give the town and the village a bad name.*'

'I wouldn't disagree with him – anyway, I went up to the place to check it over ...' he continued.

'What!'

'It's all right, I just pretended to fiddle with the bike while I was getting a look at what went on. There weren't too many people arriving, but maybe it's always quiet on a Tuesday. Everyone was wearing evening dress, and there were some very smart cars pulling up outside, I can tell you.'

'So Stanley lost all his money there?'

'That's what I'm going to find out, I'm going to try and get in there tomorrow night –'

'No!' She sat up sharply and Ben's hand slipped from her shoulders.

'Yes – Lucy, I have to find out about this Spink fellow, what Stanley was doing there.'

'You can't do that, it's far too dangerous, this man might have killed Stanley. Haven't you got enough to go to the police now?'

He shook his head. 'No, but there's no danger in trying to get in, they won't know who I am,' he said.

'It's too dangerous,' she insisted, taking his hand and squeezing it.

Ben laid his free hand gently on her cheek, then pushed a strand of hair back behind her ear. 'It could provide me with something else to go on, some other line on the whole matter. I haven't got anything right now. I think that Stanley ran up his debts gambling, and it might have been at this club – but that's hardly something I can take to the police without an explanation of why he was killed for it, if he was killed for it. Think of the embarrassment for Mrs Arbethwaite if the police investigate and there's nothing more, just all these debts and Stanley, a failed gambler mixed up with dodgy people and clubs ...'

Lucy frowned. She let go of his hand. Then, after a moment's stillness, she leaned down and turned his shoes round. The warmth from the range was dying.

He wrapped the blanket back around them both. 'I promised Mrs Arbethwaite I'd keep this thing quiet until we have some real evidence,' he told her.

'Do you *have* to go?' she said. 'There has to be another way – what do real detectives do?'

'I'll be careful, Lucy, truly I will, although ...'

'What?'

'It would be nice if all the people we're trying to help could be a bit more cooperative. What with your father organising the pickets, and Mrs Arbethwaite not even wanting to talk about the debts, I feel a bit like Sisyphus pushing his bloody rock up that hill.'

She didn't know who Sisyphus was, or what rock he pushed up what hill, and she certainly wasn't going to ask – she'd check at the library later. So she nodded as wisely as she could, relaxing into him as she did so.

'You haven't told anyone about the debts, have you?' he asked.

'Of course not,' she replied.

'It's just that she's very sensitive about appearances and such like ...'

'I know, Ben, I know,' retorted Lucy, rather more sharply than she'd intended.

'Sorry,' he said, 'this is a nightmare for you too.'

It was her turn to push back a lock of hair that had fallen across his eyes. He smiled warmly at her and Lucy luxuriated in the moment, the feeling of his body close to hers, his breath on her hair. Then she felt him shift under her.

'I should go,' he said, standing. 'I know ... but we agreed it was better for me to stay out of your father's way for a while, and he could be home any time.'

'But it's awful that we don't have anywhere to be together, not here, not Mrs Arbethwaite's, not even out there ...' she trailed off, waving at the wind and rain that beat at the windowpane.

'I know, but ...' He shook his head, frowned and left the sentence unfinished. He crouched down to put his shoes back on, lacing them with swift accurate actions, before moving to get his coat. She watched in silence, unable to think of anything to say. There was just the beat of the rain from that broken guttering.

He stood. 'Give me a hug before I go,' he said.

And in a moment she was in his arms, wriggling in close, feeling him shift his weight so they fit together, so perfectly. For a long while he just held her tightly, as though he couldn't let go. And then something made her turn her face upwards, and he was looking down at her, eyes quite still, a half smile on his face. He made a tiny movement towards her and she reached up as he bent his head. Their lips touched, her stomach fluttered uncontrollably, a tingle chased up her spine. She couldn't stop a breathless little sigh as he pulled her into him. He slid his cheek against hers, his breath in her ear, and that's all there was of her, just the fall of his breath. God, she wanted him so badly ...

'Lucy' – his voice was so soft she had to strain to hear him – 'will you marry me?'

For one wild uncomprehending moment, she thought she might have misheard – but the look in his eyes banished all doubts. 'Yes, yes! YES! Oh Ben, oh, I ...'

'Bloody hell!' he hissed, and suddenly he was breaking away from her. 'Your father! I saw ...' With a lightning motion he turned and silently flicked the deadbolt on the door. A moment later it rattled as someone tried to open it from outside.

'Lucy?' yelled the unmistakeable voice of her father.

She looked at Ben, who shook his head violently, then grabbed her hand and tugged her towards the back door. They covered the distance in a few strides, and Ben heaved it open. A flurry of March rain pattered around them. He turned to her.

'He mustn't know, not until ... not until things have settled down again; promise me, no one must know. I have no ring, and I haven't asked him, and I can't until this business is over ...'

She hesitated for a moment. She wanted to tell the world, to run up the High Street and fling open the doors of all the pubs, screaming the news. But this wasn't the time to argue about it. She nodded and he smiled – a wonderful smile that lit up her world. And then he was gone. She watched the darkness until his shadow faded, then slipped the door shut, the angry rattle from the kitchen door making little impression on her. They were engaged. It seemed impossible after all this time, but ... Then there was a thunderous hammering at the front door, and she heard Tom moving on the stairs. She rushed through to the kitchen. Tom hesitated when he saw her, looking puzzled.

'It's all right, I just forgot I'd latched the door,' she said, letting her father in.

Chapter 14

Ben clicked the engine off and Mrs Arbethwaite's little Morris Eight juddered reluctantly into silence. He'd approached The Avenue from the east and parked in a side street just short of his goal. He didn't want anyone at the club to see the lowly nature of the borrowed vehicle. He put both hands on the steering wheel, arms straight, gripping it tight, trying to release the tension that throbbed through his neck and shoulders. He relaxed with a quick exhalation, closing his eyes for a moment. Then he pushed the door open and levered himself out against the tilt of the car into the gutter. He glanced up and down the silent street. A white cat slunk across the edge of a pool of street light. Nothing else moved. He did up a button on the dinner jacket, straightened his bow tie and wiped the tops of his shoes across his calves. Then he fetched his overcoat and the black homburg off the back seat, pushed a hand through his Brylcreemed hair, put the hat on and let the car door fall shut.

He shrugged into the overcoat as he walked down to Lodge Road, where he turned right, steel heels clipping on the stone pavement. The air was clear and cold, the sky soaked with dense splashes of stars. He arrived on The Avenue; to his left, towards the city, a Belisha beacon flashed dull orange. He turned right and quickly passed the Blackshirt Club. The houses along this stretch were impressive – gravel drives with stones of military precision, gardens with individually groomed blades of grass. There was little traffic, just a cyclist headed towards town, accompanied by the light wind sighing through the ancient trees. He felt a preparatory rush of adrenaline, his heart upping its tempo. This was the one – the white sculpted gateposts and black iron gate. He coughed to clear his throat and started up the path. There was no one else around. All the downstairs lights were on, filtering out past heavy curtains, while upstairs was completely dark.

His footfalls echoed faintly as he got closer to the imposing stone facade. Polished white steps led up to an immaculate black door, no sign or nameplate, just a bell push. He'd watched the arrival of others a couple of evenings previously and knew the routine – ring the bell, wait patiently, exchange a few authoritative words with the doorman and enter. It couldn't be simpler. Unless there was some sort of code or password. He stepped up to the door, pushed the bell and stepped back. There was a distant low chime. He waited, hands in his pockets, nonchalantly spinning on one heel. A little too nonchalantly – he realised he was overdoing it and stopped. The door opened and he was met by a bewhiskered doorman, dressed in what looked like a Boer War uniform: red tunic, red piping down the blue trousers, white sergeant's stripes.

'Sir?' the man enquired in a stentorian voice, one hand gripping the door, his bulk filling the opening.

Ben had no fixed plan for what to say beyond an opening gambit, a bluff. 'I've come for the game, my man,' he said, stepping up into the doorway.

The Boer War veteran didn't move a muscle and Ben was forced to stop a pace short of him, half in, half out of the entrance, and uncomfortably close to the other man.

'And what game would that be, sir?' said the doorman, his blue eyes levelled at Ben, the words almost in his ear, a faint trace of alcohol on the man's breath.

'The card game, of course,' he replied.

'I'm sure you're mistaken, sir, there's no card game here – perhaps a game of snap for the master's children.' The moustache twitched at its owner's humour.

Ben took a step back and down, relinquishing whatever advantage he might have gained from his height. There was a further studied silence from above, and he filled it. 'I'm a friend of Stanley Arbethwaite's; he sent me down here, said you offered excellent sport.'

The moustache twitched again, just enough to indicate that the doorman might have recognised the name. 'Did he indeed,' he replied, and for a moment, Ben thought he might have done it. Then the doorman went on, 'Which is interesting, considering that no one in this house has ever seen nor 'eard of anyone by the name of Stanley Arbethwaite.'

The ringing pronouncement of the Christian name and the ridiculous mangling of the syllables of the surname were enough to tell Ben that all was lost. He took a further step back.

'I'll thank you to leave the premises now, sir,' announced the doorman. 'Before I shall 'ave to call the constabulary. We don't want trouble with trespassing,' he added.

'Any more than you want trouble with the constabulary, I'm sure,' retorted Ben, digging his hands in his overcoat pockets. The other man frowned for a moment, then the door started to swing shut and Ben turned back down the path. His heart was doing two hundred a minute. That hadn't gone as well as he'd hoped. He was halfway back to the road when there was a heavy scrunch of gravel and the deep beat of an engine as a big Rolls-Royce swept into the drive. For a moment he was bathed in its lights. He ducked away to avoid the glare but glanced in as the car eased past. The moon threw a blue light onto the occupants of the vehicle. He stopped dead. One of them was Anna, and she was looking straight at him. Their eyes met.

He bolted for the deep shadow of the hedge that

marked the front boundary along The Avenue. The car eased to a halt at the foot of the steps, and the rear door on his side opened. Lerup got out of the car, while the driver opened the offside door for Anna. She took the first two steps quite quickly, then hesitated and let Lerup past before following him up to the door. He rang the bell and they waited. She was wearing a backless black dress and matching elbow-length gloves, her shoulders covered by a fur. The door opened quickly, and as they were ushered inside Anna half turned and gazed into the night. There was no doubt in his mind that she was looking for him. Then the door closed and she was gone.

The Rolls pulled away and started to swing into a turn that would sweep its headlights across his position. He darted through the gate and started to walk away from the house as the car crunched over the gravel and bumped out onto the road behind him. What had he seen in that look as she'd turned back at the door – recognition, curiosity, indifference? Recognition was a disaster. If Anna just made a comment or query to the doorman about him, Spink would be able to link his name with Stanley's. It had been a risk mentioning his friend, and now if Spink was in some way connected to Stanley's death, he would know that Ben was suspicious. But how could he have predicted that Anna would turn up to identify him?

He swivelled on his toe in mid-stride and then stopped. There was no one behind him, just the silent grand houses and the sweep of trees running north from the junction with London Road. A dog padded up to him, halting a couple of feet away. It was a mongrel, its mangy, dark brown fur spotted with patches of black. The dog nosed forward and sniffed his hand. He stroked it for a while, thinking ... then he started back towards the house. The dog followed and he had to shoo it away. When he reached the gate, he stepped inside and found a place in the shadows. He wasn't sure why. Perhaps he didn't like to turn his back on a man who might be out to kill him. Or maybe just watching the house qualified as doing something; it might tell him more than the pitiful amount he knew at the moment.

He settled into his vigil; more cars arrived, rolling up the drive and emptying elegant figures onto the steps. The sergeant seemed to know all of them personally; he could hear the man using their names. He recognised a few of them, serious people – money, status, power. This man Spink would have formidable protectors should he be able to call on them. What had Stanley been doing here? This secret life that he had managed to lead, to hide, what had it got him mixed up in? What had it got them both mixed up in, given that Ben now found himself skulking around someone else's property like a cat burglar casing a joint?

If that consequence wasn't improbable enough, it seemed scarcely possible that his friend, his workmate, had been gambling here with the likes of Lerup and his imperious aristocratic ilk. Perhaps Lerup was even connected to Stanley's death ... but no, as much as he disliked Lerup, the idea that he was involved in murder was ridiculous. So was it just coincidence that both Lerup and Stanley had attended this card game? At work, Lerup had always been as brusque with Stanley as everyone else; there was no hint of friendship or any connection beyond work. And whatever went on behind that immaculate closed door probably didn't have too much competition this side of London – two men looking for what that house offered would gravitate to the same place. Still, it nagged at Ben; he didn't like coincidences.

Eventually, the arrivals slowed and stopped, and The Avenue fell quiet on the other side of the hedge. Ben found himself thinking of Lucy and their engagement. It was the right thing to do, he had no doubts. He loved her, and he was sure that she loved him. There was no point in waiting, but nevertheless ... he'd just blurted it out. It would have been so much better to have had a ring, a plan, to have picked the right moment, but most of all to have dealt with his parents first. Now he had to face them, and he had to do it soon. He brooded awhile, but there was the letter from his mother. He would open it, maybe it would help.

The city was starting to empty. A couple scurried past, chattering about a movie – Hitchcock's *The 39 Steps.* They were going home, chased by the ghostly lunar cloud shadows that swept up the road. A light drizzle was drifting on the breeze, and thickening perceptibly. Soon, it was raining. It didn't take long for it to find its way through the shoulder seams of his overcoat, and to trickle down his neck. It dripped off the hem of the coat onto his trousers, and before long he could squelch his toes in the puddles in his dress shoes. Nobody else came or went from the house, nothing changed. An uncontrollable shiver struck him. He acknowledged that standing in the freezing rain was ridiculous, and decided to give it five more minutes and then go home. Then there was a cough behind him, and he spun round. A huge figure loomed over him. He whirled back towards the gate, one foot sliding out from under him as the smooth leather soles of his shoes slipped on the wet grass, but it was already too late. Another man emerged through the gate to block his escape. They were both taller with advantages of reach and weight, but he wasn't going to fight. The edge he needed was agility, but that was impossible in what was turning out to be highly unsuitable footwear. The voice of the man behind him was studiously gruff.

'Gentleman that owns the house is wondering if he can help you, sir; standing out here in the cold all night, you'll catch a chill. Perhaps you'd like to accompany us inside for a hot toddy, and a warm-up by the fire. Sir.'

Ben faced him. In the darkness, he couldn't see anything more of the man than his bulk, but the last thing he wanted to do was to accompany him anywhere. 'No, I'm just on my way, thanks,' he said, responding automatically to the man's politeness.

'Unfortunately, I can't let you do that, sir, since you're trespassing,' the voice rumbled like gravel coming off a dump truck. 'You have been for some time. You'll have to accompany us inside while we sort this out, what with trespass on private property being against the law, as I'm sure you know, sir. Unless, of course, you was to be a member of the constabulary yourself, and had some good reason for standing out here in the dark and the rain, in which case I'm sure you'll be just as happy to explain your presence to Mr Spink, while we call the station to check on your identity.'

Spink – he was going to be taken to meet Spink. He felt huge hands grasp his elbows, the weight of the men propelling him forward. For a moment it looked as if they were going in via the front door. He had a sickening vision of being paraded past the guests, past Anna and Lerup, dripping, shivering and captive. But the two men led him round the side of the house – *keep it tidy, don't scare the punters*. He tried to gather scattered thoughts. His captors had suggested that maybe they'd caught a policeman snooping on their game. No doubt the cards were long gone, some genteel alternative entertainment taking place for the benefit of the visiting policeman. The whole episode used to embarrass the constabulary into backing off for a while – if he really was the police. The trouble was ... he wasn't.

They reached a small wooden door at the back of the property. Water dripped from a gutter onto dirty concrete. There was a smell of rotting food. The gruff-voiced man opened the door and let him pass inside. Ben suddenly realised the opportunity it presented and instinctively hunched his shoulders for a blow from behind. But the only sound was the click of a switch. He looked around in the dim light. He was in some kind of a storeroom, a huge larder, with racks of tinned goods – beer, wine, boxes and sacks – but only the smell of dust and cardboard.

'Wait, I'll see whether the boss wants to come down, or see you up in his office,' said the gruff voice, a whiff of malt on his breath. In the dingy light he was revealed as every bit as solid as he'd appeared in the dark. He hung his trilby on a hook on the wall, then shook off the overcoat to join the hat, revealing a beautifully tailored dinner suit. He swept back his oiled hair before exiting through a door on the far side of the storeroom.

Ben took his homburg off and tapped it against a shelf to get rid of the loose water. He carefully placed it on one of the boxes of dried goods, as he wiped his neck dry with his handkerchief. The action calmed him considerably, and he took a better look at his guard, the shorter of the two men. He was a little more than Ben's height, just over six foot, and as heavily built as his colleague. The man kept his hat on, leaving his face in shadow. He said nothing, taking up a station by the door they had entered through. Ben looked down at his feet. He was already making a puddle on the tiled floor.

All right, he thought, *you just need to stay calm.* The chances were that they wouldn't risk killing him tonight; the possibility that he'd told others where he was going would be enough to make it too dangerous for them. If they were going to kill him, it would be later, in an accident, just like Stanley. Tonight, they would merely want to confirm who he was and what he was doing there. He needed a story, a good one, to explain his presence. But he was given no time to think. The first man returned, and an inclined head indicated that Ben should follow. He picked up his hat and went out into a badly lit passage. From immediately opposite he could hear the chatter and clatter of a busy kitchen. Ten yards along they came to an open staircase leading up.

At the top of the stairs was another tiled hallway, empty of all decoration, which finished in double swing doors with small round frosted windows. Bright light glowed through them, the only light in the corridor. He could hear music – he recognised a Fletcher Henderson arrangement – and a buzz of excited conversation from behind the doors. He briefly wondered how the upstairs appeared so silent and empty from outside, when there was so much life and light in it. Then a waiter pushed through the doors and Ben caught a glimpse of an enormous chandelier and a dazzling marble floor. People exuding an extraordinary glamour were dancing, a gilded, beautiful gathering; pearls, silk and gold. And there, amidst the colour and glitter, her perfect creamy white skin contrasting with her ebony hair and dress, was Anna. Then the doors flipped shut and she was gone, the waiter brushing past him without a glance as he hurried downstairs.

The guard prodded Ben in the back, pushing him down the gloomy corridor. They stopped at a door on the left, and the man knocked a couple of times before opening it. He was waved inside, and he heard the door close behind him.

A man sat reading papers at an oak leather-topped desk that dominated the room. The man looked up, and then motioned towards the matching leather armchair in front of the desk. Ben sat down, his attention focused on his interrogator, who had much in common with the other two – particularly size, the jet-black oiled hair and the immaculately tailored dinner jacket. But this man's complexion was greyer, his hair was thinning and his fat lips were joined at the edges by hard lines running up to a shunted nose. There was no sympathy in the expression. This was a hard man, living in a tough world.

On the heavy oak sideboard that lined one wall was a row of trophies, including a golden statuette of a boxer. A cut-throat razor with an ivory handle lay amongst the prizes. Photos adorned the wall behind it, images of men in the ring; Ben recognised some of them: Jack 'Kid' Berg, Teddy Baldock and Nipper Pat Daly. It was ludicrously at odds with the floral wallpaper. It looked as though the room might once have been a bedroom and had never been redecorated. Thick blood-red curtains with embroidered roses covered the back window. The other wall was taken up with a couple of filing cabinets and a fireplace filled with the glowing red embers of a coal fire. He could feel some of the warmth starting to seep into him. There was a knock at the door and the man looked up and shuffled the papers together – this was what he'd been waiting for.

'Enter,' he said.

Ben turned towards the opening door, but he already knew whom to expect. The blue eyes of the sergeant settled on Ben for a moment, before flicking over his shoulder to the grey man behind the desk.

'That's him,' said the sergeant, and then withdrew, shutting the door.

Slowly, Ben swivelled back round until he was facing the desk again. The thick lips smiled without showing any teeth, and then the man leaned forward and flipped up the lid on a beautiful wooden cigarette box with intricate pearl inlays. He took one and lit it with a big table lighter in the shape of an elephant. Then he got up and walked towards the sideboard, where he pulled out a crystal decanter and poured a long shot of whisky into a tumbler. Ben watched in silence as the man returned to his seat, placed the drink in front of him and took a long luxurious drag from the cigarette. Each action was economical – a man who knew that he might need every ounce of strength at any moment.

'So, *Mr Clayton*, what were you doing poking around my house?' asked the man, in a voice as measured as his movements.

Anna must have told the doorman who he was. There was no point denying it. 'I'm a friend of Stanley Arbethwaite's,' he said.

'So I understand, but what does that mean to me?'

Ben's gaze flickered over the man's face and he noticed his eyes, black as the coal in the scuttle, protruding slightly, and levelled at him like shotgun barrels. Somehow, he kept the sputter of fear down in his guts and off his face. 'Are you Mr Spink?' he asked.

A thick finger came off the desk momentarily, but the man said nothing.

'If you're Mr Spink, then I believe that Mr Arbethwaite might owe you some money. I'm trying to help his widow, to settle his affairs. There are a lot of debts; we're trying to discover the extent of them. I don't want any trouble. I just want matters settled for the widow.'

Spink took a sip of his whisky before he answered. 'If that's the case, why didn't you tell my doorman that? I'd have seen you immediately, put you straight, instead of this tosh about coming for a card game, then hanging around outside like some character in a John Buchan spy story.'

'The information I've got is limited, we're piecing things together. I wasn't sure what I was dealing with and wanted to be better informed before I talked to you. Mr Arbethwaite doesn't appear to have left any records; it's been very difficult for his widow.' He watched carefully, but Spink didn't twitch a muscle at the mention of Stanley's accounting records – silent, face blank, just the one finger tapping steadily on the papers in front of him. So Spink either had the perfect poker player's face, or it hadn't been him that had searched the Arbethwaites' house.

The interlude extended unbearably while Spink smoked the cigarette down, until finally he straightened in his chair, leaned forward to stub out the butt and placed two bulky forearms on the desk.

'All right, Mr Clayton, I'm going to be straight with you. Stanley Arbethwaite has been here on occasions, but – whatever you've heard about card games – this is a respectable house, and I frequently have some very powerful and important guests here who wouldn't be happy if someone were to level ridiculous accusations at me. Now, Stanley doesn't owe me any money, and I haven't seen him for over a month. I only heard of his accident tonight.' There was a pause. 'Most unfortunate,' he added, 'I liked Stanley.'

'So,' said Ben, after a short hesitation, 'is the matter closed, from your point of view? You won't be making any calls on the estate?'

'There was never a matter to close,' said Spink. 'And I

think that we're finished here, Mr Clayton. *I'm sure*' – he laid a rasping emphasis on the words – 'that I won't be seeing you again.' Spink tapped an ornate silver bell at the side of his desk, and the door opened.

Was that really it? Ben started to rise.

'I understand that some fishermen are saying it wasn't an accident,' said Spink, his black eyes locked on Ben.

'The yacht's owner, the police, they all think it was an accident,' he replied. 'It's only the crew that disagrees.'

Spink leaned back in his chair, a sheaf of papers looking very fragile in his powerful hand. 'And you, Mr Clayton, what do you think?' The words were polite, but the eyes, the manner, the tone, all seeped menace like a smoking volcano.

'I agree with the police, they're the ones with all the information,' he said, with a great deal more composure than he felt.

'Good,' murmured Spink. 'I'm sure that's the correct view. Let's hope everyone comes to see that very soon. Goodnight, Mr Clayton.'

Ben turned to the door.

'And by the way' – Spink's voice held him back again – 'you were good, Clayton. Very good. I was there that night when that boy Slater went down. You should never have given up.'

He didn't reply, just walked out without a backward glance. But he imagined those shotgun eyes on him all the way down the corridor, down the stairs and out into the black rain of the night. It wasn't until he was in his car and halfway home that he began to feel even vaguely safe.

Chapter 15

The rain had stopped by the following morning, but it had left the roads wet, slippery and muddy. Ben rode a cautious journey to Gosport, nostrils filled with the smell of damp earth and the metallic tang of exhaust fumes. When he came round the corner onto Castle Row, he saw what was ahead of him at the gate to Camper and Nicholsons and slammed the brakes on. A group of five men, with placards, flat caps, scarves and tin mugs of tea, stood by a brazier. It looked like a scene out of a newsreel from the troubled industrial areas. So this was the picket line. He cursed them. He didn't need it, not on top of everything else, not this morning, when he felt like he was coming down with something, every bone in his body aching, head throbbing.

He pulled the goggles down from where they were perched on his leather flying helmet, and adjusted his scarf to cover up the rest of his face. It wouldn't make any difference because they all knew the bike, but it might make the encounter less personal. However, when he kicked the Scott into gear and popped up the throttle, he did it a good bit more sharply than he'd intended. The machine leapt forward, and the men's heads turned. As he closed on the gates, he kept the speed high, reckoning it would take a madman to step out in front of him. None the less, there were two candidates, moving away from the brazier, raising their arms. He recognised Kirk, still beside the fire, yelling at the others. The words were lost to him in the engine roar and wind, but the two men lowered their arms and remained motionless as he swept by into the yard.

He jabbed on the brakes, just controlling the back wheel's urge to slip out from under him, and then coasted down the yard wall until he found a spot to put the bike out of view of the picket. He dropped the helmet, gloves and goggles into his knapsack, and headed over to have a look at the mast. The rig was going back in today ahead of the new crew's arrival at the weekend, and he must put all thoughts of Spink aside. He sneezed, violently – *bloody hell, too long standing in the rain* – as he looked at the mast, trying to formulate some sort of a checklist in his mind. *Weather* – a leaden day, gunmetal water unruffled by breeze, seamless low grey cloud sitting heavy above it, the still air carrying the sounds of labour. It might dull the spirit and deaden the heart, but it was perfect for putting a mast in a yacht.

What else? His head was pounding, and any sudden movement seemed to set it spinning. He watched as a barge was towed out to the harbour entrance. Spectators were lined up on the ferry landing stage off the Esplanade Gardens. Word must have got round that the problematic mast was about to get another turn – a mast that had cost more than all their houses put together, had been the death of one man and would be the ruin of many more if the strike dragged on.

'Clayton?'

He jumped a little, startled out of his reverie, and turned to the voice. 'Good morning, Mr Dunwood, you're here early,' he replied. There was no sign of Lerup. Perhaps he had stayed late at the club, and now he was paying for it.

'The yard called me about the picketing,' said Dunwood, trailing cigar smoke like a battle flag, a beautiful Hermes camel overcoat slung over his shoulders. 'They're worried that more men are joining in. I wanted to get down here and make sure nothing went wrong.'

'I didn't have any trouble,' he said. 'I'm sure it's just a peaceful protest.'

'Bloody commies' – Dunwood sniffed disdainfully – 'about as trustworthy as a fox in a chicken coop.' Then he turned to the mast and puffed hard on the cigar. 'It's looking great, Clayton. So are you all ready to go?'

'Yes sir, as ready as we'll ever be. I came over yesterday afternoon for one final check.'

'Excellent, excellent, and I see we've got an audience.' He waved at the ferry jetty, looking pleased. 'And what about your new chaps, did you get enough?'

'If they all turn up we've got a full crew,' he replied.

'I'm sure they all will, they're gentlemen after all, not like dealing with these scoundrels.' Dunwood took half a glance over his shoulder towards the gate, and then eyed Ben. 'I've told Personnel to put a little extra into your pay packet from now on,' he said, 'you're doing a stout job. Bartlett tells me you've still managed to be very helpful to him, on top of assembling the crew and getting the mast ready. When I'm grateful, I like people to know it.'

'That's very kind, thank you,' said Ben, a bit taken aback. He wondered how much a 'little extra' might be.

'And, I ...' Dunwood hesitated, adjusted his peaked yachting cap. 'Well, I understand that you lodge with Stanley Arbethwaite's widow.'

'That's right.' He sneezed. He'd forgotten to pick up a clean handkerchief.

'And she's, er ... all right, is she?' Dunwood gave him a look.

He meant money. Was this the real reason for his pay rise? Did Dunwood know something about Stanley's debts? No, that was impossible. But the pay rise was a generous gesture, showing that Dunwood's heart could reach the right place, despite his ruthless treatment of the striking crew. But Mrs Arbethwaite would never forgive him if he told Dunwood the truth and revealed the shame of her debts. It was a pity – *my God, how the man could help.*

'Things aren't too bad, she's getting over it ...' he replied, as vaguely as he could.

'Well,' said Dunwood, with more of his usual aplomb, 'let me know if there's anything I can do to help.' There was a momentary silence, broken by the whine of a bandsaw from the boat shed behind them. 'And d'you know,' he continued, 'if you have a list of the new crew, I'd be interested to see it, see who's coming, and what they've done and such like. It's different having an amateur crew; I feel I should know a little bit about the gentlemen coming to sail on my yacht.'

'I have it with me,' he said. He glanced at his watch. 'The crane won't be ready for another half hour at least. Shall we go through it now?'

'Yes, let's take it up to the office,' replied Dunwood, after a moment's hesitation, holding out an expansive arm to indicate that Ben should lead the way.

Matthew Faden glanced behind him for the fourth time in less than two minutes, the westerly wind flapping his coat-tails and whipping a ripe London smell of horse dung up to him. A tall man with a battered bowler hat and a shabby fur staggered down Broadwick Street, kicking at a loose newspaper that threatened to wrap itself around his feet. But he didn't look familiar, nor did the other half-dozen people scurrying from one place to the next, faces and bodies scrunched up against the wind. Faden was absolutely sure that he'd been followed out of the Red Lion and onto Soho's Great Windmill Street an hour ago. He was much less sure that he'd lost the tail either before the meeting with White or on his way back up here afterwards. Worse, he had absolutely no idea who the tail might be – it seemed unlikely that White would have had him followed when the man knew exactly where he was going. So had Leon decided to keep an eye on him? Or was there a third player? Neither alternative was palatable.

He lit a cigarette with difficulty, noting in a detached

way that his hands were shaking, and then, head down, he walked on, conscious now that everywhere he went this was his routine, his private paranoia. Maybe there was no one, perhaps it was all in his mind – perhaps not. Things were running out of control. What White had just asked him to do was plainly illegal. Equally plainly, Faden knew that he would be on his own should he be caught. There was no way that he could prove the instructions had come from MI5. White's reassurances that there would be no more for him to do after this were all very good – but of little use if he ended up in a jail cell trying to explain it all to his father's lawyers.

The issues came at him thick and fast, like the dust and blown paper on the westerly wind. If he did White's bidding, then was he still 'stringing him along' as Leon had called it – or would this be enough to let White succeed? For the life of him, he couldn't see how – or what White's instructions were intended to achieve.

The possibility that Leon was now having him followed was the most troubling of all. Faden knew what the man was capable of when people betrayed him, and the acquisition of a tail meant a leaking of trust. He knew his position in the group was relatively weak. He didn't share the class bonds of the others; he knew he would always be regarded warily, as an outsider. And he was only too aware of the urgency with which Leon had wanted Clayton's loyalty confirmed, but he'd not wanted to rush. The coming weekend's yachting provided the perfect opportunity. Now it seemed possible that Leon was getting impatient and had decided to take the matter into his own hands. God only knew that he had the capacity; he'd already managed to penetrate the Foreign Office.

The weekend loomed – both enticing, as it gave him the opportunity to see Clayton and resolve the issue of loyalty, and horrifying, because he'd have to decide whether or not to do White's bidding. He tossed the cigarette and grimly crushed it with his foot, then glanced behind him again. He'd turn back west and head for Regent Street; he could be pretty sure that he would lose a tail amongst the West End shoppers. Then he would head east and leave another message for Leon; he had to get instructions before the journey south to the coast. And perhaps he'd get a hint as to whether it was Leon having him tailed or not – maybe it would be better if it were; he really didn't want to consider the other possibilities.

It was a sullen overcast evening, a fitting end to a grim day when the sun had come and gone unseen. Anxious to get home and approaching too fast in the darkness, Ben missed the lowered kerb into Mrs Arbethwaite's drive. The bike bucked and almost stalled as it bumped up onto the pavement. He only just held on to it, a leg jabbing out to stop it falling – he would go straight to bed, he couldn't eat anything. Slowly, he straightened and rode the bike up the drive beside the house. He killed the engine, cranked the stand down and eased his weight off the seat. He was so stiff he almost lost his balance, catching himself with an arm on the wall.

'Ben?'

He turned to where the whisper had come from. Lucy appeared round the front corner of the house, her blond hair pale in the gloom.

'Over here,' he croaked.

'I've been waiting forever; I thought you'd never get back. I'm freezing,' she said.

'Sorry, long day ...'

'Are you all right? You sound awful,' she said.

'I've got a cold or something ...'

'You poor thing, did the mast go in all right?'

'Yes, thank God,' he replied.

'Good, I don't have long, but there's so much to talk about – perhaps we could meet later?'

'I ... er ...'

She reached out and he felt her hand on his forehead.

'You've got a temperature,' she said, 'you probably should be in bed ... oh, and there's so much to discuss. But Ben, I'm so happy.'

'I know.' He hesitated, but only for a moment. He had to tell her before things went any further. 'Lucy ...'

'What?'

'There's ... there's something I need to tell you. It's my parents, we don't talk. We haven't for a long while.'

'I ... Oh.'

'Actually, I swore that I'd never speak to them again, and now ... you see the problem with the wedding. I have to tell them, and I suppose they have to be there, but I don't know ... I don't know where to start.'

'Oh Ben, that's awful.' She slipped her arms around him and laid her head on his chest. 'What happened?'

He stroked her hair gently. 'It was the boxing accident, the boy, Slater, who was hurt.'

'Yes, I remember you telling me about that; it was awful, but it wasn't your fault, you said ...'

'I know, but afterwards, I couldn't fight any more. I just had no stomach for it. I didn't feel that I could ever hurt anyone again; it just made me feel sick at the thought ... Then we had to move out of London to Colchester because there was trouble with his brothers. My father knew I wouldn't face up to them and defend myself. We had terrible arguments about it ...' He shook his head. 'But I think that even after that, he always thought that I'd eventually go back into the ring. He wanted me to be a professional. Maybe he thought I would earn him his keep or something ...' He stared up at the stars and for a few seconds fell silent, remembering. 'But I just couldn't do it,' he continued, more decisively. 'And then once I got to Cambridge and I told him I'd gone further and taken up with pacifism, we had a terrible scrap. It was awful, and I've never been back home since. I've not spoken to them since that day. I still get letters from my mother; goodness knows how she keeps tracking me down, but I never read them, and so now, you see ... I don't know how it will go with them, but you'll be wanting a proper wedding ...'

'It doesn't matter, it really doesn't matter,' said Lucy, pulling away and looking at him. 'I want you, not the wedding. We can do it at the registry office for all I care, just you, me and Dad and Tom – that would be perfect.'

'Truly?'

'Truly. Cross my heart and hope to die.'

He caught a quick half smile, a flicker of light at her lips. He could see that there was nothing to worry about. Now she eased away from him, her eyes still on his.

'I'm sad for you,' she said, 'sad that you don't have them in your life, but that's another thing, for another time. It doesn't matter for the wedding; if you don't want to talk to them, you don't have to do it for my sake, for the wedding.'

'Thank you,' he said, simply.

'I'm just glad you're here. I've been so worried about you going to that club ...'

'It was all right,' he replied. 'I ended up talking to Spink ...'

'You saw Spink!' Lucy shrieked in a whisper.

'I didn't have much choice,' he said, and outlined the events of the previous evening before finishing up. 'So Spink says that Stanley doesn't owe him any money. And then he told me that I should just accept that it's an accident. Maybe that's where all the money went – Stanley used it all to pay off Spink. He could be telling the truth about Stanley not owing him anything – maybe it wasn't Spink that killed him ...'

'But Spink would say that, wouldn't he – if Stanley did owe him money and Spink killed him for it?' she replied, the concern clear in her voice. 'I knew you shouldn't have gone to that place.'

He leaned back against the wall. He loathed Spink and his type, and he was strongly inclined to agree with Lucy, but they had to look at all the possibilities – and he wanted to reassure her. 'But Spink's business is definitely a bit off the map, so it could be that he's just warning me, to stop me poking around – it doesn't necessarily follow that he had anything to do with the murder.' *I almost made that sound convincing*, he thought.

'Maybe.' Lucy shifted her weight to lean on the wall beside him in the dark. 'But I still think he's the most likely one.'

'Either way, he's the only line we have on it all, and it's going to be difficult to keep asking questions now.'

'But there are things we can investigate without Spink knowing,' she replied.

'What do you mean?' he asked.

'To start with, who could have got onto the boat, cut the downhaul away unseen and replaced the rope in the time between Dad splicing it on and when the chair was used the day after? And who understood that Stanley would be first in that chair and up the mast? If we just answered those two questions, we could narrow it down a lot. We already know that Spink isn't going to be on that list – so if he was responsible, then he must have got someone else to actually do it. If we can find that man, they will lead us to whoever was behind it anyway, without having to go near Spink.'

'Yes, of course,' he replied, staring skywards again. How could he have missed that? He'd been too focused on the debt as his line of enquiry. He needed to get his fevered weary brain working – he massaged his temples. 'But we must assume that Spink has someone inside the crew or at Camper, so we'll have to be a bit careful, or they'll know quick enough that we're poking around.' He hesitated, before adding, 'I hate the thought that it was one of the crew.'

'There's a good chance it was meant to be a warning accident that went wrong,' replied Lucy. 'If the plan was just to teach Stanley a lesson, I can certainly think of one or two of the crew who might do it for a few pounds in their pocket.'

'Jim Rails for one.' He sneezed again.

'Exactly,' affirmed Lucy, 'and we already know of one connection between Spink and the crew – Lerup. You said he was at the club last night.'

Ben shook his head, wiping at his nose with a workshop rag that he'd pocketed. 'But I can't believe he'd be mixed up in something like that with Spink,' he said.

'What do you know about Lerup?' asked Lucy.

'Not much,' he admitted, 'but I could ask the chaps in the new crew tomorrow, some of them must know him pretty well.'

'If they're your friends, it should be safe, but be careful; ask about his sailing maybe, and see what else they tell you,' she advised. 'And I think we should both make a list of the people who knew that Stanley would be first up the mast, then we can compare. And there's one other thing we should do straight away. It's not likely that anyone would mess with that downhaul during the day when everyone was around – too easy for it to be seen and remembered. So we need to check who could have got onto the boat the night before Stanley died.'

He thought for a moment. 'I could ask at the yard about night watchmen. But I don't want Dunwood or Lerup hearing that I'm investigating the murder – that would really stir up trouble. They're totally set against the idea. They'd see me as siding with your dad.'

'No, it would be better if I talk to my dad and see if I can get him to remember when was the last time he saw the finished splice, see if he can ask some questions. He's got friends at the yard, he can find out who could have got on the boat that night. There's no way Spink or Dunwood will connect that to you.'

'All right, that should be safe,' he murmured.

'Now you should go inside and get warm – but please come round tomorrow night for tea.'

He was silent.

'You promised you'd help Tom with the radio, remember?' she added.

'Yes, but here, not at your house – what about your father?'

'It'll be all right; he'll see you're helping Tom, and it'll be all right. We won't say anything about the wedding yet, but you'll see, when you're with him, that everything is fine between you.'

He hesitated; he wasn't sure, but he couldn't refuse her. 'All right, tomorrow night, I'll come round straight after sailing,' he said, and she smiled.

'Goodnight, my love,' she said, 'I wish I could come and look after you. But soon, very soon, I will be able to – sleep well. I hope you feel better in the morning,' and then she kissed him briefly on the cheek, and was gone.

Chapter 16

Ben Clayton peered out of the first-floor window of Camper and Nicholsons's yard office, his hands cradling the cup of tea he'd just made himself. From there he could see the gates – and no pickets, just the brazier sitting there, unlit and lonely. But it was early; he'd left before dawn after sleeping solidly the previous night. God knows what Mrs Arbethwaite put in the special winter soup she'd insisted he eat, but it had knocked him out as soon as his head hit the pillow. He'd woken again with a suddenness that was quite unnerving, eight and a half hours later. He couldn't believe how much better he felt. The streaming nose was gone, the fever, the aching body a memory. And today the new crew would arrive to sail the *Windflower*.

He put the tea down, lit a cigarette and glanced again at the deck plan of the yacht sitting in front of him. He had an idea for a modification that he wanted to suggest to Dunwood, but he needed to work through it first. He pushed the hair out of his eyes as he looked back up towards Portsmouth, where HMS *Victory*'s masts poked into a blood-red skyline amidst the drab grey bulk of the modern Navy. Then he made another effort to concentrate. He set up his T-square and drew the first line.

Three-quarters of an hour had gone by when he next picked up his cup and got a mouthful of cold tea; he grimaced and checked out of the window. Dark cat's paws were chasing whitecaps across the harbour – damn, too much wind for a first sail. He glanced over towards the gate. There were men by the brazier now, rubbing their hands. The collars on their dark jackets were turned up against the cold, and their flat caps were pulled down around their ears. Firewood – broken crates – sat in a pile. He watched as they tamped down the ashes from yesterday and broke up some kindling, then pulled out a newspaper and rolled it into wads, before relighting the brazier. Others arrived in ones and twos, stamping their feet, jostling for space by the fire. He counted as the group grew quickly: seventeen, eighteen ...

Preoccupied with the cold and each other, none of them noticed the first of his new crew in the Riley saloon until it was way too late. The car was on top of the pickets before either side knew who was what. A cry went up as the Riley swerved past and through the gate. A couple of fists were waved angrily. But he hadn't even had time to open the window and yell to his new teammates before he saw Dunwood's Bentley come into view from the High Street. The picket line spotted it a second later. Their mood darkened; they stopped yelling at the Riley and spread across the gate. Dunwood's driver appeared to hesitate at first, the car slowing as it approached. Then he stamped on the accelerator, and the full eight litres of the Bentley Muliner sports sedan kicked in. The car careered forward, struggling for grip on the damp surface. The line of men started to wobble, arms out, legs spread like goalkeepers.

The men scattered, diving for cover as the car hurtled into the boatyard. The brakes locked on and it slid to a halt with a spray of dirt. Dunwood immediately got out and Ben watched, knuckles white on the windowsill, as the occupants of the Riley gathered round him. He recognised Matthew Faden – so the others must be Thorpe and Burleigh, whom Ben had never met before. He looked back to the gate, where the pickets were rallying. It didn't seem as though anyone had been hurt. Rails was leading them now, organising them back into a line. Where was Joe Kirk? He spotted him at the back. Damn. It looked ugly with Rails in charge. What the hell could he do? The police! Of course, he could call the police, they would deal with this – the yard manager had a phone. He ran out of the office.

Matthew Faden was the first to greet Harold Dunwood as he climbed out of the Bentley. 'Mr Dunwood, how do you do, it's good to see you again.'

'Ah, Faden isn't it? What the devil's going on here?' Dunwood's face was flushed and unhappy, a cigar clamped between his fingers while the other hand buttoned the double-breasted Scholte jacket.

'Seems to be some sort of a picket, sir. We got here first and were through before they really noticed us, but it woke them up, and they're alive to it now.'

'I know that, they've been here all week. It's a damnable business. But did they try to stop you?

'They were certainly ...' started Faden.

'How are we going to get those other fellows through?' continued Dunwood.

A cheer from outside the gate ensured that the question remained unanswered. They all turned, but could see nothing through the jostling picket line.

Matthew Faden ran back to his car, climbed onto the bonnet and then scrambled up onto the roof with little regard for his paintwork. 'It's Hawtree, Teddy Hawtree, in his Rover,' he called down to the others in the yard. 'He's stopped, but my God, I think the picket is going to charge them!' Faden couldn't keep the excitement out of his voice. The picket was led by a big, burly fellow with a beard, and he was now whipping them up to violence. Faden rubbed anxiously at the back of his neck, his sympathies badly divided. Instinctively he was for the working man. He wouldn't be here at all – scabbing, as he thought of it – if it weren't for White, Ben, Leon and the bigger agenda. But if it got ugly and punches were thrown, then that was different, even if they were thrown at a louche roué like Teddy Hawtree, an Oxford man a couple of years older than him with quite a reputation.

Now someone with some common sense appeared at the head of the picket, an older man, shorter and slighter, but obviously respected, and under his lead they appeared to settle for barracking and jeering. Meanwhile, another couple of cars had arrived and pulled up behind the Rover. He watched as Hawtree – fedora set at a jaunty angle, apparently unperturbed – got out and took a seat on the running board, then stretched out his legs and lit a cigarette. The occupants of the cars behind soon joined him, gathering round with their hands in their pockets. They were a very picture of modern nonchalance in jackets, short-sleeved woollen sweaters and Oxford bags. Faden called down to where the others were stood around the Riley, a group that now included Dunwood and his driver, and a handful of bemused yard workers. 'I have to say that old Hawtree is showing some dashed nerve. He and the other chaps are having a cigarette and a natter just across the street. I don't see how they are going to get in though ... Uh-oh.'

'What?' asked Dunwood.

It was the engine blip of the Bugatti going up through the gears that was the first sign of trouble. Then the sunbeam-yellow 35A came around the corner, and tore down the road towards the gate.

'Oh my God!' yelled Faden.

'What!?' demanded Dunwood, just as the Bugatti slammed its brakes on and slid to a stop beside Hawtree's Rover.

'I thought he was going to charge the line!'

'Who!?' came back Dunwood.

'It's a Bugatti, 35A I think, a yellow one ... it's Lerup.' *Damn it,* thought Faden. *This could mean real trouble.*

'Ah, he'll sort things out, I'm sure those fellows will be inside in a moment,' said Dunwood, chomping on his cigar as he turned back to his car. 'I'm going to get my coat,' he added, and his driver hurried after him.

Faden watched as Lerup jumped up on the Bugatti's front seat and addressed Hawtree and the others. He couldn't hear what was said, but he got a bad feeling from the forceful gestures of the speaker. Then they all started to disperse back to their cars at a trot. The new energy in the group was visible even from that distance. The picket line responded in kind and a chant started up: 'All the gear but no idea, all the gear but no idea!'

The Bugatti crawled forward as soon as everyone was aboard the cars and they formed up in line astern. Lerup was revving to the red line, and the others started to follow.

'Oh mother of God, they *are* going to charge the picket line!' Faden shouted to those below. More yard workers had gathered to see what all the noise was about. 'I think people are going to get hurt ...' added Faden, but his last words were lost. The strikers were chanting, taunting, and the junction was a swirl of smoke and noise as all the engines hit max revs. Then Lerup let up the clutch.

'Take cover, those cars are coming through that gate at full pelt!' Faden screamed at the knot of spectators. This time they heard him. Thorpe and Burleigh led the way, some getting behind the Riley, others dashing for the protection of the office building. Faden saw a stone fly from the picket line towards Lerup. But there was no more time to watch; he leapt to the ground, absolutely certain that someone would be killed in the melee.

The picket line broke like a dam before the Bugatti, bodies hurling themselves clear. The yellow blaze burst into the yard in a hail of dust, stones and exhaust fumes. But Lerup clearly hadn't anticipated the cars already parked inside the yard, and only just managed to haul the tortured tyres of the Bugatti around Dunwood's Bentley. He jammed the brakes on and skidded towards the dock wall ... with everyone holding their breath.

The car stopped five feet short of the drop and Lerup

immediately leapt to his feet on the car seat. Faden had already turned back towards the gate, where he could see men on the ground. An angry, anxious and frightened scream made it through the engine noise as Hawtree's Rover followed through the passage forced by Lerup. Hawtree wasn't going as fast and he manoeuvred to a standstill by the Bentley. He almost fell out of the Rover in his haste, as the third car came through at a more sedate pace. The picket line was broken, beaten.

Faden's view of the striking workers was now lost behind the newcomers. The yard was full of dust, cars and people laughing and yelling. He watched as Dunwood walked towards Lerup's Bugatti clapping and calling, 'Bravo!' Thorpe, Burleigh and others now joined Dunwood in the cheering as they started to congregate around the car. Lerup, still standing on the seat, bowed and bowed again, complete with a flourish of the panama.

Ben Clayton turned the corner from the yard manager's office just in time to see Lerup milking the moment for all he could get. He'd heard the noise while he was on the phone, and it was clear enough what had happened. Worried that someone had been hurt, he started to skirt round the crowd towards the gate. As the view cleared he saw that all the strikers were gathered around a figure on the ground. Several of the men were kneeling; another took off his jacket to cover the prone figure. Seagulls squawked over them. Ben ran an agitated hand through his hair, dreading the worst, unsure what more he could do to help. Then he heard the first whistles, and the strikers started to move away from the approaching police – he was relieved to see that they had responded quickly to his call, and in numbers. He watched as the crowd cleared. Joe Kirk was left tending the man. A policeman bent to help, and Ben turned back into the yard.

Calm was being restored; the drivers were back in their vehicles and moving them out of the way. Soon, just the Bugatti remained, with Lerup sitting on the bonnet, Dunwood, Thorpe and Burleigh talking to him. Ben shied away, feeling isolated from the exuberant atmosphere of the picket-line breakers, angry that no one else appeared to have noticed the injured man. He glanced up at the sky. The red dawn was giving way to ugly clouds crowding up from the west, jostling for position. A gust of wind swooped down and rattled stray paper. There was no chance they could hoist any sail today. So let Lerup work out what they could all do instead – he'd got the floor, let him use it. Ben looked around. He should find Matthew Faden and say hello, perhaps he was with that group looking over the *Windflower*.

'Clayton!'

He heard Lerup as he headed towards the dock, but didn't stop.

'Clayton, old man,' this time accompanied by footsteps.

He pulled up, trying to compose a neutral expression. Lerup was the hero of the hour – this would be a bad moment to antagonise him.

'I've heard some gossip about you,' Lerup glanced over his shoulder as he spoke.

Ben shrugged, followed the look – Dunwood and the others were approaching.

'You're with Joe Kirk.' Lerup's tone was silky.

Ben forced a smile. 'No, I'm here, and Kirk's out there.' He waved at the gate.

'No, you're with Joe Kirk and the rest of the commie scum. I can't believe what I've heard about you,' repeated Lerup.

Dunwood drew level with them. 'What's all this about?' he asked, face set, puzzled. Thorpe and Burleigh were a few paces further back, listening.

'I'm not sure I know,' said Ben, but then it hit him – *bloody hell, no ...*

'Clayton has got something to tell us. Something about him and those scum outside the gate,' said Lerup.

Ben glanced around, looking for an escape, but all he saw were a couple of yard workers pretending not to watch.

'*Mr* Clayton here is *courting* – if I may be permitted to do the word such disservice – *Joe Kirk's daughter*,' announced Lerup.

There was a long moment in which time appeared to stand still. Ben shifted his stance automatically, unknowingly, as old reflexes kicked in; his stomach muscles tensed, legs braced, fingers curled into fists. Then he saw the encouraging, inviting flicker in Lerup's eyes and forced an effort to relax. *No, you can't hit him, you can't hit anyone ... but especially not him ... not here ... not now ...*

'Is that true, Clayton?' said Dunwood, finally.

He tried to swallow, but it felt as if there was something stuck in his throat. He should just tell them the truth – tell them that he loved Lucy. But it would end everything, get him kicked off *Windflower* ... and destroy their chances of proving her father right and any hope of sorting out this mess.

'No,' he mumbled.

'It's not true?' Lerup's tone was mocking.

Ben looked down, struggled for a breath, but his chest had tightened in some spectral grip, the urge to lash out just barely held in check. *One good punch would push that bastard's chin through his brains.* A heartbeat. Then from somewhere he found the control to look from Lerup to Dunwood and back, but without meeting either man's gaze. He shook his head.

'No,' he repeated.

'I must say that I do find it hard to believe,' said Dunwood. 'Why on earth would he want to consort with some peasant fishing girl from the family of a known communist agitator? Bad enough form at any time, but in these circumstances? Where on earth did you get this from, Lerup?'

'A good source,' said Lerup, jaw grinding under his flat cheeks.

Ben couldn't trust himself to speak – *what had he done?*

'Well, Clayton says not, and his response seems satisfactory to me. Now, if there's nothing else to be said, we need to get organised. We can't have all these people milling about. Come on, Lerup, let's get going; move your car, they're trying to run a boatyard,' instructed Dunwood.

'Better make sure you aren't lying to us about the girl, Clayton,' said Lerup, with a final sardonic smile, as he headed for his Bugatti. Ben was aware that Dunwood was still looking at him curiously. He turned quickly and started towards the office. *What would Lucy say? What would Joe Kirk say?*

He headed straight for the toilets and stumbled into a cubicle, slammed and locked the door. He flipped the toilet lid shut and sat, head in his hands. What else could he have done? He hadn't seen this coming – why had he not seen this coming? Because he didn't see the world with the same eyes as the likes of Lerup and Dunwood, that was why – *peasant fishing girl* ... What the hell was he going to do now? How could he tell Lucy? How could he not tell Lucy? *That bastard* – he could just imagine Lerup getting the information, the pleasure he would have taken in planning that scene and how he'd act it out. Ben slammed his fist into the partition wall. Impossible, stupid – he wanted to scream, rage, tear something up ...

'Ben?'

Ben froze. The voice was distant, not in the toilet block. 'Yes?' he yelled back.

'It's Matthew Faden, old chap!' Footsteps, the voice getting closer. 'Lerup's getting us started out here.'

Matthew would be sympathetic, but he couldn't begin to explain this to him. 'I'll be right out,' he said.

'Good man.'

He listened to Faden's retreat. He had to pull himself together and get out there and put a brave face on it. He flushed the toilet for good measure, washed his hands to give himself a little more time and then went outside. Everyone was gathered on the dock, and he silently joined the back of the group.

Chapter 17

'Little chap's doing terribly well, already playing scrum half for the under-15s, and he's only just thirteen,' said Graham Thorpe to the assembled table, picking up his knife and fork.

The threatening storm had eventually unloaded its burden of horizontal rain, and the *Windflower* crew had moved down to the Bell Hotel for lunch. Ben had notified the dining room in advance, and re-established a little bit of credibility with Dunwood, after a morning dominated by Lerup's grandstanding efforts to train the new crew in the basics of sailing the yacht.

The remains of the eggs Florentine were being cleared from the linen and lace by a waiter in white tie, while Ben's table companions had collected platefuls of cold meats, salad and vegetables from a buffet laid out for the main course. A string quartet scraped their way gently through their weekend lunchtime repertoire, barely disturbing the noisy hum of conversation from the crew, seated at tables around them. Only Lerup and Dunwood were missing; they were lunching aboard the latter's motor yacht, the MV *May*.

'What school's he at?' asked Teddy Hawtree, arranging his napkin.

'Marlborough,' replied Thorpe, pushing his fringe back with a habitual motion of the right hand. His mousy-brown hair was left long on the top and cut short at the sides, worn without oil, the haircut accentuating the flash of grey above his ears.

'Marlborough – that's where you went, isn't it, Johnners?' asked Hawtree, his black eyes settling on Matthew Faden, who made up the table of four. 'Johnners?'

Faden looked up from his newspaper with a white-toothed smile. 'I'm sorry?' he said.

'Marlborough – you went there, didn't you?' repeated Hawtree. 'Although they obviously didn't teach you any table manners. Put that damn paper away, man, and talk to us.'

'Sorry,' said Faden, folding the paper up and pushing it to one side. 'I wouldn't send a boy there anyway,' he added, taking a first mouthful of the honeyed ham.

'As you've pointed out at every opportunity, my dear fellow,' replied Thorpe. 'Our Johnners is making a name for himself as something of a left-wing rabble-rouser. He got a small pamphlet published by a Marxist press down in the East End,' he continued.

Faden chewed, his blue eyes watchful.

'My goodness, Johnners, never would have thought it of you,' said Hawtree, swigging a mouthful of Merlot. 'What does your old man think?' he added, replacing the glass on the table, gaze narrowing onto Faden. Hawtree's face was puffy, and the dark eyes were red-rimmed, the only colour in a white complexion, framed by slicked black hair. It looked to Ben as though Hawtree had had a proper night out – but then, he was famous for it.

'He thinks it's a bit of bore,' Faden replied, and Thorpe snorted. Faden rubbed the back of his neck, tugging at the auburn hair in a gesture that was very familiar to Ben. 'But that was a couple of years ago – I'm going to have to knuckle under, the writing isn't going terribly well,' Faden finished.

'More pamphlets?' asked Hawtree, struggling to hide his smile by raising his glass again.

'No,' said Faden, 'a novel – sort of a sub–Eric Blair thing.' His gaze flickered round the table to each of them in turn.

'Who's Eric Blair?' asked Hawtree.

'He writes as George Orwell – do you know *Down and Out in Paris and London*, or *Burmese Days*, perhaps?' replied Faden.

'Sorry, old chap, I don't read much, probably not my bag anyway,' said Hawtree, shaking his head. 'Bloody hell, Clayton,' he continued, 'steady on, man, it's wine not beer – not a very good one, I grant you, but still, you didn't use to be much of a drinker.'

'Ugh,' said Ben, grimacing at the taste, looking at the empty glass. 'I got a bit carried away,' he added.

'Anyway, father's putting the big squeeze on me now,' Faden was saying. 'He's still on about me joining his wretched bank. Oh,' he said, looking at Thorpe, 'no offence.'

'None taken,' replied Thorpe.

'Why would you be taking offence, Thorpe? Do you work for his old man?' asked Hawtree, waving at Faden with his knife.

'It is my deep and abiding privilege,' Thorpe grinned, but his carefully balanced forkful of peas spilled. Now he frowned as he speared a piece of potato, before continuing, 'I've been trying to get Johnners to sail in my Eight Metre with me. His old man put me in touch, but I can't get him away from the drudgery of Marxist pamphlet writing.'

'Novels, actually,' repeated Faden, darting a sharp look in Thorpe's direction.

'Still, I imagine the old boy's grateful for Thorpe-oh's efforts,' said Hawtree, with a wicked half smile.

Thorpe's thin cheeks bulged as he struggled momentarily to swallow. Ben doubted that he was the only one who'd noticed the man's discomfort at Hawtree's remark. Had Thorpe been given the job at the bank just so he could try to entice Matthew Faden away from his Marxist writing, and back to yachting and society? If Ben knew anything about Matthew, it would never work; he knew his own mind, his own path. Ben wished he shared a little more of his friend's ability to move around in the world, to move amongst the classes. He could use that skill.

'Anyway, it's about time you had to knuckle under, Johnners,' continued Hawtree, 'country needs a smart chap like you in harness, not frittering your energies away on this book rubbish – how old are you now?'

'Twenty-six, same as Clayton,' said Faden, 'and it's not rubbish.'

'Of course, that's right, you two were starting to sail together when I left Balliol, you had a couple of years to go at Cambridge,' said Hawtree.

'I thought I might try the RAF, actually,' announced Faden, looking at Ben.

Ben returned the gaze, his surprise showing through his grim mood.

'What?' asked Thorpe.

'Yes, I've always wanted to fly.' Faden scratched at the back of his neck again as he spoke.

'So tell me the part of this I've got wrong,' replied Thorpe. He put down his knife and fork and folded his arms. 'Last summer, you explained to me that as a committed pacifist, you'd decided to join the Peace Pledge Union. And now, a mere – what? – seven months later, you've decided to join the RAF, which, last time I checked, was still part of this country's fighting services. Now, how exactly do those two things square?'

'Father can't possibly complain about the RAF,' said Faden, defensively. 'It gets me away from him and I learn to fly, all at once. Besides, there isn't going to *be* another war, people won't have it. Look at that peace ballot last year, eleven million people voted and over ten million opposed rearmament. So I'll go in, do a few years, learn to fly, father will forgive my sins, all will be sweetness and light again, and then I can beetle off and see the world and maybe write a book about my travels.'

'So, a man of great principle then,' said Hawtree, amusement never far from the surface, even in the hooded eyes.

'It does seem a little expedient to me,' replied Thorpe, resuming his meal, 'if not rather contrary. And I suspect the RAF may require you to renounce your earlier pledge – that's if they'll have you at all.'

'Oh, don't say that, old boy, I thought it was a whiz idea,' replied Faden, pulling off the guernsey he was wearing. 'It's getting hot in here,' he added, as he put the sweater on the back of his chair, and then smoothed the blue cotton shirt he was wearing.

'You say there isn't going to be another war, but what about this Rhineland business?' Ben directed the question at Matthew. Despite his dreadful morning, he was curious about what seemed an astonishing change of direction by his friend.

'It *is* German territory,' replied Faden.

'Versailles was too harsh on the Germans anyway,' added Hawtree. 'And it's really about time we slackened off on them a bit – if we give 'em what they want, they'll stop bothering us.'

'Whole thing's a lot of fuss for no reason, nothing will come of it – Baldwin will see to that. Appeasement, old boy, that's the name of the game,' finished Thorpe.

There was a pause. And then once again, Ben fired a question directly at Matthew. 'And if you're wrong, if there's a war, and you have to fight?'

'I'm not, there won't be.' Faden looked straight back at him.

Ben nodded, and let it go. He could see from his expression that Matthew was trying to tell him something that wasn't for general consumption. He forked another piece of the ham. He wanted to be convinced by them anyway, to believe that the politicians would make sure it was all right, to feel more of the reassurance that he'd given Lucy.

'Frankly, I think that Hitler fellow might be on to something,' said Hawtree. 'Strong leadership and all that –

I was reading a story in the *Daily Mail* the other –'

'No!' said Faden. A hush fell over the room's conversation for a moment, but it passed quickly and the hubbub renewed itself. Faden leaned forward, jabbed at Hawtree with a finger and said more softly, but no less intently, 'I can't believe you could say that, have you any idea what he's up to? He has a prison camp, Dachau, where he puts people for no better reason than that they disagree with him, or he doesn't like them ...'

'Bloody good idea, I'd say,' retorted Hawtree, 'we could do with a bit of that in this country.'

'And torture them?' demanded Faden.

'I suppose that might be going a bit far,' conceded Hawtree, after a pause.

'A bit far?' Faden's voice had gone up an octave with indignation. He coughed and cleared his throat, just as the music stopped and a chair scraped loudly behind him. They all turned and looked. The violinist was carefully placing his instrument in a case; the other players were stretching fingers and necks. Ben's gaze flickered around the table. He'd never had much enthusiasm for politics before he met Faden, but after sailing with him for a couple of years, it had been impossible not to have some interest. He knew enough to be on Faden's side in any argument about the merits or otherwise of Herr Hitler, anyway.

'Enough of that stuff,' said Thorpe, 'what I want to know about is the serious news – this fishing girl that Lerup was ragging Clayton about, what's the story there?'

Ben loaded his fork with ham.

'I thought I saw something going on, what *did* I miss?' asked Faden.

'After Lerup smashed through the picket line this morning, he was on about Clayton and the daughter of some fisherman,' said Thorpe.

'What-ho, Clayton strikes again – bet she goes like a rabbit,' said Hawtree, through a mouthful of potato. 'But what's it got to do with Lerup?'

'Indeed, what the hell does it have to do with Lerup?' said Ben, before chewing on the mouthful of ham.

'Her father is leading the strikers and Lerup's concerned about a conflict of interest for Clayton here,' Thorpe filled in.

'Ruddy hell,' gulped Hawtree, as he swallowed.

Ben just chewed, playing for time to think on a response, and praying for some kind of intervention. A bolt of lightning blasting these two from the table would do just fine.

'I don't see what's wrong with Clayton courting this girl if he wants to,' said Faden. 'He's not the kind of chap to let it affect his judgement over *Windflower*,' he added.

There was a silence, and then Thorpe laughed. 'That's a bit off the map, Johnners,' he said. 'I don't mind Clayton doing a bit of rough once in a while, plenty of chaps have got away with that, but let's not get carried away – *courting*?'

Ben closed his eyes and, for the second time that day, fought an internal battle to maintain his pacifist principles. He put down his knife and fork before he stabbed Thorpe with them, then balled and gripped his napkin under the table until his knuckles were white. Thorpe might know instinctively that Ben wasn't quite of his own kind, but it seemed that Ben's reformed accent and smooth manners were still good enough to make the idea of marriage to a fisherman's daughter horrifying. *Beyond pompous, beyond idiots* ... Once again he found himself wishing for a little more of Matthew's ease in the world.

'Frankly, I think Lerup should be more concerned with that fellow who was injured this morning, rather than ragging Clayton,' said Faden, quickly. 'Does anyone know what happened to him? Because I'm damn sure Lerup hasn't checked,' he added, before swallowing his final mouthful and pushing his plate to one side.

'Broken arm,' said Ben, quickly, to keep the new line of conversation going. 'They took him off to the War

Memorial Hospital. God knows how he's going to pay for it though,' he said.

'There's a fairy godmother out there for him somewhere,' said Faden. 'I'll have a wander down there after lunch, if you'll tell me the way, see what I can do.'

'That's good of you,' replied Ben.

'I might as well put the old man's cash to good use, while I've still got some.'

'But Johnners, those fellows were well out of order, trying to keep a man from his sport, I think they deserve all they got,' drawled Hawtree, before dabbing at his lips with a napkin.

'Oh, come on,' replied Faden. 'Lerup's a thug, there was no need for that – another couple of minutes and the police would have cleared the gate. Clayton told us that they were called in plenty of time, he had it under control. Lerup made it a lot worse than it need have been. Have the police had a word with him?'

'With Lerup – for breaking a picket line and cracking the arm of some worker?' asked Hawtree, black eyebrows raised exaggeratedly high into a question mark.

'You're a cynic,' replied Faden, 'you shouldn't have joined in with him.'

'Actually, Johnners is right about Lerup,' said Thorpe, pushing his knife and fork to the side of a plate still half full of food. 'He's a frightful chap, no one takes him seriously. He came up to Oxford the year I was going down. He was a terrible bore even then.' He eased his chair back a little from the table and crossed his legs. 'Not a bad piece of ham, shame about the wine,' he added.

'You were with Lerup at Oxford?' asked Ben, focusing on this new opportunity, the anger subsiding.

'Yes, but only for my final year, thank God. We still have some mutual friends; I hear about him occasionally. But I try to avoid him if I possibly can,' said Thorpe.

'Did he sail, back in those days?' asked Ben – was the question too probing? He had to be careful.

'No. Cards were about as active as he got as far as I remember, he started sailing after Oxford.' Thorpe glanced briefly over his shoulder. Then he asked, 'Pudding, cheese, anyone?' Heads shook in response. 'Can we smoke, then?' he went on.

'A couple of the others have started,' said Faden, looking around the room as he pulled out a silver cigarette case. He flipped the lid and offered it round. Everyone took one. Thorpe produced an engraved ivory cigarette holder, then passed the matching lighter around, and they all settled back.

'So where's Lerup's estate?' asked Hawtree, before exhaling the first lungful with some relish.

'What's left of it, you mean,' replied Thorpe, head down as he fiddled with his cravat, hair flopping over his face. 'Berkshire way, I think, he was always a bit cagey about that. What I understood was that his father got it handed on to him just after the war.' Thorpe straightened, pushed his hair clear and took another draw on the cigarette. 'It was a bad time for the old man to shuffle off this mortal coil, what with the crippling death duties levied to pay for the aforementioned bloody war. The family had to sell most of it just to get the books to balance. It's been downhill from there – plummeting agricultural prices and so on. One story has it that Lerup was pulled out of Eton because his father couldn't pay the fees any more, but that might be apocryphal – more likely he was thrown out for bad behaviour.'

'And his father's still alive?' asked Faden.

'Just, I believe. But from what I hear, Lerup's already given the rest of the estate away at card tables. No one's quite sure how he keeps going, seems to spend a lot of time in the company of the nouveau riche, like Dunwood.'

'Ah,' said Hawtree, 'trading status for hard cash, perhaps?'

'Nothing so gauche, I'm sure,' replied Thorpe, smirking.

'But did you hear the rubbish he was spouting this morning about crewing *Windflower*?' asked Faden. 'We'd be better off working it out amongst ourselves; I think he's got less idea of what goes on forward of the wheels than I have.'

'I don't think he's got a damn clue about any of it,' added Thorpe. 'Still, that's not our problem, we've just got to pull the sails up and down – can't be that tricky, can it? These fishermen manage it all right, don't they?'

'They did,' said Hawtree. 'But it's still a shame that Dunwood seems to think the sun shines out of Lerup's behind.'

'So, Clayton – how did you get involved with Dunwood?' asked Thorpe.

'I happened to be there when the fishermen went on strike,' replied Ben. 'And he knew I had the sailing contacts to find an amateur crew.'

'So you got involved when the strike started, like the rest of us?'

There was a moment's silence. Ben rolled the ash off his cigarette into the ashtray. 'No – a friend and I did the engineering and oversaw the mast construction,' he said.

'Oh ...' murmured Thorpe.

And now he understands, thought Ben, as the silence extended. Now he knows I'm not like him. Engineers were rarely gentlemen.

Faden saved him again, stubbing his own cigarette out vigorously and rising to stand. 'Shall I go and see if I can rustle us up a coffee before we head back to the yacht?' he said. There were murmurs of agreement.

But before Faden could get any further, Ben was on his feet. 'I'll go,' he said, already moving.

Matthew Faden shrugged. 'I need some more cigarettes anyway, chaps,' he said to the others. He caught up by the dessert trolley, filled with cakes and strawberry flan, spotted dick and plum pie. 'Ben.'

Ben looked round – his expression was bleak, but the

arctic-blue eyes were as clear and as glorious as ever.

'I'm sorry about those two, they just ...'

'I've heard it all before,' replied Ben.

'I know, but it doesn't make it all right, here ...' He offered him another cigarette. Ben lit it from the butt of the first, coughing a little as he did so and looking around. 'Can I buy you a drink?' Faden waved towards the bar and an ashtray.

'We can probably get the coffee over there as well,' said Ben.

Faden placed the order, and they watched in silence as the barman poured his brandy and a whisky for Ben. 'Cheers,' said Faden, offering his glass. 'It's good to see you again, old man, it's been a long while. We should have kept in better touch.' There was a rich clinking sound as they made the toast, and once again Ben's blue eyes settled on him.

'Different worlds, Matt,' he said, smiling pensively.

'Not necessarily,' he replied. 'These days, my world is not what you think.'

Ben shrugged, took a drag on the cigarette. 'It certainly seems different to what I remember. What's all this about the RAF? You were such a strong pacifist when we were at Cambridge.'

'Ah yes, well, still a believer, old boy. The RAF is just an idea, a rather expedient way to deal with the ever-troublesome pater, probably never happen. What about you? I thought you were going to land a stiff right-hook on Lerup this morning, that wouldn't have sat easily with the pacifist principles.' Faden smiled as he spoke, but he knew it wasn't reaching his eyes.

'I nearly did, not to mention Thorpe a couple of minutes ago,' replied Ben. 'But the principles are still intact, and I go to those No More War Movement meetings whenever I can, although I've been so busy these past few months ...'

'Main thing is not to lend any succour to the bloody

warmongers,' said Faden, feeling the relief start to flow through him. 'There's lots of talk about rearmament which I find rather disturbing; you think Dunwood will get involved with that? He's got the factories, and there could be plenty of money to be made. Look at old Sopwith in the Great War.'

Ben shook his head. 'He seems dead set against it. I can't imagine him changing his mind.'

'Anyone trying to?' nudged Faden.

'To what?'

'Change his mind.'

Ben shrugged, obviously bemused. 'I wouldn't know; he hardly talks to me much about it. Why do you ask?'

'Oh, nothing, just some rumours that friends in the Movement were trying to tie down. Doesn't matter.' He took a sip of his brandy. 'So, what about this girl – is it serious?' he asked.

Ben gave him a hard appraising look, and Faden felt himself withering.

'Serious, Matthew? Only in so far as I'm engaged to her,' said Ben, finally.

'Bloody hell ...' breathed Faden. 'I mean, congratulations,' he corrected, before glancing back at where Thorpe and Hawtree were deep in conversation.

'Their views aren't the half of it,' continued Ben. 'I had to tell Lerup that I didn't even know her, otherwise I'd have been out of a job and on my way home ...' He shook his head. 'It was awful, Faden, I feel like I've betrayed her, I just wanted to tell them the truth ...'

'How bloody, how utterly bloody.' He softened his face sympathetically before continuing, 'But Dunwood would have cut you faster than you can say knife and butter, old man, and I know how desperately you've always wanted to sail these boats.'

'One day, I'm going to teach those idiots ...'

'Come the glorious day, comrade, they'll be up against the wall, and I'll be at your shoulder, handing you the rifle.'

Ben smiled, grimly, but didn't reply.

'She'll be all right though, won't she? She'll understand when she finds out – true love and all that?' he consoled him.

'If I thought that, I wouldn't be here now. I'd be back in Hamble getting it over with,' replied Ben.

'You poor old thing, is there anything I can do?'

Ben shook his head. 'Apart from not telling anyone – no, but thanks, Matt, you've always been a pal.'

Faden smiled encouragingly. 'I'm sure it'll all work out. Now, I need to get some cigarettes – I saw a machine on the way in. See you back at the table for coffee?'

'Maybe,' replied Ben.

Faden nodded, tipped back the brandy and headed for the lobby, fishing in his pocket for change, and still feeling the gaze of those blue eyes. Gorgeous Ben Clayton, engaged – and to a working-class girl! Faden wondered what she looked like; she would be fabulous, obviously, in a gritty homely sort of way, but was she blond, dark, petite, curvy? Dark, he thought, Ben had always had a weakness for brunettes at university. He couldn't help but get a little thrill at the romance of the whole idea. The sacrifices these lovers would have to make for each other across the class boundaries ... it was the stuff of storybooks, or at least some gossip; the comrades would love it.

He pulled up at the cigarette machine, pushed in the first penny and stared at the choice of brands. And now he could finally be confident that White would get nowhere with Ben. It would appease Leon – or at least it would once he could tell him. His efforts to contact him before he had travelled south had come to nothing. Faden slid the second penny into the machine. He needed to get back to London as quickly as possible to report to Leon, but he couldn't just ignore the task that White had set him. Judging by the news in this morning's paper the pressure was building – Churchill hadn't got the new Ministerial job for Coordination of Defence. It had gone to the Attorney

General, Sir Thomas Inskip. Faden knew that White would be fuming; it was almost as though the Prime Minister was trying to make a statement, to tell everyone he didn't take rearmament seriously. White and his cronies would be even more desperate to lean on private industry to get on with the job.

He pushed in the third penny. It seemed very likely, given the snub to Churchill, that if he didn't do the deed that White had asked of him, then the brute would go to his father, rather than give him another chance. But while he might come up with a viable excuse for failing, there was no possible excuse for a failure to even try, particularly as White's men were surely watching him. And as it seemed likely that Leon's men were watching him too ... He should never have given Ben's name to Fleming White. He'd been too anxious to get out from under the heartless press of MI5 scheming. If he'd just held off until after he'd contacted Leon, he wouldn't be trapped in this nightmare. And now, with no instructions or guidance from Leon, he had to decide what to do. What to do? Oh, what to do? He pushed in the fourth penny, pulled the drawer out and realised he'd got the wrong ones. 'Dammit all to hell!' he cursed. He was out of change. He picked up the packet of ten Park Lanes anyway, and headed back to the table.

Chapter 18

Lucy spent the day cleaning the house and preparing a meal for Ben's visit. She went up to Spake's and used some of her savings on a fresh young rabbit – so fresh the shotgun pellets were still warm, the butcher had said. And then, after the skinning was done, she cut it up and fried it with an onion, an apple, and some streaky bacon. She added a bit of cider and some prunes and nutmeg, and then made up some pastry – it was a proper rabbit pie. She made an apple-and-prune tart with the leftover pastry and the rest of the fruit, and with the whole lot in the oven and the potatoes on for some mash, she just had to clear the mess up. She didn't bake very often, and it had been a hard day. Tom had bowled through the door at a critical moment – soaking wet and bursting with tales of his day's crabbing and the prospect of getting his radio fixed. When he saw the mess, he had retreated to his room. She didn't blame him. Frankly, if this was cooking, she would rather haul scallops out of the Channel. But there were some things you had to do for your man, and she would learn to like it.

She sat down at the kitchen table and methodically rolled herself a cigarette, smoking and picking at the pastry and dried rabbit guts on her apron. Flour smeared her forearms and there were smudges of it on her skirt and blouse. She should be getting on with the clearing up, give herself time to change before Ben arrived, not sitting here relaxing. Her favourite yellow blouse needed ironing too, but Tom could set the table and watch the potatoes, that would help. This was the perfect occasion to try the tiny bottle of Coty Asuma perfume that she had got at Christmas, and to wear the beautiful silver necklace that had been her mother's.

The cottage smelled deliciously of baking. The range was roaring – to hell with the cost of it – the room was warm and cosy, and the sound of the rain drumming helplessly onto the roof tiles made it seem all the more welcoming. But the noise of the broken gutter flushing straight onto the dirt was as loud as ever – she must remember to speak to her father, she thought. And at that moment, he burst through the door, cursing the weather and shaking water everywhere.

'Oh Dad! I just scrubbed that floor this morning,' she said.

'Huh?' Joe Kirk looked round, took in the aftermath of cooking, the smell of baking, the tidy shelves and spotless floor. 'Whose birthday?' he asked.

'No one,' she said, defiantly. 'Ben's coming round to help Tom with his radio, and having some tea with us; you remember, I told you at breakfast.'

Joe looked at her for a moment, and then slowly hung the oilskin coat and hat on the hook behind the door.

'Is something wrong?' she said, stubbing out the cigarette. 'What's happened?'

'I don't think he'll be coming round here tonight, not unless he wants a horse whipping,' said Joe.

'What's happened?' she asked again, rising to her feet. Her father didn't reply. 'Tell me,' she insisted.

Joe looked at her with weary heavy-lidded eyes. He wiped the rain from his face and beard with his forearm and sank into his chair. 'There were all kinds of trouble – that maniac Lerup charged the picket line with his car, and one of the lads ended up in hospital with a broken arm. We've been there all day – but some gentleman sailor came and paid his bill with the doctors. Right decent thing to do, that was ...' He stared at the floor.

'And, what else?' She knew she hadn't heard the worst of it.

'Ben Clayton. He denied you, Lucy.'

'What? What do you mean, denied me?' She leaned forward across the table on her arms, gaze locked on her father's face.

'Lerup said that courting you was treachery to Mr Dunwood – so Clayton said there weren't nothing between you. Right there in front of everybody, dismissed you just like ...' He waved his hand.

She sat down, trying to take it in. 'Tell me again,' she commanded. 'Lerup said what?'

Joe Kirk's forearms and palms were flat on the table, his head sunk to his chest. He looked up. 'He said that having Clayton court you, while he was working for Dunwood, was being treacherous, 'cause of me and the strike. So to wriggle out of it, Clayton told him there weren't nothing between you.' He closed his eyes again and lowered his head. 'I'm all done in,' he mumbled.

She bit her lower lip, realising what had happened. Ben had been too successful getting the new crew, and Lerup, feeling his position threatened, had struck back. A rush of anger and confusion came over her, and she picked up the chopping board and carried it towards the sink. She didn't want her father to see her reaction. Ben would still come round to see her tonight, she knew he would. He'd want to explain this to her.

'I should never have let him near you, fancy type with degrees and all that can't be bloody trusted with a good girl like you.' Joe looked up at her suddenly, his eyebrows set, intense. 'He never ...'

'No!' she lied, glaring at him. She should clear up the mess, he'd be here soon, she was sure he would be here – those potatoes were nearly ready ...

'I wanted something better for you than your mother

got, that's all,' said Joe.

She could hear the strain in his voice. His fists were balled on the table. And those were tears, not raindrops, on his cheeks, running into the grey-flecked beard. Suddenly the tension between them slipped away, the strain that had been there for more than a decade. The ten long years and more since her mother had died, all that pushing and tugging at each other, all that blaming and misunderstanding – but now it seemed so clear.

'Oh Dad,' she whispered, dropping the chopping board with a clatter, a hand to her forehead, tears streaming down her face. She heard the chair scrape back, his boots on the stone floor, and then he was holding her for the first time since she was a child, and she was wrapped in his arms again, a crying child who had lost something precious.

Ben Clayton shrugged his collar up a little higher, pulling his hat down around his ears as he walked. But it was limited protection against the rain that gusted across the High Street. It was quiet – most people were at home, and just a few figures scurried to and from the cosy fraternity of the pubs. But not for him, there was no more of a welcome in there than there would be at the Kirks'. He'd soaked for a long while in a hot bath, hoping for an Archimedean revelation about what he might say to Lucy – but he could think of nothing but the truth. It could not be put off any longer. He wished he'd had a chance to get flowers. At least he had the list that he had promised her in his pocket, all the people who knew that Stanley would be the first one up the mast. It wasn't much, but it was the only thing he could think of to show her that he was still on her side. He just had to hope that Faden had been right and that she would understand.

He reached the quay and turned right along the foreshore. Absorbed in his thoughts, his regret, he heard nothing but the final footstep behind him. Something about it – the scratch of gravel from a slight loss of grip – jerked his senses away from his introspection, and he started to turn. But it was too late, the blow caught him, and although it was across the temple rather than the back of the head, the effect was the same. His legs crumpled. He had enough awareness to get his arms out in front of him as he fell, but that was all. There was a stab of pain in his shoulder as he hit the dirt, and he could feel wetness under his cheek. Instinct kicked in and he rolled – *keep moving* – but his reactions were hopelessly dulled by the blow. Another caught him on the injured shoulder, and with the rush of pain everything darkened, narrowed and slowed. He slumped.

'Ruddy hell, how 'ard did you 'it him? You can't teach 'im a bleedin' lesson if 'e's dead.'

There was something about the voice that he recognised. Hands grabbed his overcoat lapels, hauling him up a couple of feet. He felt a brush of beard and harsh breath on his face – the smell of beer and neglect.

'See here, Clayton – mind y'own bleedin' business, or the next beatin'll be the last.'

The hands pushed him back into the dirt. He just had time to curl his legs up defensively and get his head in his arms. The first kick cracked into his elbows, accompanied by a grunt of exertion, and for him a wave of giddying pain that almost broke his fragile hold on consciousness. Another boot slammed into his back, and another – he had to hang on until it stopped. If he let himself slide under, he would take the blows defenceless and it would be a lot worse. But then there were hands rummaging through his pockets; his wallet was stripped and thrown back in his face. The retreat of footsteps and the patter of rain and the whine of the wind took over from the steady tempo of the beating. He let himself relax and felt the slip of perception, knew that he was over the edge, knew that in a moment the pain would be gone. He sank into darkness.

Lucy's tears lasted a long while. But they had almost

stopped when the creak of the stairs brought her head up off her father's shoulder. She wiped at her face with her hand, and saw Tom peer round the corner into the kitchen. Their eyes met, and she realised that he looked frightened.

'Tom,' she said, and her father let go of her and turned. 'It's all right,' she continued. She moved towards Tom, wiping her face with quick motions. 'Don't look so worried, we've got a nice rabbit pie for tea. Special.'

Tom's face relaxed a little.

'Let's see your hands,' she said.

Tom held them out, surprisingly dutiful. He must have been listening.

'Not bad,' she said, 'maybe just have one more go under those nails.'

Tom nodded, seriously. 'Is Mr Clayton still coming?' he asked, looking at her with an unnerving directness.

'I don't know,' she said. Lucy glanced up at her father, and she realised that she'd never seen him look at them like that before. *That's what love is,* she thought – that look. She could feel her throat tighten again. 'I'll save some pie for Mr Clayton, just in case he gets here later.'

'All right,' said Tom.

'Now, go and wash your hands and I'll start serving up,' she said.

Tom stepped past and out to the back bathroom.

'What'll you say to him if he does turn up?' she asked her father softly.

'That'd be your choice. You know how I feel – but your mother wouldn't let me rest a day in heaven if she knew I'd kept you from what you wanted.'

She could feel tears welling up again, and tried to compose herself. This was not like her. She didn't know whether she wanted Ben to arrive or not. No, that wasn't true. She knew she wanted him to come and tell her it was all a mistake. But she didn't want him to do it in front of Tom and her father.

'Let's eat now, I don't want it to spoil, I spent all day

on it,' she said.

'All right, love, I'll go and change into some dry clothes,' he replied, touching her with surprising tenderness on the arm, as he passed her on the way upstairs.

At first, Ben thought he was in bed. He could hear the wind in the trees, and the rain sounded as it did when it landed on the roof in his attic room. But then the pounding in his head started and the rain and the wind receded, until all he could hear and feel was the throbbing at his temple. Giddiness rushed through him; he felt as if he was stumbling, falling. Then he realised he was already lying in the dirt. He started to feel a cold wet pressure up the side of his body, and with it came an urgent rush of pain. A chill convulsed him. How long had he been out? He tried to isolate the sensations, to judge the damage. He hurt almost everywhere, but he didn't think anything was broken. He had to get home.

He pushed up with his good left arm and dragged his legs under him into a squat. For a moment the pain ramped up and threatened to overwhelm him, dizziness in his head looping like some crazy fairground ride. But slowly it settled again. A thought came to him. They went through his wallet. Where was it? He groped about blindly in the dark until he found it, the sodden leather soft under his touch. He pushed it into a pocket and staggered towards the fuzzy lights from the cottages on the quay. He stumbled into a wall, and stopped there for a few moments, leaning on his left shoulder, forehead resting on the cool brick, nursing his right arm.

The walk back up the High Street, across the Square and down Satchell Lane seemed to take forever. He lurched in agony from walls to gates to keep himself upright. At Mrs Arbethwaite's the kitchen lights were still on. The door wasn't locked and he pushed it open. It banged back on its hinges into the dresser. Mrs Arbethwaite was at the sink, washing up the dishes. She turned at the noise, as he burst into the room, catching himself on the kitchen table. She grabbed his elbow and guided him into a chair, pushing the door shut as she did so. There was a light touch on his temple and he flinched.

'No bleeding. What happened, did you get knocked out?' she asked.

'For a little while, not sure how long, took a while to get back here,' he mumbled.

'And your arm?'

He was still supporting his right forearm. 'I think it's just bruised,' he replied, 'my shoulder hurts too, where I hit the ground.'

'Anything else?'

'My ribs just below the shoulder blade, and my left shin; don't think anything's broken, it's not too bad, really ...' Something compelled him to try to stand. But she kept good pressure on his undamaged left shoulder and he didn't even get an inch out of the chair.

'Sit right there, we'll get those things off you and have a proper look.'

In the Kirks' aromatic kitchen, nothing remained of the meal that Lucy had spent all day cooking except dirty dishes and a single serving of rabbit pie and apple-and-prune tart, both of which still stood on the range. They had eaten in silence, just the thrum of the rain on the roof and garden. Tom straightened his spoon in the empty dish and looked up.

'Can I get down now?' he asked.

'Did you enjoy that?' replied Lucy, as she picked up his spoon, and placed her own dish on top of his with a clatter.

Tom nodded his head, a big exaggerated motion, chin to his chest and then all the way back, eyes wide.

'All right, then.' She smiled.

Tom slipped off the chair, still a bit big for him, got as far as the stairs and then hesitated. 'Dad?'

'Yes, boy.' Joe looked up from where he was chasing the final piece of apple round his plate.

'Can *you* help me with my radio valve?'

'Not tonight, another night maybe.' Joe Kirk frowned as he spoke.

'Half an hour to read and then put the light out,' she added. Tom nodded, doing well to hide his disappointment, she thought.

She cleared up the meal, then joined her father at the table, rolling and smoking a cigarette, while Joe fiddled with his pipe.

'He isn't coming,' said Joe, finally. 'Probably for the best, give you a chance to think.'

She nodded, tucking the matches under the leather tie-ups of her pouch of rolling tobacco.

'I'll ask around the lads and see if anyone else knows about radio valves and stuff, I'm not much use to Tom on that score,' Joe added.

She looked up. 'Let's not give up on Ben completely, not just yet, please.'

Joe Kirk frowned, rubbed his hand across his beard a couple of times. 'As you like.'

She put the tobacco down. 'Ben was trying to help us. He had a plan – he wanted to prove that Stanley was murdered, just like you said he was. He thought that if he could do that, Dunwood's excuse for sacking the Captain would be gone, and he'd have to give him his job back – thought he might do the same for the rest of you too.'

'That's the bobbies' business, proving murders.'

'But the police aren't going to do anything,' she said. 'Lerup told them your evidence of the downhaul is just a ploy to get Captain Emerton back. Ben wanted to find something more, something that would force the police to look at it again.'

'Like what?' Her father kept his eyes on the pipe.

She sat back in her chair and put her hands in her lap, trying to relax a little. 'Whoever cut the downhaul off and changed the rope probably did it at night; there are too many people around during the day. We wanted to find out who could have got onto *Windflower* the night before the accident.'

'And this investigation was Ben's idea?'

'To start with, he wanted to help everyone get their jobs back. But we were working on it together – it was my idea to try and find out who could have cut the downhaul off. What with the picketing and everything, it's maybe gone too far to get anyone's job back now. But I'd still love to show them that *you* were right. And to show people round here that Ben didn't betray them, that he was doing his best for them, even while he *was* working for Dunwood.' Her father didn't reply immediately, and Lucy picked at some more of the pastry that had stuck to her apron. 'So, can you help find out who could've cut the downhaul that night?' she asked.

Joe tapped his pipe gently against the table, frowning. Then he said, 'The Gosport lads will be in the pub tomorrow, a few of them are usually in the Castle Tavern right by the yard, even on the weekend. I can go and have a pint with them at lunchtime.'

'Thanks, Dad.'

'No promises, but I'll ask.'

'And you're going to man the picket line again?'

'I should say so, we can't let people think we've been beat, there's a lot of anger still, amongst the men.'

She was silent, watching him.

'We'll keep it orderly,' he went on, 'that Jim Rails was there today and he's trouble. A few of us have had a word, and we'll keep it under control tomorrow.'

'And when you see Ben, you won't be too hard on him, will you?' she asked.

Joe Kirk took a deep breath. 'Nothing'll happen to Ben Clayton. But you talk to him and sort out what's what between you two – he can't go on behaving like this.'

'All right, thanks, Dad.'

Joe stood, pushing himself up stiffly. 'I'm off upstairs, early start tomorrow; it's bloody hard to get to the yard without Dunwood's lorry.'

Lucy watched her father climb the stairs. His limp looked worse than usual. *Poor Dad.* She turned and her eyes fell on the meal sitting on the range, waiting for Ben. She put it away in the larder.

Mrs Arbethwaite knelt at the kitchen cupboard, carefully returning the herbs and ointments to their correct places on the shelves, taking them one by one from the woven basket. Ben watched her, spooning soup clumsily with his left hand, his right arm now in a sling. She had checked each of his injuries with an unexpected care and expertise. Then she had filled a bath, shaking in dark powders from old tea tins and pouring milky viscous liquids from former jam jars until the water was a pungent grey-green colour. He had soaked in her potion until it was cold, staring at the bathroom ceiling with its brown patch where the rain had got through the roof the previous winter. And now she was feeding him more of her life-saving soup.

She shut the cupboard door and pushed herself onto her feet. 'Your coat's a mess,' she said. 'I'll dry it out, but I think it'll need to go to the cleaners.' She put his wallet, a few coins and his keys onto the kitchen table.

He put down his spoon to reach out and flip open the damp wallet. The money was gone, but the receipts and a picture of Lucy in her red cloche hat were still there. He remembered the list that he'd made for her. 'You didn't find a piece of paper with a list of names on it, by any chance?' he asked.

'No, that's everything that was in the pockets.' The chair scraped as Mrs Arbethwaite sat down. 'Was the list important?' she asked.

'They got all my money, must have been a couple of quid in there,' he said, avoiding the question.

'So what happened?' asked Mrs Arbethwaite.

'Robbery,' he said, picking the easy answer, his deceit in the omission. 'They clipped me round the head with a cosh, biffed me a few times, pulled my wallet and then left me in the mud on the foreshore.' He swallowed another spoonful of the hot spicy broth. 'Maybe it was some of the crew of *Windflower* – they're not overjoyed that I'm working for Dunwood, and especially not with me finding him another crew. There was some trouble today on the picket line at the yard, one of the men got hurt, and someone might have decided on revenge.'

Mrs Arbethwaite nodded. 'I thought as much. I heard a few mutterings around the village. You're not much liked at the minute.'

He looked up at her.

'Those fishing folk are a rough lot,' she added. 'Are you going to the police?'

'No, I don't think that would be the thing to do,' he replied, raising another spoonful of soup.

'And how are you feeling?'

'A lot better.' He managed a smile. 'You certainly know what you're doing.'

'I used to be a nurse. I worked at the Royal Victoria in Netley for the last couple of years of the war.' As she spoke her shoulders sagged and her head lowered as though she was physically deflating in front of his eyes.

'I had no idea,' he replied. He had seen the hospital from Southampton Water – a Victorian monstrosity which stretched for a full quarter mile along the estuary.

'It was awful,' she said, 'all those young boys like you, so many lives destroyed, terrible injuries, terrible ... Worse than not coming back at all, I used to think.'

'Did you lose someone?' he asked, gently.

'We all lost someone,' she replied. 'Everyone lost someone. I met him at the hospital in the summer of 1918, there wasn't long to go. Just a little bit too long. He got sent back to the front in September ... and died the last day. The last day,' she repeated, touching the black-and-silver brooch on her lapel.

He stared at her. 'I'm so sorry ... that's awful.'

'It took a long while to get over it,' she said, her voice softer than he'd ever heard it. 'A couple of months into the new year, his lieutenant turned up on the door. He told me it was his fault, he'd thought they should fight to the end, show them it wasn't over until they surrendered. He took them out on a final patrol, the morning of the armistice.' She looked down. 'I often wondered what happened to him, that lieutenant – but I couldn't help him.' There was a silence before she continued. 'And then for a long while after that ... well, when Stanley came along ... I'd been all on my own for so long.'

He could find nothing more to say.

'Anyway, no point crying over spilt milk,' said Mrs Arbethwaite eventually, straightening her back. 'What's done is done,' she continued, her voice more solid. 'I just can't believe what they're saying about another war.'

'They won't let it happen again, really, they won't,' he said.

Mrs Arbethwaite nodded, perfunctorily, as though nothing in this life would surprise her, least of all another war before the last was even twenty years gone. 'I've got something for you,' she said, rising. Her heavy footsteps receded up the stairs. She returned to hand him a tiny notebook fashioned from a couple of staples and some thin paper. 'You remember you asked me to search for something unusual?' she asked.

He nodded, taking the notebook and flicking through it – the paper was so thin that the whole thing was hardly bulkier than a folded ten-pound note. He felt a buzz of excitement surge through him.

'Do you think that's it?' she asked. 'I found it in the shed. I was looking for the decent scissors Stanley had out there. I found it in one of the drawers, under a great pile of tools.'

Several pages were filled with tiny columns of

numbers and letters, all in Stanley's neat script. It looked like a code, the records of a man with something to hide. Ben glanced up at Mrs Arbethwaite. Her expression was carefully blank, but her eyes hovered on the notebook for a moment, before she picked up his empty soup bowl and moved away to the sink.

'It looks promising,' he replied. 'I'll have a proper look tomorrow, I'll feel brighter then and it'll make more sense.' He tucked it into his wallet.

'What are you going to do in the morning?' asked Mrs Arbethwaite, filling the kettle.

'Could I use the car?' he replied. 'I don't think I'll be able to ride my bike.'

'Yes, of course,' she said, turning off the tap. 'So are you going to work?'

'I have to – but do you mind not telling anyone about what happened tonight?'

Mrs Arbethwaite put the kettle on the range and then leaned back against it, arms folded. 'So how are you going to hide that bruise on your head?' she asked.

'I'll keep my hat on,' he replied. 'I'll come up with a story for it,' he added, easing himself upright.

'No one'll hear about it from me, you can be sure of that.'

'Thank you,' he said. He hobbled to the door and then hesitated. 'Thanks again for all your help.'

'We will talk about that notebook again before you do anything, won't we?' she asked.

'Of course,' he replied, with a smile of what he hoped was comforting reassurance.

Chapter 19

Ben Clayton attracted no interest from the surly men around the brazier as he drove into the Camper and Nicholsons boatyard the next day. None of them recognised Mrs Arbethwaite's car, and only the bored gaze of a policeman followed him through the gates. He parked the Morris Eight by the office, climbed out awkwardly and went looking for Dunwood. He found him watching six men unload sails from the lorry. The *Windflower* was going out on a beautiful spring morning. The low sun glittered off the water of the calm harbour, a couple of seagulls fought noisily over a piece of fish.

Dunwood smiled as Ben approached. 'Ah, there you are, I've been looking for you.'

'Sorry I'm late, Mr Dunwood. I had an accident last night, I fell off the bike.' As he spoke, Ben removed his hat, revealing the bandage that Mrs Arbethwaite had applied.

Dunwood flinched. 'The old Scott give you a spot of bother?'

'More my fault than the bike, sir, I ran her off that sharp corner going into the village, on Satchell Lane, hit a pothole and went over the handlebars.'

'Any other damage?'

'A few bruises, but nothing broken – not a scratch on the bike.'

'Could have been worse, then.' Dunwood smiled in

obvious relief. 'Since there's no wind at all,' he continued, 'we thought we might tow out into the Solent so the crew can walk round some of the manoeuvres, be a good shakedown for everyone.'

'That's wonderful news.' Ben brightened at the thought of getting out on the water, of sailing the *Windflower* at last.

'But do y'think you'll be all right to sail with that lump on your head?' asked Dunwood.

'Certainly, sir,' replied Ben.

Dunwood pursed his lips, considering. 'Well, at the moment we can't leave the mooring anyway. There's a problem with the *May*, something to do with the engines. Captain McDonald's got his mechanic working on it, but there's no one around from Camper's to help. I was wondering if you might go and take a look, I know you're a whiz with anything mechanical.'

'Of course,' replied Ben, trying to hide his disappointment. He'd have much preferred to spend the morning in the spring sunshine with the crew than buried in the murk of the *May*'s engine room.

'Good man, get her fired up as soon as you can, and we'll get out there. The chaps are all itching to go.'

Ben limped along the dock until he found one of the rowing dinghies used for getting out to the moorings. He eased himself down the steps, got aboard, untied it and started to row out to the *May*. Church bells pealed out across the water. He wasn't wearing the sling, but moving his right arm was painful. He tied the dinghy up at the foot of the boarding ladder on the starboard side of the *May*, climbed up to the main deck and found himself halfway along an open passageway that ran the length of the superstructure. He must find Captain McDonald, report Dunwood's request and get down to the engine room.

'Hello,' said a warm husky voice.

Ben jumped. Anna had appeared, leaning against a doorway, right elbow propped in the palm of her left hand, cigarette by her ear, smoke drifting across her face. 'Hello,' he replied.

'So how can we be of service to you aboard the beautiful MV *May* on this fine spring morning?' she asked, moving back inside the door as she spoke.

Ben followed her into what was obviously the main saloon, stepping onto a lush white carpet that stretched away to beech-panelled walls. Two gorgeous cream-coloured upholstered sofas dominated the room, the sweeping white wood varnished and polished to a finish that seemed to make the grain almost three-dimensional – he'd never seen work like it. On the opposite wall was a swirling monochrome painting of fountain-like lotus flowers. To his right was an extraordinary image of a sprawling nude – was it Man Ray? Yes, and it was signed. And the music! It was Bubber Miley's trumpet wailing mournfully from the gramophone in the corner. Ben's opinion of Dunwood ratcheted up several notches. This, he thought, is how he would furnish a house, if he could ever afford it.

Anna flung herself onto the sofa in the centre of the room, looking completely comfortable – looking, in fact, as though she didn't just belong but was essential, the finishing touch. She kicked off her espadrilles and tucked her white-linen-clad legs underneath her. The trousers contrasted with a simple knitted black top. Her raven hair was loose around her shoulders, set off by a necklace of pearls. She was examining him. And he was suddenly acutely conscious of his shabby work clothes, and the old navy-surplus reefer jacket, a leftover from university that he'd dug out for the day. He took his hat off.

'Oh, that looks painful,' she said, forehead creasing in a frown. 'What happened to you?'

Ben's hand went up, his fingers brushing the soft bandage. 'Motorbike accident,' he said. He didn't mention that his head was pounding, and that his arm, shin and shoulder were throbbing and his ribs stabbed pain every time he breathed.

'Oh dear.' Then she leaned forward. 'Motorbikes look so exciting – are they? I've never been on one.'

Was she suggesting he offer her a ride? Thorpe's comment about 'doing a bit of rough' popped into his head at the same time as an image of her on the back of the Scott, her arms wrapped around him and holding on tight. He nodded. 'Yes, they are,' he said, politely.

She stubbed out her cigarette and sat back. 'So, are you our guest today, if you are injured and cannot sail?'

'No, Mr Dunwood sent me over here to help with the engines. I was looking for Captain McDonald.'

'Ah.' She leaned across, and pressed a button set in the side panel of the sofa. 'He'll be along in a moment.'

'I don't want to put him to any trouble. I can go and find him.'

'Oh no, I've heard you're the man of the moment – so I'm quite sure the Captain can come to you,' she said, watching him as she continued. 'I'm so glad we've finally got to meet again, it was such a shame that we missed you at the club the other night.'

Ben's heart thumped in his throat. 'Yes ...'

'I sensed you watching me.'

'If I may say so, you're ... mistaken ...'

'No,' she cut in, confidently, hands pushing her hair up, and then sweeping it back behind her ears and down onto her back. 'Women can tell these things – do you think that's something Mr Einstein's new science will be able to explain?' She was not expecting an answer, and immediately added, 'I heard that you had some trouble getting in.'

'I'd been told there was a card game there. Seemed I was wrong,' he said, thinking, *Stick to the story you had for Spink*. There was no reason to trust her.

'Oh no, you were quite correct,' she replied, matter-of-factly, leaning forward to pick up a magazine from the coffee table. 'A heavenly *Tatler* day,' she added, 'the new one does so help with the *aching* boredom of it all ... But there doesn't seem to be a picture of me in it this time ...' She glanced back up at him.

'An oversight, I'm sure,' he offered. *What does she know?* Then he said, 'Perhaps my face just doesn't fit at this club.'

'Oh, I think your face would fit, Ben Clayton,' she said. 'Even in *Tatler* – you just need the right friends.'

'It's a pity my friend Stanley isn't around to make the introductions,' he replied.

She looked puzzled for a moment. Then she said, 'Oh, do you mean the Stanley that was killed in that terrible accident?'

'Yes,' replied Ben.

'I'm so sorry. I didn't know you were friends. But you should ask Lerup, he played there with Stanley – I'm sure he'll get you in if you want to go. You two know each other.' She smiled sweetly and plucked at a page without looking at the magazine.

Didn't she know about the trouble between him and Lerup?

'So, do you think that poor Stanley was murdered, like these people claim?' continued Anna.

'Not at all, I side with Mr Dunwood,' said Ben.

'I think the police should have made some further effort.' Anna frowned. 'Just because it's the word of a fisherman, it doesn't make it any less valuable, does it?'

For a moment her chocolate-brown eyes settled on him, and the effect was insistent. But it was only for a moment, before they shifted, restlessly, back to the magazine. She flicked another page. 'But you think just like all the others ...' she continued.

'No, I ...' Ben stopped, realizing the trap, if it was one, as the gaze came back to him, as wide-eyed and innocent as a newborn foal. 'Actually, I probably do think just like all the others,' he said.

Anna laughed a throaty, sexy chuckle that was interrupted by a knock on the door. 'Come,' she said.

The door opened and a thickset man dressed in crisp white ducks and a matching shirt with shoulder boards entered. 'Miss Annabelle,' he murmured, in a soft Scots accent.

'Captain, I discovered Mr Clayton here, lost and wandering our decks; he says he's been sent to help with the engines,' she replied, rising to head towards the gramophone, where the needle was clicking helplessly in the exit groove.

'Great,' he said, with a thick burring of the *r*, 'the boss mentioned that you'd come and help us.' He held out a right hand to Ben before continuing. 'I'm Captain McDonald.'

'How do you do.' Ben smiled, shaking his hand. McDonald was an ex–Merchant Marine captain; Ben knew that he had been with Dunwood for a couple of years, but had never met him before.

'Come and say goodbye before you leave – perhaps you'll have a drink with me?' asked Anna.

Ben looked back – her head was set at a slight angle, and she was playing with the pearl necklace with her right hand, her smile guileless – and he half nodded, half bowed.

'Come on then, laddie, no time to waste,' said McDonald. And with a hand at his elbow, he ushered Ben from the room.

Outside, Ben took a deep breath. 'I'm sorry you were called up here, I could've come and found you, but Miss Venuti insisted.'

'Don't worry, I know what she's like. I'm glad to have your help, laddie, the boss is fair frantic to get out there. Come and have a look, it's this way.' McDonald strode forward.

Bloody great lumps of recalcitrant metal – a little easier to deal with, thought Ben, as he followed McDonald down a companionway into the bowels of the ship.

Chapter 20

When Ben followed Captain McDonald back into the main saloon a few hours later, Anna was still sitting on the sofa, a magazine on her lap, head down. Just along from her was a second woman, also reading a magazine – older, but no less elegant, although not quite a match for Anna's beauty. He recognised Mrs Dunwood, and remembered the monkey.

'Ah, the Captain ... and Clayton,' said Harold Dunwood. He and Lerup sat at opposite ends of the other sofa – Lerup in an immaculate white suit, his panama on the seat beside him. McDonald pulled up a few yards short of the two men. Ben stood at his shoulder and took an idle glance at Lerup – the man looked far too composed.

'Clayton, have you met my wife?' said Dunwood.

'This is the young man who was so helpful finding me a cage for Dennis,' said May Dunwood, nodding approvingly at Ben.

'Very pleased to see you again,' he replied, smiling. He thought highly of Harold Dunwood's wife, but Dennis – what kind of name was that for a monkey?

'And you know Anna,' added Dunwood. She looked up from the magazine at the mention of her name, smiled at Ben, then returned to the page. 'So what's happening in the engine room? We're still sitting on the mooring,' continued Dunwood.

'We've got a serious problem, sir, we've been

sabotaged,' replied McDonald, his hands respectfully clasped in front of him.

'Sabotaged?' Dunwood repeated, leaning forward, elbows on his knees, intent, shocked.

'Someone has put sugar in the diesel tanks,' added McDonald.

'Sugar? I don't understand,' said Dunwood, aghast.

'I think the idea is that it dissolves and gets into the engine and damages it through the combustion process by melting or burning,' said Ben, taking over, 'but it certainly hasn't all dissolved. The filters and fuel lines are thick with it. But we're not sure how much has dissolved, and what damage it's done internally – the engineer's still stripping it down.'

'Deliberate sabotage,' said Dunwood, an icy edge to his voice.

'Aye, no other way it could have got in the tank,' replied McDonald.

'My God, are you serious?' Lerup uncoiled at the other end of the sofa. 'How would they do such a thing?'

'Easy, the tank fills from the deck,' replied McDonald.

'You mean there's no security?' said Lerup.

McDonald shifted on his feet. 'This is a British-flagged ship in Portsmouth harbour, with half the Royal Navy on the wharves opposite. We always have a man on anchor watch, but there's never been any need for security as such, not till now, anyway,' he retorted.

Lerup hesitated for a moment, looking at McDonald, before turning his attention to Ben. 'It must be Kirk,' he said. 'You're pretty thick with him, Clayton. Do you know anything about this?'

'That's ridiculous, Lerup, and you know it,' Ben snapped back.

Lerup grinned. 'Nasty bump too, old man, did you bang your head on a door, or fall out with your fishermen pals?'

'Lerup, please,' said Dunwood, 'the boy fell off his

motorbike.'

'Ah, right,' replied Lerup, sarcasm in the tiny dismissive movement of his left hand where it lay on the sofa. Nicely judged, thought Ben, just enough scepticism to indicate that he thought the motorbike story was a cover-up, but not enough to indicate that he knew it for sure.

'We shall have to get the constabulary to look into this,' said Dunwood.

'Damn right we will, we'll have Kirk up on a charge before the end of the day,' said Lerup.

'It doesn't help us get the *Windflower* out on the water, though, and that's obviously where they want us – stuck on the mooring,' said Dunwood.

'I could try to charter something, but there's not much in commission at this time of year,' said Lerup, shaking his head. 'Damn those pinko scum.' Then he looked across at McDonald. 'And Captain, this really is negligent – I think we need to review your duties.'

'Please, Lerup,' said May Dunwood, glancing up from the magazine she obviously wasn't reading, interrupting before the skipper could react. 'Captain McDonald had no way of knowing the situation was going to deteriorate in this fashion. In fact, you were in a much better position to judge the mood of those men, and should have warned him to take precautions.'

Lerup's lips tightened, disappearing under his thin moustache, then he crossed his legs and adjusted his trouser crease with an effort at nonchalance. He didn't reply. *Bravo, Mrs Dunwood*, thought Ben.

'How quickly can we repair it, Captain?' asked Harold Dunwood.

McDonald turned to Ben.

'It's a German engine,' he obliged, 'and it's quite possible that some of the parts will have to come from over there.'

'Is there anyone we can talk to about that, a supplier perhaps?' asked Dunwood.

'Not on a Sunday, sir, but first thing tomorrow morning we can get onto it,' said McDonald.

Dunwood relapsed into silence, pulling a silver cigar case out of the inside pocket of his blazer.

'Please, darling,' said May Dunwood, 'surely that can wait till after lunch.'

'Huh?' Dunwood looked round at her, deep in thought, and she inclined her head towards the cigars, raising a single immaculate eyebrow. 'Oh, yes,' he said, looking down at the case as if surprised to see it in his hands, before rather reluctantly pushing it back into his pocket. He exhaled a deep sigh, then stood and paced over to the window behind the sofa, hands thrust deep in his blazer pockets, while he stared out towards the *Windflower* for what seemed to Ben like a very long time. The sound of a brass band drifted across the water from Esplanade Gardens. Everyone else in the room remained silent – even Lerup, presumably still smarting from May Dunwood's rebuke.

Harold Dunwood turned back to them. 'Clayton, I want you to fly to Germany this afternoon; you can be at the factory tomorrow, and on your way back here with the parts the day after. Having a man on the spot is the only way to be certain that we get the stuff as quickly as possible. We can't trust the Germans to understand the urgency, we could be waiting weeks.'

Ben felt a chill wash over his skin. He glanced towards Lerup, who was struggling to disguise a smirk.

'But darling, what if these parts are available in England somewhere?' asked May Dunwood.

'If we wait till tomorrow to find that out and they aren't, we'll have lost another day.' Dunwood pulled his hands out of his pockets and leaned on the back of the sofa. He glared round the room. 'I'm not having those damn fishermen lose me another day's sailing. And I need someone to go to that factory anyway, to talk about the engines for the new motor yacht. We've been trying to get

Lerup out there for weeks, but he's just been far too busy with *Windflower*.'

Ben managed to maintain a neutral expression. He was being demoted to delivery boy, while Lerup stayed here with the yacht. Worse, he wasn't even going to make a good delivery boy – he'd never been abroad before, and he had no idea how to organise a trip like this at such short notice. And ... 'I don't speak any German,' he said.

'I do,' replied Anna, folding the *Vogue* magazine shut, and leaning forward to toss it back onto the coffee table. 'I could go with him,' she added, looking at Dunwood. Ben stared at his rival's girlfriend.

'What a marvellous idea, Anna,' exclaimed May Dunwood, 'you can visit your friends.'

'I didn't have a holiday in mind,' said Dunwood, with a trace of irritation, 'there's business to be done. We need the equipment back here.'

Ben glanced momentarily at Lerup – the hand on the sofa was now balled into a fist.

'But darling,' May Dunwood was saying, 'things never go smoothly, that's why you're sending Mr Clayton over there; there are bound to be delays, time when Anna can see her friends.'

'Well,' Dunwood sighed more obviously this time, 'only if the friends live close to the factory.'

Anna looked at Ben. 'Where are we going?' she said, with an expression that told him that she had decided, even if Dunwood had not.

'It's a M.A.N. engine ...' he started.

'They're in Augsburg, it's near Munich,' said Dunwood, frowning.

'Perfect,' replied Anna, smiling conspiratorially at May. 'We can stay at the Vier Jahreszeiten.'

'Oh, the divine Mr Walterspiel – I am *so* envious,' replied May.

Harold Dunwood rolled his eyes.

'So why don't you come with us.' Anna touched May

lightly on the arm as she spoke.

'I couldn't possibly, we're tied up in London all week. Now do admit, darling,' said May to her husband, 'as long as they are back in time for Captain McDonald to have the boat ready for next weekend's sailing, you'll be happy, won't you?' It was really a statement rather than a question. 'And it's a wonderful opportunity for Anna to go back for a couple of days, she's been talking about it for months – but as you say, Mr Lerup here is always *so* busy with the yacht. Now Mr Clayton can provide the proper company, and Anna can help him with the arrangements – it's perfectly ideal for everyone.'

'Well, I suppose I have no objection, so long as the boat is ready for next Saturday. Lerup?' Dunwood glanced at the other man.

Lerup was looking at Anna, the smirk replaced by a blank, even cold, expression. 'If it's best for the *Windflower* ...' he said, his left hand now on the hat that lay beside him, raising it a fraction, letting it drop back down.

'Why can't he go with Anna, darling?' asked May.

'No, no, I need Lerup here,' replied Dunwood. 'There's far too much work to do on *Windflower*; some of the new crew have offered to stay down and help out, they'll need direction and we can't expect them to take it from the yard. I can't possibly spare him,' said Dunwood, straightening, hands back in the blazer pockets, grasping at some semblance of control over the situation.

'That's settled then,' said Anna. 'You do have a passport?' she added, turning to Ben.

'Yes ...' he replied, wondering a moment too late if a lie would have been advantageous.

'Good.' She glanced at Dunwood. 'I shall take the tender over and use the telephone to see if we can get tickets for the aeroplane.'

Dunwood nodded.

'We can get there tonight if we're quick.' She glanced at her watch. 'Imperial Airways flight four fifty-five leaves

Croydon at six thirty, gets into Cologne just after ten. We can get a sleeper train down to Munich for breakfast. I've done it several times.' She looked at Ben. 'I lived there for nearly four years,' she added, by way of explanation. 'What else do you need to do?'

'I need to get my passport and some clothes and things from Hamble,' he replied. 'And I'll need the part numbers from the engineer.'

'All right, I'll have one of our servants meet me at the airfield with the things I need. So I'll arrange the tickets and then pick you up in Hamble. How does that sound?' Anna replied.

'Fine,' he said, with another glance at Lerup, who was examining the headband of the panama.

'What about lunch, Anna?' said May, pulling a powder compact out of her handbag.

'No time for that, I'm afraid,' replied Anna, 'I need to get straight over to the office.'

'I'll come with you,' said Lerup. 'I want to telephone the police and get Kirk arrested before he can do any more damage ...'

'Nonsense, Lerup,' May Dunwood interrupted him with a commanding voice. 'What can they do before lunch? Eat with us.' Her Jean Patou handbag snapped shut.

'Quite right,' agreed Dunwood.

Lerup's eyes flickered round each of them, then he nodded with the slightest of exaggerations to May Dunwood. 'Of course,' he said, with the trace of a smile.

After giving Anna his address, Ben hurried below to get the information about the engine parts. Things were happening very quickly, but he was starting to get some traction on the new landscape. He would have to be careful – and he *must* talk to Lucy before he left. He jumped down the companionway; the engineer was bent over a manual, a thick cheese sandwich in one grimy hand, a pencil in the other.

'I need the part numbers,' said Ben, 'of *everything* we

might need to fix it, and I need them now ...’

Chapter 21

'Lucy, Lucy!' Tom burst breathless through the front door.

Lucy's heart jumped. She was at the sink, elbow deep in washing, the kitchen filled with the steam and smell of laundry.

'Mr Clayton's at his house,' exclaimed Tom, with a melodramatic struggle for breath, leaning forward, hands on his knees, the door banging shut behind him.

She started to dry her hands on her apron. 'How did he look?'

'I only saw the car, I came straight here,' said Tom, still wheezing.

'I'd best get up there then,' she replied, pulling off her apron. It was early, why was he back so soon? But it was a Sunday. She grabbed her coat and hat off the hook on the front door, and started down the path, putting them on as she went. 'Mind the house for me, Tom, I won't be long,' she called.

'What about this?' Tom shouted after her.

She stopped. Tom was standing at the front door, holding out Ben's bedraggled hat – he'd found it by the river that morning. She had dried it out on the range, and then brushed off the worst of the mud. How had it got into that state and ended up on the foreshore? She turned back and took it from Tom; he looked up at her, brow set anxiously – *just like his dad*, she thought. He knows something's wrong.

'Thank you, Tom,' she said, and crouched down to give him a kiss on the cheek. 'I won't be long.' She set off along the foreshore, not rushing – she didn't want to arrive beetroot red, breathless and sweaty. She hoped Mrs Arbethwaite wasn't home; that old witch would rather have seagull shit land in her tea than a Hamble fisher girl up to her house. And she still had no idea what she was going to say to Ben when she saw him.

Ben pulled a final clean shirt off the hanger and pushed it into the case. That should be enough – they were only going to be away for four or five days at the most. He glanced at his watch; Anna would be here soon and he had to get to Lucy's. He was halfway to the door when he remembered his passport. He dropped the bags and stepped over to the dressing table, fumbling amongst the litter of paperwork in the top drawer until he found it. He slipped it into his jacket pocket with his wallet, and then heard the car squeal to a halt outside. Light, quick footsteps crunched up the drive. *Bloody hell* – she couldn't be here already. How fast did she drive? He hurried unevenly down the attic stairs, the case bumping against the wall, the pain jabbing from his injuries.

'Ben, someone to see you,' called Mrs Arbethwaite, and there was no mistaking the approval in her tone.

Bloody, bloody hell ... He should have gone to see Lucy as soon as he'd got back to the village, then come here and packed.

'Can I offer you a cup of tea, while you're waiting?' he heard Mrs Arbethwaite say.

'No, thank you, we really have to go,' was Anna's reply, as he started down the final flight of stairs. 'Hello,' she said as he appeared, 'are you ready? We simply must dash if we're to catch the plane. There isn't a minute to lose.'

Ben hesitated. He'd thought to ask Anna to wait while he went round to see Lucy. But it wasn't the kind of conversation that could be rushed, particularly by a society beauty tapping her foot at the Kirks' door. And if they missed this flight because of him, they'd lose a whole day, and that was the entire point of Dunwood sending him. He couldn't afford to fail this task; it was a vital chance to recover some credibility. 'Yes, let's go,' he said, grabbing his Sunday-best hat off the rack. Lucy would understand.

Anna's car was sitting on Satchell Lane at the end of the drive. 'Oh! It's a 6C,' he exclaimed, as he saw it.

Anna tapped the rack on the back of the open-topped red Alfa, indicating where Ben should put his suitcase.

'It was second-hand. Daddy bought it for me for my twenty-fifth birthday.'

Ben heaved his suitcase up and pulled the leather straps over to fasten it in place. He hadn't imagined her owning a car as beautiful and quick as this. 'Is it the seventeen-fifty version?' he asked.

'No, the fifteen hundred. I thought we'd have the top down as it's such a beautiful day, so you'll need your coat on.'

Ben nodded, shrugging into the overcoat as soon as he'd finished with the suitcase. Anna was already in the driver's seat, the engine fired and running. She pulled on a pair of blood-red kid-leather driving gloves as he climbed in beside her, and then let the clutch up and they were off. The car shot towards the Square, Ben clutching at his hat in the wind. They dipped into the right-hand corner to go up Hamble Lane with such force that he slid into the door. He glanced across, and met the gaze from her big chocolate-brown eyes, a faint smile on her full lips. And then she turned back to the road and stamped on the accelerator, and the engine roar mixed with the gale in his ears as they hurtled out of the village.

Lucy was almost at the top of the High Street when she saw the red Alfa squat into its suspension at the corner of the Square. She recognised Ben immediately, raised a hand and started forward. But the shout of greeting died in her throat as she saw the way the woman in the driving seat was looking across at him. Lucy stopped in her tracks, arm falling limply to her side as the Alfa disappeared up Hamble Lane, the image stuck in her head. The woman's expression had been unmistakeable.

Finally, she started to wander after the Alfa in a daze, but then at the School Lane turning she drifted down towards the Common. How could things have turned upside down so quickly? One minute she'd been as happy as she could remember, and now ... and now everything seemed to be falling apart faster than she could keep up. She found a hidden spot on a fallen tree trunk, close to the whispering reeds and the cold flowing river. A pigeon settled on a nearby branch, its chest puffed out, head squat on its shoulders, watching her. She returned the gaze, wishing it could talk. The pigeon shuffled a couple of inches along the branch and flew off. She watched it go. *Would he really betray me*?

They were so different, from such different worlds: Ben with his safe, smart life of a college degree and office job, with his motorbike and yachts; and her, dumped out of school early for a life of fishing boats, bicycles, buses and fish-and-chip shops. Until now, there had never been any sign or hint from him that this was a problem, and that was the source of much of her confidence. She knew that others thought it was wrong; Mrs Arbethwaite was a long way from being alone in her disapproval. But she hadn't cared what anyone else had thought while Ben had seemed completely indifferent, completely blind to his superior station. Until now, until the moment when he'd driven off in a fancy red sports car, with a fancy-looking woman in matching red driving gloves. And now she could feel her belief in him, in them, seeping away like warmth into the cold still air.

'What the bloody hell do you think you're doing, coming here?' asked Leon.

Matthew Faden scratched at the birthmark on his neck and cast an anxious glance over his shoulder, back out through the fug of cigarette smoke and the grease-stained window of the East End betting shop. He was sure that no one had followed him.

'You know the protocol: dead-letter drop, reply, meet.' Leon tapped the Geordie beat of the words out with a fist into his palm as he spoke. 'Never. Ever. Come here. Especially now ...'

'There's no time for all that – we have to talk, a lot has happened,' insisted Faden. Leon stared at him for a long moment, and then licked his lips. Faden knew it was a telltale sign of tension in the man, but he had no idea how he would react next.

'This had better be good,' said Leon. Then he pointed at the two bruisers by the door. 'Get the rest of the boys and check every last soul on the streets within a mile of here. I want you to follow anyone we don't know to their final destination – home, work, whatever – and then report that to me. And I want to know about anyone they talk to on the way. Go.' Leon's final gesticulation was a four-fingered stab out of the door. The little bell on the door frame tinkled as the men departed with no shortage of urgency.

Leon led the way up a staircase to the first floor. Faden followed him; it was dark, the treads creaked and it smelt of cat pee. Leon slumped into a threadbare armchair in the back room and started to roll a cigarette. Feeble flames flickered in the hearth. A gust of wind whined around the chimney above, pushing a swirl of smoke back into the room. Faden briefly covered his mouth with his handkerchief as he took a seat on the opposite side of the fire. It was another worn armchair and the only other piece of furniture on the bare floorboards. It also smelt of cat pee. Horsehair poked through the cheap, worn upholstery and into his thighs. He should have stopped at a roadhouse on the drive back to London, and now he badly wanted a cup of tea, but he wasn't going to ask.

'So, what the hell's going on to justify this?' said Leon, out of the side of his mouth as he held a match to the cigarette.

'I talked to Clayton, just as you asked ...'

'About bloody time.'

'Yes, well, he's on our side. Utterly. He still goes to Movement meetings, and I saw that he won't use violence even when he's badly provoked.'

'He used to box, didn't he? He was pretty good from what I heard.'

'Yes, but that was before. He's a true pacifist now, I was there yesterday when he had every reason to punch a man on the nose – but he didn't. He really is with us.'

Leon spat a stray piece of tobacco into the spluttering fire. 'That's good news, but it damn well isn't enough to justify breaking the contact rules.'

'No, there's more. I'm sure that White hadn't approached Clayton before I saw him yesterday at lunchtime, but I tipped White off about Ben nearly a week ago, and he's not someone who'd sit on his hands. White must have been up to something in the meantime, and now Clayton's left for Germany on an errand for Dunwood.'

'An errand for Dunwood – to Germany – do you know what?' Leon exhaled smoke as he spoke.

'I was told that it was to fetch urgently needed parts for Dunwood's motor yacht, which does have an engine problem. Dunwood could have sent him, but so could Charles Lerup, who's Dunwood's right-hand man for his yachts,' replied Faden. He hesitated for effect. 'They're going to the Augsburg factory of M.A.N. Diesel.'

'Innocent enough,' shrugged Leon.

Faden faltered; Leon wasn't normally inclined to regard anything as innocent. 'But Clayton isn't alone either, he went with Annabelle Venuti, and her current beau is none other than the aforementioned Honourable Charles Lerup. And I caught the pair of them coming out of the Russian Tea Rooms owned by that foul admiral with lots of fascist pals. Venuti's a good friend from university days and I could vouch for her back then. But she's just returned after living in Germany for several years, and although her mother was born Jewish, they don't have anything to do with all that. Who knows what happened out there and what she might support now. And as for Lerup, I could believe anything of him.'

'I know of the Russian admiral, but what can you tell me about Lerup?'

Faden outlined what he knew and had learned over lunch at the Bell Hotel, while Leon sucked his teeth and smoked, but otherwise listened in silence. When Faden was finished, Leon flicked the cigarette butt towards the fire. It bounced off the chimney jamb and back onto the floor. It stayed there amongst the fish-and-chip papers and beer bottles as Leon started to roll another. Whatever else the revolution was going to be, it wasn't going to be tidy, thought Faden.

The second cigarette was alight before Leon spoke again. 'So to summarise: White believes that Clayton is someone that can help him persuade Dunwood to build warplanes; Clayton is now going to Germany to visit what's historically been a major arms supplier to their military, accompanied by someone with unknown political affiliations; we think Dunwood or Lerup was directly responsible for sending him, but you're speculating that White's hand is also somehow involved in this journey.'

'Yes,' Faden retorted. Too quick, he thought.

'How?' asked Leon.

'I don't know, it just seems a coincidence that Clayton is going out there now.'

'Most of the time coincidence is more likely than conspiracy,' said Leon. He smoked the cigarette down to his fingers without saying anything more. Faden sat still and watched him. It appeared that he had just about justified coming directly to the betting shop, and he wasn't going to say anything more that might risk overturning that impression. He stared at some damp that had lifted a patch of faded and stained wallpaper off the chimney breast. Eventually, Leon got up and walked to the fireplace. He threw the second cigarette butt into the flames as he spoke. 'It's a mess, there's no obvious plot or motive and there may be nothing happening at all.' He turned to Faden. 'I don't have anywhere near enough information to even judge if this was worth the risk of you coming here.'

Faden nodded obediently, warily.

'But the stakes are very, very high – if Dunwood and the others start to build weapons, they'll eventually persuade the government to buy 'em and use 'em ...'

Faden stood. 'What can I do?'

Leon licked his lips. 'We've already got a watch on White, but we're getting short of certain types of people. I want you to keep an eye on this Lerup character; you should fit in to his part of the jungle.'

'Of course.'

'I want to know as much as you can tell me – where he goes, who he meets and for how long. If you think he's spotted you, or if he might be getting suspicious, call this number and let it ring five times, hang up, then call back thirty seconds later and let it ring four times. Hang up again. Then go home. I'll contact you there.' Leon jotted the number down on the back of a betting slip from the mantelpiece and handed it over.

Faden glanced down at the scrawl. 'Five times, wait thirty seconds, four times. All right, I've got it.'

'Memorise it and throw it away before you leave here. No more risks, Matthew. No more chances.'

When Lucy returned to the cottage, Albert Parks was sitting at the kitchen table with Tom.

'Hello, Lucy,' he said as she opened the door, gazing at her levelly with grey eyes, his huge hands wrapped around a teacup. 'Tom thought you wouldn't be long, so I made us a pot of tea and waited.'

'What's wrong?' she asked. As one of Captain Emerton's long-serving hands, she knew that Parks had been on the picket line with her father all week.

Parks hesitated, glanced at Tom, who was sorting some cigarette cards that he'd traded. Then Parks said, 'It's your dad, there's been a bit of trouble with the, er ... authorities in Gosport.'

'Oh,' she exclaimed. She shut the door and hung her coat and hat up. Sinking her head into them for a moment, she took a deep breath, then turned back to the room. 'Tom, can you let the grown-ups talk for a minute? Weren't you going to play with Michael this afternoon?'

Tom nodded. 'You told me to stay here,' he said, gathering the cards.

'Of course, and you've done a grand job, but now I'm back and you can go and play,' she replied, holding the door open again.

He got to her and then stopped. 'Is Mr Clayton all right?' he asked, looking at her earnestly.

'He's fine, Tom, thanks for asking ...'

'Will he be able to help with my radio soon?'

She hesitated. 'He's busy working,' she managed, 'but as soon as he has time, we'll get him to do it, now off you go.' She shooed him out of the door, calling after him, 'Don't be late for your tea.' As soon as he was gone and the door shut, she turned to Parks. 'What sort of trouble?'

'The bogeys arrested him just after lunch, from off the picket line. He's been taken to Gosport nick. It's to do with damage to the *May*, Dunwood's motor yacht. I guess Dunwood must have filed some sort of complaint with the bogeys, but I don't know what they can prove. Your dad won't be up in court till tomorrow at least. He certainly won't be home tonight.'

She sank into the kitchen chair opposite Parks, stunned at the news. For a moment a flood of self-pity threatened. 'Is that all you know, have they charged him with anything?'

'They wouldn't talk to us, said there were an investigation going on and that were that,' replied Parks.

'Why would anyone damage the *May*?' she asked.

'To stop Dunwood going sailing, I'd reckon; without the *May* they can't tow the *Windflower* off the dock and out to sea,' replied Parks, scratching at his tanned forehead. 'With the J Class boats not having any engines in them, it's far too dangerous to try to sail her out, her not being tested or anything yet,' he added. He pushed a hand back through thick dark brown hair. 'There are a lot of angry lads after yesterday.'

'What was the damage?' she asked. 'It must be serious to stop that motor yacht going to sea.'

'I spoke to a fellow I know, works on the *May*, and he says there were sugar in the fuel tanks, done deliberate,' said Parks.

'But Dad wouldn't do a thing like that.'

'It weren't him, but someone done it, and Dunwood or Lerup'll make sure the coppers'll have him till they get a better story.'

'What about Rails?'

'Like as not, but it'd be a brave man as says so without some proof.'

A sudden thought – *my father had been going to speak to the Gosport lads today.* 'When did you say this happened?' she asked.

'Just after lunch, your dad went and had a pint and a sandwich in the Castle Tavern, then he came back on the picket line, and they took him as soon as they saw him. Lerup was there as well.'

So, it was likely that her father had spoken to the yard workers. He might have learned something about access to the *Windflower* the night before the accident, something that could solve the murder. But now she was the only one who could do anything about it and sort out this terrible mess.

'I heard that Dunwood sent your Ben to Germany to

get the replacement parts for the *May*'s engines,' said Parks, pausing before he added, 'and that fancy woman of Lerup's went with him.'

Lucy glanced up at Parks, who was watching her. 'I know,' she said. Was that woman really Lerup's girlfriend, could that be possible? But what about the look she'd given Ben? She hesitated; she wanted to know the woman's name, but didn't want to ask Parks.

He pushed himself up from the kitchen table and took his mug over to the sink. 'I best be going. If you want to see your dad tomorrow, there're a few of us going to Gosport in the morning, to keep up the picketing; we can't let the bloody bosses beat us down. Meet us up at the Square at about six thirty.'

She frowned, thoughts clouded by all the bad news. She had to see her dad. She'd have to get a message to Miss Ritchie and go in to work later. 'All right, I'll be there, and thanks for coming by and letting me know.'

'S'all right, sorry for your troubles, and if you ever need anything, you know where to find me.' He put his flat cap on, tipped it with his index finger and left.

Chapter 22

The plane's wheels touched down with a jolt, and Ben jerked awake with no idea of where he was. Then there was a second bump and a squeal of rubber and he remembered. Damn – he'd worked on planes since he'd come down from Cambridge, but this was the first time he'd ever flown and he'd slept for most of it. He stretched cautiously in his comfortable Pullman-style upholstered seat. Everything ached, but they had been served a decent meal by the stewards and now here they were just hours later, rested, well fed and in Cologne. It was extraordinary. He felt he owed it to the Handley Page H.P. 45 to have paid a little more attention. He looked across to where Anna sat opposite, staring out of the window into the darkness. Both of them had a view – she'd insisted on it. There was a table between them, and an elderly couple occupied the aisle seats beside them. The engine noise made polite get-to-know-you conversation impossible, just as it had in the Alfa – especially the way Anna had been driving it. He had been grateful. He'd needed time to think.

He was worried about Lucy. He hoped she'd understand, but he knew this would be testing her, he knew how he would feel if it were the other way around. He just had to use this opportunity to discover what had happened to Stanley – to decode the notebook. And perhaps to win Anna's confidence and learn to what extent he could trust her, and find out what she knew about Lerup and Spink. Why had she chosen to accompany him – was it just to see Germany again? It certainly hadn't appeared that she was doing so as part of some ploy of Lerup's. Or was Ben missing something? He had to be careful – but he also had to believe that whatever Lucy was thinking now, however angry she was, solving the murder would mean everything could be forgiven and put right.

'Thank God we're here,' said Anna, unmistakeable relief in her voice. The plane had slowed, the engine note easing as they started to taxi towards the apron.

He looked at her quizzically.

'I hate flying,' she said, vehemently. 'It just doesn't seem natural.'

'I would never have known, you're very calm,' he told her.

'I'm like the swan – serene on the surface, paddling frantically out of sight,' she replied, as the plane came to a halt outside a brightly lit building. Around them the passengers started to get up, stretching, shuffling, waiting for the door to open. 'I must confess to feeling quite tired now,' she added.

He nodded, massaging his neck. 'I didn't sleep well last night either.'

'We'll be on the train in a jiffy. I've arranged for a car to meet us and take us straight to the station. It's only about twenty minutes.'

He nodded – *I can't fault the organisation*, he thought, as they filed off the plane into the dark night.

They were met by an officious man with a military bearing and a uniform to match – Ben presumed he was a customs officer. After presenting their passports, Anna fielded his questions in German. Ben understood only the tone of the exchange, which was pleasant enough, and soon they were making their way across the concrete. Their luggage followed after them on a trolley, pushed by a man in another, rather plainer, uniform. Flags snapped and fluttered in the breeze above him, black crosses on a white background with a red surround. The chill wind plucked at his trouser legs and overcoat. *Swastikas,* he thought. He hadn't expected to see them like this – but there they were, and plenty of them. It left no doubt about who was running Cologne airfield in the recently re-militarised Rhineland.

The car was a big black Mercedes Benz saloon, a model he didn't recognise in the dark. The driver held the door for them; Anna stepped inside and he followed her. The warm interior had a strong smell of new leather. Ben sank back into the seat. He heard the thump as the luggage was put in the boot behind them, then the driver got in and they were away. The car bumped off the airfield and onto an access road, quickly leaving the lights behind and heading towards the glow of the city in the distance. He watched the rural darkness slide by – he had an idea, something that might help appease Lucy. It was a question of how best to put it to Anna.

By the time he finally spoke, the first feeble street lights had just begun to appear around them as they entered the city. 'I was thinking ...'

She was searching in her quilted Chanel handbag. 'You were thinking?' There was a teasing quality in her voice.

'I was thinking about how we would ship the new parts back to England. Does Mr Dunwood want us to travel with them?'

'Yes, I'm sure he does.' She rustled in the handbag, holding it up to the weak light.

'It's going to be very heavy, it's possible they won't let us take it on the plane as luggage – and even if they do, it will be very expensive. It will be a lot cheaper to ship it by sea.'

The rustling stopped. 'I wouldn't worry too much about the cost – the only thing is to get the parts back in time.'

'But that's exactly it.' He leaned forward. 'We could

get one of the Hamble fishing boats to come over and pick it up from a North Sea port – Emden perhaps. We could meet them there, take the equipment up on a train.'

She was still for a moment, looking at him. He saw her in the flashes of overhead light from the street lamps. Her face was just shadows and shapes, and he couldn't detect her expression. Was it interest, disapproval, disappointment? It would cut short their time in Munich and lengthen the trip home. But if she'd agree, then there was a good chance that Lucy would hear about it, and perhaps not think quite so badly of him. It meant work and money for a couple of the fishermen. It was a gesture, not much, but better than nothing.

'That's a good idea,' she said. 'We'd be able to travel right through Germany, south to north, we'd see the whole country, and they have a wonderful railway system here. The *Luxus Zug* express service is quite a treat ... and the boat could take everything straight to the *May*, how clever. They said you were a bright one, Ben Clayton.'

'You won't have much time to visit friends,' he replied. *Who said I was a bright one*, he thought, *who have you talked to about me?*

'That's true,' she said, a little wistfully, 'but I like the idea of travelling by train with you, it will be an adventure.'

'Emden would be the closest port for the fishing boat to reach,' he said. Emden – right in the middle of the *Riddle of the Sands* country that he had always wanted to see.

'That sounds perfectly fine,' replied Anna. 'We can get the train to Bremen or Hamburg from there and fly home, or even get a ferry.' Her excitement at the notion of not having to fly again was now evident in her voice. 'Actually, it's a wonderful idea – I shall start looking into it first thing tomorrow morning.'

'And we can telegraph Hamble?'

'Perhaps even tonight, I shall ask at the station.'

'That's marvellous, thank you for everything,' he said, as the car drew to a halt in a broad, open square. Ahead and to their right a Gothic cathedral soared into the air; on their left was a wall of stone and glass adorned with towers and a broad entrance that must belong to the railway station.

'I'm here to look after it all,' replied Anna.

'Yes, but ... it's been so efficient.'

'It's really no trouble,' she replied, leaning forward to touch him on the forearm, head tilted slightly to one side. 'Quite the opposite, in fact,' she added, with a quick radiant smile. Then the driver opened her door; she eased back, pulled some Reichsmark notes from her handbag and got out.

Ben stretched quickly, like a dog rising for a long-awaited walk, as the luggage was transferred once again, this time from the train back into the boot of another big black Mercedes. Anna was talking to the driver, and Ben hesitated on the other side of the car. It was good to be out in the open for a few minutes – another beautiful day of clear skies and weak morning sunshine, with the same cold wind snapping at the flags here in Munich as back in Cologne. He had fallen into the comfortable bed in his cabin on the train, and slept through the steward's knock at the door to warn him of breakfast. When he finally responded to more energetic efforts to wake him, it was so close to Munich that he barely had time to dress. He was now much in need of a bath, a shave and something to eat. Hopefully, that was next on the agenda, as Anna continued to smoothly administer the journey for them like the Red Sea parting for Moses.

The driver closed the door on Anna as Ben slid into the car beside her. She smiled. 'I didn't see you at breakfast.'

'I slept through it,' he replied, a little sheepishly.

'I know a great spot for coffee and sausages, we shall go there as soon as we've checked in at the hotel.' The car jerked into motion, sweeping into a turn in the broad square in front of the station. 'But tonight is the real treat,' continued Anna, 'we are staying at the Vier Jahreszeiten, and the restaurant is presided over by the magnificent Alfred Walterspiel, one of the finest chefs in Europe. People visit Munich just to have a meal there, and we have a good table booked. I still have some connections in this city, and Mr Dunwood kindly gave me plenty of money for our expenses,' she continued. 'We can't be sent traipsing around Europe at short notice and not have a few comforts, can we?'

'No, of course not ...'

'Just leave everything to me,' she said, 'I'm telling everyone that you are a brilliant and famous British engineer and I am your assistant. People are much more impressed by engineers here in Germany than they are at home; they wouldn't expect you to trouble yourself with such trifles as taxis, restaurants and money.'

He smiled at the image: this beautiful sophisticated woman as his assistant, catering for his every whim. It was something he could get used to, he thought, watching as she delved into her handbag. She flipped open a plain silver case. 'Cigarette?'

'Er ...' He tapped his pockets. 'Yes, thanks – sorry, I'm out again.' And now would have been a good moment to flourish a lighter, if only he'd had one. She lit both cigarettes. He twisted to exhale away from her. The wide perfectly kept boulevard was lined with elegant buildings – baroque, Gothic, classical styles – but all appeared to be relatively recent; this was a modern city.

'Those are the courts,' she said, following his gaze.

He nodded to acknowledge her comment. 'The flags, they're everywhere,' he said.

'This is the Nazis' spiritual home and they like to make a show,' she told him. 'It's very beguiling – when you see the torchlight parades, the flags and the lighting effects, the slogans and salutes. The year before we left there was a pageant called the Night of the Amazons, part of a big horse race; you should have seen it – semi-nude gold-painted women on horseback.'

'Semi-nude women,' he said, 'on horseback, how terribly cultured.'

She laughed, the smoke spilling from her mouth. 'Nudity is all the rage over here.'

'Really?' he replied – was she pulling his leg?

'Oh yes, madly, we all used to go to a marvellous little holiday town by a lake, and no one had a stitch on. It's considered quite the thing for health, *Nacktkultur* they call it. If there was a little more time, I could take you out there.'

His mental image was all too vivid. 'I'm sure it would be a most bracing distraction at this time of year,' he said.

Her quick laugh was very sexy. 'I went with my family, everyone does, we all had these little cottages – but father wouldn't allow me to bring boys ...' The last was accompanied by a light touch of her hand on his knee.

'I'm sure that was a terrible disappointment for them, but quite correct of your father – they're dreadful troublemakers, nude boys.' He turned to look out of the window, seeking safer territory. 'Where are we?' he asked. They were traversing a busy square, their taxi weaving between trams under the ramparts of another huge Gothic building.

'This is the Marien-Platz, the centre of the old town, and that's the new town hall,' said Anna, the humour still in her voice. 'We're nearly at the hotel.'

Under the awnings, shoppers thronged the busy pavements. Some of the people were clearly wealthy – he noted their furs, jewels, impeccably styled overcoats, polished shoes and crisply angled hats. But there was also a double amputee with a tray of matches for sale, a dog dragging his owner along in a wheelchair, a cart filled with scrap iron being pulled by a skeletal pony, shoeshine stands, women selling flowers, and amongst them all, beggars and tramps. You might see such things in any European city, especially those whose men had fought in the Great War. But he felt it was different to London – the tailoring and the hats people wore, the bearing of the wealthy, and there was something else. What was it?

Before he could identify it, Anna touched his elbow and then pointed. 'That's where we're having *Weisswurst*, the Franziskaner,' she said. He caught a glimpse of people crowding into a late-medieval building. 'They do the most divine veal sausages,' she continued, glancing at her watch. She gave him a big smile. 'We shall be just in time, it's absolutely forbidden to eat *Weisswurst* after midday – and the freshest and finest are served about an hour before that.'

'Midday?'

'Seriously – the Germans insist those little sausages don't see the clock strike twelve.'

Then the car turned right. 'This is the Maximilianstrasse,' Anna told him, 'the hotel is just down here on the left.' They pulled up outside the deep arches of the Vier Jahreszeiten. The door opened, and Anna got out and took a couple of steps onto the pavement before she turned and watched him follow her. 'Welcome to Munich,' she said, with a little curtsey.

He smiled, and she led the way under the arches into the muted glow of the lobby.

As Anna approached the front desk, the receptionist nodded and saluted. 'Heil Hitler,' he said.

'Heil Hitler,' responded Anna, with a more perfunctory raise of the hand, before continuing in German.

He gazed around the lobby, panelled in dark wood, with soft light falling like mist from a glass cupola. There were two other people there, both men. They lounged on the sofas, black boots up on the coffee table, smoking from long cigarette holders – watching. Uniforms. That was it. That was the difference. There were a lot more uniforms around than you'd see in London. These two men were in black with plenty of silver embroidery. And when Ben returned the stares, one of them held his gaze for a long while, before finally smiling sardonically and turning away to talk to his colleague.

'Here we are,' said Anna, and held out a key. 'Second floor, it's a suite, and I think you'll like it. I'm just down the corridor. Let's freshen up and meet back here in half an hour, and we'll go in search of *Weisswurst*.'

'That sounds splendid, what about my luggage?'

'It's probably already in your room.'

She was right. The suite consisted of four rooms. Ben wandered from the dining area to a lounge, and then to the bedroom. Each was lavishly decorated with a stylish modernism – but what did you expect in the home of Bauhaus? He tried out the tubular-steel-and-leather dining chairs, flopped onto the matching sofa and had a gentle exploratory bounce on the vast bed, all chrome and curves. He felt the gorgeous softness of the linen sheets, his slow smile widening to a grin of satisfaction.

In the bathroom there was a tub the size of a small swimming pool, with gold taps the colour of a clear spring sunrise over the Hamble River. He turned one on and hot water flowed smoothly out. At home it would be spitting like a sixty-a-day smoker clearing his lungs. He ran a good deep bath, and gingerly started to pull the jacket off his aching body. He would shave and spruce up as best he could. As he stripped and lowered himself into the wonderful hot water, he felt a lot less anxious than before. Her light, teasing mood was infectious and friendly, and he started to think that he might just get the information about Spink and Lerup that he needed from Anna.

Chapter 23

Lucy felt chill damp air on her neck as the door slammed shut behind her. The policeman turned the key in the lock with a harsh metallic clacking. Then he motioned for her to walk ahead of him. She started down the long corridor, her basket clasped tight in front of her. There was a smell of mouldering blankets, human sweat and shit. Halfway down the corridor a single naked bulb did little to push back the gloom. There would be rats as big as dogs down here, she thought. Well, small dogs, anyway.

'Here,' muttered the policeman, and pulled up. More clanking of a key in a lock, and the door opened.

Lucy peered into the unlit cell, the light from the corridor barely illuminating the inside. She recoiled from the virulent smell of an open latrine. 'Dad?' She saw a shape move on the bunk, huddled under a blanket, a head lifting, slow and jerky.

'Lucy?' came his voice.

She stepped into the cell, the policeman following her until she hesitated. 'Officer, please may I see him alone?' she asked. She could feel his eyes on her, conscious of the close-fitting dress and jacket that she had chosen. She'd had to look as good as she could to talk her way in here.

'Sorry, miss, I can't leave you unattended with the prisoner,' he mumbled, but there was a hint of genuineness about the apology.

'Oh please, officer, just a few minutes.' Lucy gave those seven words everything she had, and was duly rewarded.

His nose wrinkled. 'Ten minutes, I'll be by the door.' He stepped into the corridor, leaving the door ajar. Lucy smiled gratefully.

Her father was sitting up now. Holding out the basket, she stepped forward. 'I brought you some food,' she said. Joe didn't reply, and she put it on the bunk beside him and sat the other side of it. They looked at each other. Lucy could feel her throat tightening. She bit her lip. She was shocked by how small and frail he looked.

Joe examined the contents of the basket and pulled out a pasty. 'I didn't do it,' he said, chewing the first mouthful.

'I know,' replied Lucy, 'but who did?'

Joe glanced at the policeman, who was leaning against the door jamb, staring down the corridor. 'I don't know,' he replied.

'But ... they can't keep you in here when you didn't do it.' She was looking at her hands in her lap, her eyes slowly getting accustomed to the poor light.

'Nothing to be done about it.' Kirk bit another chunk off the pasty. 'Even if I did know, I wouldn't tell the bogeys. There's no other way if a man's going to face his friends afterwards. Don't you worry about it, those who deserve it will get their comeuppance,' he added, his brow set with some of his old belligerence.

She glanced around the cell – a piss pot, a bunk, a blanket, dark red glazed tiles and that door. She shivered; the cold and damp were going straight to her bones.

'My hearing is later today,' said Joe, through another mouthful. He ate as though he were starving.

'Will they give you bail?' she asked. She had to get him out of here.

'Bail? It would take more than we have – and you and Tom need the money to feed yourselves.' He hesitated. 'How much is left?'

'Enough for a couple of weeks at the most.' She could hear the tremor in her voice.

'Christ.' Joe's stoicism faltered, the pasty dropped to his lap, the chewing slowed as though the mouthful had dried to sawdust.

In the silence, Lucy pulled a flask out of her basket and poured her father a cup of tea. Gratefully, he took a few mouthfuls, and then started to finish the pasty. It was a while longer before Lucy had herself under enough control to speak. 'The only way out of this is to prove that Stanley Arbethwaite's death wasn't an accident,' she said. 'Then Mr Dunwood might listen to our side of the story. Did you manage to talk to any of the yard men before they arrested you?'

'Yes, I did.'

'What did they say?' asked Lucy.

'I talked to old Horace Jack, the night watchman.'

'And?' she asked, handing him an apple as he finished the pasty.

'Horace was there the night before Stanley died' – Joe rubbed the apple on his shirt – 'and he said the only people he saw were Lerup and his fancy girlfriend. They turned up in the middle of the night. They'd had some sauce and told Horace they were going to christen the boat.' He took a crisp bite from the apple.

'What did they mean by that?' asked Lucy.

Her father raised his eyebrows, gave her a meaningful look.

'Oh,' she said, as it dawned on her. *That slut's gone off to Germany with my Ben.* She clutched at the bunk, cold hard stone beneath her fingers.

'No one is going to believe Lerup did it,' said Joe. He slurped at the tea.

'But Lerup is the one who wouldn't believe you. He caused all this,' she hissed at him.

Joe looked at her thoughtfully, chewing the apple.

'Why would Lerup want to kill Mr Arbethwaite?'

Lucy could tell her dad about Stanley's debts, about the club, about Spink – but the policeman might hear it. And Ben had asked her to tell no one. She realised that despite it all, she wasn't going to let him down. She really hadn't given up on him.

'Time's up,' said the policeman, with a self-conscious look at his watch.

'That's not ten minutes,' said Lucy.

''Fraid so, miss.'

Lucy and her father stared sombrely at one another. 'We'll pull the cloth out of the basket and wrap the rest of the food in it,' she said, starting on the task. Tears were pricking at her eyes, and she forced herself to be practical. 'You can eat it later. Keep the flask, there's more tea in there. We've got another, I'll bring it tomorrow and swap it. There's a blanket under here for you too, and I brought your book.' She set the food on the bunk with the copy of Orwell's *Down and Out in Paris and London.*

Her father pulled the blanket out of the basket. The door creaked as the policeman impatiently opened it a little further.

'Looks like I've got to go,' she said, standing. 'I'll be back tomorrow.'

'You'll be all right. Do you know who to go to in the village if you have any trouble?' he asked, concern in every line of his weathered face.

'Albert Parks has already been round and offered his services,' she said.

Joe looked at her, curiosity overcoming the worry. 'Has he now.' He hesitated. 'What happened when you talked to Ben Clayton?'

'I haven't. Dunwood sent him to Germany yesterday to get the parts for the *May*.'

'Oh ...' Joe stood up, the blanket wrapped around him like a shawl.

But that's only the half of it, she thought, *if you knew about our engagement, and Lerup's girl ...* She stepped towards him and he opened the blanket out and wrapped it around her in a hug, his beard rough against her face.

'It's going to be all right, Lucy,' he whispered, 'just you look after Tom, and I'll be out of here before you know it.'

Lucy choked back the tears, heard the policeman shuffling impatiently outside.

'Miss?'

She didn't trust herself to say anything; she broke away and stepped through the door, which started to shut behind her. She waved, catching a last glimpse of him by the bunk, the apple still in his right hand. The door clanked shut with an ugly finality. *That was my father, old and vulnerable.* How could this be? She clutched her hand to her mouth and hurried up the corridor, the policeman a couple of paces behind her. They arrived at the outer door, and he stepped past her to open it.

'When are you going to let him out of there to empty the bucket?' she whispered, as the door opened.

'Soon as I've got rid of you, miss, so you come right along.' He waved her out and into the brighter hallway that led to the rest of the police station.

Lucy had one last chance to look down the gloomy corridor to where her father was imprisoned. 'I'll get you out of there, Dad,' she whispered, with a fierce determination.

Ben looked at himself critically in the mirror. Anna set a high standard, and he didn't want to feel shabby beside her. He ran his hands across his face – shaving in the endless hot water of the bathroom had been so different to the hurried scrape across cold rough skin that he suffered at Mrs Arbethwaite's. His shirt too had been warm and comfortable when he'd put it on, not damp and chilly as it would have been in his attic room. It was as though someone had stretched out summer so it lasted all year long – blissful. Gingerly, he reached out and touched the bruise on his head, and winced at the little throb of pain. But the lump had gone down significantly, and he would be able to take the wrap of bandage off soon – it was starting to look grubby. He gently stretched onto his toes; the hot water had soaked out the aches, and he felt almost normal. Adrenaline would have to get him through the rest, he thought, as he adjusted his tie and smoothed it into his jacket. His best suit wasn't too bad, even if it wasn't Savile Row tailoring. He glanced at his watch. He was due to meet Anna downstairs in a couple of minutes. He picked up his overcoat, hat and gloves and headed for the lobby.

Anna was waiting for him, looking like a princess from the Russian Steppes in a dark fur coat and hat lit up by discreet diamond earrings. 'How smart you look,' she said, as he approached, 'although you could do with a haircut ...'

He pushed at the fringe that flopped over the bandage and remembered Lucy with a pang of longing. 'You're not the first to notice,' he said.

'I've spoken to the people at M.A.N. and they've agreed to see us this afternoon. The hotel is organising a car, and we leave at twelve thirty. So we still have time for sausages, not too many though' – she tapped him lightly on the arm with her black leather gloves – 'you must save your appetite for tonight's feast.'

'That sounds terrific.' He hesitated. 'Has there been any word from Captain Emerton?' They had sent a telegram from the station office before boarding the train in Cologne. It had asked the Captain to prepare for a voyage to Emden to pick up an urgent cargo. *Name your price*, it had said, and asked him to let them know his earliest time of arrival, by return.

'No message yet,' she replied, 'but we should give him a little longer, we're an hour ahead here.'

'Of course.'

She was setting off towards the door when he said, 'Would it be possible to find out about the train times going north?'

'Of course, yes, that's a good idea.' She spoke swiftly in German to the concierge, who sported a heavy waxed moustache and a lugubrious cast to his bushy eyebrows. 'I've asked him,' she explained to Ben as they resumed the walk across the foyer, 'and he says he'll have them for us when we come back for the car.'

'They're amazing, these people,' he said, shaking his head.

'No, it's their job, we pay them a great deal of money, and in return they smooth out every detail in our lives for as long as we're here.'

He stopped again just as they reached the door. 'Wait, Anna, I need to change some sterling ...' No sooner were the words out of his mouth than he realised that he was penniless – his wallet was still empty from the robbery.

'Oh! But we don't want to waste time with that.' She looked in the Chanel handbag, and quickly offered him a handful of notes and change, silver marks and bronze pfennigs. 'One Reichsmark is worth about a shilling.'

Ben hesitated, trying to mitigate the embarrassment of having to accept.

'Don't be silly, you're here in Mr Dunwood's employ.'

'Thank you,' he said, stuffing the cash into his pocket.

'I hope you have gloves,' she continued. 'The weather can change fast in Munich; it's because of the mountains.' She smiled at him, dazzlingly. 'So, now we can promenade, like real Germans.'

As they emerged from the lobby, he could see the breeze ripping through the flags on the buildings opposite. It tugged at his hat as soon as they stepped out onto the pavement. It was a glorious day, with a sky of cobalt blue. He pulled his coat a little tighter, flipping up the collar. It would have been just the day for a sail, he thought – if it wasn't for the temperature. They turned right and joined the stream of people strolling along Maximilianstrasse. There was a poster for the coming Olympics in a shop window. He would love to be sailing at Kiel – but one thing at a time, perhaps in the next Olympic regatta in 1940.

All the buildings had a remarkably uniform look, nothing like the hotchpotch of styles and designs along Southampton's High Street. A bit too tidy for his liking, he thought, as Anna leaned into him and said, 'It's quiet now, but after the shops close, everyone is out, salesmen and salesgirls, clerks and managers – everyone says hello and good evening and how do you do. On Sundays, whole families come out to walk, and there are courting couples, and you should see the girls! They wear their best clothes and parade along, trying to catch the eye of a good-looking boy. There's lots of hat doffing and handshaking and chatter and gossip before they go off for a beer or a coffee.'

'I've heard all about the beer halls of Munich,' he said, with a grin.

'Oh yes, they're quite the thing, you'll see a little bit of the reason at this café today – *gemütlichkeit* they call it, it's a sort of sense of national friendliness, quite hard to translate, better to show you.' She took his arm, smiling up at him as she did so, with the guileless wide-eyed look he was coming to know well.

Then he noticed a couple coming towards them. The girl's blond hair was swept up under a wide-brimmed black felt hat. She wore a matching snug black sweater jacket and very little make-up. Ben glanced at the man she was with. He had a uniform cap with a skull insignia like the two men who'd been in the lobby the previous night. He was scowling, dark eyes beady, clouded. At first, Ben thought the man was angry with him, as if he had caught him looking at his girl for too long. But then he realised that it was Anna whom the man was scowling at. And for a second, Ben thought he was going to spit at them. He tensed quickly with a rush of adrenaline – no one was going to insult a girl on his arm – but then, they were past and nothing had happened.

Ben walked another ten paces, wondering if he'd

imagined it. But other people around them had slowed down or sped up, whatever took them furthest from the confrontation. Or had he just imagined that as well? But Anna's reaction had been real enough – a turn of the cheek, a little falter in the step and the tension on his arm tightening. He cleared his throat. 'That man we just passed, the one wearing the black leather overcoat, with the blond girl – did you see his cap? There were two men in the hotel lobby last night wearing a uniform like that. Who are they?'

Anna leaned into him again. 'They're SS, or perhaps Gestapo, Hitler's bodyguards and secret police. You must be very polite and careful when they are around. They have almost limitless power.'

Ben glanced over his shoulder; the couple was lost in the crowd, but there were others, he realised, the black-and-silver caps and leather overcoats, and lots of grey uniform greatcoats – his impression of the night before was accurate. But what, exactly, did they have against Anna?

'Here we are,' she said.

Inside the Franziskaner it was warm with a fug of cigar, cigarette and pipe smokes. He unbuttoned his overcoat. Long tables stretched away. Many of the benches were filled with young men, singing. They drank big glasses of a light-coloured beer – and they were eating sausages. Anna led him through the crowds until she found a table a little less cramped than the others, with more of a mix of people, including some women. Some of the older men were sporting grey whiskers and the Bavarian chamois-skin breeches with embroidered braces. There were other more distinguished-looking gentlemen, who might have been academics, with dark softly cut suits.

There was a polite ripple along the table, as everyone shuffled up to make more room for them to sit. The beer glasses and sausage plates, the homburgs and the green velour hats of the Tyrol were all moved a few inches along the bench to accompany their owners. Then there were enquiries of the new arrivals. Anna replied in German, before asking in English if anyone spoke that language. There were blank looks, so she smiled disarmingly, went back to German and explained that Ben was new to their country and had not yet had a chance to learn the language. There were nods and smiles, and much fuss was made of getting a waiter for the guests. Anna placed their order and a cheer went up, because – as she also explained to Ben – they had ordered *Weisswurst* and must, therefore, be good fellows.

Finally, things settled enough for Ben to get a word in. 'They're very friendly,' he said, leaning close to her. He felt more relaxed now they were inside, the fight-or-flight reflex provoked by the near confrontation on the street ebbing away.

'This' – Anna waved expansively around the café, at the singing, at a toast being proposed, at the eager chatter up and down and between the tables – 'is *gemütlichkeit*. Many of these people won't have met before – and you see how the classes mix.' She leaned towards him, their faces almost touching. 'It's very important when the sausages arrive that you do it right, Ben. Otherwise you will lose us all the credit we've gained for ordering them – don't use the knife and fork, eat it with your fingers and put a good layer of mustard on first. Then they'll know you're one of them.'

'All right.' He smiled.

They both sat back, the moment of intimacy fading. He nodded towards one of the big tables of young men. 'Don't they have any work to do?' he asked.

'Many of them are students – some will be intellectuals, professors, writers, and there'll be a few peasants who have come into town for a market.'

He nodded. That made sense – the atmosphere was nothing like the quiet reserve of most English pubs of his experience. The closest equivalent would be a college bar on a Saturday after a rugby game.

'A couple of years ago you could come in here and the students would all be wearing their corporation caps and sashes,' went on Anna. 'That was very colourful.'

'Corporations?'

'A bit like our college houses – although German university corps are more like American fraternities. A group of them were getting drunk, just like this, in a Heidelberg tavern, when someone got up and questioned Hitler's knowledge of the correct etiquette for eating asparagus.' She smiled. Ben didn't know the right way to eat asparagus either, but he had a feeling that Anna did. 'The insult didn't go down well,' she continued, 'and the corps were banned. But the tradition goes on, even if it isn't so open.'

Ben looked around him more curiously. So was that what it meant to live with fascism? You can't be mildly rude about the Prime Minister? It wouldn't last long in England, he thought. 'How long did you say you lived here?' he asked.

'Nearly four years in Germany, and that's the thing, you see, once the Kaiser had gone it just unleashed this huge wave of new thinking. When I first got here we lived in Berlin for a year, and the atmosphere was so different – the modern attitudes, the art and literature, Bauhaus – there was none of the stuffiness of England. It was more liberated even than Paris, never mind London. You could go to a restaurant and strangers would come up, introduce themselves and ask for a dance, and it was all considered perfectly proper. But when we moved down here to Munich, we found it was much more conservative – and home to the Nazis.'

'That fellow this morning, what did you call him?'

'Gestapo.' Anna glanced up the table as she spoke. But no one was paying any attention to them now.

'He didn't seem exactly friendly – is that resentment from the Great War?'

Anna gave him a quick wry smile. 'No,' she said, leaning a little closer again, 'the Nazis don't like the Jews.'

Ben nodded. 'And you're Jewish?' he asked.

'My father's half Italian, and my mother's half Jewish,

but she repeated the sins of her mother and married a Catholic. So she hasn't had much to do with the Jewish side of her family. I just look Jewish, and that's what he didn't like. But they held the Winter Olympics near here at Garmisch-Partenkirchen a month ago, and with the Summer Games still to come in Berlin and so many foreign visitors around, I suspect that they are on their best behaviour.' She pulled her cigarettes out of her handbag, offered one to Ben and then quickly lit both. 'A year ago he would have spat on me,' she added, matter-of-factly.

Ben was silent for a moment, wondering what would have happened if his reaction to that event had actually been tested. And then he said, 'I've never understood quite what it was that the Nazis have against the Jews.'

'Apart from their virulent anti-Semitism?' She smiled, disarmingly. 'In his speeches, Hitler blames the Jews for Germany losing the Great War. The Nazis want people to think that it was the unrest at home in 1918 – behind the front, back in Germany – that brought about the country's surrender, and they identify that unrest with Bolshevik agitation, led by the Jews ...' She stopped as the waiter arrived with their food. They stubbed out the cigarettes as he put down a plate of *Weisswurst* between them, and a small glass of beer for each of them. Ben glanced up the table – everyone was watching them, the conversation hushed. So he pulled the spoon out of the mustard pot, smeared a long drizzle down the length of the sausage, then picked it up with his fingers and took a good-sized bite. There was a ripple of nods and satisfied approval. He had passed the test.

'What do you think?' asked Anna, as he swallowed his first mouthful.

'Excellent,' he replied.

'Bottoms up,' she said, and they toasted each other.

He took his first sip; it was different, not just in colour but in taste.

'All right?' asked Anna. 'Perhaps I should have got

you the *Dunkles*, the dark beer.'

'No, no, this is fine, really,' and he took another, bigger, swig, and then nodded his approval. 'So you came to live out here with your parents?' he asked.

'That's right, I'd just come down from Oxford when Daddy got offered the job. It seemed like a good opportunity to learn German.'

'You were at Oxford?' He realised that too much of his surprise had strayed into his voice. 'I'm sorry ...'

She smiled, the teasing glitter back in her eyes. 'Somerville College, reading PPE.'

He managed to keep his face straight this time, thinking, *bloody hell – Politics, Philosophy and Economics ... degrees didn't get much more elite.* The society girl worried about her picture in *Tatler* had come into focus as someone to be taken much more seriously. 'Very impressive,' he murmured, wondering what class of degree she had got, but knowing it would be too crass to ask. 'So did you go back to England because of how the Jews are being treated here?'

'No, my father's job came to an end, and his next post was back in England.' She paused for a moment to take another quick, tiny bite of sausage. She had nothing like Lucy's hearty appetite, he noticed with disapproval. 'But I think some of the Jews are leaving,' she went on. 'The Nazis are *encouraging* emigration. I heard that they're even working with the Zionist organisations to smuggle them into Palestine. But I fear most of the Jews believe that everything will be fine, that the anti-Semitism will die down, that they're good Germans – they have a stake here and don't want to leave.' Her eyes flickered over his face. 'What would you do, if you were them?'

He hesitated, sausage halfway to his mouth. What he'd seen so far of Nazism had just reinforced earlier beliefs from his newspaper reading in England. He remembered the little sailing cruiser struggling up the River Hamble, with the Jewish couple and everything they owned on board. 'If I wasn't strong enough to fight it, then I'd get out –

people shouldn't have to live like this,' he said.

She nodded slowly, a more thoughtful, knowing smile emerging.

He glanced at his watch. 'We must eat up. We have to get back to the hotel,' he said. They finished up the sausages and beer, paid the bill, wished their new friends 'auf wiedersehen' and left. Despite the friendliness of the Franziskaner, some tension from the earlier incident stayed with him on the walk back. It was like crossing a school courtyard when you knew you were the one the bullies were going to pick on.

'I'll see if there are any messages,' said Anna, as they entered the lobby, and she let go of his arm and headed to the desk. He watched her take a piece of paper from the girl at reception and read it as she walked back towards him. 'Captain Emerton says he can be there on Wednesday around midday, if he leaves this afternoon. And the price he's asking seems very cheap, don't you think?' She handed the paper over as she spoke, so he could see for himself.

He scanned the lines, nodding. 'Very reasonable – and it would give them time to get back to Gosport and leave us with most of Friday to fit the engine parts,' he said, looking up. 'We should telegraph him to depart as soon as possible.'

'Don't you think we should wait to check that we can get the parts?' she enquired, with a slight arch of the perfect eyebrows.

'Yes, I suppose so,' he replied, a little unwillingly. 'But we should tell him to get ready at least, and stand by for further instructions.'

'Good idea – and we must check on the trains.' Anna was already moving towards the concierge's desk and Ben followed her. Another piece of paper was handed over, and she frowned with concentration as she examined it. 'The most direct route will take eighteen hours – so we can easily get there before Wednesday.' She looked up. 'We even have time to stop, maybe in Hanover?'

'I was wondering about having a look around the

Emden area, I believe there's some wonderful country around the Frisian Islands ...'

'Oh?' she asked, looking up at him curiously, encouraging him to go on.

'It's just that, well, I read *Riddle of the Sands* when I was a child, and perhaps it was something to do with where I grew up, but the sailing caught my imagination, and I've always wanted to see those places.'

She looked at him in surprise, and then she started to laugh. He was startled – but Anna stopped instantly. She reached out a hand, touched him on the arm, contrite. 'It's nothing to be embarrassed about, that's not why I was laughing ...' She hesitated for a moment. 'My father loves that book, it's quite a coincidence. And I understand the islands are beautiful ...' And then came the smile. 'I'd love to do that – we'll go straight up there and have a look around while we wait for the Captain on Wednesday.'

Chapter 24

Lucy trudged down Hamble High Street on her return from Gosport. She was struggling to hold back tears, her thoughts as captive as her father in his cell. She was convinced that Lerup and his woman were involved in Stanley's death, convinced that Ben was in danger, and convinced that he held the key to freeing her father. She stumbled over a pothole and grabbed at the wall of the butcher's, then slumped against it in her misery. She heard the bell clink on the door, caught a whiff of blood and sawdust. She wiped at her face with her sleeve. She was a mess. She couldn't let people see her like this. She had to get home. Blindly, she pushed off the wall and bumped straight into a solid figure.

'Easy there, Lucy. Are you all right?'

She looked up at the sound of the familiar voice, dabbing at her eyes. It was Captain Emerton. 'I will be in a minute,' she said.

'You don't look all right. I heard what happened to your dad. I'm right sorry, I blame myself. We should have just knuckled under like we always do, but your dad was so keen to make a fight of it, and I agreed with him at the time ...'

'It's not your fault, Captain Emerton, don't blame yourself. It was just seeing him in prison upset me ...' She could feel the tears welling again, tried blinking them back.

'I'm putting to sea this afternoon, so I can't stop,' Emerton told her softly. 'I've got provisions and diesel to get, and I need to find a deckie – all for that job I got from your Ben.'

'Ben? What job?' she exclaimed.

'I thought you'd know all about it. He's in Germany. I'm going to Emden to pick up some parts for him.'

'Emden?' she said, the blood starting to drum in her ears.

'That's right, I've got a feeling it's for Dunwood. But I don't mind, I charged him a good price, it ought to get me through a few weeks till I can find work.'

'Emden,' she repeated – if the crashing in her head would stop, she might remember why that was familiar. 'Where's Emden?'

'At the mouth of the Ems, just inside the East Frisian Islands,' replied Emerton.

Riddle of the Sands, she thought, instantly. Thank God she'd finally read that book a couple of months previously. 'So you're going to meet Ben in Emden, and you're leaving today?' she asked.

'I don't know if we're meeting Ben or not. I'm waiting for final instructions.' He pulled a telegram out of the top pocket of his blue seaman's coat. 'It says to get ready to put to sea. It's from a hotel in Munich.' He offered it.

Lucy studied the message. Emden. It was too much of a coincidence – hadn't he told her that he would take her there? Perhaps he was in trouble. This could be a cry for help. 'I'm coming with you,' she said.

'What?'

'You said you needed a deckie,' she replied.

'What about your father in jail? And Tom?'

She looked at him for a moment – she would have to tell him, it was only fair. 'I think Ben's in some kind of difficulty,' she blurted out. 'I think that's why he wants you to meet him at Emden – this is a kind of message.' She waved the telegram. 'I'm supposed to understand it – it's a private thing. It's to do with Stanley's murder.'

Captain Emerton was silent for a long moment, and then he gently took the paper from her. 'You sure you're all right, Miss Lucy? That does sound a bit ...' He hesitated. '... unusual, don't you think? I mean, how would he know that I'd show it to you?'

She shifted agitatedly; it was a good point, but still, she had a feeling about it, and she was sure. 'Please, I'm not mad, you have to understand. Ben and I were investigating the murder, there's a lot I still can't tell you, not until we get it all straightened out, but you have to trust me, please, Captain, please.' She saw him wilt a little. 'If I'm wrong and it's just an ordinary trip, then you need a deckie anyway. And I could really use the money, with Dad in jail.'

Emerton pushed his cap back on his head and scratched at his forehead, then pulled the remains of a roll-up from behind his ear, put it in his mouth and patted his pockets till he came up with some matches. It wasn't until it was alight and he'd taken the first couple of puffs that he finally said, 'All right, but what about your dad, and Tom?'

'Albert Parks can get a message to Dad. And I'm sure I can find someone to have Tom.'

Emerton sucked deeply on the roll-up until it was down to his fingers. Then he dropped it on the floor and stepped on it decisively. 'My missus'll look after Tom, she'd love to have him. You bring him by the house straight after school. Bring your seabag too, and we'll be down to the boat and on our way, if I get the go-ahead from Germany. In the meantime, if you've got a minute, you can help me get ready, there're some stores I need fetching.'

'That's just ... just bloody brilliant, Captain Emerton,' she said, almost overwhelmed. 'This will work out all right, it really will.'

At twelve thirty, Ben and Anna walked out of the hotel to wait by the kerb. The car was on its way round to pick them up for the journey out to the M.A.N. factory. The breeze chased a loose sheet of newspaper down the street, and he gently pushed his hat a little harder onto his head. His bones had started to throb, and he'd had to ask the concierge for an aspirin to help his headache. Then he heard the sound of marching. A unit of black-booted, brown-shirted, swastika-flag-waving men came into view. He watched, intrigued, as they got closer – the leather-cross-belt, tie, breeches and riding boots gave the marchers a military look. There was a tug at his arm; he looked at Anna.

'Salute!' she whispered. 'It's the SA, the storm troopers, salute the flag, like me, now,' and she raised her hand in a straight-arm salute.

'Really?' he said. 'What – these characters?' He and Anna were foreigners, strangers here, and he wouldn't salute the army or the police at home, never mind a political party ...

'Do it.' She started to lift his arm.

He began to resist, something about it just didn't seem right, but then he realised that everyone else on the street was stopping to salute. If he hadn't been so astonished, he'd have laughed – but several of the marchers were looking at them with the same ugly expressions he'd seen on the face of the Gestapo officer earlier. A couple of them even exchanged looks and made ready to break step. They were twenty yards away now and he had a sudden intimation of real danger. The tension he'd felt that morning condensed into a visible threat as Anna hauled at his arm.

'You can't do anything for Dunwood in the hospital or jail,' she hissed.

And he gave way, raising his arm and staring fixedly into the middle distance, over the heads of the marching storm troopers, above the grand buildings with their swastika flags, and up into the clear blue sky. The unit passed at the bottom of his peripheral vision. And a moment later the car pulled up in front of them. Anna didn't wait for the driver to open the door, she did it herself and Ben followed her inside.

They sat in silence as the car pulled off, overtaking the storm troopers. He turned away from them to look at Anna, who was digging in her handbag. She came up with her cigarettes, and glanced at him.

'Yes, please,' he said.

She flipped open the case for him, took one herself and lit both.

Then he said, 'It just didn't seem right.'

Anna slid across the seat, drawing so close she was whispering in his ear. 'Keep your voice down; if the driver speaks English he might report what you say to the Gestapo.' She smiled coyly, as though this were some lover's secret, her eyebrows twitched up for a moment, then she exhaled a cloud of smoke towards the front seats.

Ben looked at the fat neck of the driver – layers bulging over the tight collar, tufts of hair missed in an uneven shave – and inhaled deeply on his cigarette.

'A couple of years ago' – Anna moved so close that he could feel her breath on his skin – 'an eminent American physician was here to advise on lung treatments. He didn't salute an SA unit as they passed him on the streets and he was beaten unconscious.'

Instinctively, he reached up and touched his forehead.

'There's no law against not saluting,' she continued, 'but the public prosecutors regard it as provocative not to – so they won't help you. Did you hear about the 'Night of the Long Knives' in England?'

'I remember the phrase, but not much else ...' he admitted.

'Hitler accused the leader of the SA, Ernst Roehm, of homosexuality. He arrested him personally and had him shot. Then Hitler purged Roehm's officers and since then, the survivors have been forced to kowtow to the SS and the Gestapo – but it means that the rest of us really *cannot* afford to be rude.'

He nodded. 'What a madhouse,' he said.

'As my German friends commented at the time, the affair did at least shed new light on Roehm's previous announcement that "out of every Hitler Youth a Storm Trooper will emerge",' replied Anna, with an ironic smile as she eased back to the other side of the car.

The chauffeur had his foot hard on the accelerator, and soon the streets gave way to fields. The car found every pothole and rut in the road in the driver's efforts to overtake everything they came upon – bicycles, oxen, horses and carts and a handful of muddy cars were all forced into the gutter. Ben could have sworn that the man was actually aiming the big Mercedes at people, using the horn to chase them onto the dusty pavements of the small towns. And he spent the journey staring out of the window with an increasingly tight knot in his stomach as the population scattered, all bundled against the cold in their layers of leather waistcoats, battered wool coats and jackets.

The fields were thinned out by houses as they came down to a river and Gothic spires rose in the distance ahead. They crossed a bridge and turned right onto an orbital road, going round the city to their left. Chimneys became visible ahead of them, and they continued beside the river towards a factory district until they turned left by another bridge. Immediately, they were faced with a muscular frontage of buildings, a towering chimney beyond. They were under the ramparts of a veritable fortress of German industrial might. Supermarine was the only place Ben had to compare it to, and that was a two-bedroom semi compared to this castle. The car pulled up outside big double doors, and Anna finally broke their silence.

'We made it,' she said.

He smiled after the long silence of the unnervingly fast journey. There were a couple of times when he'd thought that they would not make it. He got out of the car, his body aching again, and opened the door for her. They were met by a smiling man in an immaculate charcoal suit that matched a full head of grey-flecked dark hair. He clicked his heels for a low-key, 'Heil Hitler' – to which they both responded, this time without Ben having to be encouraged – and introduced himself in perfect, but accented, English as Herr Rosenfeld. They were shown into a boardroom of leather-upholstered chairs, matching leather-panelled doors and a potent smell of polish – with a traditional oak table so huge that Ben felt it would have seated most of the workforce at Supermarine. A distant hum of machinery, of production, infiltrated the calm.

Rosenfeld ordered coffee for them, and asked to see their list of parts. Ben handed it over, and by the time he was halfway through the coffee – dark and bitter in neat white cups – news was brought that they could be supplied immediately.

'Will it be possible to deliver the equipment to the railway station in Munich for tomorrow morning, perhaps by six o'clock?' asked Anna. 'You see, we're in a terrible rush, and want to take it up to Emden for our boat to collect.'

'There is some paperwork – will it be charged to the shipyard, to Camper and Nicholsons or to Herr Dunwood directly?' replied Rosenfeld, sipping his coffee.

'Camper's,' said Ben.

'Then we can deliver tomorrow morning and I will arrange the paperwork afterwards. We do a great deal of business with our English friends at Camper's and this can go through the normal channels.' Rosenfeld put his coffee cup down, stretched his long legs out and leaned back in the chair, hands folded comfortably in his lap.

'Mr Dunwood is also building a new motor yacht, and he asked me to talk to you about the engines,' replied Ben.

'I have already prepared the material,' said Rosenfeld, pushing forward a manila folder that had been lying on the boardroom table.

Ben opened it and flicked slowly through the pages of specifications and drawings. He asked a handful of questions, made some notes, but the document was very thorough and appeared to contain everything that he needed. He was impressed by the efficiency, by Rosenfeld's relaxed, polished manner. This was the kind of company he'd like to work for, he thought.

'If you have any further questions, you can always telephone me,' added Rosenfeld. 'I understand Camper's is building the new motor yacht?'

'Yes,' said Ben.

'They build everything, eh?'

'And you supply the engines,' replied Ben, swivelling his chair towards Anna with a creak of leather and wood. 'They invented the diesel engine here, at the turn of the century,' he told her, then looking back to Rosenfeld, 'and still manufacture the best-designed and built engines in the world.'

Rosenfeld smiled. 'You are too kind. We had a head start – Rudolf Diesel brought his patent to us and the rest is history. We have so many extraordinary machines from those early days.'

'Really?' said Ben, leaning forward in his seat.

'Yes, but not somewhere you can see them, though there is talk of a museum.'

'Oh.' He didn't attempt to hide his disappointment.

'But I can show you the factory, if you're interested.' Rosenfeld sat up straight as he spoke, scratched at his earlobe.

'Oh yes, please,' he said, and then looked at Anna – would she be terribly bored?

But Anna smiled generously. 'I wouldn't dream of stopping you, but there's one thing you might do for us first, Herr Rosenfeld.'

'Anything, madam,' he said, with a nod of the head.

'We would like to send a telegram, do you have the facility?'

'Of course.' He tore off the sheet he had been using and then pushed forward the notepad and Mont Blanc fountain pen in front of him. Ben took it, and wrote a short message to Captain Emerton.

When he was finished, Rosenfeld took the paper and led them down marbled corridors – more like a cathedral than a factory – turning right and left until they stopped outside an office. Rosenfeld entered to drop off the telegram. There was no pause in the clatter of typewriters as the door opened and shut. Ben and Anna stood in silence; the hallway seemed to demand it. Anna flipped open a powder compact and glanced at herself in the mirror.

'You don't mind? Looking around?' he asked, finally.

'Not at all – I didn't realise it was such a famous place for you engineers, almost holy ground.' The compact snapped shut and she tucked it back in the handbag.

'Almost,' he replied. 'It's certainly an interesting comparison with where I work.'

'Then we should both be alert, we might learn something useful,' she said, with her teasing smile.

The door opened again and Rosenfeld emerged. He held out the original note and a copy of the telegram to Ben.

'For your records – I have added some details on the back about where you will find the package tomorrow, Munich is a big station,' he said.

Ben took it, thanked Rosenfeld and slipped it into his pocket. They proceeded to the end of the corridor and a door that led outside. There they turned right, the noise building quickly, arriving at a T-junction, halfway along a road that ran between enormous factory walls. *Now we're getting down to the business end of things*, he thought, as they followed Rosenfeld back inside and ever deeper into the complex.

They passed power generators, omnibus motors and ship engines of all sizes, some in pieces, some in boxes, some in jigs or clamps and others suspended from cranes. The noise and energy of man and machine ebbed and flowed around them as they moved from huge halls to spotless workshops. When he could be heard, Rosenfeld pointed out the more exotic destinations for Anna – Chile, China, Iran, Mexico, a diamond mine in South Africa – while keeping up a technical commentary for Ben, of power output, efficiency and innovations. He absorbed it like a sponge, asking the occasional question to help his analysis of the M.A.N. proposal for the motor-yacht engines. And he took keen notes of some ideas in their assembly-line system that he could take back to Dunwood's factory.

Finally, with the workers disappearing off the shop floor in response to a bell, Rosenfeld stopped. He smiled at them both as they pulled up beside him. In the background was the hiss and thump of a huge press at the other end of the shed. Rosenfeld pointed to a big half-built engine, its guts open, the precision steel glistening.

'This is the six-cylinder, four-stroke M6V 40/46,' he announced, momentously. 'It produces up to two thousand three hundred and ten brake horsepower – a most impressive unit. We have twenty of these engines for the ten new Type VII U-boats.'

Neither Ben nor Anna responded for several seconds. Ben just looked at the engine blankly, unsure that he'd heard correctly. 'Ten new U-boats?' he asked, turning to Rosenfeld.

'Yes, ten,' said Rosenfeld, quite deliberately. 'Submerged tonnage – fully loaded and manned – of a little over nine hundred tons.' He stood with his hands casually in his trouser pockets, a posture surreally at odds with the magnitude of what he was telling them. 'And they will all be launched by the end of the year. We are also supplying the eight-cylinder version for the Type IA U-boat, but only a couple of them are being built at the moment. And everyone here was very disappointed to lose the order for the Type II to Motoren-Werke Mannheim – that was another forty-eight engines, twenty-four boats. Many are in the water already; the rest should be launched by the end of the year.'

Sun from the skylight hit the floor just behind Rosenfeld, and he was slightly silhouetted against the beam of light, his presence seemingly dissipated into the billions of dust particles caught drifting in the air. Ben would remember that moment for a long while. 'That's thirty-six submarines,' he said in disbelief.

'Hmm,' replied Rosenfeld, raising his eyebrows and scratching his earlobe. 'And there's the Type IX on the drawing board too, we are very hopeful for the engine order for those – there is talk of eight boats.' He hesitated, then said, 'Rearmament is good business,' and he held Ben's gaze for just a moment, before he pointed to an exit. 'This way, please.'

Ben and Anna followed him outside, the sun bright and the air cool above them, just the occasional gust of wind making it down into the dark ravines between the factory walls. A single bird sang.

'I'm sorry, but I have another meeting soon,' said Rosenfeld as they walked, Ben on one side of him, Anna on the other, both silent. 'But I hope I have shown you enough,' he added.

'Yes, yes ...' said Ben, distractedly – thirty-six or possibly even *forty-four* new German U-boats, he could scarcely believe it. Hadn't the Germans been forbidden by treaty from building submarines? He glanced at Anna, but she was intent on her handbag, pulling out her cigarettes. He looked at Rosenfeld. 'Excuse me, but ...'

'Oh, damn,' exclaimed Anna, the cigarette and lighter spilling onto the floor. She bent down to pick them up, but he was quicker, and as they both crouched, she looked him in the eye and her meaning was clear. *Shut up.*

Ben stood in silence as Anna pulled out another cigarette. He shook his head when she offered him one, then lit hers and returned her lighter, before stepping a couple of paces to drop the first cigarette into a bin.

'I'm sorry, Herr Rosenfeld, I forgot, how rude – do you smoke?' asked Anna, offering the cigarette case.

'No, thank you, it aggravates my lungs,' he replied, starting to walk again. 'The mustard gas,' he added in explanation.

They fell in behind Rosenfeld, leaving the factory blocks and heading back towards the office buildings. Then Ben felt her take his hand, and she raised it to her lips with her index finger extended.

'Later,' she mouthed, lowering his hand and letting go.

Trees appeared ahead, growing in an expanse of tousled grass which was ready for its first spring trim. He recognised the landscaping at the entrance; they had come full circle. Around the next corner he saw that they were back to the car.

'It's good that our two countries are at peace now, so that we can build engines for your pleasure yachts,' Rosenfeld was saying.

'It's been many years,' replied Anna, 'and the Kaiser was a great racing yachtsman, often with British crews.'

'Yes, it's important that we mix and learn from one another, I think,' said Rosenfeld, arriving at the Mercedes. 'I was taught many a lesson by your flyers over the Western Front.' He smiled.

'You were in the Imperial Army Air Service?' Ben asked.

'Yes, for two years.'

'My boss, Captain Dunwood as he was then, flew with the RFC,' said Ben.

'I knew his reputation, an excellent shot, but I don't think I ever had the pleasure of meeting him over France. Probably for the best, so now he can buy his engines from us.' Rosenfeld smiled again. 'Let us hope that this spirit of peaceful cooperation stays with us for many, many years,' he added, but there was more hope than confidence in his tone. Then he pulled himself upright, held out his hand. 'Leutnant Hans Rosenfeld, Jasta 34b. Give Captain Dunwood my regards. I wish you a safe journey home, Mr Clayton.' They shook, and he turned to Anna. 'Miss Venuti.'

Anna exhaled quickly, stepped on the cigarette to extinguish it and held out her hand. Rosenfeld took it and bowed to grace it with a gentle brush of the lips.

She nodded demurely. 'Thank you for *all* your help, Herr Rosenfeld, perhaps we will meet again if there are more problems.'

'Always at your service, madam.' Rosenfeld clicked his heels and bowed his head. Then he raised his right arm. 'Heil Hitler,' he said, with a slightly wistful smile.

Anna and Ben saluted in response, and he eased in front of her to open the door.

'Don't say a word,' she hissed, 'I'll find us somewhere to get out of the car and talk on the way back.'

Chapter 25

They had been moving through the outskirts of Munich for several minutes before Anna finally got the driver to stop by the wrought-iron gates of a small park. There was a short exchange in German and then she said to Ben, 'There's a nice café by a pond in this park; it's such a beautiful day. I thought we might get a little fresh air and a coffee.'

'That sounds all right,' he replied, pushing the door open. He walked round to her side and helped her out. She kept a grip of his hand and led him into the park. A puff of breeze scattered petals from the blossom of a pink flowering cherry tree onto the path.

'I'm sure he thinks we're sneaking away for an illicit few minutes, it'll be all over the hotel when we get back ...' she said.

He glanced down at where she was holding his hand. He could feel each of her fingers, slim and delicately boned under the leather. 'So what about those damn submarines – why didn't you want me to tackle Rosenfeld?' he asked.

'If someone had overheard you, there might have been trouble for him. Do you think the führer would be happy if he knew Herr Rosenfeld was telling you all about his secret U-boat construction programme?'

'So the treaties *don't* allow them to build subs,' he replied.

'Actually, they do – it happened after Hitler's announcement that Germany would rearm a year ago,' she replied. 'Our dear Prime Minister Baldwin signed a Naval Agreement that allows Germany to build roughly thirty-five per cent of Britain's tonnage, and sixty per cent of our submarines. As you can see, they are well on the way.'

'Sixty per cent, bloody hell – what was Baldwin thinking? The U-boats are how they nearly beat us in the Great War!'

'The Naval Agreement was a particularly vile piece of politics on the part of Baldwin and his cronies,' she said. 'It managed to stab our potential allies in the back by allowing Germany to build a large-enough navy to challenge the French and Italians. Not just that, but by accepting it we effectively acquiesced with Hitler when he tore up the Treaty of Versailles. So our government must know in principle about the German submarine programme, but I doubt the Führer would be happy to hear Rosenfeld giving out such detailed information on their progress. He gave us overall numbers and specifications – the displacement figures he mentioned, the engine sizes and ratings – could you work out top speeds from that?'

'I'm not sure, I'd have to assume a fair bit ...'

'Could you try?'

There was an intensity in her tone that he couldn't refuse. 'I can look at it.'

'D'you need to write it down?'

Ben hesitated for a moment, and then patted his pockets for pen and paper, finally jotting the numbers down on the back of his train ticket.

'Don't make it obvious what they are,' she warned.

He nodded, and as he finished he said, 'So Rosenfeld was taking a big chance that this didn't get back to the Gestapo. I wonder why he picked us.'

'Perhaps he recognised that I have Jewish blood, and would be unlikely to be harbouring Nazi sympathies,' she said, and then moved closer and took him by both hands.

'But it's you that has to decide whose side you're on.'

'England's, of course,' he replied.

'Yes ... but there are two sides in England, and you must decide which you are on. What did you vote in the election last November?'

He frowned.

'You didn't vote?'

'No. Lerup had just brought forward the launch date and we were busy trying to work out how to get the mast built on time, I just never got there ...'

'But you understood the campaign arguments, didn't you?' She was looking at him hopefully. 'Chamberlain and Churchill spoke up, said that the Tories were for rearmament, then the Labour Party painted them as scaremongering warriors with no money for the unemployed, the depressed areas and social services.'

'And then Baldwin came out and flatly contradicted them both – "I give you my word there will be no great armaments",' he said. He'd heard about that at a Movement meeting after the election.

'That's right,' she smiled, relieved, pleased with him. Anna started to walk again, the path winding between the trees and limp, damp grass littered with blossom. 'Nothing's really changed – Churchill and a handful of others are the only ones calling for rearmament, but Winston blotted his copybook so badly by switching parties that no one trusts him or his motives. There are some in the Foreign Office – Robert Vansittart for one – that have been warning of the dangers for months or years, but Baldwin won't listen because it's politically inconvenient to do anything about it. And now it's worse than just doing nothing – we're selling Rolls-Royce engines to the Germans so they can test-fly their Messerschmitt fighters. It's extraordinary, when you think about it.' She shook her head.

'It's Baldwin's cynicism that really sickens me though,' she continued. 'He bought votes with his 'peace by collective security' slogan and a platform of using the League of Nations to meet any threat from Germany.' She lifted her hand in an exasperated movement. 'Then his government's *very next act* was to betray Abyssinia and the League of Nations sanctions when Mussolini invaded.' She seemed to sense his gaze and looked up, her eyebrows knitted, her lips tight with disapproval. 'This came on top of the naval pact, making the French and Italians hopelessly distrustful of our motives. If collective security requires anything, it's *trust*. And collective security doesn't work if *no one* in the League rearms in response to the German threat. But Baldwin can't see it, or won't see it, and certainly won't do anything about it. It was awful, being here and watching the Nazis gather more power to themselves with every passing day, and then coming home to England and finding such wilful blindness. Damn!' Anna stopped dead.

They had arrived at the pond, small and green, a sad willow drooping on the other side, stirring occasionally in the breeze. A flock of ducks had settled on the muddy bank under its sinewy branches. Closer, a rusty shed stood barred and shuttered at the edge of a paved area, now green with slime and duck droppings. 'They're still shut for the winter,' said Anna, 'normally there are chairs and tables all round here, and lots of people – it's very popular. And very fine coffee.'

There was just a single bench seat, looking out over the duck pond, and she headed for it. 'Never mind,' she said, 'we can talk for a little while and then have coffee back at the hotel.' He followed her, brushing the seat clear with a gloved hand and his handkerchief before they sat down. A single mallard stirred from its sloth. It paddled slowly towards them from the congregated mass on the other shore.

'You've seen the Germany that Hitler's building,' she said, 'the militarised Germany that we face. Soon, the only political tool left to Baldwin will be to give Hitler what he wants – but where does it stop? The Rhineland? No – nor

Austria, Czechoslovakia, Poland, France, Russia nor even Britain.' The mallard swam up and down in front of them, hopefully, before it emitted a single bleak quack. 'I wish I had something to give the ducks,' she added.

'At least there won't be a war that way,' he replied.

She turned to study him for several seconds. 'Yes, there will. In the end we won't stand for it. We won't live in a country where they beat and execute any opposition, spy on each other, where racial persecution is normal. When the Nazis truly threaten England, there will be a war.'

Is it really possible? he wondered, watching the ducks and not returning her gaze. Others were waddling into the water. Could there really be more years of death and sacrifice stretching out to ... what end? He shook his head, wanting to deny it. 'Surely something can be done, it can't be inevitable,' he said.

'Rearm,' she replied.

'And then fight anyway,' he added, looking at her now.

She sighed. 'Probably, yes, but if we start by matching Germany's rearmament, then at least we send the right kind of message to Hitler. We could stand up to his next move from a position of strength. Instead, everything we do is an invitation for him to carry on – like just standing by while he moves into the Rhineland ...'

'There must be another way, we can't fight another war like the last one.'

'Tragically, I think it will come to that in the end. Hitler has no qualms about violence, and his ambition is limitless. But we will have to stop him sooner or later, and the only way will be to fight.'

He shook his head. 'Not me.'

'What?'

'I took a vow of pacifism.'

'What? Why?'

'Something happened when I was at school ...' he trailed off. Anna was looking at him, her expression fixed, unsure what to expect.

'Go on,' she said, after several more seconds had passed.

'I ...' A breath. 'I used to box when I was a lad ... and I was pretty good,' he said. 'Then one night when I was thirteen I was in a really tough fight. I could feel it slipping away and ... I just hit this boy with everything I had left. I was desperate ... The doctor told me afterwards that I came very close to killing him.'

'My God,' said Anna. 'Was he all right?'

'Not really.' Ben shivered and took a deep breath. He stood and walked forward to the edge of the pond, shrugging deeper into his coat, pushing his hands into the pockets. A ripple went through the ducks, the bolder ones coming forward, and their more cautious comrades backing away. He picked up a stone, a flat one, and skimmed it across the pond. It skipped twice and then leapt ashore and buried itself in a hedge on the other side. He sensed that Anna had moved to stand behind him. It was almost as though he could step out of the scene, see it from afar. A tall man in a dark overcoat, hunched against the cold or his feelings, with his back turned to the beautiful woman, elegant in her furs just a few feet away. He ran his tongue along dry lips.

'I didn't want to hit anyone ever again,' he said. 'So I stopped boxing, and to start with that was enough – and I got in plenty enough trouble with my father for hanging up my gloves – but then I met Matt Faden at Cambridge and he introduced me to the No More War Movement. I just felt it was right.'

'Everyone would understand that,' she replied, 'no one decent wants to hurt anyone – but what if the man you had to fight was a murderer, and you knew that he'd go on to murder others – women, children, family, a lover? Wouldn't you fight back then?'

'I took a vow of pacifism ...' he muttered.

'And you'd stand by and watch someone rape your mother and not raise a hand?'

Clayton was silent. They both knew the answer.

'So shouldn't you fight this threat?' she continued. 'Isn't that what all our fathers did?'

'My father suffered horribly from that war,' he said, turning to her now, 'but when I told him that I'd taken a vow of pacifism, it was as though I'd stabbed him to the heart. It was the last time we spoke. I still don't understand, if anyone should be against another war, it ought to be those who fought the last one.'

'I'm quite sure they are all against it,' she replied, gently, 'but those men more than any of us understand the human capacity for violence, and while that still exists, pacifism is at best an unrealistic position.'

He shook his head. 'Not for all of them – Dunwood fought, but he's building planes for the Royal Mail, not the Royal Air Force.'

'Of course ...' she gasped.

'What is it?'

'Don't you see it?'

'What?'

'We know Harold Dunwood, and he knows Sopwith and Fairey, and between them they control a huge piece of the military aviation industry. None of them need politicians to start building planes, we don't need the government to rearm!'

He looked at her for a long moment, her brown eyes wide open, her mouth set with determination.

She stepped closer to him and said, 'What if you told Harold what you've seen here? He won't listen to me – I'm a woman – but he'll listen to you, he thinks a lot of you, and if you can persuade him, he could take you to Sopwith and Fairey. If we could persuade them all to start building planes ...' She tailed off.

Will he try to talk his boss into arming for a war whose very idea, whose very principle, they both loathe?

'Surely you see it; we can't let this go unchallenged any longer, it'll just end in a worse disaster.' She waved back towards the Mercedes on the road.

He picked up another stone, but this one caught an edge or a ripple. It skipped off at an angle, clipped through the branches and slammed into the trunk of the willow just above the remaining snoozing ducks. There was a lot of ruffling of feathers and beating of wings, and a great deal of quacking.

'I hope you're not trying to hit those ducks,' said Anna, as the rest of birds retreated to the other side of the pond.

'No, God, no, I'd never hurt anything ...' He stopped. A gust of wind crept down and flapped his coat round his legs. He turned to look at her again and found some comfort in her steady, unblinking gaze. 'If I do this and England rearms, and then there's a war, I will have a responsibility for the fighting, for the ... consequences. How will I feel then?' he asked.

'That you did the right thing. There will almost certainly be a war anyway, but the longer we wait to confront Hitler, the more blood and gold it will cost to defeat him. If the German forces reach full strength ... well, just look at the Great War. We have to stop this madness as quickly as we can, and if we don't rearm, it won't be stopped before the Nazis are marching down The Mall. If we rearm, we can face them down, or win; the seeds of their destruction are already sown – brave people like Rosenfeld, and the scientists they've purged from once-great universities just because they're Jewish. The enemy is already within. But they're going to need our help – *your help.*'

He shook his head. 'Even if I was to try to help, Mr Dunwood's set against building bombers and fighters ...'

'But you could try?

He let out another long, slow, deep breath. He had seen the Nazis and their altered reality. He didn't doubt Hitler's ambitions or intent, and he knew that she was right – Englishmen would not live with it. In the end, enough of them would fight. And if they were going to fight, they might as well be prepared. Finally, he nodded. 'All right, I can try; we'll tell Mr Dunwood and see what he says, but he's very strongly minded about this.'

'Thank you,' she said, and leaned forward, her breath on his skin, warm and soft, her lips brushing his cheek.

'If we tell Dunwood, do you think Rosenfeld will be all right?' he asked.

'I think so, I'm sure Mr Dunwood is discreet. But no one has to know how we came across the information – you could have seen something lying on a workbench.'

Ben nodded. 'So why did he do what he did?' he asked. 'He's German; he fought in the last war.'

'He's also Jewish,' said Anna. 'Many of the Jews are great Germans, great patriots, but the Nazis have made them outsiders. Herr Rosenfeld has seen what's coming, he knows that only Britain, France and perhaps Russia can now stop the Nazi machine – so that's where he has to go for help. He's very brave. If the Gestapo knew what he'd done, I don't think he'd last long.' She frowned, and then added, 'We should get back to the car, the driver will be wondering.'

They started towards the gate, walking in silence until they were almost out of the park. Then Anna turned and smiled up at him. 'It will be cocktail hour soon, it's such a gay time in the Vier Jahreszeiten, down in the cellar, perhaps we will see someone famous – there are often writers and actors there. And then tonight' – her eyes widened – 'a meal from the masterful Herr Walterspiel, such exquisite flavours – ohhh.' She shuddered theatrically. 'So, are you ready to play the part of my illicit lover again?'

Chapter 26

Ben Clayton stepped out of the bath and pulled the enormous towel from the rail. He wrapped it around himself and buried his face in the impossibly thick, soft, warm cotton. The long soak had again eased much of the pain from his body. But his head was still full of Rosenfeld's revelations. Another war, he kept thinking, what would that mean – more hideous years in the trenches in France? Or would it be different this time? Suddenly, as he towelled his wet hair, he had a flash of memory – himself as a child, running into the kitchen with a stick for a rifle. *Daddy, what did you do in the war?* The old man hadn't shouted at him, just a glance filled with something that had pierced even the incomprehension of a nine-year-old. His mother had whisked him back out of the house, and then set him down, brushed the dirt off his knees and told him that he mustn't play soldiers near Daddy, and he mustn't ask Daddy about the war. Ever.

He tried to put it out of his mind, rubbing himself carefully, gingerly patting at all the bruises. He nudged his thoughts to Anna – what had he learned? He had sided with her desire for a rearming Britain, but would she be for him against Lerup? She no longer seemed much like the aristocrat's type. Or perhaps he was just being prejudiced – but why had she come with him to Germany, when it could only embarrass Lerup? Did she want to revisit the country that badly? Or was there something else? The thought that he had been suppressing bubbled to the surface – *The something else might be me.* In which case, perhaps he could use her against Lerup. But it was a fraught notion, from every aspect.

He threw the towel over the rim of the bath and went into the bedroom to find some clothes. He pulled on underwear, socks and trousers, and was halfway through buttoning a crisp white dress shirt when it hit him – Stanley's tiny coded notebook, he'd not looked at it at all. He glanced at his watch; he had a few minutes before he had to meet her, he could make a start now. He lit a cigarette, and then pulled the notebook out of his wallet and went through to the lounge. There he found a neat stack of letterheaded paper and a pencil, and he settled down at the dining table to try to crack the code.

A quick canter through the basics of cryptology had been part of one of his maths courses at Cambridge. He smoothed the tiny book out in front of him. All right, from first principles, each letter or number must have been transposed to another letter or number in a way that Stanley could do in his head. Having gone to all the trouble of making the book itself so small and easily hidden, there was no point if he had to carry around some sort of table to cipher it. Ben looked at the first page; it was laid out exactly as a set of accounts might be, with five columns that could be the date, a comment and then the debit, credit and balance figures. The key had to be the numbers because numbers had to add up, had to balance. That was it – he felt the pulse of recognition, of excitement – accounts had the underlying logic of maths, and that would mean recognisable patterns in whatever transposition of symbols Stanley had used for a code. He just had to look for the patterns, symbols that always combined to form the same result. He started to scan the pages. Half an hour later there was a knock at the door and Ben jumped, completely lost in his task.

It opened slightly, and Anna's voice called, 'Hello?'

'Come in,' he said, the tiny notebook in his hand as he got up to walk to the door. 'What time is it?' he asked, already glancing at his watch as she stepped into the room. Then he looked back at her. 'Oh, I'm sorry ...' His voice faded. She had put her hair up and the nape of her long neck swept into the silk of a black dress, silk that wrapped across her shoulders and then flowed down her body, skintight all the way to her knees, where it loosened and tumbled in folds around her feet.

'What have you been doing?' she asked, looking at the mess of paper spread across the dining table, then at the notebook in his left hand.

He hesitated, but only momentarily. 'This belonged to my friend, Stanley Arbethwaite,' he said. 'His wife thinks it's his accounts, but they seem to be in some sort of code – no idea why, obviously not a very trusting sort of fellow. But she asked me to see if I could work out what it meant; poor old Stanley wasn't expecting to go so soon and left his affairs in a bit of a mess. She's hoping this might shed some light on it.' He held up the notebook as he finished – had he said too much?

'And that's why you've kept me waiting for the best part of fifteen minutes?' replied Anna, folding her arms – and showing no interest whatsoever in the notebook.

'I am sorry ... I just got involved, completely forgot the time ...' he said, grabbing for his wallet and tucking the notebook back in as he made a move for his jacket. 'Right,' he said, as he picked it up, 'ready.'

'And where's your bow tie?' she asked, the impatience plain. He felt his neck – damn. He retrieved the tie from his inside jacket pocket.

'Let me, it'll be quicker,' she said, stepping forward and taking it from him, then reaching over his shoulders to place the tie round his collar. For a moment he breathed in her scent – exotic, unknown – then as she eased back, he saw her gaze concentrate on the tie. No doubting that she was angry with him. He closed his eyes, feeling the slim, dextrous fingers at his neck – a touch, the briefest brush, against his skin above the collar. He jolted, as he did sometimes just before he fell asleep. She murmured something to the effect of 'keep still'. Eyes open now, he watched her lips. Tiny movements, as though she was repeating some rhyme that reminded her how to tie the knot. There were details in her face that he hadn't seen before – a black fleck in the brown of one eye, a single faint freckle on her cheek, the way the corners of her nose sloped down at the same angle as her upper lip, a little square portion to the round of her chin.

Then her eyes came up to meet his, and he was suddenly self-conscious and looked down. He had a perfect view of her breasts folding into the sheer black silk of the dress. And now he didn't know where to look. Instinctively, he started to pull away from her. There was tension in his collar as she held on to the almost-complete bow tie, like a dog pulled up on a lead. He caught her eyes – impatient, questioning, the anger still there. He fell still. *Think of something useful to say, something that will placate her – you need her on your side.* Then he had an inspiration.

'I've been looking at what Rosenfeld said about the engine power and displacement, to work out a top speed underwater and ...' Her hand flattened across his mouth and he found himself staring straight into wild wide eyes. Then she took her hand away and kissed him.

The lipstick had a smooth, silky feel as it touched, then brushed across his lips. A faint tension as she squeezed his lower lip between hers. He felt a strand of her hair fall against the line of his jaw. Then her hand touched his temple and ran into his hair, but so lightly it was scarcely a contact at all. There was the faint smell of almonds or marzipan. And then that exotic scent again, intoxicatingly strong in comparison, just for a moment before her tongue touched his and there was nothing else. Then she was gone, pulling back, one hand on his chest, the other holding a finger to her lips.

'Perfect,' she said, admiring her handiwork.

He stared into her eyes, reaching automatically up to the tie.

'Don't you want to check it in the mirror?' she asked.

'I'm sure it's fine.'

'Good, now, we don't want to keep Herr Walterspiel waiting any longer, do we?' She took his jacket from him and held it out for him to get into. He picked the key off the sideboard, and she led the way out into the corridor.

They were almost back to the lobby before either of them said anything more. Then she leaned towards him and said, 'It's possible they have the room arranged so they can eavesdrop through microphones.'

It took him several moments to shift the sentence around in his head, to get it into something he understood, it was so out of the context of his thoughts. Then he realised – the Gestapo, he'd been babbling about Rosenfeld and submarines just before she kissed him. She had kissed him to shut him up.

'It's not very likely that they'd be interested in us, but it is possible, so please, let's not talk of these matters again until we are safely back in England, unless we're outdoors and absolutely sure we're alone.'

He nodded.

'Now let's eat this wonderful food,' she said, and took his hand to lead the way to the restaurant.

'You all right there, Lucy?' asked Captain Emerton from the wheel of the *Silver Crescent*.

'Aye, skipper,' she replied, swallowing a mouthful of bread and cheese, 'it's a beautiful evening for it.'

'Not a breath of wind. Be handy if it stayed like this all the way there.'

'You never know your luck.' She peered up at the stars from her spot beside Emerton in the wheelhouse. Not a cloud in the sky, and with the moon in its final quarter the stars jumped out – close enough to touch. The sea's glassy surface rose and fell under them, like a fairground crazy mirror, long, slow waves rolling at the urging of some distant storm. It was good to be back at sea again, things were simpler out here. All she had to worry about for the next couple of days was helping the Captain get to Emden on time.

A memory came back to her, of stowing away on a twenty-ton yacht that her father and a friend were taking over to France for the owner. It had been a night much like this – cold, clear skies – but with a little more breeze. They'd had no engine, and she could remember the creak of blocks and ropes as the wind had pushed fitfully at the sails. She had been comfortably hidden in the aft cabin, and had no reason to show herself until she was confident they were well offshore. But she hadn't realised how slowly they were going, battling a tide. And she was young, time was still slippery – and more practically, she was hungry, lonely and in need of a toilet. So, after staying out of sight for what had seemed like forever, certainly long enough to be closer to France than England, she had finally crept out and into the main cabin.

Both men were on deck, but her father had seen her first – she'd heard his exclamation as she peeked up through the cockpit hatch. But she hadn't been able to see his face in the weak moonlight, and there had been a stomach-boiling moment while she had worked out his reaction. Then she had realised her mistake: they were barely out of the Solent. There had been an argument, the other man – an old Itchen Ferry sailor called Harry with a terrifyingly swollen red nose – had been anxious to get her off the boat. But her father had won and she had been allowed to stay – tucked under his arm, warm and safe inside his oilskins, wafts of his smell mingling with the salt air, gazing hypnotised at the foaming luminescence flashing along the lee rail as the breeze filled in and they charged across the Channel. But the joy of that moment had been tempered; the thrill of the empty sea and the plunging yacht, the strong, confident and reassuring presence of her father – even then, at just twelve years old, she had been frightened that she would never be quite that happy again. It was not long after that voyage that her mother had died.

She took another swig of her tea. And then something struck her with a clarity which made it all the more extraordinary that she hadn't seen it before. She looked like her mother. People had often commented on it as she was growing up – *She's got her father's eyes, but everything else is you, Mary*. Her father must see his lost wife every time he looked at her, more so as she got older. *My God*, she thought, *how much must that hurt?* And now she started to see how little they'd understood each other. How her battles to leave the kitchen – to get back the freedom she had lost along with her mother – must have seemed just like she was trying to leave home, to leave him. She had been struggling to recover something from her loss, while reminding him constantly of his – both of them seeing only what was gone, and not what they still had: each other and Tom. She leaned back against the deckhouse wall, shaky, her stomach fluttering. Things were changing now, but there were so many years when she could have gone to her father, told him how she really felt, swallowed her anger, forgiven him for what had gone before. But she had been too young, too confused. She wouldn't make the same mistake with Ben.

The jerk of the train as it pulled out of the station nudged Ben just above the line separating sleep from consciousness. He shifted his position, his hip and neck stiff and cramped, the injuries from the beating adding their dull ache. He pushed the hair from his eyes and gazed groggily out of the window – another town, another Gothic church spire – where were they? He had no idea. He glanced around the empty compartment – *Powdering her nose*, he thought. They had eaten an excellent lunch in the Mitropa dining car before the change at Leipzig, and ever since he had been dozing to the soporific clack of wheels and tracks as the train edged its way north-west in the spring sunshine.

The compartment door opened. He stood up to hold it while Anna entered with a tray, which she placed on the small table between them. It held two cups of the bouillon and a plate with half a dozen of the little sausages they favoured on board.

'The attendant made a terrible fuss about me bringing this myself – I sort of stole it, I think it was intended for someone else – but I told him not to be silly. Did you see Halle? It's where Handel was born, and there's supposed to be a wonderful ruined castle,' she said.

He shook his head. She had kept up a cultural commentary right through the journey: magnificent churches and the Germanic Museum in Nuremberg, Wagner anecdotes in Bayreuth, a nice castle in Altenburg, Blüthner's piano factory in Leipzig ...

'It's such a shame we can't get off at any of these places – I suppose you slept through it?' she added, picking up her cup.

'Sorry,' he replied, taking a sausage, chewing slowly and thinking, *Now is as good a time as any*. 'When we talked yesterday,' he began, 'it was clear that you have a real passion from your time living here ... about the situation, about Germany ...' He hesitated. 'But I wondered how Lerup feels about it all, does he agree with you?'

'Ah, Lerup.' Her eyes went demurely to the cup, and then to the window.

He followed her gaze; a farmer and his horse toiled up the incline towards them as they flashed past, ploughing lines that weren't quite straight.

'We don't talk about politics any more,' she went on. 'Since I got to know him better, it's become clear that he's rather more ...' She hesitated, shrugged and then sipped at the cup. 'Different. We don't really talk about much at all these days,' she added.

'That doesn't sound much fun,' he replied.

He was still staring out of the window. But now he could see Anna, reflected in the glass – real but unreal, there but not there. She was unaware of his gaze; her eyes came up towards him, and for several moments he watched her watching him. There was something that he didn't quite understand in the look – or was it just the ghostly, deceptive quality of the reflection? But to look at her properly, to check, would destroy the very thing he wanted to see, like catching a snowflake. Then the light, or the background, changed, and she was gone as quickly as the thought itself.

'I think,' she said, 'if I may borrow a metaphor from our journey, that Lerup and I have left the last stop before the terminus.'

He turned back to her. He should find some way to tell her about Lucy, but he couldn't even do that without first establishing whose side she was on. He put the cup down again, clasped his hands on the table. He had to take the chance.

'There's something I'd like to ask you,' he said.

Her eyebrows lifted a fraction and she turned her head slightly.

'It's about Stanley Arbethwaite,' he added.

'Your friend who was killed?'

'That's right.' He leaned forward, staring at her hands on her cup, the faint wisp of steam struggling off it. He lifted his gaze to meet hers. 'But if Lerup were to hear that I held certain views and was to tell Mr Dunwood ... that might finish off my chances of sailing on the *Windflower*, which would be a disaster for me, but I suspect would make Lerup rather happy.'

Anna nodded solemnly to acknowledge the trust he was placing in her. 'I understand. I won't speak of it to Lerup, or anyone else.'

'Thank you,' he said. 'In that case, I have to say that ... I rather agree with the striking fishermen, that Stanley was murdered.'

There was half a breath of pause, before she replied, 'As I said before, the police should have investigated further, at least to be sure.'

'Exactly,' he went on, pulling out his wallet and then the notebook. 'That's why I wanted to ask you about it. You see, there is some evidence from these accounts and ... elsewhere that Stanley lost a great deal of money gambling.'

Anna's perfect dark eyebrows arched again.

'So I was wondering – as you'd seen Stanley playing with Lerup at Spink's club – if you were aware of any large debts that Stanley might have had with someone like Spink, or even Spink himself. Maybe Lerup mentioned something?'

She put her cup down, and frowned.

'It's just that, why would anyone kill Stanley?' he continued. 'It does seem that all this money he owed is too much of a coincidence – I can't help feeling that the reason he was killed is in here somewhere.' He waved the notebook. 'If I can decode this properly, it might tell me what I want to know ...'

'I hope you're not planning to try now,' interrupted Anna.

He looked at her quizzically.

'Given the state of relations between England and Germany, travelling through the countryside with coded material in front of you might be misinterpreted ...'

He held her gaze for a moment, then put the notebook back in the wallet, shaking his head. 'This bloody country,' he said. 'Anyway, I wanted to see if you knew anything. That's also why I was at the club – trying to find out if Stanley owed them any money.'

'And what did you discover?'

'Spink claimed that Stanley owed him nothing.'

Anna pulled her handbag towards her, got out her cigarettes and offered them. He took one, and she said, 'But what I don't understand, is why anyone would want to kill

Mr Arbethwaite when he owed them money.' She paused to light the cigarettes. 'How does that do them any good?'

'It would have been a warning to others, and the incident could in fact just have been a warning to Stanley – he was unlucky. If his head had missed the strut, then he'd probably have got away with a few bruises, maybe a broken bone or two – and a big scare.'

'That's a good point about it being a warning – did you tell the constabulary that? You have talked to them, I take it.' She drew deeply on the cigarette.

'No, Mrs Arbethwaite was very anxious that no one should know about the debts until there was some evidence of foul play. I shouldn't even have told you, but I've been getting desperate to find some way into the puzzle.'

Anna continued to watch him for a long moment before she spoke. 'Did it occur to you that Lerup might have had a motive for coming out against the strike, and the idea of the murder?'

He didn't reply, just watched her and waited.

'I know a couple of things – when they're combined with what you've told me ...'

He rolled the ash off his cigarette. His hand was steady.

'Stanley Arbethwaite did owe Spink a lot of money,' she said. 'I heard Lerup refer to it when he was talking to Spink the day before the accident. They're associates, those two; I don't know the extent, but they definitely have some business dealings.'

'And the other thing?'

'Lerup was at the yard, the night before Mr Arbethwaite was murdered. I was with him. He could easily ...' She shrugged.

'Lerup was on *Windflower*, the night before the accident?' he echoed.

'Yes,' she said.

He sat back with a long sigh. 'At last,' he murmured.

Anna was staring out of the window again, right

elbow propped in the palm of her left hand, cigarette by her ear, smoke drifting across her face – a now-familiar pose to him.

'But I don't understand,' he said, drawing quickly on his own cigarette, 'why didn't you tell anyone this before?'

'I had no idea that Mr Arbethwaite had serious money trouble; except for the fact that he owed Spink, I knew nothing about the fellow – who was to say that he couldn't pay the debt? So Lerup's association with Spink, our presence at the yard – there was nothing suspicious about any of it. Until now, when you come along with your little black book, saying that Spink denies the debt ...'

'And together we have the whole story.' *What had Thorpe said? "Lerup's already pissed the rest of the estate away at card tables."*

'Will you come to the police with me, when we get back to England?' he asked.

'Of course, we have crucial evidence.' She finished the cigarette with a long drag, and then stubbed the butt out, rather harder than necessary. 'I hope you're right – that it was supposed to be a warning, that he didn't intend to kill poor Mr Arbethwaite.'

No, he thought, the intent may not have been murder. The anticipated outcome may well have been a few bruises and maybe a broken bone. But murder was the result, and now his friend would be avenged and everything could be put straight. With Lerup discredited and gone from the scene, Dunwood would fall back on him for advice. He could make the case that the strikers had been right all along, get Joe Kirk out of prison and probably get a lot of them their jobs back. Mrs Arbethwaite might even get some of Stanley's money returned when Spink's illegal business was wrapped up. And Lucy, she would surely forgive him for denying her to Lerup, for dashing off to Germany, and they could get back to normal. An overwhelming relief flooded through him as he sat there, the cigarette burning unnoticed down to his fingers. Then he caught the look in

Anna's chocolate-brown eyes.

Chapter 27

In the limited wattage of a single light, Ben watched as the red-capped stationmaster bustled about his business, gathering up parcels and checking all the doors were shut, before finally waving his lighted fan to release them. The conductor blew his horn, and the train jerked into motion. A row of white faces watched along the iron fence, the disembarking passengers patiently waiting by the wicker gate for their tickets to be checked before they could depart into the night to their homes. This final, late-night stage of their journey on a rattling train of lonely second-class carriages – which stopped at every barnyard between Leer and Emden – was the antithesis of the express services. But it would get them there, and that meant dinner, a bath and a bed.

He glanced at his watch. Anna had bought a paper at Leer while they waited for the connecting train and disappeared with it almost as soon as they'd boarded. Then the door unlatched and she entered, turning and slamming it shut before lowering the blinds on the internal compartment windows. She dropped the Chanel bag and the newspaper down on the seat and sat beside him.

'We have to get off the train,' she said, in an urgent whisper.

'Yes, of course, at Emden,' he replied.

'No, before then, as soon as we can,' she said.

He sat up straight.

'I think the Gestapo are probably waiting for us in Emden.'

He stared at her.

'They went to M.A.N. and arrested Rosenfeld earlier today; I'm sure they've had him in interrogation since then, they must know he's passed us the information about the U-boats.'

'But ...' he started, struggling against the impossible weight of her statement. 'How do you know that?' He followed her gaze down to the newspaper. 'It's in the paper? But we didn't ask him to tell us anything, and we're British citizens – what can they do to us?'

'Shoot us or hang us as spies,' she said. 'We've got one of theirs at the Old Bailey right now – Dr Hermann Goertz, I think – so getting us on some charges will be the Nazis' perfect response.'

He held her gaze for another second, but his mind was already responding to the threat. A moment later, he calmly stood and pulled his case off the overhead rack. 'Better get ready to do some walking. Emden is the next stop.' He flipped the catches and lifted the lid.

She remained motionless. 'Emden is the next stop? What are we going to do?'

'Jump. The closer we are to Emden when we get off the train, the greater the risk. So let's get off first and then think about the rest. We have no time to waste.'

'I hate walking,' she muttered, watching as he started to rummage through his clothes.

'We need to get rid of the suitcases, then hopefully they'll think we got off at a station long before Emden and will start looking somewhere else. We can't carry them or anything inessential, so we'll throw them off and then hide them. Did you bring any warm, practical clothes?'

'The dress I wore last night is by Madeleine Vionnet, it was a twenty-first birthday present ...'

'And now it's going to end up feathering the bed of

some lucky fox,' he replied. 'Find something warm to wear,' he insisted, pulling her suitcase off the rack and opening it. Slowly, mechanically, she stood up and started to follow his instructions. He returned to his own clothes, choosing a short-sleeved sweater that would go under his jacket, another thick shirt he could put on over the one he was wearing and a couple of extra vests to stuff in his pockets just in case. He stripped his jacket off.

'Don't forget your passport,' he said, 'we'll need it once we get to Holland.'

'And don't you forget that notebook,' she replied, moving more quickly now, catching up with his urgency.

He put his passport into an inside jacket pocket along with his wallet, buttoned it shut and then pulled on the extra shirt. 'We need a dark section on a bend, or a hill – or both – somewhere the damn train will slow down enough,' he said.

'Not much chance of a hill around here,' Anna replied, sweeping her hair up under a black beret.

'I hope you're feeling brave then,' he said, pushing his suitcase towards the door with his feet as he buttoned the shirt. He glanced forward, out of the window. The flat land stretched away, there wasn't much of a moon, but there were no clouds either – the cold blue light would pick out anything that moved in open country. 'Lights up ahead,' he said. It was Emden glittering in the darkness.

He closed the blinds on the outside windows, then shrugged into the jumper and put his jacket on over the extra clothes – he was already starting to sweat. Anna shut the lid on her case and dragged it up to his, then she sat beside the door, where she could see forward through a crack in the blinds. He pulled on his coat and gloves, peering over her shoulder to see outside as he sat down beside her; there were lights from left to right all across the horizon in front of them.

'You go first, I'll push the suitcases out and shut the door,' he said.

'It's going too fast,' she replied.

'It'll have to slow down somewhere before it gets to the platform,' he said.

'And by then we'll be jumping into the arms of the Gestapo.'

He didn't respond; the train had steadied its speed again. They passed the first lonely building. Seconds ticked by, long, silent seconds, with just the rhythmic clatter of the train as background. Then he remembered his hat and stuffed it under his coat. He saw the newspaper and picked it off the seat.

'We should take this,' he said, thinking that if he saw the story it might make it all seem more real. Anna's shoulders tightened, but she didn't reply. There was something in the movement that bothered him. 'What page was the Rosenfeld story?' he asked, with a sudden intuition. The Nazis controlled everything in Germany, so why would they allow the story into the paper when it might warn him and Anna?

'It's slowing,' she murmured.

'It wasn't in the paper, was it?' he asked.

'This is not the time,' she replied, reaching up to turn off the compartment's gas lights as she spoke.

He stared at her, all the possibilities running through his mind. 'This isn't some charade ...' he started, more in hope than belief.

'No,' she snapped, finally looking at him. 'We have to get off this train. Please. Trust me.'

'I want to know exactly what's happening,' he said, grabbing her wrist. If anything was going to make them look guilty, it was running.

'It's slowing, and those trees ...' she said, twisting her arm, desperation in her voice now. 'Please.'

He glanced through the gap in the blinds. The train had slowed for a corner in some woodland. It was likely now or never. He looked into her frightened, darkly troubled eyes for a moment, then he opened and held the door.

'Oh God, now I don't think I can do it ...' she said, braced in the doorway as the wind roared in. So he pushed her. She disappeared in silence. The cases followed without hesitation. Then he quickly felt for the step, got a foot onto one corner and slid outside, hanging on to the window. It rattled under his grip. He squeezed the door shut round his body and it clicked quietly. He glanced ahead – the front of the train was already out of the trees, back in the weak moonlight. He twisted to face outwards, nothing but black, no idea what was down there. He jumped. Time seemed to extend indefinitely – how far was it? How hard was he going to land?

Then his feet hit the ground and his knees caved. But the forward speed he had taken from the train tumbled him onwards, clutched into a ball, his bruised head tucked in with his hands, rolling once, twice, three times, each impact crushing the air out of him, before he slid to a stop in the grass. He sucked back a breath, the pain in his ribs shot up and he yelped. It felt like someone had jabbed a red-hot poker into all the old injuries. He lay quietly for a while, waiting for it to subside, trying to get his breathing under control, listening to the train recede, the silence expand. No brakes, no whistles or horns. No one had seen them jump. No one had pulled the emergency cord.

He uncoiled a little – no new stabs of pain. Gently, he felt up and down his body, growing in confidence. He started to ease himself to a sitting position, and realised he had landed on a shallow embankment, covered in thick grass growing out of soft mud. They could not have picked a better spot. *And that is the kind of luck we are going to need.* He looked around. He was at the edge of a little copse of trees, and it was the only thing breaking the landscape before the collection of lights that marked the town – they could not have waited any longer.

'Ben?' His name was cooed softly.

'Over here,' he hissed. He pulled his hat out from under his coat, pushed it back into shape and put it on. Not much Sunday-best about it any more. Then he heard the swish of the grass and a few moments later Anna was beside him, panting heavily.

'I found the cases,' she said, businesslike, 'they stayed in one piece, the train wasn't going that fast – are you all right?'

'Wet and muddy, but no serious damage,' he replied. 'What about you?'

'The same,' she said, laying a concerned hand on his shoulder as he started to push himself to his feet. He didn't get far, leaning forward, hands on his knees, and then crouching back down again as a wave of giddiness washed through him. 'Are you sure you're all right?' she asked again.

He nodded.

'Well done for shoving me, it was our last chance,' she told him.

'So, what the hell is going on?' he asked, eventually, looking up at her.

'Let's get the cases under cover,' she replied, turning away.

'No.' He grabbed her arm again as he spoke. 'Nothing happens until I know what's going on.'

'But what if there's another train?'

'We'll hear it in plenty of time.'

She didn't reply for a moment. 'It's better, safer, if you know as little as possible.'

He shook his head. 'I don't care, I'm in this with you and I'm not going anywhere until I know what's going on.' He shrugged, let go of her arm, and then slid from a crouch to sit on the wet grass again.

Still she hesitated. And then finally she sat down beside him and said, 'When my family came back from Germany, I was approached by people from British Intelligence; there are a few people there who see the Nazi threat seriously. They wanted to debrief me on what I knew, and to encourage me to keep my eyes open should I either go back or have any contact with friends who still lived there – nothing formal, just give them a hand if I could.'

'Bloody hell,' he said.

'I let them know I was coming here with you, and they gave me a contact in Munich. After you started telling me how you were going to work out the U-boat's top speed in your hotel room, I got a bit worried. The contact established a way for them to communicate as we travelled up here, in case there was any trouble. At Leer, the newspaper I bought had a coded message that told me Rosenfeld had been arrested.'

'But ...' he said, 'has this happened because of what I said in the hotel?'

'Not necessarily,' replied Anna. 'They could have been watching him for a while – we can't possibly know. But Rosenfeld knew the chance he was taking, and we can't worry about him now. We have to get ourselves out of this.'

Ben was silent.

'Ben, please – all we can do is get to Holland.'

'But what about Captain Emerton? Is he in any danger? Maybe that's why they've waited until Emden to pick us up – they want to get us all together.'

'Or they could have waited till Emden because they've only just got what they need from Rosenfeld. In either case, Emerton will be all right because we won't show up, and there's nothing incriminating in the packages. There's no reason for the Germans to involve him.'

He rubbed at his cheek. He could only hope that she was right.

'I didn't want to lie to you,' she said, 'but really it would have been better if you knew nothing.' She sighed. 'And it took me too damn long to decode that message, otherwise we wouldn't have ended up so close to Emden. I never was any good with numbers and things.' She waved up the track. 'And now the Gestapo can't be more than a mile or two up there, wondering where the hell we are – so please, can we get the cases hidden and get going?'

He started to push himself to his feet. Anna was quickly up and moving back down the tracks. He hobbled along behind, towards where the two suitcases had landed and bounced to the edge of the copse. But they couldn't push them into the undergrowth without leaving an obvious trail for anyone looking out from the next daytime train. So he picked the cases up and carried them to the end of the trees, over a wooden fence and then back along the boundary, till they found a track leading in. Once inside the copse, Anna retrieved her handbag before they buried the cases in the scrub.

'Someone will find them eventually,' he said, 'children, hunters.' He was sweating, breathing heavily after the exertion. But his ribs didn't hurt too much any more, the physical pain was bearable. 'So, can those contacts of yours help us now?' he asked.

'No, there wasn't enough time to arrange anything – we're on our own,' she replied, fumbling in the handbag. 'I wish I had the Baedeker, that's got all the information we need.' She pulled out the large-scale map she'd bought in Leipzig station to show him their journey on the train. He took it and they ducked down into the undergrowth so she could use her lighter.

He pointed. 'So, the first bridge that will get us across the Ems estuary is at Leer. We could walk back there, find the bridge and then the Dutch border is, um ...' He took a quick measurement off the scale with his thumb. '... about ten miles the other side; it's a long way to walk,' he said, before asking, 'Is the border fortified?'

'Probably, but I don't know for sure.'

'It's got to be a good fifteen miles back to Leer anyway, if we're almost in Emden,' he said. 'In the dark, staying out of sight, that's two nights' walk to the border, then another night trying to find somewhere to get across – we've got no food or water, and no idea of the intensity of the search.'

'Or ...?' she asked.

'Or we can go into Emden, find a boat we can steal

and we'll be across tonight,' he replied.

The lighter clicked off. 'It sounds a lot better than walking twenty-five miles,' she said. 'But don't you think they'll be looking for us in Emden?'

'Not to start with, they'll need to ask questions of the people on that train, try to find out if we were on it at all, or where we got off. Did you see the conductor, acknowledge anyone on board?'

'No,' she said.

He remembered the red-capped stationmaster, a line of white faces above an iron fence, passengers on the platform at Leer – would he or Anna have registered with any of them? If they had a picture or a decent description, then for certain, he thought. She was too beautiful for anything else. They had to assume that the Gestapo would establish that they had left Leer, but hopefully not too quickly. 'There's a good chance that they won't get any further than asking questions before the morning,' he replied, thinking that Emden was still a lot better prospect than going back to Leer. He was a lot more comfortable with the idea of a boat than a twenty-five-mile walk through what was now effectively enemy territory. He started to fold the map back up.

'We'll follow the railway line, to start with at least, it'll be easier than through the fields,' he told her. They set off into the night, but it was too dark to see the sleepers clearly, and he stumbled along, struggling to concentrate on what he was doing and not get distracted by the reasons he found himself doing it. Their footfalls rang out into the silence that stretched towards the town. On any other occasion it would have been a beautiful night, a calm velvet sky touching down in a faint haze that might be mist, or distance. His breath steamed past his ears as he walked, his nose running a little in the cold. But the rest of him was warm enough under the layers of wool and cotton.

'Damn!'

'Shhh!' He spun round, looking for Anna in the

darkness and finding her sitting in a heap.

'It's these bloody shoes. I keep stumbling on the rocks between these bloody sleepers. And I hate bloody walking,' she hissed, waving one of the shoes at him.

'Shhh!' he said again. 'Do you want the whole of Emden to hear?' He grabbed the shoe from her, felt the heel. 'I'm not surprised – is this the most practical thing you've got?'

'I didn't pack for a bloody walking tour!'

'All right, all right ...' He felt for where the heel connected to the shoe, and was just about to snap it off.

'No!' she whispered.

'Why?'

'How will I look if I meet someone, stumbling around Emden in a pair of shoes with no heels?'

He had to concede that she had a point. He handed the shoe back and she pushed it on. 'Here, take my hand,' he said, and helped her up to her feet.

'Thank you,' she replied, in a more conciliatory voice, as she smoothed her coat down and continued. 'Let me use you for support, then at least if I do go head over heels I won't break an ankle.' He held out his arm, and they started on towards Emden.

Eventually, they came to a bridge over a wide double-channelled canal. 'Let's stop a minute,' he told her, 'there's good cover under this bridge; we can use the lighter, I want to have a quick look at that map before we get any closer.'

They slithered down the muddy embankment, arms flapping frantically. He caught Anna just short of the water. Then he pulled the map out and opened it, and when he was ready she lit the lighter.

'From this it's not even clear that Emden is beside the sea,' he said, peering doubtfully at the map in the fitful illumination.

'Emden's definitely a port. I used the Vier Jahreszeiten's Baedeker to book our hotel for tonight. I read the entry – although it did say something about being separated from the Ems by a big harbour.'

He looked up and the lighter clicked off; the darkness crept back in to them. 'I was wondering why there are lights down where the water should be, and I thought I saw some high chimneys.' It had been troubling him, the sense that they were heading inland. But there was no doubt that the town itself was in front of them, it wasn't just the lights – he could feel its bulk looming.

'So isn't that the way we want to go?' queried Anna. 'Surely we want the port rather than the town – why don't we just follow this canal south till we get there?' She waved at the water at their feet.

'I suspect,' he said, thoughtfully, 'that it's all industrial docks down there; this is flat, marshy countryside, chances are the town started a little way inland on a river, to make it safer from flooding. The land between here and the sea has probably been reclaimed to expand the docks and put factories on. We're not going to find the type of boat we need down there. We want a fishing boat, or a yacht, and we'll find that in the old docks, probably in the centre of town, where they could unload everything straight into the market and shops.'

Anna was quiet for a few seconds before she said, 'All right, so we go into the town, and then turn back towards the sea until we find the old docks?'

'Yes, I think so, but ...'

'What?'

He tapped the map with a fingernail in the darkness. 'Nothing, let's go,' he said, folding the map up and putting it in his pocket. Something was bothering him, but he didn't know what it was.

They scrambled back up the embankment, struggling and sweating in their thick clothes, and then continued along the railway. They took the second road that crossed the tracks, just after a cut through another embankment, heading towards the town, and avoiding the station. A right fork then followed the line of the embankment, and a wood materialized on their left. Anna led them onto open ground beneath the dark sombre shapes of the trees. She kept just close enough to follow the direction of the road, and they picked their way carefully forward with a faint squish of mulch. Even that was enough to startle an owl into flight, a phantom movement through the branches that stopped them both in their tracks, hearts pounding. Soon they were forced out onto the road again by a hedge, backed by a row of solid buildings. Walking side by side, she took his hand. They passed a water tower and one crossroads, then another.

'Bahnhof Strasse,' whispered Anna, 'the station's down there.' She pointed to their left.

'That looks about right,' he replied.

They were on a wide tree-lined avenue now, the buildings tall, silent and shuttered. The water was close, he could feel it, there was a change in the air, and an emptiness ahead at the end of the road that couldn't be explained by anything other than the harbour. As they approached the final building, the water appeared in front of them, running at right angles to the direction they'd been walking. Fishing boats edged the dockside, just as he had hoped. The town was to their right, and to their left were the industrial port and the railway yards. Anna squeezed his hand and he turned to follow her gaze, up to their left, at the building beside them. There was a light on in one of the front windows, overlooking the water.

She pointed to a sign. '*Hafen Verwalt* – harbour master,' she whispered.

'It looks as if there might be someone on duty up there,' he replied, 'damn tricky taking something out from under his nose.' He glanced back at the harbour. 'At least it's high water.' And then it hit him – the thing that had been troubling him. 'Bloody hell!' he hissed.

'What?'

'Look at all the water, remember how flat the land is – how far are we from the sea? There's almost bound to be a bloody lock gate! This coast is tidal, and this is a decent-sized town with a port and all that industry to the south – they couldn't run all that with the water disappearing twice a day. We have no hope of getting past a lock in a stolen boat tonight or any other night.'

'Oh God!' Her voice was a terse whisper, hoarse with anger and fear. 'Why didn't you think of that before!'

For several seconds they looked at each other in silence, and he was a breath away from saying, *You got us into this mess.* But he didn't – because he wasn't sure it was true, it wouldn't do them any good and he was too startled by her flash of anger.

'Why didn't we go back the other way, maybe that last train stop was on the coast, a little fishing village ...' she continued.

'Because this was a lot closer and you don't like walking,' he replied. 'And we didn't think of it,' he added.

There was a long silence. Then she said, plaintively, 'Can we get back there tonight?'

'I don't know, it must be miles,' he replied. 'Let's not do anything in a rush, we need to find somewhere safe, so we can have a look at the map and think. Maybe we could wait and check the water level in an hour or two and see if it's changed – just in case. But I feel too bloody conspicuous out here. We'll head up towards the town. I don't like that light on in the harbour master's, and the station's the other side of it – the Gestapo could still be around there.'

He took Anna's arm and they turned down towards the town. A street light flickered, and he jumped as a tabby slunk across the road in the short-lived strobe. The muscular, industrial tone of the port buildings softened to residential property.

'Here, walk in as though we own the place,' he said.

The ground-floor windows on the next block of flats were all boarded up. He just made out some writing scrawled across the bare wood, paint uneven on the rough timber, as they made their way up a path paved with pink and white slabs. *Juden sind hier unerwunscht.*

'What does that mean?' he asked into her ear.

'*Jews are not welcome* – it looks like they've been harassed out of here, must have boarded the place up before they left, perhaps hoping for better times to come back to; come on.'

They walked around the side of the building, passing steps up to the higher floors. The front door was also boarded and decorated with swastikas. They followed the path round into the backyard. Several boards had been peeled away from the back wall of the ground-floor flat, and underneath a window had been broken.

'Can you get through it?' he asked.

Anna felt carefully around the edge of the shattered glass. 'It's not too bad, I think so, what about you?' she whispered.

'Let me try first, hold my coat,' he replied, giving her his hat and then peeling the coat off. He checked around him as he did so – there were dustbins, a cracked concrete patio, weeds and a washing line; the rest of the garden receded into the dark. Several other buildings overlooked them, but only one of the windows showed a light, and that had its curtains closed. He turned back to the flat, found a clean grip on the window frame on either side and then levered himself up till his knees were on the sill. He poked his head in and the smell assailed him – it stank like a sewer, it was so strong and so fresh that he wondered if there was still someone there. He tried not to breathe, peering into the gloom, but he could see nothing. Outside, and not far away, a dog barked, followed by a sharp metallic rattle.

'It's all right, carry on,' whispered Anna.

He pushed his shoulders into the hole, feeling the sharp scrape of glass along his arm – it was a tight fit. He wriggled through, climbing onto and then over what turned out to be a sink. Once past that, the smell seemed to ease a little. He lowered himself to the floor carefully, and was rewarded with the very faintest crunch of broken glass. Anna was already pushing his coat and hat, and her handbag through. He took it all from her, put the hat on, shrugged into the coat and pushed the handbag onto his shoulder, unwilling to put anything down, given the smell. He leaned into the window.

'Careful, there's a sink this side, and I think it's full of ... shit.'

'Ugh, disgusting,' she muttered, and then added, 'Damn children,' as she pushed herself up into the gap.

He cleared the glass from under his feet, and once he had a good stance, with her hands on his shoulders, he was able to lift Anna by the waist over the sink. 'Watch the glass on the floor,' he whispered.

She pulled herself into him, arms around his neck, as he gently lowered her the last couple of inches. She sank her head into his chest and held on.

'I'm exhausted,' she whispered.

'It's all right, we're going to be all right. I think we just need some rest, it's been a very long day.' He could feel her breathing, the thump of her heart. She gave a little shudder – cold, fear, relief – he didn't know why and it didn't matter. She was suddenly almost overwhelmingly real to him. The effect was quite startling, like cuddling a favourite toy bear that comes alive in your arms and hugs you back.

Then she straightened and said, 'My God, let's get away from this smell.' She let go of him, feeling for his hand, taking it as she groped forward.

The boards cut out almost all of the light that might have found its way through the windows. It took a minute just to find a door out of the kitchen, and into what he assumed was the hallway off the entrance they had passed outside. But once there, it was possible to be more methodical, and Anna turned right and felt her way round the wall until they came to another door. She opened it with almost-painful care and he followed her in, shutting it just as cautiously behind him. They stood for several seconds, sensing the empty room – a tiny echo to the slight sounds they made, the smell of damp and a vague perfume.

'Try the lighter,' he whispered, 'I don't think there can be any windows.'

He heard Anna pull it from her pocket, but even so the flame was shockingly bright to his dark-adapted eyes. They were in a windowless bathroom, which had been stripped from floorboards to ceiling except for the bath, sink and toilet. Smears of old soap scum and water stains were just visible under a layer of dust. Holes in the wall showed where towel rails, mirrors and cupboards had been ripped away. He let out a silent sigh of relief, and sat beside Anna on the edge of the bath. He pulled out the map. A glance told him that the first settlements marked on the coast either side of Emden were Leer to the south, and a place called Greetsiel to the north.

'There are other little fishing villages along there,' he said, pointing to the strip of coast, 'I remember seeing the moon on the water from the train soon after Leer, so some of the places we stopped at must have harbours. The question is which ones, and how far back are they?' He looked at his watch. 'One thirty – it can't be much more than five hours till sunrise. Even if we left now and found a boat at that last train stop and everything went smoothly – like there's enough water in the harbour – we'd be lucky to clear the German coast before daylight.'

Anna clicked the lighter off as she dropped her head into her hands. The darkness pressed in on them again, and with it the air of abandonment, sorrow and neglect that had soaked into the flat.

'I was hoping that we could get out of Germany tonight,' she said in frustration. 'The quicker we get out of here, the better.'

'We still might, there's a chance there's no lock gate,' he reminded her.

'You think it's worth waiting to check?'

'Rather that I don't like the alternative. There's so little time before sunrise. We could get caught with nowhere to hide – the landscape was so flat and empty. And in all those tiny villages a strange face will stand out much more than in a town. This place feels safe. And there's still a slim chance that we can find a boat and get out of here tonight.' Anna was silent. There was something strange, he thought, about having a conversation in such complete darkness. It was as though they were on the telephone.

'But then we're stuck here tomorrow,' she said.

'What about trying to get on the Captain's boat when it arrives?' he suggested.

'It'll be watched,' she replied.

'True, but I rather like the idea of going straight home.' He thought for a moment, then said, 'Turn the lighter on again.' Anna did as he instructed and again he pointed. 'The closest place marked on the coast is north of here, Greetsiel, where this branch railway runs up to – it's about ten miles away. We could easily walk there tomorrow night if we set off at sunset, then get a boat. I think there's a lot less chance of them looking for us in the north – surely they'll concentrate any search the other side of Emden.'

'I suppose that makes sense,' she said, the light flickering under her face, giving her a hollow-eyed look that only accentuated the tiredness in her voice.

'So what about this for a plan – we wait here for a couple of hours and see if the water goes out. If it does, we can just steal one of the fishing boats and leave. If not, we can look at the chance of getting aboard Emerton's boat when he arrives tomorrow. Or maybe we can try to get a message to him somehow, to meet him out on the Ems – Greetsiel would be ideal for that, it's halfway to the open water past the islands. Otherwise, we just head for Greetsiel anyway, and take a boat and go straight to Holland.' He looked up from the map and caught a shake of Anna's head, just before she turned off the lighter.

'I was really hoping we could get out of here tonight,'

she said.

'Yes, me too – but we have to be sensible, let's not get panicked into a mistake, we've had a bloody long day already. If we start stumbling about out there again now, there's a pretty good chance we'll do something stupid. Give us a day to rest and it might all be a lot easier.'

There was another long, tired silence filled with all the other unspoken fears of their situation. Then she said, 'All right.'

'Let's see what the room at the front is like, check that we can see the water, then you get some sleep and I'll take the first watch.'

Chapter 28

The cramp in Ben's leg became unbearable and he shifted. Anna stirred immediately with a sigh, and he thought what a light sleeper she must be.

'What time is it?' she asked, in a hoarse voice.

'I don't know, I can't read my watch without the street lights, but I think it's time to check the tide.' There was a silence that lasted for several seconds, then, with a little exclamation of effort, she pushed herself up onto an elbow. He slid out and turned to look over the windowsill and through the boards. The lights on the quay opposite sparkled darkly in water whose level hadn't moved. He checked his watch in the glow coming through the crack. It was just after three – plenty of time to see a difference, if there was to be one.

'Well?' came the anxious whisper from beside him.

'No change,' he said.

'Damn it,' she hissed, slumping back to the floor.

He didn't respond.

Then she said, 'It's my turn to keep a lookout. Someone needs to stay awake.'

'No, I'll do it, you sleep.'

'Definitely not.' Sounds of movement and shuffling. 'I'm awake, I'm up and I'm on watch. Here, use me as a pillow.'

He felt her sit back against the wall beside him.

'You'll get terrible cramp,' he said.

'I'll wake you when I have to move, and you can have a turn.'

'Do we have to have someone on watch?' he asked.

'It's safer, as the town gets up – to make sure we're all right here. It's better than being woken by some brat of a Hitler Youth, or a caretaker come to fix the window.'

'Someone will fix that?'

'Of course, they're not all Nazi monsters – whoever owned the place would have organised something.'

He took a last look across the silent dock, the fishing boats sitting obediently, just waiting for someone to cast them off. It crossed his mind that they could stow away, but what if the boat didn't go out for a couple of days? And he somehow didn't see himself forcing Teutonic fishermen to take them to Holland. No, they were trapped here for the day, and he'd better get used to it.

Matt Faden marked his page and carefully shut the copy of John Maynard Keynes's new opus, *The General Theory of Employment, Interest and Money.* He pushed the chair back from his seat at a window table in Chelsea's public library. The scrape of the legs on the battered floorboards was loud in the silence, and the plump tweedy woman opposite meaningfully lifted her gaze over her glasses and up from the *Illustrated London News.* Faden ignored her, stretched and lit a cigarette.

The first inhalation of smoke dispelled the room's musty damp smell. The steady stream of morning visitors had arrived shaking umbrellas and tapping the rain off their hats, forming a small puddle by the door. A glance out of the window established that while the rain had stopped, it was probably a temporary state of affairs. Faden pulled his shepherd's-check overcoat off the back of the chair and put it on. The plump woman had gone back to her magazine, and no one else was paying him any attention. Leaving the book where it was, along with his notes and a scarf tactically positioned on the chair, he strolled out into the corridor.

The vaulted ceilings and black and white tiles of the Old Town Hall's rather grand entrance led him out onto the King's Road. It was just after ten o'clock and he was right on time. The street was still dark with the thick blanket of cloud. The handful of people out and about were not tarrying. He tossed the cigarette into a puddle glittering with the amber light of a Belisha beacon, turned left and walked west – the positioning of a bicycle parked outside his flat each morning told him which way to go.

He took one more look up to the first-floor windows of 151b Sydney Street. There was still no light on. There had been no sign of occupation for the four days that he had been watching. Charles Lerup was not at home. Where the hell had he gone? The news from Leon's network that Ben's girl, Lucy, had left Hamble aboard a fishing boat made some sense – apparently headed for Germany with the *Windflower*'s former Captain. They could be using the fishing boat to bring back the engine parts. But there was no obvious explanation for Lerup's absence. He had simply disappeared, straight after Dunwood had abandoned sailing and sent everyone home on Sunday afternoon. And Faden was worried, but not as worried as Leon.

He walked for a couple of minutes before he found the chestnut barrow just before the corner with Oakley Street. Leon was stomping his feet and rubbing his hands, water dripping from the jeweller's canopy that he had used for shelter. He didn't look happy.

'I'll take a bag, my good man,' announced Faden as he approached.

'I've had a bit of a run on 'em just recently, sir, but these'll be ready in a couple of minutes if you don't mind waiting.'

Faden nodded, pulled out his cigarettes again and lit another, then shuffled closer, palms up to get some warmth from the brazier.

'Bloody hell, that last cloud just threw it down,' said Leon under his breath, as he bent to pick up his poker.

Faden didn't reply.

'Anything?' asked Leon, head down still, opening the fire grate.

Faden tapped his foot once. *No.*

'No sign of the others either – not Venuti, Clayton or his girl. The whole bloody lot have gone to ground. I've got a bad feeling, a really bad feeling. I've called on the comrades for help. We still have some Comintern friends in Germany, not many, but someone might be able to tell us something.' Leon poked at the fire aggressively as he spoke, and his donkey jacket flapped open. Faden caught a momentary glimpse of what looked like a pistol butt protruding from the poacher's pocket on the inside. He started to draw breath to say something, and then stopped. His instructions were to say as little as possible, just answer yes or no with a tap of the foot whenever he could.

'I've got to say I'm bloody worried about your friend Clayton,' continued Leon, giving the fire another vicious poke; ash and sparks spat back at him. 'Could he have gone over to White?'

Faden tapped his foot again, just the once. *No.*

Leon grunted disbelievingly. 'We've got to be ready for anything.'

'So I see,' said Faden, and immediately regretted his inability to keep his mouth shut, as Leon glanced up at him with an ugly look. An anxious ball of nausea lodged in his guts.

But Leon flipped the grate shut and propped the poker against the barrow so he could button his coat to the top. 'Bloody right,' he said, picking up a small serving shovel and starting to flip the chestnuts. 'It'd be better if we can persuade your friend Clayton to go public with White's plot, but you never know what those MI5 bastards will do when you poke around inside their dark, sordid little cave with a stick.'

'It's not very ...' started Faden.

Again Leon's expression contained a warning. 'We're trying to stop a war here, stop the workers getting slaughtered and robbed. If we have to break a few eggs to make the omelette, then so be it,' he muttered, barely audible even to Faden. 'This is life and death for the working class. Not a game.'

Faden said nothing, the implication and the insult stung. What the hell had he got wrapped up in? What the hell had he started? He tried to finish his cigarette nonchalantly, but mostly he just tried to hide his shaking hands. Finally, Leon shovelled up some chestnuts and served them into a wrap of newspaper.

'Better get back to your books,' he said, handing it over. 'And that Keynes stuff is shite, by the way,' he added, as Faden took the packet from him. 'What the hell are you doing reading it?'

Faden hesitated with the packet of chestnuts hot in his hands. So the watcher was being watched. 'Know your enemy,' he said. Then he turned and walked back to his seat in the library.

Ben knelt by the window, squinting into a sun which was dropping towards the buildings on the other side of the quay, creeping shadows about to snuff out the dancing light on the water. He was trying to think about something other than his thirst and his hunger. A short exploration just after dawn had established that the water was turned off. There was nothing in the lounge but the discolouration on the ghastly flock wallpaper where paintings and furniture had protected it from the light. And the rest of the flat was no different – two bedrooms, the bathroom and the kitchen were all completely stripped.

'Do you think they're actually coming? Maybe there were difficulties, it's a long trip,' whispered Anna. She was sitting beside him, brushing fitfully at her shoes with her hairbrush. They had got as much of the previous night's mud off as they possibly could without the help of soap and water.

He glanced at his watch, nearly four o'clock. 'Nothing's come into the harbour since that final fishing boat late this morning; maybe no one has been able to get in since then because of the tide. Emerton might have been waiting outside in the channel since lunchtime.'

'Or it might just be a quiet day,' mumbled Anna. 'God, I need a cigarette,' she added, with a lot more conviction. The last one had been smoked hours ago.

'I'd much rather have a drink,' he replied.

'That too, but mostly a cigarette for me,' she sighed.

He wondered how it was possible, at that moment, for anything to be worse than thirst. At least there was no sign of any search. A single policeman had strolled down the other side of the dock a couple of hours earlier. But as Anna had pointed out, it could be part of a trap, designed to make them feel safe. He massaged his forehead bleakly; he had a roasting headache. Then he stiffened. He reached out a hand to prod Anna.

'What?' she asked.

'Coming down our channel right now,' he hissed. 'I'm not sure if it's Emerton, but it's a fishing boat.' He peered up the waterway, wishing he had a pair of binoculars. The boat was framed for a moment between each pair of the row of trees that lined the bank, ticking them off one by one, slowly coming closer. 'It's him! I'm sure of it.'

The old crabber still had its stubby mast forward, but the aft one had gone when Emerton had fitted a big engine, putting a wheelhouse in its place – it had created a distinctive shape. Now it was close enough to almost see the faces through the glass, it looked as if it was going to tie up just past a coaster on the opposite side – the returning fishing fleet had filled the nearer quay. Then a figure separated from the wheelhouse and went forward to a mooring line and his intestines flipped. It was Lucy.

'Bloody hell,' he said.

'What?' Anna was beside him now.

He was dumbstruck – why had Lucy come? To earn the money, of course, Emerton would be sympathetic to the Kirks' plight. But did she know he was here? He tried to remember what he'd said in the last telegram; had he indicated that they would be accompanying the parts? He thought he had. Would she be as angry as he feared? Would she even want anything to do with him?

'What's wrong, Ben?' asked Anna, again, a touch on his elbow.

'The girl – I know her,' he said.

'You know her, or you *know* her?' replied Anna.

He just frowned.

She stared out of the window. 'So she's the one. A very pretty girl, but then, that isn't a surprise.'

He turned and found himself trapped by her calm gaze, the faint smile on her lips.

'Lerup mentioned her,' she said, 'he thought you were betraying your class. I told him that was ridiculous.'

He looked back out of the window. Emerton was just bringing the boat alongside.

'But I ...' she started. It was an uncharacteristic hesitation. 'You do have a choice – you know that, don't you?' She placed her hand on his arm for a moment. 'I really ... like you, Ben ...' she said. 'When this is over ... when you've had a chance to think about it ...'

And there it was, not just a possibility any longer. How that would show Lerup. Of course, it was impossible, but could he risk telling her that? There was a chance, however faint, that her affection for him was the foundation of her support against Lerup. In silence they stared out at Emerton's boat – at Lucy tying her up.

'Having Lucy on board will make it easier to organise a rendezvous,' he said, finally.

'How?'

'Have you still got your powder compact?' he replied, looking at her.

Anna pulled the handbag towards her and fumbled around inside for a few moments. When she pulled it out, she said, 'Morse code, with the sun?'

'That's right.' He took it from her, flipped it open and looked at himself in the mirror. Bloodshot eyes peered bleakly back at him from under dark lids. He snapped it back shut; the smooth ivory finish had a little elephant engraved on it. 'In the *Riddle of the Sands*, one of the characters goes off to explore a salvage site and they arrange a rendezvous on the island of Memmert. It's the perfect spot for us too, since it's somewhere I'm sure I can find without a chart – and as I know Lucy's read the book recently, I can use that as a reference.'

'Will she understand?'

'I'm certain of it.'

'But what if she does something silly when she realises it's you on the signalling mirror?'

'I can wait until Emerton is the only one on deck. He's bound to share the message with her.'

There was a short silence. 'Where do you think you can signal from?' she asked.

He scanned the quay, looking to the right, the direction they'd have to go to leave town to the north. There was a bridge further up, and on the other side of it a small park.

He pointed. 'Down amongst those trees at the end of the bridge. We'll be completely hidden. I can make the signal straight up the harbour. Then we can slip out the back of the park and away.' This time, Anna was quiet for almost half a minute. He waited patiently.

'All right, it's worth trying,' she said, finally.

Two men in uniform were approaching the fishing boat. 'Who are they?' he asked.

'Customs.'

Ben watched as Emerton invited the officials on board. Lucy stood back, arms folded, looking around the dockside. There was a discussion, a lot of pointing up towards the harbour master's building and the station. Then Emerton took the officials down below, and Lucy jumped off the boat and started to walk down the quay towards the bridge.

'She's coming this way. I think Emerton has sent her round to the station to see about the delivery. We should go as soon as she's gone past, it's the perfect opportunity,' he said.

'You can't signal until those customs officers are gone.'

'No, of course not,' he replied.

'And you can't wait there forever, for the right opportunity.'

'I'll give it fifteen minutes, and then I'll leave regardless.'

'All right, we should go separately – they're looking for a couple,' she said.

He looked at her. 'That could be dangerous if anyone talks to me.'

'I'll be right behind you,' she said, 'just a few yards. I'll sit this side of the water while you do the signal. Then when you're finished, walk north and I'll catch up once we're out of the town. If anyone approaches you I'll be there in a jiffy, just pretend you have a sore throat. They're looking for a couple, remember.'

He nodded, she was right, but he was only too aware that the main risk to them was his lack of German. He followed Lucy's progress as she temporarily disappeared behind the moored fishing boats, reappearing again as she approached up the road on their side of the harbour. She was wearing an old blue seaman's jacket a couple of sizes too big, and dark trousers that were stuffed into a pair of sea boots with the tops turned over. She wasn't wearing a hat, and her blond hair was tousled and spiky with the salt air and sunshine. She looked improbably desirable – something only Lucy could manage in those circumstances. But she also looked tense, wary, as though she were expecting trouble.

'I don't see anyone following her, perhaps they don't

think we're here,' said Anna, rising and starting to button her coat. 'We'd better get on with it. We don't know how long she'll be up there.'

He struggled to his feet, taking the compact from where it lay beside Anna's handbag and slipping it into his jacket pocket. He picked up his hat and gloves and made his way carefully to the kitchen. The smell didn't seem as bad. He edged a little closer to the window and saw a single skinny stool fast drying in the sink, a couple of lethargic, early-season flies buzzing fitfully around it. He peered through the window from all angles. Much of the garden was already in dark shadow – unkempt, with the first signs of new growth. A cat strolled in a leisurely fashion across the grass, tail high and flicking with a proprietorial air. But there was no life that he could see in any of the windows overlooking the flat. He peeled off his coat, put it on the floor with his hat and gloves, then levered himself up onto the sink and stepped his feet through the hole. At least he could see what he was doing this time, but then again, so might other people.

He wriggled and sweated, finally managing to get his feet to the ground without knocking any glass out. He checked the surrounding buildings again – still nothing moved. There was a tap on the glass behind him; Anna was at the window. She passed out his things and her handbag, and then he lifted her through as before. But this time she let him go as her feet touched the ground – brisk, businesslike, straightening her clothes. He pulled his coat back on, flipped the collar up and pushed his hat down to hide his face. He tugged his fingers tight into his gloves and straightened his tie.

'All right?' he asked.

Anna ran a critical eye over him as she tidied her distinctive hair back under her beret. 'You could do with a shave, but quite decent, really.'

They looked at each other for a moment. Then she said, 'I'll be right behind you, good luck.'

'You too,' he replied.

He walked out to the pavement and glanced up to the left, but Lucy was gone from sight. So he turned right and strode down towards the bridge, staying on the inland side of the road, in case Emerton and the customs men emerged back on deck. Emerton probably wouldn't recognise him from that distance, but he wasn't taking the risk. He would need to give a time for the rendezvous. If he was right about the tide, it would be about four thirty in the morning before Emerton could get through the lock, and then it would take them another three or four hours to get to Memmert. If he told them nine o'clock that would be plenty of time, and it would give him and Anna seventeen hours to get to Greetsiel, find a boat and row, motor or sail to the rendezvous.

By now, he was almost at the bridge. A handful of people on the other side of the road were enjoying the spring sunshine. Two dogs sniffed each other while their owners talked, a bareheaded man and a younger woman whose mousy-brown hair stuck out at angles from under a cloche hat. Ben stepped out to cross the road and, in a blur of wind rush and horn, flying metal brushed his sleeve. He jumped back onto the pavement, the flash of anger driving an involuntary shout of rage up his throat ... *They drive on the right.* He choked back the words as the realisation coursed through him – the immensity of the error, just the tiniest fraction of a second had saved him.

The dog owners were watching, alerted by the horn. The woman called out. He stared at her blankly. Then Anna was at his side, a gentle touch on his elbow. She spoke some words in loud German, and he had the wit to just nod as though he understood. She smiled, turned and shouted to the couple, who waved and went back to their conversation.

'They drive on the right,' she said, in the softest voice, as she held out a hand to let him cross in front of her, with a glance over her shoulder to check for traffic. He nodded, stumbling back into life, into motion. He made it to the opposite pavement, and headed for the bridge. He sensed Anna drop back to just a few steps behind him. It was all right, he told himself, he'd got away with it. *Calm down and for God's sake, concentrate.* By the time he was on the bridge, his body had restored a reasonable pulse and breathing rate. He slowed his walk, examining the park and picking out a wooden seat dappled by light. He followed a path down across the grass. He glanced over his shoulder, but Anna had gone.

A couple was approaching along the quayside from the opposite direction – an elderly gentleman with sunken cheeks, his charcoal-grey coat hanging off him, a plump younger woman providing support under the fragile grasp of his right hand. They stopped and sat on the bench Ben was heading for – he ducked into the trees and halted in a pool of sunlight. He leaned back against the smooth grey bark of a beech tree. A red squirrel darted across the grass in front of him and scampered up another trunk. It hesitated at the first branch and eyed him curiously. But the tree hid him from the road and he had a clear view all the way up to the boat. He would look a bit odd just standing there, particularly to anyone coming up the quay towards him, but he could always stop and move if that happened.

He realised that Emerton and the customs men had come back on deck while he'd been getting himself into position. He wouldn't have recognised the Captain from this distance, which encouraged him – all Emerton needed to see was the flash of light. As he watched, the three men shook hands and parted, the portly customs officers hauling weighty frames onto the dock and then jamming themselves into a small black car. He heard it shudder into life, and watched as it crashed into gear and pulled off. What would Emerton do now? *Please don't go back below* – but the Captain took a seat propped against the port rail, pulled out his tobacco pouch and started to roll himself a cigarette.

Ben pulled the compact out and, still leaning against

the tree with his arms folded, flipped it open. With the mirror resting in the crook of his left arm he experimented. He could use tiny movements of his right hand to break the light and create the pattern he needed. Emerton was smoking, his gaze flicking around the harbour. Now he was looking straight at the park. Ben began with a quick SOS: *dot, dot, dot – dash, dash, dash – dot, dot dot.* He repeated it, then stopped, wondering how Emerton would react. Would he jump up, look away? ... Ben thought his heart was going to squeeze itself out through the gaps in his ribcage it was pounding so hard. But no, Emerton just sat, still looking at him, a slow drag on the cigarette ... was he nodding? Had Ben imagined it? He repeated the SOS, then went straight into the message – *police trouble need help stop tell lucy meet at carruthers and davies salvage site rdz stop at 0900 ben.*

When he'd finished he glanced around, feeling horribly vulnerable. But nothing had changed – it remained a quiet provincial harbour on a late afternoon in early spring. Two men were overhauling nets on one of the fishing boats. The couple on the seat burst into conversation, broken by the old man's raucous coughing. A car rumbled across the bridge behind him, and a child screamed briefly on the other side of the water. He looked back at Emerton, who nipped the cigarette out and stuck it behind his ear, before pulling what appeared to be paper and pencil out of the top pocket of his coat. A massive elated rush poured through Ben. It had been a nod, Emerton had got the message. But don't make it too bloody obvious, he thought, as he started the signal again.

This time he forced himself to go more slowly, giving Emerton the opportunity to write, relax a little at the breaks and look around the quays – just as though he were writing a job or provisioning list. It was agonising, Ben felt conspicuous and exposed – but eventually, message complete, he watched Emerton tuck the paper into his pocket, pull the cigarette from behind his ear and wander off into the wheelhouse. Ben snapped the compact shut, dropped it into his pocket and pushed himself off the tree. *Now get the hell away from here.*

Chapter 29

Ben walked out of the park, following the harbour channel north. Cautiously, he crossed the road coming off the bridge, concentrating on keeping his pace steady, hands in his pockets and head down. Almost immediately he was confronted by another channel splitting off to the left, and he had no choice but to go with it, down a pleasant tree-lined street, now travelling what he reckoned to be north-west. He passed a window full of butchered meat on marble slabs, whole legs hanging from hooks. There was a grocer's ahead, a whiff of pastry on the air – food! But it was torture, all so painfully, frustratingly out of his grasp. And where was Anna? Was she still behind him as they'd originally planned, or had she gone ahead to wait, after her intervention at the near accident?

There was another bridge coming up, and he had to make a decision – which way might she have gone? These roads seemed to be gridded north-east and north-west, or perhaps they were north and east, or even north and west, he couldn't be sure. Then he saw her, sitting at an outside café table, smoking – a cup of coffee, two glasses of water and two slices of cake in front of her. *Bloody hell,* he thought, *the plan has changed.* She caught his eye, and indicated the chair opposite as he approached. He did not want to sit down. The situation felt too vulnerable, the danger too random, too out of his control – his lack of

German was a terrible liability. But the smell of pastry and coffee was powerful, his hunger and thirst immense. He sat. She smiled and greeted him in German. All he could do was nod and smile. She pushed the glass of water towards him. The desire to pour it all back at once was almost overpowering, but he could feel her reproachful gaze even as he picked it up. Never had plain water tasted better.

The crisp white linen tablecloth brushed against his hand as he put the glass down, and suddenly he felt filthy. Surely everyone who walked past could see that. But Anna indicated the plate as she leaned back in her chair, and then looked over her shoulder into the café, quickly attracting an attentive waiter as Ben took a piece of the cake. Sugar and fat melted in his mouth; the blissful sensation was overwhelming and for a moment he didn't care about anything else. She was digging in her purse for money. He finished the cake slowly, steadily. Anna sipped her coffee, smoked another cigarette and watched him, eyes flicking up momentarily at everyone who approached along the pavement. A second glass of water arrived just as he swallowed the final mouthful. He drank steadily, feeling it flow through him, feeling stronger as they stood to leave.

Then she took his arm and they were moving. He wanted to get off the busy waterfront and they turned into a wide boulevard, which terminated after a couple of hundred yards in a grand Renaissance building. They both headed for the next right turn, a smaller street, homelier, despite the bare trees. Their pace lifted, more comfortable away from the crowds, following their instincts. Crossing one canal, they converged on another, passing an empty barge, high in the water, towed at a stately speed by a sagging blinkered horse.

They dog-legged right and left through the old defensive earthworks and moat that had protected the town. On the second bend someone had daubed a comment under a road sign. He nudged Anna and nodded towards it.

'It's a warning about the dangerous corner,' she

whispered into his ear, 'and underneath someone has added *Jews drive faster*.' He had a brief image of a child in a family car – *Mummy, why do they hate us?* Then the road straightened ahead of them and the houses dropped away. He felt a rising elation; there was something hopeful about being in the open and on the move again, with the sun slipping towards the horizon. Another hour and they would be hidden by darkness. By daylight they would be gone from this land. He hadn't realised how tense he'd become, trapped in that awful, oppressive, degraded flat.

They continued in silence until they had passed the last of the houses, but as soon as they were clear, Anna asked, 'So, tell me, what happened?'

'It worked, he definitely got the message,' he replied.

'Really! How could you tell?'

'I saw him write it down.'

Her mouth opened and her eyes widened.

'It's all right, it was a great piece of acting,' he reassured her. 'I did it slowly and Emerton wrote it down as though he was making a shopping list – Oscar-winning stuff. They'll definitely be there, I'm sure of it.'

She took a deep breath and let it out. 'So ...' she started, 'are you happy staying on the roads? We could go along the railway line like last night, it isn't far.' She waved out to the west, where a smudge of smoke, still visible on the air, indicated a passing train.

'As long as we keep a good lookout, I don't see why we can't use the roads,' he replied. 'It's a lot faster, especially with your shoes, and we don't end up looking like we've been in the trenches for a week.'

'I was hoping you'd say that.' Anna hesitated, then added, 'I was a little concerned when you decided to throw yourself in front of that car.'

He looked at her, not quite sure if the tone was amused or annoyed. 'I know, I'm sorry about that – I just wasn't thinking, or not about that, anyway.'

'We were lucky.'

Now he could see the trace of a smile. 'And that stop in the café – when did you decide on that?' he asked.

'Oh, don't tell me you minded!' she scolded him, laughing.

'Well ...' he said. It was plain that she shared his sense of relief at being out of Emden.

'So you won't want any of the bread, sausages or milk I got then?' She held up a paper bag that Ben, in his focus on escape, hadn't even noticed.

He looked at her. 'You bought food as well?'

'I had some spare time. I thought I was more likely to attract attention standing around doing nothing – and you took so long.'

There was some sense in that, he thought. He stopped. 'I'm so hungry,' he said.

'We'll have half now, and half when we get to the rendezvous. It can be our reward.' Her smile faded. 'I'm going to need a reward after walking *ten bloody miles*.'

They had already passed through several tiny hamlets, as well as the bigger villages of Hinte and Krummhorn. There were few people about, and those that were they avoided easily enough. The only scare had been the attention of one particularly curious and loud dog. Fortunately, it had been chained up, and they had hurried on before any human could come to investigate the racket. The road threaded a lonely route through flat countryside, past dykes and looming windmills, huge blades impotent in the still air.

'Ben, please, I must stop.'

He halted – Anna had flagged in the last half an hour, her weight dragging on his arm. Even her complaints had dried up. 'How are your feet?' he asked.

'Agony, I have terrible blisters.'

'Here, sit down a moment,' he said, and helped her to the side of the road. He pulled her shoes off and felt her feet. She yelped with pain, and his fingertips came away wet with blood. 'You'd be better off with bare feet,' he said.

'Not on these wretched stones,' she replied, waving at the dirt road.

'I'll carry you for a while,' he suggested. 'There's no one about.'

'Really, do you think you can?'

He remembered her weight as he had lifted her through the window of the flat. 'For a while, we'll see how we get on.'

'Thank you, darling.' She sounded pathetically grateful.

He pushed her shoes into his overcoat pockets along with the vests, then knelt on one knee so that she could climb onto his back. She draped her arms tiredly round his neck, but he got a good grip on her legs, pressing her thighs tightly against his hips. She laid her head on his shoulder and he felt her body relax into his. He stood, balancing carefully under the extra weight, and started down the road.

'Can you read it?' asked Anna, as he peered at the sign in the darkness.

'More feel it than read it, but this is it,' he said. 'Greetsiel.'

'Thank God,' she replied, her voice an exhausted whisper.

They both stared ahead towards the church spire looming out of the horizon, a sprinkling of lights scattered around it. It had taken a little over four hours, and he had carried Anna for much of the last thirty minutes.

'You'll have to walk, I'm afraid,' he told her. 'We could easily meet someone.'

'I know. I'll try bare feet now that the surface is smoother.'

A canal ran parallel to the road, and they followed that in the hope that it led to the harbour, Anna limping slowly beside him. It was a beautiful clear night, just like the previous one. But there was a hint on the southern rim of the infinite horizon – perhaps an absence of stars, a darker, more threatening black than the soft velvet that wrapped the rest of the landscape. Or perhaps it was just a rise of the land. If there was to be a change in the weather, he hoped it would hold off until they were safely with Emerton and Lucy. Everything would be harder in a gale.

The village slowly embraced them, much of its character shrouded by the darkness. Eventually their canal joined a second at a T-junction, and the road bridged across it. They chose the right-hand fork, and then another, as it seemed to run into a bigger stretch of open water. It was a dead end. They retreated to the junction, and turned deeper into the village. Anna clutched his arm, hobbling along the tight little cobbled streets. His frustration was building – why was it so difficult to find the sea? But finally, a silhouetted roofline – curiously curved in places – stretched away opposite, with an erratic pattern of lit windows pointing the way. They were rewarded with the cold glitter of moonlight on water. A lock gate leaked a steady jet out into the narrow inland neck of a small harbour, in which nestled a row of fishing boats, nets strung up from their masts.

They took the bridge across the top of the lock, and then followed the road around in front of the houses until they found a path that led down to the quay, some fifteen or twenty feet below the buildings. They strolled along the dock, Anna moving as casually as she could manage, hesitating by one of the fishing boats as a cart rumbled past above them. Then a door banged and a short burst of excited chatter flew over their heads and away into the salt flats beyond. The door creaked, and then quiet returned.

'The problem with taking one of these fishing boats is that its absence is likely to be noticed pretty quickly tomorrow morning, if not tonight,' he said. 'A search party could have time to make life awkward for us.'

'That's if we could get it out of here at all,' replied Anna. 'Those houses are so close – they'll hear an engine start and see a mast move.'

He reluctantly agreed. 'We need something smaller, let's look further up,' he added. There had to be a boat that they could propel without breeze or an engine.

They walked the hundred yards to the end of the quay, his anxiety rising with each glance down into empty inky-black water. But then their prize revealed itself, tucked in tight under the stern of the final fishing smack – a fifteen-foot-long open rowing boat.

'Our luck holds,' he said, glancing over his shoulder towards the road. Nothing moved, not even a sigh of wind through the grass. Perhaps a couple of the lights had gone out in the windows. 'You keep a lookout; if you see anyone, tap three times and then walk away. Come back and do the same when it's safe.'

Without waiting for a reply, he let himself over the edge of the quay, feeling with his feet for the boat, before he gently eased himself down onto the floorboards. He felt it move beneath him. That was a good feeling, he thought, the suck of the tide. There was still plenty of water, but it was properly away now, and it would be so much easier to get to Memmert with the help of the ebb.

Again, he wondered at their luck – he couldn't have timed this much better if he'd checked the tide tables in the almanac. How much longer could their run hold up? *Just find some oars*, he told himself. He groped under the prow of the boat, and came up with a galvanised steel bucket, anchor, chain and some line. Then he moved cautiously back, weight solid on the front foot before he lifted the second, the boat alive under him. He bent to check, and found the oars tucked under the thwarts. The rowlocks were notches carved into the gunwales. He had all that he needed to get them to the rendezvous. He looked up – Anna stood silently, staring back towards the road, silhouetted against the moonlight.

'Untie her,' he hissed.

Without a word, she knelt. He took her shoes and one dock-line from her, then held on while she undid the other and climbed down to join him. She sat in the stern, a hand on the quay, while he, with painstaking care, pulled the oars clear from under the thwarts. Then he got the two vests out of his overcoat pockets and, feeling along the wood, found the area of chafe where the oar bore on the rowlocks. He tied a vest round each one to muffle the sound.

Then he whispered, 'Push her off, out into the middle.'

The boat glided away from the dockside. It was unnaturally quiet. It felt as though a single drop of water dripping from an oar would wake the whole village. So he did nothing, just let Anna's shove carry them out to where the unseen hand of the current began to move them more quickly downstream. They sat, absorbed whole into the silence, watching each other and the shore behind them.

The narrow harbour quickly opened up into a bigger channel, and the critical moment passed – the high banks soon hid them from the houses. Ahead, he could see a sharp corner, and he carefully put the oars into place to steer them around it. The only sign of a human presence was the faint loom of light from the village, and this soon faded beneath the dykes that hid them and herded them onwards. He started to row with more effort. He followed the trickle of reflected moonlight, like Ariadne's thread, round a long curve to the left, then another sharper turn back to the right. Neither he nor Anna spoke, not wanting to break the silent spell of their efforts before they'd left the land far behind. But the channel seemed endless, and more oppressive with every turn, with no outlook beyond the water they had just travelled and the beckoning glitter ahead. He rowed mechanically, every sense twitching for change in the silence emanating from the land – anything could lie ahead or behind those dykes. It was just an act of faith that this channel, the flow of an ebb tide, would eventually take them to the sea.

Abruptly, the dyke fell away on their starboard side. He saw that there were green and red channel lights ahead. They must mark the entrance to this tributary. Finally, it would lead them out into the open estuary of the Ems. And after what seemed like a thousand more strokes of the oars and a last narrowing of the dykes on either side, the horizon flattened and expanded. Occasional, distant lights beckoned in all directions. Watching astern, he saw the channel entrance start to move to his left and realised they had hit a deeper, stronger flow than the one exiting their river.

'We're into open water,' he whispered. 'We need to go west before we can go north; there are shallows between here and Memmert.' He pulled harder on his left stroke to turn the boat as he spoke.

'All right,' said Anna. 'I think there's a locker back here, under the aft deck. I'm just going to have a look, see if there's anything useful.'

He watched her outline twist and bend, heard wood grind and screech and then what might have been a bolt being thrown. In the pause, he could imagine her probing the darkness with nervous fingers.

'There's an engine,' she whispered back over her shoulder.

'Terrific!' He wasn't going to have to row the whole bloody way – that was almost as good as getting clear of those endless dykes. He waited; there was the noise of a canister being lifted and replaced, before finally a rustling as she looked back to him.

'It's a little outboard engine, with a half-full petrol can. And I think this might be a compass.'

He heaved the oars inboard, and took what was indeed a compass from her. 'We might as well have a look with the lighter, we're well clear now,' he said. The tide was sweeping them along quickly, the channel lights were diminishing.

Anna was already going through her pockets, and soon he could see that the tide was swirling them north-west. That was all right, he thought, but only for a while. He knew that they had to find the northern edge of this channel and follow it as it turned north, up the eastern edge of the Ems estuary. That would lead them straight to the southern tip of Memmert. He decided to save as much of the limited petrol as he could, and set to the oars again. But the adrenaline charge of their escape from Greetsiel faded quickly, the cumulative effect of the past two nights' endeavour and the limited food had drained him. After half an hour of rowing, he reluctantly turned to the engine. It took him some time to work out how to fasten it to the stern. But once it was in place it started at the third tug of the greasy rope, and they chugged north under the sliver of waning moon. The ebb was running out fast now, and ghostly sandbanks started to ease their way clear of the receding water. Soon they were travelling beside a steep beach of darkly glistening sand and mud, just the moan of the little engine as they slid across the black mirror of water, their wake arcing away behind them, the wash rocking gently onto the shore.

It was cold now that he wasn't rowing. He said as much to Anna and heard in her juddering reply an uncontrollable shivering. They both moved onto the floorboards, sheltering from the chilling wind created by their motion. He wrapped his overcoat around her, holding her as close as he could. Only his head poked over the gunwale, watching the thin black line on the horizon slowly resolve itself into the island of Juist. Memmert jutted up out of the Nordland Sand at its western extremity. It was easy to find their rendezvous on such a still, clear night – the beacon on the southern tip of Memmert. They nudged the nose of the boat into the mud right under it, tall and angular on its tripod at the visible limit of the steeply rising sands. The early flood was just starting to build inshore, and he threw the anchor out ahead of them to hold their position, while Anna pulled out the remaining milk, bread and sausage.

'Should we leave a little for the morning?' she said, voice still shaky with the cold, as he stumbled, stiff and uncoordinated, back down the boat.

He hesitated – if all went to plan, they would be aboard the fishing boat for hot tea and a proper breakfast in the morning. But that wasn't till nine – if they made it at all. 'All right,' he conceded.

She handed him a piece of sausage wrapped in the rye bread. 'I should have got more,' she said, as he slumped down beside her, both of them curling into the turn of the bilge.

'It'll do until Emerton finds us,' he replied, but it was gone in three bites, spicy and bitter.

Anna handed him the milk. 'Maybe a couple of mouthfuls.'

He felt the weight of the bottle, the glass cold to his touch, clean against his dirty grip. He swallowed a single swig as slowly as possible. 'We made it this far,' he said, handing the bottle back.

Anna screwed the cap on and propped it up in the bilge beside her. 'Well done, us,' she replied, slipping back under his overcoat, leaning her head on his chest and wrapping her arms around him. He didn't even try to suppress the yawn that overtook him, and didn't reply.

Chapter 30

It was the slap of waves against the hull that woke Ben, the wash from some unseen distant passing boat. He half opened his eyes, and then wished he hadn't – the daylight seared in. Quickly, he glanced at his watch.

'What time is it?' asked Anna, still huddled under his coat.

'Eight, an hour to go – have you been awake for long?'

'A while, I didn't sleep much.'

He was about to reply, but something wasn't right about the day, the sky was all fuzzy. He rubbed at sore eyes and started to shuffle upright to get a better look around.

Anna shifted and moaned.

'Sorry, but ... damn,' he said, as he peered over the gunwale, 'look at this bloody fog! It's a bloody pea-souper, not more than ten or twenty yards visibility. I can't even see the beacon and I could have hit it with a stone last night.'

She sat upright beside him. 'Oh my God,' she said, 'they'll never find us.'

They stared out into the grey murk that drifted amorphously around them, a foot or two above the dull glaze of the water. 'It'll burn off pretty quickly; the sun's up, the sky's clear, this won't last long,' he said, almost sounding as if he believed it.

She looked at him, her brown eyes doubtful.

He frowned. 'Emerton is the best – if anyone can find us, it's him.'

She sank back with a desperate sigh, then rolled over to reach for the bottle of milk. 'We might as well finish this,' she said, offering it to him.

'What if they don't find us?' he asked, eyes flicking from her to the milk.

'Now or later, this sip isn't going to make a lot of difference,' she replied, unscrewing the top. They shared the milk and the remainder of the bread and sausage. He wasn't sure if he felt better for the nourishment, or worse for the knowledge that it was all gone.

There was nothing to do but wait and hope the fog lifted. The grey shapes shifted around them as they sat together on the aft thwart. Every now and again it would clear for a few seconds, but always in the seaward direction, so it was hard to tell how much further they could see – there was just more water. Anna shivered.

'Are you still cold?' he asked.

She nodded. 'But not as bad as last night.'

'Come here.' Once again he pulled her against him, wrapping his coat around both of them. He could feel little tremors running through her. She must be exhausted, he thought, being cold drained so much energy.

'Do you think he'll even leave Emden in this?' she asked.

'It might not be this thick on the coast, there might not be any fog at all. And he should do most of the trip on the flood tide, so if he goes on the mud, it'll lift him off again pretty quickly.' She didn't reply and he was happy to let the silence roll on, her head on his chest, tucked under the overcoat. He could smell her hair, her body – the sophisticated perfumes long gone. He could also smell his own unwashed self. He could feel the grime ingrained in his cuffs, the stickiness around his eyes, his itching hair, the metallic, furry, corrosive tang in his mouth and the stubble starting to chafe his collar. He eased his tie loose and pushed it into his jacket pocket. Then he undid the top button of his shirt, pulled the grey bandage off and brushed the hair from his forehead and out of his eyes.

Eventually a weak blood-red sun broke through the fog, and they could feel faint warmth from its rays. *Red sky in morning, sailor's warning*, he thought, and remembered the dark line on the southern horizon the night before.

'The weather's going to break, I'd say we're in for a thrashing,' he said. As if in response to his words, the fog stirred as a gust of wind swirled down to the water. The glassy surface broke up into ripples.

'What?' mumbled Anna, pulling her head clear of the overcoat and looking up at him.

'There's a south-westerly coming in,' he said, 'an offshore breeze. If we don't see them by ten, we should go round to the north of Borkum with the rest of the ebb. We'll be sheltered there, and then we can nip across the western Ems to the first of the Dutch Frisian Islands.'

Anna nodded, leaning back into him. In the distance, an engine thrummed its way past, coming and fading quickly, a long way off, out to sea – perhaps the fog had already dispersed out there. But there were no other sounds, not even a foghorn – no one anchored in the channel waiting for this to clear. He shuddered. There was an eerie chill to the air. *Come on, Emerton*, he thought, *I've had enough of this.*

It was fifteen endless minutes later that he heard it – an engine, the revs low. It faded for a moment, but then it was back, louder and much more distinct, revealed by the fog like a magician with a swirling cape. He straightened and Anna, who had dozed off leaning on him, awoke.

'What is it?' she asked.

He put a finger to his lips, and she cocked her head slightly, sweeping the hair away from her ears to listen. He tried to get a bearing on the sound, peering into the swirl of fog. Holes were appearing in it, and for a moment he thought he caught a glimpse of something ... then it was gone. But the wind was strengthening – it was starting to get the better of the fog. The boat rocked a little in the waves, and he realised they were now held side on to the wind by the current. He took a compass bearing down the centreline to check – the tide was rushing out through the channel. Should he lift the anchor and try to go towards the sound of the boat? But it would be too easy to lose the beacon and never find it again. He must be patient; they were at the rendezvous, moving would only make things harder and it might not even be Emerton. So they waited, listening to the engine throb and then fade through the fog.

Suddenly there was a voice. It was Lucy. She was calling the depths for the lead line.

'Lucy!' His whisper cracked into a shout. They listened – nothing. He repeated the call, louder again. This time the engine audibly clicked back to neutral.

Then they heard her, startlingly clear. 'Ben Clayton?'

'Lucy! Keep calling, we'll come to you!' he yelled, all caution forgotten, the boat rolling under his weight as he stumbled to the anchor line. The tension of the escape had broken inside him and he was caught up with a feverish desire to be aboard the fishing boat, not to lose them, not to miss this chance to get away. He hauled on the rope that held them to the shallow bottom and soon had the chain and anchor back in the bow. Anna had shipped the oars, and he stepped into his place and took them from her.

She shuffled back onto the aft thwart. 'I'll point to the sound,' she said.

He started to row, powering into the strokes, keeping it as smooth and quiet as possible, so that Anna could get the bearing. He watched her arm – a little to the left, another shout, now to the right. Straight ahead, he gave it a good solid stroke with both hands, and another. Lucy's voice was much closer.

'I see them!' Anna exclaimed. 'Fifty yards' she added, still pointing straight ahead.

He wanted to look, but he wanted to get there even

more, and he rowed that final handful of strokes as though Lucy might disappear into the fog forever.

'Hold water starboard! We're going to hit them!'

He dug the starboard oar into the water at Anna's instruction and flicked the port one aboard. A moment later they crashed sideways into the hull, and both of them stood to grab hold as the rowing boat rocked wildly.

'Here, take this,' said Lucy, dropping a rope down.

'It's all right, I've got it,' replied Anna, hanging on to the fishing boat's rail, the two women just feet apart. 'But thanks anyway,' she added, with a sweet smile.

Lucy's expression would have turned wine to vinegar, but she said nothing as Ben moved forward to hurl the anchor and line over the bow. It might end up back with the owner this way, he thought, better than letting it just get swept out to sea. Then he turned to Anna, the boat still unstable under his hurried movements.

'I'll give you a lift up,' he said, grabbing the rail with one hand and making a stirrup for her with the other. She stepped lightly into it, and he heaved himself after her. He tumbled onto the deck, hearing the engine bite as Emerton engaged gear and the propeller churned. They were moving. They were safe. He lay there, his lungs heaving, the salty grain of the deck under his fingers.

'Are you all right?' said Lucy.

He pushed himself to his feet, glancing across at Anna. 'I can't believe you found us,' he said, looking at Lucy. 'And you understood the message,' he went on, brushing at his filthy trousers. She was angry, he thought. What could he say, with Anna right there? *Lucy, I'm sorry, I love you – forgive me ...* There was no more brutal way to tell Anna that she wasn't the one.

'I knew you were in trouble when the Captain said he was meeting you in Emden,' said Lucy, her mouth a firm line.

'You saved us,' he said.

'Us?' replied Lucy, her voice icy, glancing at Anna,

who had moved off towards the stern.

He followed Lucy's gaze – Anna was almost in the wheelhouse. 'There's nothing between us, I can't believe you could think such a thing,' he whispered.

'Believe? After you told Lerup you didn't even know me ...'

'I'm desperately sorry for that, but I had to, you know that's true,' he insisted. 'We'd be completely finished if I lost the job and any chance to prove your dad right ...'

'And then you cleared out to Germany without a word, with ... with her ...' Lucy blazed on, with a dismissive wave towards the back of the boat. 'I've seen how she looks at you!'

'What? But ...?' Ben couldn't hide his confusion, realising too late how guilty it made him look.

'I saw you leaving the village in that damn car of hers!'

Bloody hell, he thought – this was much worse than he'd imagined. 'But Lucy, I can't control what she feels,' he said, 'only what I feel, and *nothing happened*. And *we need her* – she makes the case against Lerup; he killed Stanley, and she was there the night he cut the downhaul off, she didn't realise at the time, but ...'

'Is that what she told you?'

'Yes ...'

'And you believed her?'

'Of course, why not ...?'

'Lucy, get back on that damn lead afore we put her on the mud!' Emerton's hard whisper came hissing down the deck. A moment later, Lucy hit Ben with a stinging slap that jerked his face through a quarter turn.

Ben raised a hand to his cheek, but she was gone, forward to the bow, picking up the lead line. He retrieved his hat from where it had fallen, rubbing his face. For a moment, he started after her – then pulled up. He had to let her calm down. Nothing would be gained by a huge row, not now, with Emerton struggling to get them clear of the coast in this fog.

As he reached the wheelhouse, Emerton jerked a thumb over his shoulder towards the little cubbyhole that served as a kitchen. 'Tea's on the way, plenty of food in the tins,' he said.

'Thanks,' replied Ben, 'I don't know how the hell you found us.'

'More luck than judgement, I'd reckon,' replied Emerton.

Ben tossed his hat down, leaned on the chart table with folded arms and stared in silence towards the bow. Soon Anna was handing him a cup of tea. He took it wordlessly. He gulped at the liquid – strong, sweet and milky – and felt the warmth hit his gut.

Emerton pushed his cap back off his forehead and scratched at his hair. He glanced at Ben, and then returned to the compass. 'I don't know what you two have done, lad, but it's serious. First they said we couldn't leave, then they went through those packages of yours and half pulled the boat apart. Then they ordered us out. A couple of patrol boats went in the lock with us. They followed us up the estuary and when we hit the fog – it isn't so bad inland – we more or less gave 'em the slip. But I think I hear them every now and again. We need to get clear of here before this burns off. We've got no chance of outrunning the German navy.'

'Bloody hell,' breathed Ben, running a hand through his hair. He glanced at Anna, who had halted her examination of the contents of the biscuit tins that littered the cubbyhole and was listening. 'It all seemed quiet when you first docked,' he said, looking back at Emerton.

'All hell broke loose a couple of hours after your message,' said the Captain. 'A staff car turned up with a big fellow in a leather coat and a fedora. He spoke proper English, but he still wouldn't tell us what was going on, just some tale about smuggling.'

'Perhaps we should go back to the rowing boat, we

could hide on Memmert until nightfall, then get across to Holland,' said Anna.

Emerton shook his head slowly. 'I don't think I could find that boat again. You know where you left it – how far from the beacon?'

Ben grimaced. 'I didn't look, didn't think to even try ...'

'We could be hours trying to find it, better to get away from here while we can,' concluded Emerton.

'Do you have a dinghy?' asked Anna.

Emerton glanced at her, shook his head. 'We left it in Hamble. Didn't see how we'd need it.' He leaned on the wheel spokes. 'If it weren't for the fog I'd have left you there anyways, would've been no point leading the Hun patrol boats to you.' He glanced at Ben again. 'Lucy wanted to have a crack at finding you pretty badly.'

Ben didn't reply, just stared forward out of the windows to where Lucy was still swinging the lead.

'So what kind of trouble you in?' Emerton went on.

'They want us for spying, it's just a story, but ...' Anna tailed off. She took the empty mug from Ben.

Emerton shook his head. 'You can't trust the Hun,' he said. Then Lucy called from the bow, and he adjusted the wheel by one spoke. 'Best make sure they don't catch you then,' he finished.

'Here, eat this,' said Anna, pushing rye bread and Edam cheese into Ben's hand.

He bit into the bread, remembering how hungry he was – but there was a solid ball of tension twisting his stomach, and, despite his hunger, the food dried and gagged in his mouth. He took his refilled mug from Anna and swilled it down with tea. Even as he watched, he could see the fog slowly breaking up at the urging of this fresher, warmer wind. The sun was coming through more solidly as it burned off the top, and a thick line of black cloud was visible, rearing up to the south – the storm system that was driving the change.

'We're safe in the channel so long as we don't turn west and head for home too quickly,' said Emerton, relighting a cigarette from behind his ear, and then rapping the chart to the west of Memmert.

Ben looked – soon tide and wind would flush them through the gap between Juist and Borkum and they would be out in the North Sea and safe.

Emerton leaned out of the wheelhouse door and shouted forward, 'All done, Lucy.'

Ben watched her coil the line for the last time, and put a couple of hitches around the top to hold it together. Then she started towards the wheelhouse. Had she calmed down? Would she listen to reason? Either way, he was going to have to say something. And it was going to have to be good. Would Anna defend her story about Lerup, and back him up? Or would she take badly against him? *Bloody hell, they could lose everything ...*

Then the world rolled on its ear, as Emerton spun the wheel hard. Ben's bread, cheese and mug hit the floor as he grabbed frantically for a hold. Lucy was hurled across the deck, shrieking as she was slammed into the rail. And then he saw it, rising out of the murk, its threatening grey paint shrouded in fog. There was the simultaneous roar of powerful engines and a klaxon. Emerton kept the wheel hard to starboard until they were heading away from the patrol boat. It had just been sitting in the channel, waiting. Ben threw himself into the doorway so he could watch behind. He saw a huge boil of wash under the stern of the German boat as the propellers bit, and then everything was engulfed in the muffling blanket of fog.

'We're hidden again,' he said.

Emerton turned the wheel and they jinked ninety degrees to starboard, taking them back the way they'd come. 'Ben – you steer, I'll work the chart,' he snapped, flicking his cigarette out of the door.

He took the wheel without saying a word as Lucy appeared at the door, breathing hard.

'Lucy, you watch aft on the port side,' ordered Emerton, more coolly, glancing up at the clock above the windows and making a note. 'And Miss Venuti –'

'It's Anna,' she interrupted.

'Miss Anna, could you keep a lookout aft on the starboard side, please.'

'Just Anna,' she insisted, as the women took up their positions on opposite sides of the wheelhouse.

The fog thickened even more in front of them. The damp cloying cloud swallowed them whole, and he could no longer even see their bow. But he could still hear the diesel throb of the patrol boat. 'Where is he?' asked Ben.

'He's just crossed our track behind us, going from starboard to port,' called Lucy.

'That takes him towards Juist or Memmert,' said Emerton. 'Let's hope the bugger runs aground. Turn to starboard, please, Mr Clayton, two-four-zero degrees' he added, looking down at the chart.

Ben obeyed the instruction.

'Now we should be heading away from him on opposite courses, give or take a bit,' said Emerton, glancing up. 'Trouble is we're headed straight at Borkum.'

'This fog bank could be moving north-ish with the breeze,' Ben advised, glancing at the compass.

Emerton made a note on the chart, and then said, 'Turn to starboard, a course of three-two-zero degrees. That will still take us away from him, and might keep us in this thick fog. It's also the direction home.'

Ben did as he was told, and within seconds they hit some waves. 'That'll be his wash,' he commented.

'I can't hear his engines any more,' said Anna.

'Me neither,' agreed Lucy, as Ben throttled right back. 'I still can't hear him,' she added.

'Shall we turn ours off?' asked Ben.

Emerton nodded and hit the switch, and the engine died.

'He can't hear us with those bloody great diesels on, so

he can either listen or move, but not both,' said Ben, softly, almost to himself.

'What the bloody hell is going on,' hissed Lucy, 'why are they after you?'

'They've got some story that these two have been spying,' offered Emerton.

Ben heard Lucy draw breath, but she said nothing, and he guessed it was because of a silencing look from the Captain. Suddenly, the patrol boat's engines fired up with a hoarse booming, and they all turned to the noise.

'He thinks he's got a bearing on us,' said Emerton, turning on their engines.

'He'll expect us to carry on and head for open water,' said Ben, hand hovering over the throttle.

'So that's what we do, double-bluff him,' replied Emerton, as the fishing boat spluttered back into life.

Ben pressed the throttle down hard and glanced at the Captain. But Emerton just nodded confidently, and no one dissented. Lucy left the wheelhouse doorway for the aft deck, to keep a watch to starboard. The visibility was slowly increasing, clearing to a hundred yards on that side. And the patrol boat's engines were getting steadily louder, the deep sonic thrum rolling out of the fog from different places at different times, as the sound energy filtered through the moist air. There was no certainty other than that they were going to pass very close by. No one breathed.

'He's missed us, he's gone behind,' said Lucy, reappearing.

There was a long pause. 'I agree,' added Anna.

'All right, if he cuts his engines again we'll do the same,' said Ben, pushing pointlessly down on a throttle already at the maximum. The fishing boat churned her way towards England – cupboard doors, biscuit tins and scattered tools rattling along to the frantic rev count.

'Now,' said Lucy, 'switch off!'

Ben slammed it into neutral and a moment later the fishing boat's diesels died. They coasted onwards, silent in the threatening grey fog with its eerie omnipresence. The only sound was an occasional bigger wave reaching up to smack against the hull. And then suddenly they were in bright sunshine, the fog bank falling away astern, a ragged broken line stretching as far as the eye could see in both directions.

'Bloody hell,' he whispered, craning to look aft as they drifted inexorably away from concealment.

'If I put the engines on to go back in there he'll come this way,' murmured Emerton, beside him.

'We've rolled the dice,' said Ben, 'if he goes further into the fog to look for us, the game's ours.'

'And if he comes this way?' replied Emerton.

'We've lost,' he replied.

Emerton looked at him for a moment, and then produced a faint smile. 'Kind of gives it an extra edge when you know they want blood, don't it?' he said.

They waited in silence. The breeze had got up, and dark ripples chased towards them across the building waves. He looked to the south – the line of black cloud towered over the fast-disappearing fog. If that rain and wind arrived quickly enough, it would give them another chance to slip away. Then the patrol boat's diesels rumbled back into life, but this time there was no great roar of power, just a gentle tick over. *He's lost us,* thought Ben. The slow speed implied he didn't know which way to look. But was the engine noise getting louder or quieter?

'No point moving until we know which way to go,' he said, as Emerton leaned down to the engine switch. The Captain looked up and nodded. But was the patrol boat getting louder, or had they just increased the revs? Seconds ticked past, everyone listening. He caught a sudden fearful flicker in Anna's eye. She was right. He was coming this way.

'Back into the fog, quick!' shouted Ben. The diesels coughed and choked and finally caught. He eased the power on as quickly as he dared and spun the wheel. They turned back, racing for cover.

The patrol boat's engine note also picked up as the German commander accelerated. But again the noise seemed to be coming from everywhere and nowhere along the whole wall of fog, the distance and bearing impossible to judge. Ben was only aware of the gap between them and safety. He urged the old fishing boat on, pushing on the wheel spokes. One hundred yards, seventy-five yards, fifty yards ... And then, right in front of them, the grey prow burst out of the fog, white foam flicking down its flanks. Both helmsmen spun their wheels to the right in a seaman's reflex to avoid the collision. And for an instant he thought they'd made it. Then the patrol boat struck them on the port quarter. The combination of the hard turn and the impact threw all of them to the deck. The engine cut out and the fishing boat sat lifeless in the water, rolling to the wind and waves.

Chapter 31

Ben Clayton was the first back on his feet. The patrol boat's trajectory had barely been affected by the impact, and it was now turning a tight circle towards them. He could see the men on the deck hanging on as it heeled into the manoeuvre, the wake peeling off the quarter, the aft gun already trained on the fishing boat. It was over. Even hiding wasn't an option; the only place was down below and that was reached from a hatch in full view of the German crew. He checked the others – Emerton had pushed himself up to a sitting position and was holding on to his wrist, with Lucy crouched beside him. But Anna wasn't moving, lying just inside the starboard doorway, thrown to the floor like a broken doll.

Ben knelt down to her and put a hand on her shoulder – she didn't respond. Gently he brushed back her hair and saw blood from an ugly cut on her forehead, bruised and stark against the pale skin. He grabbed the jerrycan and poured a cup of water, splashed it on the wound, across her face – she moved groggily.

'Are you all right?' he asked. She didn't answer, slumping back with her head on her arm. He pulled out his handkerchief and dabbed at the cut with it, before drying her face and carefully pulling loose hair from the wound, tucking it behind her ear.

'What's going to happen now?' Lucy was getting a

bandage from a cupboard as she spoke.

'I don't know,' he said, 'they want me and Anna, perhaps they'll let you go with the boat ...' Then he shook his head. 'I don't know,' he repeated.

Lucy was unrolling the bandage. She hesitated and looked up at him, her mouth set angrily, but her eyes skittered across his face, frightened and hopeless. He had nothing to reassure her with.

'Have a look at the damage,' instructed Emerton. 'The boat feels sluggish.'

Ben put his handkerchief in Anna's hand and lifted it to the wound. 'Hold it there, Anna, do you understand me?' She didn't acknowledge him in any way, but the handkerchief stayed where he had put it. He pushed himself up with his hands on his knees and went outside. There were no obviously splintered timbers, but as he peered over the rail he saw a crease running all the way to the waterline and beyond. Several planks – although intact – had been started open, there were gaps between them. They were taking on water fast. He looked astern to where the patrol boat was approaching on their starboard side. Men in black uniforms were lined up along the rail beside the bridge. He ducked back into the wheelhouse. Lucy was strapping Emerton's wrist, and Anna hadn't moved.

'We're shipping water,' he told them.

Emerton wiped the back of his hand across his mouth. 'She's all I've got, lad, this boat,' he said. 'There are pumps below, the handle's starboard side amidships.'

Ben nodded and went back outside, glancing at the patrol boat – it looked as if they planned to come alongside. He turned his back to them and bent to the hatch.

'*Stay on deck, or we will open fire.*'

The metallic accented voice rang out across the water. Ben straightened, heaving open the hatch cover as he did so – the floorboards were already afloat.

'We're sinking,' he yelled; several of the uniformed figures had raised machine guns at him, as if the heavy weapon on the stern was not enough.

'Stay on deck.'

Ben stood still, wondering what to do – would they really open fire? Aboard the patrol boat, a man in a light brown overcoat stepped out of the bridge. Ben glanced at him. And then he looked again, not believing what he plainly saw – because it made no sense at all. For several seconds he thought it was just his own shocked confusion. But there could be no doubt. Ben moved back into the wheelhouse with his grip on the world shaken to a fingertip hold.

'Lerup is on the patrol boat,' he said.

'What the hell would Lerup be doing with the German navy?' replied Emerton.

'I bet she knows,' Lucy accused Anna.

But Anna didn't even seem to have registered the news.

'Ben,' continued Lucy, 'whatever she's told you – it's all lies. Those two are in this together – something awful's happening, you must understand that ...' Then there was a thud, and the deck shifted under Ben's feet as the patrol boat came alongside.

'Clayton!' Lerup was coming straight at him from the rail, soldiers climbing aboard behind him. 'This need never have happened, if you'd just done as you were told, taken the warnings and minded your own bloody business,' he yelled.

One clear thought went through Ben – *This man killed my best friend.*

'And now you've dragged Anna into this – who the hell d'you think you are? Richard bloody Hannay?' hissed Lerup in his face.

Ben's hand came up with lightning quickness and hit Lerup in the stomach. The thick clothing took the killing edge off the blow, but Lerup doubled over, hat flying off, staggering backwards across the deck towards the rail, racked by a choking wheeze of pain. Ben hesitated for a moment – he had broken his vow, all those years of careful pacifist control lay wrecked, gasping, collapsed across the railing. So be it. He went after Lerup again, arms swinging, but the second or so of hesitation was enough for the soldiers. One of them hit Ben with a shoulder charge from the side. It knocked him off balance, and before he could recover another had kicked his legs out and slammed him down to the deck. All the breath exploded out of him and he lay motionless, struggling for air. A gun barrel clattered past his teeth and jammed up against the back of his throat. It started a gag reaction and he retched, thrashed onto his side, coughing – and helpless.

By the time Ben managed to breathe, three machine guns were levelled at him. He spat and snorted, wiping mucus away with the back of his hand, the strong acid taste of vomit lingering in his mouth. Lerup was still bent over the rail, rocking, moaning – and protected by the soldiers. One of them waved his gun, indicating that Ben should get up.

A heavily accented voice added in English, 'Everyone outside, line up in front of the wheelhouse, all of you. Now.'

Ben lurched onto all fours as the boat rolled to a wave. He looked for the new voice – a big pasty-faced man dressed in a black leather raincoat and a fedora, clearly the officer in charge. But before Ben could take in any more he was dragged forward by a hand on each arm, stumbling to his feet, pulled and then pushed into place by the wheelhouse.

A sullen Lucy came round the corner next and Ben tried to catch her eye, but she didn't look up from the deck. Emerton followed her, protecting his wrist, and then Anna, supported by one of the Germans, who propped her against the wheelhouse. There were four soldiers in the black SS uniforms that Ben had first seen in Munich, lightning flashes on the lapels, all young, none of them within four inches of his height, but all armed with machine guns. They now lined up in an arc in front of him and the others. There were two more men who appeared to be sailors. One of them had disappeared to the port side astern. Ben presumed he was checking the damage from the collision. The other was organising a towline, as the patrol boat pulled ahead of the crippled fishing boat. Behind it, the sky was streaked with towering grey-black cloud, the wind already whipping the tops off the waves, swirling around the wheelhouse. The fog had gone. *We never stood a chance.*

Lerup was still creased at the waist with both arms across his stomach. He moved slowly to sit on the rail behind the SS men. He was bareheaded, face white against his oiled black hair. He pointed a finger at Ben. 'You'll pay for that.'

'Enough,' said the big man in the leather coat, stepping in front of his soldiers. 'We are only here for one thing,' he continued, turning to Ben. 'The notebook – we know you have it. We overheard you talking about it in the hotel in Munich.' He held out a black leather-gloved hand.

The notebook, thought Ben, this was nothing to do with Rosenfeld. Lerup must need the notebook. It must prove his guilt for Stanley's murder, and somehow he'd got the Germans to help him get it back.

Then the Nazi pulled a Luger from a holster inside his raincoat and held it to Anna's head. 'Herr Clayton,' he said, 'if you do not give me the notebook by the count of ten, I will kill the girl. One.'

'Wrong girl,' muttered Lerup, hunching his shoulders to light a cigarette as he spoke.

'I think this one will do; if not, we will try the other one,' replied the German. 'Two.'

A trickle of blood had run down Anna's cheek to her neck. Her head was down, her face half hidden, her hair strewn by the wind. Ben felt utter despair. If this was because of the notebook, then he was in some way responsible. He looked back to where Lerup hid behind the four soldiers. It was impossible to reach him. Ben wanted to have at least a chance.

'Three.'

'Don't be a fool, Clayton, see what you're going to do? Give us the notebook and we'll be on our way,' said Lerup, taking a quick, anxious puff on the cigarette.

'Will you let us go if I give you the notebook?' Ben asked the German officer.

'Of course they won't,' Anna spoke suddenly, her voice thick and hoarse.

Ben turned to her; she was looking at him, and her eyes were alight.

'Clayton, just give us the notebook and we'll be on our way,' repeated Lerup.

'That is correct. Four,' added the German.

Ben was still staring at Anna, trying to work out what was in her face. He didn't trust the German, never mind Lerup – how could he let them return to England with a tale like this? But there was no alternative – so, go along with them, and wait for a chance to get at Lerup. He reached inside his jacket.

'Slowly,' said the Nazi, his thick lips pursed, watching Ben, the gun still pointed at Anna.

'My wallet,' he replied, undoing the pocket button and pulling it out. He flipped it open and reached for the notebook. It wasn't there. He looked again. It had to be there, how could it have fallen out? He fumbled inside the pocket, nothing.

'Five.'

'It was here, I don't understand.' A cold sweat filmed his body.

'Most unfortunate. Six.'

Ben scrabbled inside his jacket pockets, all of them, although he knew it couldn't possibly be anywhere else.

'Seven.'

In desperation he opened the wallet and flapped it – receipts and a picture of Lucy fluttered towards the deck before being snatched up by the wind, swirled and torn away. Ben watched them go for a moment, and then jumped towards Lerup, only to come up hard against a gun barrel in his belly.

'You bastard, you killed my best friend, now her, and then what – the rest of us?' he yelled.

'Eight,' intoned the implacable voice of the German officer.

'If you weren't so damn stupid none of this would have happened,' said Lerup. 'Arbethwaite's death was an accident. I've been telling you that for weeks. If you'd believed me, none of us would even be here now – you think I want her to die?' He threw the cigarette angrily over the side, waving at Anna.

'So why in hell do you want the notebook?' Ben almost screamed it at him.

'Nine.'

'Bloody hell, no ...' Ben spun round to Anna.

'He doesn't have it,' she said. 'It's already on its way to London.'

For several seconds no one spoke. Then the boat jolted under their feet as the towline took up the slack. Ben swayed against the wheelhouse before he could get his balance. And for a moment there might have been a chance – but he was too stunned by Anna's words to notice in time. The SS men quickly recovered their feet and closed the line again, bracing themselves against the new motion.

'My God,' said Lerup, 'you ruthless bitch.'

'Let them go,' said Anna. 'They can take their chances on the boat. You can see he knows nothing' – she waved at Ben – 'and the other two know even less. No one has any proof of anything without me and the notebook. I'll go with you and your Gestapo friends – they can have their pound of flesh. I'll make sure you get the notebook from my people in London, and that you can go back to England without any trouble. But if I don't report in forty-eight hours, then MI5 will act and you'll face treason charges and be exiled forever, Lerup – so you'd better really like Germany.'

'The Gestapo thought you might be working for British Intelligence, but I ...' Lerup shook his head as if to clear it. '... couldn't believe it.'

'So – what do you say?' demanded Anna.

The Gestapo officer glanced back at Lerup – the Luger still hadn't wavered from Anna's head – and Lerup, hunched into his overcoat, shrugged. The German barked out an order in his own language and waved his men forward with the pistol. Two of the soldiers shouldered their weapons and stepped towards Anna, one of them grabbing the leather coat and starting to tear it off her shoulders. Ben watched dumbly for a moment – but when he realised their purpose was to strip-search her, he jumped forward instinctively. The gun barrel poked hard into his chest this time, and he found himself looking straight into a pair of moist red eyes set deep in puffy white flesh. He got a whiff of gun oil and leather, then a rattle of spray blasted across them, as the bow of the sinking boat, gathering momentum, pitched heavily into a wave. The soldier didn't even flinch. His eyes were locked on Ben's face, his desire clear. Ben clenched his fists tight, just one chance, he thought, one moment of inattention ...

'All right, all right,' yelled Anna, still struggling. They had torn her coat off, and one man held her arms while the other tried to grab her bare bloodied feet.

The Gestapo officer shouted another order and they dropped her onto the deck. For a moment she didn't move, as the soldiers stepped back into line. Again, Ben butted up against the weapon, the pitiless red eyes. But then, in stages, she stood, sweeping her hair clear of her face as she did so. She pulled the notebook out from under her dark blue blouse and held it up in two fingers.

'You've picked the wrong side, Lerup, you'll lose in the end,' she said, as the Gestapo officer took it from her.

'Shut up, you stupid bitch – it's your friends that are leading us down the path to extinction. If we fight another German war, we're finished; the last one ruined the country, the next will destroy it,' hissed Lerup.

'Better that than live as Nazi slaves, you treasonous

coward,' she spat back at him. 'I can't believe you thought I was with you because I *liked* you! And MI5 knows we're here – how are you going to explain four bodies?'

'Enough!' yelled the Gestapo officer, raising the Luger at Anna again.

Lerup flipped up his collar against another gust of spray, then stepped forward and held out his hand. 'May I?' he asked. The notebook was passed over. Lerup flipped through the pages quickly. 'That's what we came for,' he said, as he tossed it into the water.

And it was gone, lost behind them as the old fishing boat strained at the tow, struggling against the wind, the waves and the water that was filling her guts. The Gestapo officer rattled out another order. The two sailors stepped forward to Anna with lengths of rope and linen padding in their hands, just as it began to rain.

'Stanley's notebook ...' said Ben, turning to Anna.

'I think you would have found that it shows that Lerup was blackmailing Stanley to get him to disrupt the Supermarine fighter trials,' replied Anna. 'That's why Lerup had to destroy it. It's proof of his treason. He's working for the Nazis – why do you think they're helping him now?' she added, as the two soldiers pulled her arms behind her back.

And then it hit him – the hot flush and tremor of a world-shifting insight. 'It was you! *You* killed Stanley,' he said.

Anna jerked as the ropes pulled tight, but said nothing.

'The test flight was just after the weekend Stanley died,' he continued, '*you* killed Stanley to stop him sabotaging the test!'

'*Obviously*,' said Lerup, from behind the soldier with the remorseless stare. 'Quite apart from anything else, I didn't have a bloody clue that you needed a downhaul on the bosun's chair.'

He stared at her. The new understanding was so raw,

the new knowledge so fresh, that its impact was still rippling out, a shock wave blasting through thought and memory, razing and rebuilding in moments. He was seeing everything, *everything*, differently, but it was all explained perfectly. Spink saying that Stanley had no gambling debts – because Lerup had paid them off in exchange for Stanley sabotaging the fighter. So Stanley's sudden desire to change jobs and get away from Supermarine was to avoid Lerup's blackmail. Lerup must have had the house searched to look for the notebook. He then tried to warn Ben off with the beating – but it was because Ben was getting too close to discovering the *blackmail*, not the murder. And Anna had been aboard the *Windflower* the night before, and she had the technical knowledge of the downhaul from sailing with her father. There was even her visit to the yacht just before the accident – to check on her handiwork, or distract him?

'For God's sake, Ben,' said Anna, as the sailors stepped away and started tying up Emerton, 'don't look at me like that. I never meant to kill him, just to break an arm or a leg. You said yourself, he was unlucky. But I had to get him away from the fighter – there was no time for anything else, and no proof. I was desperate, I wasn't even sure it would work, at best I thought he might just be hurt, be off work for a while, long enough to get something solid against Lerup.'

'You monster ...' whispered Lucy.

Ben jabbed a hand against the wheelhouse to brace himself against another sudden lurch of the boat. 'He was leaving Supermarine anyway, he had a job with Dunwood,' he said, jaw muscles clenched tight enough to lock.

'I didn't know that – he'd taken Lerup's Nazi money for a treasonous act, how was I to know he might change his mind?' She was straining against the bonds. The wind plastered her hair to her face in the rain. 'God, Ben, it's people like you, bumbling along, not even bothering to vote, that allow this sort of thing to happen. Sitting on your hands while the extremists take over – and we end up with this.' She spat at the Nazi officer. 'And then you get on your moral high horse about desperate remedies, when it's the only way left to stop the world sleepwalking to oblivion.'

It was all her fault, the whole damn thing from the very beginning. Her plotting and scheming had done for Stanley, and now it was about to do for the rest of them. The anger tore through him; he couldn't reach Lerup, but no one was protecting Anna – there was nothing between them except the sailor now tying Lucy's hands. Ben dropped his shoulder and launched himself, hitting the man in the middle of the back. The sailor cannoned off Lucy and there was a shriek as Ben's momentum took him onwards into Anna; together they tumbled against the guard rail. A wave smacked into his face, running brown and almost unbroken over him as it flowed across the deck. He spat and snorted, every nerve and synapse surging at the impact of the cold water.

Then he was wrenched back by the collar of his coat. He lurched upwards and away from Anna, crashing into the wheelhouse and then crumpling to the deck. The first of the soldiers jumped on his back, another grabbed his legs. He twisted and rolled, kicking and thrashing to free himself, but even as he fought, something didn't make sense – if they were all to die, why not just shoot them both? He caught a glimpse through the struggle of Emerton being pushed down the open hatch, Anna being dragged towards it. Lucy was nowhere to be seen. Then he remembered the linen padding, and Anna's question: *How are you going to explain four bodies?* And he realised they were to drown, otherwise unharmed, the fishing boat sunk from a collision in the fog – *Terribly sorry, nasty accident, it does happen ...* There would be suspicions at home, but no evidence – the linen padding would stop any rope burns, and once cut away there'd be no sign of the restraint if the Nazis had to return the bodies to England. *And Lucy is down there already, struggling to keep herself afloat with her hands tied.*

He found new purpose. If he could get down that

hatch, he could find her, he could hold her, free her, he could tell her that he loved her. He wouldn't let her die in darkness, cold and alone. Pinned against the deck, one man was trying to subdue his legs, another struggling to sit on his chest; two more worked on an arm each, in an effort to bring them together to tie his hands. But he'd got a firm grip round a couple of the railings and they couldn't move him. He had one last big effort in him, and it had to be made soon.

He waited till the boat was rolling with him, as thunder clocked around the horizon, like some great artillery barrage. Then, with a single convulsive jerk, he let go of the rail, swung his arms at the man on his chest, pulled his legs in towards him and twisted his whole body. The speed, violence and surprise of the combination of moves yanked him free of tired, slippery, wet hands. Ben was on his knees and then his feet, stumbling across the deck. He plunged forward as the boat shuddered into a wave – straight through the hatch into space. He fell for just an instant, and then pitched into freezing water. There was a moment of silence as he drifted downwards in the dark. Then he touched the bottom, and with a roar building in his lungs, pushed himself back up. He breached the surface, yelling for Lucy – just to crash into the deck above him. He fell back, but not before he heard the clack and whine of Luger bullets chasing him down into the murk.

He dived back down and touched bottom, grabbing at a packing case – the *May*'s engine spares. The gloom faded into total darkness. The hatch had been shut. Now the storm boards would go on and they would be trapped. He pushed up from the bilge again and surfaced into a maelstrom of heaving, plunging foam and debris. Each gasp for breath was as likely to snort back water as air, the waves lurching randomly, unseen about him. He coughed and spat, and at every opportunity cried out for Lucy. Nothing. She couldn't be gone. He had to hold her one more time, to tell her he loved her. He roared, beyond words.

There was only raw emotion left and it was all regret, hate and anger – at Lerup, at Anna, but most of all at himself. He'd failed them – Lucy, Emerton, Joe Kirk, the strikers, Mrs Arbethwaite, even Stanley, everyone and everything that meant anything to him.

He yelled and thrashed, beating against the deck above and the water and anything he touched. They were all going to die down there, trapped in that chaotic black hole, and he'd let it happen. Then a voice screamed his name. *Ben Clayton, Ben Clayton – I love you, and we're not going to die. You can save us, please listen to me, I still love you, just listen to me* – the same thing, over and over. It was a siren's song, he was sure of it, there was no way out. He stopped thrashing and held his head, hands over his ears. *Stop*, he told the voice. *It's all finished, she's dead. I've lost her and everything we had, and it's all over.* Then he felt strong legs grip him round the waist. The weight immediately started to pull him under. He had to kick hard for the surface, and when he came back up there was a body pressed tightly against him, and a voice in his ear, and it was real, and it was Lucy calling his name and telling him she loved him.

'Now listen to me because we can get out of here and only you can save us.'

He heard her and he was calm, holding her tight – there was no time for the huge bubble of emotion swelling within him. He scrabbled for the ropes that bound her, kicking hard to keep them both afloat. And he told her that he loved her, that there was no one else, that he'd always loved her and that he always would. Then she was free, yelling at him, telling him the tiny scrap of knowledge that could save them. She dived away to find Emerton, and perhaps even to find Anna. And he was left alone.

Chapter 32

Ben wrestled his heavy overcoat off. He needed something like a crowbar or a tyre lever. The toolbox was fastened to the foot of the steps leading down from the hatch, but he barely knew which way was up and which way was down. So he dived and swam, just hoping to hit something he recognised. He found the hull and turned left, thinking that he would come to the bow or stern eventually and that would tell him where he was. He heard occasional human sounds in an otherwise alien bedlam of noise and random blows from waves and flotsam – Lucy, yelling for the others, perhaps a response. And then his hand landed on exactly the kind of lever he was looking for – a long, thin piece of metal. He pulled at different angles and on the third go it came away in his hands. He felt for the ends, blunt – that wouldn't work, he needed something with a thin edge for driving into wood. But there was a cord grip woven onto the other end – it must be the pump handle. Where had Emerton said it was? Starboard side amidships – so he was moving towards the bow. He laid himself flat against the hull, arms out, twisted towards where he thought the toolbox should be, took a breath and pushed off.

He got it wrong, but he hit the packing cases and knew they had to be just forward of the steps. Holding on with one hand, he swept about him with the other until he touched solid wood, just as a lack of air forced him to the surface. He banged into the steps, took a couple of snatched breaths, dived again and found the toolbox. The clasp on the lid refused to open and the tightness in his chest made him impatient, and he started to wrench at it, hopelessly, before being driven up for air. This time he climbed the ladder, clear of the maelstrom, and sucked back deep, calming breaths. It was only a latch. It was simple enough, if he didn't try to rush it. He dived again and this time it flipped open easily. The first tray contained what felt like screwdrivers and spanners, but underneath, after discarding a couple of saws and a drill, his probing fingers found the shapes he was looking for – a big chisel and a tyre lever.

He pushed off the bottom and surged upwards, straight into the clammy grasp of a tarpaulin floating loose on the surface. It smothered him, making it impossible to get a breath. In complete darkness, it felt as if someone was trying to hold him under. A flash of panic went through him and he started to struggle wildly – almost dropping the tools. Reason cut in; he stopped, let himself sink and then kicked as hard as he could until his lungs were screaming. He came up in the open, heaving back oxygen – but he was lost again. All he could do was pick a direction, roll onto his back and kick out through the chop and the rubbish. The water had risen so high that occasionally he was pushed up into the deck beams. He fended off as well as he could, hampered by the tools in his hands, holding to the faith that he was moving steadily in one direction and not round in circles.

Finally, he clattered into the hull, and this time he turned right. Every foot of progress was a battle, as each roll of the boat and the water surging around inside it threatened to suck him away from the guiding hull – or smash him into it. He started to use the chisel and tyre lever like ice picks, stabbing them at the timber for grip. That was quicker, and he had to be quick – this old boat wouldn't last much longer, soon there would be a final roll or tip and she would plunge to the bottom. Then he hit a corner whose angle and shape could only belong to the starboard quarter. He needed to be on the other side, so he turned along the stern and struggled past what had to be the rudder stock and steering gear.

When he finally made it to the port quarter, he realised that there was an occasional easing of the blackness. As the water surged around the collision damage, some light was creeping in through the cracks between the timbers. It was not enough to be useful. A bad repair and some rot Lucy had said – *three feet inboard and a foot down from the deck.* Her instructions rang in his head as he ran his hands from the corner of the stern, bracing his legs against the beams. He realised that the water level was lower here, the boat must be sitting bow down. She was trying to help them, he thought – the old girl, in her death throes, she was doing everything she could to let them go before she plunged to the bottom. There, he had it! Along a two-foot strip, the impact from the collision had broken the joint between the old wood and the new timber of the repair.

Then he felt a hand touch his hair and a chill flashed up his spine. He lurched and roared, 'Who's that?' into the darkness.

'Emerton,' came back a feeble voice.

'Hold this,' he said, shoving the tyre lever at him, impatient until Emerton's groping hands took it from him. He was so cold now that his thick shaking fingers refused to be manipulated into anything more sophisticated than a fist. But that was enough to get a working grip on the chisel. Feeling for the spot, he stabbed the blade into the wood along the broken edge, and then pushed with as much weight as he could get behind it. It went straight in up to the haft. There was no strength in the wood at all – it was completely rotten, just like Lucy had said. With another throb of adrenaline, he realised that they had a chance. He pushed at it again, further up, and it was the same, a huge split appearing and daylight creeping in. It was a sight more beautiful to him than any sunrise would ever be – dispatching the bleak confining darkness.

They could get out, but would the patrol boat be waiting for the boat to sink, so they could mark the spot and come back later to 'find' the bodies? He jumped at another hand on his shoulder. It was Lucy, but her grip was tremulous, her attempted speech incoherent. He squeezed her hand for a moment. 'We're getting out of here right now,' he yelled encouragingly, before grabbing the tyre lever from Emerton.

It was a chance they had to take, much longer in this freezing water and they would be dead anyway. He wedged the lever into the crack he had opened, into the soft wood, and heaved against the new repaired section – but the metal just dug into the rot. He tried again, further up, with the same result. Further again, and finally he had some purchase – but the repair wasn't moving, some of the wood it was bonded to was obviously good. He shifted, braced himself into the corner, feet hard against the beams, focused his whole body on that lever, that single moment – and gave it everything he had. The repair cracked and splintered around the edges, but held. He settled himself again, took a deep breath and heaved – and the whole thing popped out like a bad tooth, spilling him headlong towards the bilge. But suddenly there was fresh air, daylight, freedom. He dropped the tyre lever, splashing and crashing back to the hole.

He stuck his head out, but could see nothing – just grey walls of drifting rain. Emerton was closest and Ben grabbed him, pushing him towards the gap, through it, out into the open. Then he turned to find Lucy, and saw a shape behind her – it must be Anna, she could follow Lucy.

'Go,' he screamed at Lucy, but she hesitated, trying to tell him something through a numb mouth and juddering teeth.

Then the old fishing boat gave up on them. Perhaps it was the sudden rent in the hull, the shift and change of the air pocket destabilising whatever delicate equilibrium had been keeping her afloat. But the bow went down, the stern tipped up and suddenly they were plunged back into darkness. A great belch of air rushed for the surface as the hull filled, and Ben was underwater before he'd had time to completely fill his lungs. But he had hold of Lucy with one hand and the shattered edge of the hole with the other – he pushed her up and away. He felt her kick and she was gone.

Then there was a jarring bump as the hull hit the seabed bow first. His precious grip on the exit was broken, the boat rotating as the stern kept sinking. A second thud and he found himself upside down, jammed against a solid unyielding surface. He scrabbled frantically for the gap. The darkness pushed in on him. His lungs were burning – just seconds more and he would breathe whether he liked it or not. Then his hand hit the edge again; he gripped, pulled, felt with the other hand, got nothing but water, twisted and pushed in one move and he was clear, rising to the surface, kicking like a man possessed. It couldn't be that deep, it just couldn't ...

He hit the surface with his mouth opening a moment too early, and got a lungful of air and spume. It stung his throat hard and he heaved and spat, thrashing for oxygen – and Lucy, where was Lucy? He saw nothing but waves, humping up, towering over him, bleeding white spray, ripped and rippled by the wind, pockmarked by rain. He tried to call for her, but all he managed was a pathetic gasp and another choking mouthful of salt water. She would be swimming ashore. She would be all right; she was a stronger swimmer than he was – but which way? The storm was on them, and the wind ought to have veered towards the west, but there was still an ebb tide sweeping him past the island and out to sea. He kicked off his shoes, wrestled free of his jacket and started to swim with the wind on his right shoulder.

He wondered briefly what Lucy had tried to tell him before the boat had gone down, but then that thought and all others slipped away as consciousness was stripped back to the struggle for existence. Random memories beset him, blasts of experience that blazed with extraordinary intensity: lying in the sun in a hidden corner of the school playing field, reading *Riddle of the Sands* with a stray dog asleep in his lap; the smell of cut grass on Hamble Green the first time he had met with Lucy after their swim. And then sinking, ebbing away – it was calmer below the surface, peaceful, the memories receded, his thoughts drifted, his eyes closed, relaxing, perhaps he should take a breath now ...

Distantly, he felt himself lifted, and then an immediate, violent slam into mud or sand, he did not know and did not care, only recognising that it was just about solid and he had it in his hands, running between his fingers, even as he was sucked back out by the receding wave. And then again, another rush, a tumble forward, and this time he found a footing and pushed and staggered and stumbled and fell, and he was clear, he was safe, he was alive. He lay there, utterly spent, not believing it, feeling the rain pound him, the wind snatching at his shirt. Then he realised how hard he was shivering. It was uncontrollable. He had to move or he would die right there. And he remembered Lucy – where was Lucy? He pushed himself up onto all fours and looked around – the sand rose to a grassy scrub. And out to sea just whitecaps and rain, clouds pouring in from the west.

No sign of the patrol boat. No sign of anything but raging sea. He rubbed at his eyes, and only succeeded in grinding in more salt, leaving them red-rimmed and weeping in the wind. Any of the other three could be fifty yards from safety and going down and he wouldn't be able to see them. He looked north, blinking and squinting – but nothing interrupted the sweep of beach, where wind and receding tide had moulded the sand into long, elegant, horizontal lines. He turned to the south and pushed himself to his feet and cupped his hands around his eyes, staring into the wind. *What was that?* Someone, something, just clear of the water.

He started a stumbling, uncoordinated run, and soon he could make out blond hair. It was Lucy. He fell onto his knees beside her; the oilskin coat and jumper were gone and she was dressed in just a shirt. He reached out and shook her shoulder. She did not react to his touch, but he could feel a tremor of exhaustion and cold – still alive. He must get them into some shelter, to the other side of the dunes, out of the wind and rain.

Carefully, and with great effort, he picked her up. She responded a little, a feeble attempt to put her arms around his neck as she brought her head up for a moment, hair plastered down her face, the wet sand sticking to it. Then she fell back, her body slack in his arms.

He got them up the sand dunes – a calf-searing effort of will – then tripped and stumbled over a clump of coarse grass, pitching them down the other side. But they were out of the wind, and the worst of the rain drove over their heads. He lay flat, holding Lucy tightly to him, scraping sand over them both, and feeling her uncontrolled shuddering. But with the shelter and her body pressed against his, he could believe they were warmer. A moment later, he passed out.

Ben came to with a jolt, as though driven to wakefulness by some terrible nightmare. He pulled himself tighter against Lucy, felt her breathing, steadier now, the trembling gone. How long had he been unconscious? He peered at his watch – it said eleven, but it had stopped. The rain and wind were just as unrelenting – surely it was minutes, not hours. Tenderly, he shook Lucy, and she awoke with a shudder, startled green eyes only relaxing when she saw his face. 'We've got to check for the others, then find the rowing boat and get to Holland,' he said. As long as it had stayed afloat, it was the best chance they had of getting out of Germany. The weather would provide cover. Even if it was still out there, the patrol boat would have to stay clear of this fearsome lee shore.

She nodded, tried twice to speak and finally croaked, 'The Captain can't swim. I tried to tell you, but there was no time ...'

'Oh please ... no ...' He shut his eyes.

Lucy held Ben tight, rocking gently. 'I thought I had him. I got his collar. A lot of the fishermen can't swim. They'd rather the end was quick. I got his collar but I couldn't hold him. Just wasn't strong enough ...'

'Oh, Lucy, it's not your fault, no one could have got him ashore in *this* ...' He choked the final word into her shoulder – a single exhalation of all the fear and tension releasing, tears following, uncontrolled.

Lucy gripped him convulsively. 'Look,' she said, after a while, as their mutual tremors subsided.

He lifted his head, wiped a sodden sleeve across his face and found himself staring into the unblinking gaze of a swan that had just landed. He looked back at Lucy – mottled cheeks, words only forming with difficulty from her numb blue lips, her eyes bloodshot by the salt and the wind, rain running clean lines through the sand on her cheeks. There was so much that he wanted to say to her. 'God, I love you, Lucy, I thought I'd lost you ...'

'No! No, never ...'

'There was only ever you, there is only you ...' he whispered.

'Really?' she replied, her gaze earnest, intent on his face.

He didn't reply, just smiled at her.

Lucy pulled herself to him again. 'I'm sorry, I was just so relieved to see you, and then this anger came from nowhere ...' she replied.

'No ... it was my fault, but it's all right now,' he said.

She pushed her face into his chest and he hung on to her for a long while. Until finally there was a stirring and beat of wings, and they both watched the swan rise rapidly on the breeze, then wheel in a huge arc and head downwind.

'We'd better look on the beach,' she said.

He slackened his grip a little. 'She killed Stanley.'

'She didn't mean to, and we can't leave her here if she made it ashore,' replied Lucy.

Another shiver gripped him. He nodded. 'I know.'

They crept to the top of the sand dune, and scanned the long storm-swept beach and ocean. There was still no sign of the patrol boat. If it had stayed in the area, it was doing it in much safer, deeper water – but neither was there any sign of Anna.

'What's that?' said Lucy, pointing to the north, in the distance.

He followed her finger – a dark smudge on the sand. 'Bloody hell,' he said, starting to rise. Lucy grabbed his hand and together they stumbled down the beach, muscles now almost rigid with the cold. By the time they had struggled the first two hundred yards, it was clear that the smudge was a body. After another couple of hundred yards, Ben could make out Anna's blouse and her mass of dark hair, but he could see no movement. A minute later they were beside her. She was spreadeagled on her stomach and had vomited, her skin a ghostly pallor against the jet-black hair. Lucy felt for a heartbeat.

'I think she's still alive,' she said. She leaned closer. 'Her breathing's faint, but I think it's still there. What do we do?' She looked up at him.

'There's nothing we can do for her here,' he said. It was the only thing that he was sure of. 'She needs warmth and food, let's do what we planned and get to the rowing boat. I'll carry her.' Lucy nodded, and once again he climbed the dunes with a woman in his arms. This time, as soon as they were out of sight from the sea, they veered right and struggled south, feet too numb to feel the stab of the tough marram grass, the stones and shells that were underfoot.

Huts emerged out of the rain, elementally battered, long neglected by whoever had put them there. It just might allow them to save her, he thought, as he broke a window.

He climbed in and found a hammer to smash the padlock and clasp off the door, and then carried a still-unconscious Anna inside. He laid her on a rough bed that Lucy made from old musty clothes she found in a battered sea chest. Lucy tried to rouse her, but although she was now breathing a little more strongly, she didn't come round. More searching turned up a jerrycan of petrol and a few rusting tins of peas – the last provided both nourishment and liquid once he had taken to the tops with an old hacksaw blade. They tried again to rouse Anna to get her to drink and eat, but without success. Eventually, they dressed her and then themselves in some of the old woollen jumpers and oilskins, and then loaded up with the fuel.

After they'd left, coming almost immediately to the beacon, he realised the huts had been exactly where Childers had described the salvage operation's base in *Riddle of the Sands*. Working their way back down the beach, they found the boat had dragged its anchor towards the shore and was just starting to dig its stern into the surf. Another ten minutes and it would have been rolled or swamped and on the bottom. He reached it with difficulty, but then rowed it into the calmer waters on the other side of the point. It was still tough, but they managed to get Anna and the fuel aboard. He fired up the engine and, clearing the beacon, steered west by north-west into the rain and the storm.

Ben guided them north of the German island of Borkum, where they were forced inshore – too close inshore – for a nerve-racking fight against the first of the new flood tide. But no one paid them any attention, and eventually he turned south-east with the current and ran down the western Ems, past Rottum and into Dutch waters. Still conscious of their closeness to Germany, they decided to avoid a landfall at Eemshaven. Instead, they picked a spot to the west, creeping inshore with the tide to beach the boat. He left Lucy with Anna, and went on alone on foot, ploughing over sandbanks and fields and through dykes to reach the nearest house.

When Ben staggered up to the door, exhausted, soaking wet and covered in mud, the elderly Dutch couple who lived there quickly accepted his explanation – drawn in the dirt – of losing his yacht. They all returned in a horse-drawn cart with dry blankets and hot food and found Lucy slumped over Anna, both now unconscious. Ben found the strength to get the two women into the cart, and the old lady fussed over them as they plodded back to the house. By the time they arrived, Lucy's green eyes were open and peering out from a tiny gap between the blanket and her hat, but Anna remained dead to the world.

Chapter 33

The house was gloriously warm, filled with rough oak furniture and the detritus of fishing boats. They dragged a straw mattress onto the dirt floor beside the fire, and Ben laid Anna down. The Dutchwoman's name was Margriet; a life eked out by the North Sea had left her with snow-white hair, a map of Holland's waterways written in broken blood vessels on her cheeks and an intimate knowledge of how to tend to the half-drowned, half-frozen and terminally exhausted. She tended to Anna with hot water and dry blankets, while Lucy and Ben cleaned themselves up. Pieter, her husband, shuffled into the room with some ill-fitting but clean clothing that he had found for them. Then Lucy and Ben were left alone with Anna, the crackling fire and a pan of steaming-hot cabbage soup.

They ate and told each other their stories – he learned how, three weeks before, Lucy had watched Jim Rails scarf the botched repair into rotting wood on the stern of Captain Emerton's boat. How she had seen her father in jail, and persuaded the Captain to take her to Emden. And he told her why he hadn't arrived for dinner that Saturday night, why he'd gone to Germany so abruptly and all that had happened since. Soon enough, the conversation turned to Anna and their current predicament. 'She was trying to do the right thing for the country,' Lucy told him. 'She didn't mean to kill Stanley, and then she tried to swap herself, as a sacrifice to save us.'

He found it hard to be that understanding. Stanley had been his friend, and while there was little doubt that Stanley's weaknesses had been the source of the whole affair, Annabelle Venuti's actions had nevertheless been the cause of his death. But Lerup was still out there somewhere, and they had no case against him beyond their own account of events. It should surely be the gallows for the man, but he had friends in the very highest places. It was not over yet, this thing ...

'I think she's coming round,' said Lucy. She was knelt beside Anna with a hand on her cheek. 'I think I saw her move,' she added, and looked over her shoulder at him. 'Don't be too hard on her.' He nodded. Anna opened her eyes. They flickered around the room and then came to rest on Lucy. 'How do you feel?' asked Lucy.

'Where am I?' she replied, trying to rise.

Lucy pressed her back down. 'We found you on the beach; we're safe, but you must eat.' She offered a spoon filled with hot soup from a fresh bowl.

'I think I can do it myself,' said Anna.

After a moment's thought, Lucy helped her to sit upright and take the bowl. 'How do you feel?' asked Lucy again.

Anna paused, spoon halfway to her mouth. 'Tired, aching, hungry and the blisters on my feet are agony, but otherwise ... all right. And the Captain ...?'

Lucy shook her head. 'He can't swim.'

Anna was silent and still for several seconds before she looked directly at Lucy. 'I'm so sorry.'

Lucy just looked down, pushing at some stray cabbage with the spoon in her soup bowl.

Anna drew a deep breath. 'So where are we? How long have I been out?'

'A few hours; we're in the home of a very kind Dutch couple, fishing people, somewhere west of Eemshaven,' said Ben. Anna's big brown eyes were steady on his face. 'I told them our yacht sank. We're safe here, for now at least.'

'I feel awful about my deception,' she said, 'for drawing you into this. I know what you must think of me, but I have great regard for you both, and I am desperately sorry about what's happened to you and your friends. I'm sorry for everything that has gone on.' She leaned forward. 'But I have contacts; I can help sort this mess out. I will do everything I can to make it up to you.'

Ben met her gaze with a flinty stare. 'I hope that one day I will come to feel differently and be able to accept your apology with good grace. In the meantime, the notebook is gone and we are stuck here with no money and no papers. So I must, at least, accept your help.'

Anna didn't take her eyes from him. 'I understand. There is a lot that I can do, and much of the damage I can repair, but I can't bring back your friends. I really am truly sorry for that.'

Ben hesitated, and then glanced across at Lucy. She nodded. He turned back to Anna. 'I know,' he said.

'All right,' said Anna. 'We need to get to a telephone.'

'We have no money,' said Lucy.

Anna put down the bowl and the spoon, and reached into her mouth with her finger and thumb. Ben heard a tiny crack. And then she produced half a tooth, in gold. 'They fitted it for me, for emergencies, and I think this qualifies. Give it to our kind hosts for their hospitality, but make sure that they will also guide us into Eemshaven, and give us enough guilders to make a short phone call to England.'

A grateful Margriet and Pieter took them into town on their cart. Anna telephoned from a backstreet hotel. She spoke for less than a minute, and a couple of hours and several coffees and pastries later the three of them were squeezing into the back seat of a black MG SA Saloon. It was just past sunset by the time they started the journey home to England. After that Ben lost track in a blur of broken sleep. He awoke when they were bundled from the car onto a small tramp steamer in a silent almost-unlit harbour, whose only distinguishing feature was a prominent church tower and a strong smell of shrimp. They were given some new and better-fitting clothes. Then Ben and Lucy were shown to a plain cabin of white-painted steel walls and two bunk beds, with clean grey blankets and no sheets. They fell into them, and Ben slept properly for the first time in three days.

Matthew Faden walked west down the King's Road towards the fast-descending sun. He had now spent six and a half days watching Charles Lerup's Chelsea flat – much of it in the Old Town Hall reading Keynes – without a single appearance by Charles Lerup. Faden's commitment wasn't wavering, but he couldn't help feeling that the time could have been better spent. He checked his watch and increased his pace a little; his duties were not quite complete for the day. The night watch had taken over till the morning, or perhaps till Monday, but Leon had set up a meeting in a local safe house so they could talk. Faden fervently hoped both that he would be given the weekend off and that there would be some sort of news, something else from Leon's network that would explain what the hell was going on.

The house was on Glebe Place, and Faden was let in moments after he delivered the required knock. He had met Leon there before; the house belonged to another writer, a politically sympathetic friend of his from Cambridge – although Faden had never seen him on these visits. Leon was waiting by the outside door into the scullery, arms folded, dressed in a green grocer's smock. A cauliflower peeked out of a stiff brown paper bag on the floor at his feet. Doubtless there was a bike outside with a basket over the front wheel. Leon didn't take chances.

'Still nothing?' asked Leon, without preamble.

Faden shook his head.

'I've got some news,' he went on. 'Last night, a Jew by the name of Rosenfeld died in Dachau at the hands of the SS. He worked at M.A.N., and on the day before his arrest he met with Clayton and Venuti.'

'Christ,' breathed Faden, a hot rush of guilt boiling through him.

'He was tortured first; the Nazis must think he passed secrets to Clayton ...'

'It's my fault,' Faden blurted out.

'What's your fault?' snapped Leon, his cold gaze locking on to Faden's distraught expression.

A shudder travelled down Matt Faden's spine. He could think of nothing to say but the truth.

'What?' insisted Leon.

'I put ...' Faden hesitated.

'For god's sake, man!' Leon stepped a pace closer.

'I put sugar ... in the *May*'s fuel tanks. Fleming White told me to ... I had no idea; I couldn't see what harm it could do.'

Leon was briefly silent as the pieces of the puzzle dropped into place. When he did speak, his voice was muted with unwilling admiration. 'So White *was* responsible for Clayton going to Germany, to the M.A.N. factory. And once Clayton got there, Rosenfeld was waiting for him – doubtless with enough evidence of German rearmament to scare Clayton into talking to Dunwood, and then to provoke Dunwood into building bombers rather than mail planes.' Leon took a breath, and now his voice built. '*Bloody hell – you couldn't see what harm it could do?* It's got Rosenfeld tortured and killed – but that's just the beginning. If he told Clayton and Venuti information that will rouse the Tory dogs of war, Rosenfeld will be the first of millions, *millions ...*'

'I never ... I just ... I thought ...' stammered out Faden.

'You didn't bloody think,' yelled Leon, stepping forward and stabbing a nicotine-stained finger into Faden's chest. 'And worse, you didn't give me a chance to think. I should have known about this as soon as White gave you the instructions.' He slammed his fist onto a draining board. 'Your idiocy is going to cost your friends dear when they get back to England ...'

'No!' yelped Faden.

'How else can we stop White now?' Leon bulldozed on, his moustache quivering, spittle flying. 'We cannot allow Clayton to deliver Rosenfeld's information to Dunwood. If he decides to build warplanes, then he'll bring Sopwith and Fairey in as well –'

'No, we can talk to him,' Faden broke in. 'You said yourself that if we could prove that MI5 are trying to manipulate rearmament it would be a massive embarrassment for the government. If we go to the papers with my story and Clayton's, then together we can show everyone what they've been up to – we might even bring Baldwin down!'

'It's too risky now – whatever it is that Clayton knows would have to come out in public. Once the papers get hold of it there's no telling ...' Leon hesitated at a sudden loud clatter, hobnailed boots running across the cobbles outside. A moment later there was a thunderous banging at the door. Leon turned and opened it. Faden recognised one of the men from the betting shop. He was breathing heavily, his hands propped on his knees as he tried to get more air into his lungs. He looked up.

'Lerup's just got back to his flat ...' A pause, stricken breathing. 'About five minutes ago. But he had a tail, there's another team watching him, some look like bogeys, but a couple of them I definitely recognise from MI5. And I saw Clayton and the girl with them ...'

'Bloody hell, we're going to be too late.' Leon licked his lips. 'They'll talk to Lerup and he'll go to Dunwood.' He turned to the messenger. 'Get the Lee-Enfields from the motor and meet me at the back of the library.'

'No! Clayton's with us!' shrieked Faden.

Leon turned back to him. 'Then why is he on his way to see Lerup?'

'I don't know, maybe they're forcing him to do this, but we can talk to him, please, Leon ... *please*.'

Leon shook his head. 'We can't reach Clayton, not now he's with MI5. No. Go home, Faden, you've done enough damage already. And you'd better hope that we can fix this mess.' And with that, he strode out of the door, pulling off the grocer's smock.

Ben Clayton stood in the marbled corridor of the first floor of number 151b Sydney Street with five armed men. One of them had been on the dock in Harwich with a car and two uniformed police officers. On the road back to London he had introduced himself as Bill Derry, and explained that Lerup was expected to fly into Croydon that afternoon. They intended to deal with him at the first opportunity. After a frantic journey through London with sirens blaring and lights blazing, they had met Fleming White at the police station on the King's Road. Tall, with a patrician's voice and a mane of blond hair, White had introduced himself to Ben as Anna's contact at the Security Service.

Ben had spent a couple of minutes persuading White that both he and Anna should be there when they arrested Lerup. He had argued that their combined presence would reinforce to Lerup how hopeless his position really was – but mostly, quietly, Ben just didn't want to miss the arrest and downfall. He had then spent another five minutes persuading Lucy that she should stay at the police station. He was glad that he had also won the second argument. White and Derry – along with the three plain-clothes policemen accompanying them – had just drawn Webley and Scott pistols.

They were all pressed back against the wall, out of sight from the peephole. White waved the building's janitor forward into view, and then rapped on Lerup's pale oak door with the revolver barrel.

'Mr Lerup. Sir?' the janitor said calmly.

There was silence. White knocked a second time, and encouraged the man to try again with a wave of his hand.

'Mr Lerup?'

There were footsteps behind the door. 'What is it?' Lerup's distinctive, imperiously nasal tones were barely muffled by the door.

'Could I just have a quick word, please, sir, there've been some problems with the electricity while you've been away, it might be a fire risk, sir.'

'Oh for goodness' sake, what now ...' said Lerup, as he unlocked the door. He got no further. Derry spun off the wall and kicked it wide open. There was a single loud exclamation from Lerup. Derry piled through the door, and the three policemen followed. Ben started to move, but White held out his arm to bar the way.

'Wait, let them make sure he's not armed,' he said.

Ben listened, frustrated, to the sounds of the scuffle on the other side of the door. It didn't last long, and within a minute Derry came to fetch them.

'All right, I'll do all the talking,' said White. 'I think the sight of you two will be enough,' he added, dryly.

Derry led the way down the hall into a modern, sparsely appointed and largely monochrome drawing room. Lerup stood looking out of the window, down onto the King's Road below. He was smoking, flanked by the plain-clothes policemen. He made no move as they entered the room, but then when White cleared his throat to speak, Lerup turned.

'Now what the devil is all this about ...' started Lerup.

Even in the soft light from the two Art Deco table lamps, Ben could see the colour drain from Lerup's face. It was the moment he had been waiting for.

'Good evening, Lerup,' said White, but that was as far as he got, before there were quick, heavy footsteps on the marble of the corridor outside.

'We left the front door open,' said White. Derry started to move, the policemen were already drawing their pistols.

'Get down!' came Matt Faden's breathless voice and running footfalls from the flat's hallway. 'Get away from the windows, there's a sniper outside ...' Too astonished to react, they watched Faden burst into the room. 'For God's sake, get down!' he yelled.

Ben didn't hear the shots, just the clatter of broken glass hitting the parquet floor. He saw Faden drop, heard him scream, writhing on the rug and clutching at his chest. Ben dived towards him and got there at the same time as Anna, bullets plinking into the aluminium frame of a divan just a few feet away. There was a deafening crash of return gunfire from within the room, as White, Derry and the three policemen opened up.

'We need something to stem the bleeding,' said Anna, as she unbuttoned Faden's coat. Ben looked around; there was a red velvet smoking jacket draped over the back of a chair fifteen feet away. He crawled cautiously towards it through glass and wood splinters, gun smoke, noise and dust. He tugged the jacket off the chair and crawled back. He found Faden now unconscious; Anna had stripped his clothes back from the wound and propped him up on a couple of cushions.

'The bullet's gone straight through his shoulder,' shouted Anna over the din. She was kneeling, pressing the palms of her bloody hands into the torn flesh of the entry and exit wounds.

Ben ripped the belt and arms off the jacket, folding the latter into compact squares. 'Here,' he replied, offering them, 'these might help.'

Anna took the thick pads of cloth from him.

'Who the hell is shooting at us?' asked Ben, as she worked.

Anna shrugged. 'No idea,' she said, glancing up to take the belt.

'Lerup! He's getting away!' yelled White.

Ben looked round just as one of the police officers crashed through a coffee table onto the floor. Lerup had already covered half the distance to the door. White got off a poorly aimed shot from the Webley and Scott, but before anyone else could react, Lerup was safely into the hall.

More bullets thudded into the room in rapid succession from the sniper, and for a moment no one moved.

'You,' yelled White, pointing at the two remaining policemen, 'keep that bloody sniper's head down. Derry, you get after Lerup.' There was another volley from the police pistols and Derry took the opportunity to escape through the door. Ben looked at Anna.

'Go,' she said, 'I'll look after Matt, there's nothing more you can do here.'

Ben hesitated for a second, and then followed. She was right about Faden, and while he knew that White had got all the exits manned, he wasn't going to take any chances. There was a score to settle.

Derry was the full length of the hall ahead of him, and didn't stop at the front door to the flat, bursting out into the corridor. This time, Ben heard the shot. It was much closer, but just as unexpected. The bullet threw Derry sideways, sprawling to his left, his gun skittering on the marble. Ben pulled up hard, just inside the door. Derry wasn't moving, and a glance told Ben that the bullet had struck him in the temple. There was nothing anyone could do for the man.

Ben tried to steady his breathing. There was more gunfire from the drawing room, and police whistles from the street outside now added to the cacophony. Lerup couldn't afford to wait long. Finally, running footsteps started down the corridor. Ben gave him a couple of seconds before he ducked his head round the door jamb. Lerup was disappearing into the stairwell. Ben picked up Derry's gun and followed. On the landing he stopped to listen and was glad that he did – the footsteps were going up, not down. He knew that there was only an attic floor above them, so Lerup had three choices as far as he could see – hide, jump or take to the roof.

Lerup's footsteps stopped, a door was pushed open and then shut. Ben followed as quietly as he could on the wooden treads of the stairs. He found a single door off the landing, which must lead into the attic – or was there another exit? If not, then he had Lerup trapped, and all he had to do was call for help. But if there was another way out, then the same shout could encourage Lerup to find it, and perhaps elude White's men on the street. Ben listened at the door for several seconds, but could hear nothing. He had to make a decision. Every second that he hesitated could be giving Lerup a head start. He looked at the gun in his hand. He'd never fired one and thought it was unlikely that he could hit Lerup unless he got very close.

He put the pistol into his jacket pocket and, taking out his handkerchief, reached up to the single bulb lighting the landing and unscrewed it. Then, gently, he turned the doorknob. It moved almost soundlessly. When he had it fully rotated, he pushed the door open as hard as he could and dived through, onto the floor. The gunshot was both dazzling and deafening in the confined space. Ben didn't see where the bullet went, but he did register the muzzle flash off to his right. He could see nothing now, but it must have also blinded Lerup. He threw the bulb to the left of where the flash had been and moved. It shattered loudly, and there was another blaze of gunfire.

Ben hit Lerup with his shoulder a fraction of a second later, but the other man's body offered little resistance. Lerup tumbled off the window ledge he had been sitting on and, barely slowed by the impact, Ben was following. He threw out both arms and just caught the edge of an iron window box with his right-hand as he went past. A moment later he crashed down onto the roof tiles, all the air flying out of him in a terrified gasp. He scrabbled with his feet and got some purchase, enough to get his left-hand onto the window box with a solid grip. A quick pull-up and he rolled safely back over the windowsill and into the attic room. Still shaking with the adrenaline, he turned to look down and could see the body on the grass below, in the light from the Sydney Street lamps. A policeman was already running towards it. There was the sound of hurried footsteps on the stairs behind him.

'What happened?' asked Fleming White from the open door. A torch picked him out and Ben held up a hand to shield his eyes. 'Where's Lerup?' asked White.

'Down there,' Ben waved. 'He was trying to get out onto the roof. I didn't mean to push him, but I couldn't see anything because of the muzzle flash. I hit him with a shoulder charge and out he went.'

'Bloody hell, well done, Benjamin.'

'What about Matt and the policeman?' asked Ben.

'They're being treated. The ambulance is on its way, but I'm afraid it'll be no use to my man Derry.' A brief sigh followed. 'All right, now I want you to stay here, shut the door and do not let anyone in except me. I won't be long.' White hesitated again, the torch beam wavering on Ben's face. 'There will be a dozen journalists crawling all over a shoot-out on the King's Road before we can say D-notice. It'll be most unwelcome publicity at this stage, and we need to get you and Lucy Kirk out of here before they arrive. I'll get one of my men to take you both down to Harold Dunwood's place. I'll join you there first thing tomorrow morning to talk. In the meantime, you will say nothing to anyone.'

Ben stared into the torchlight for a moment, and then nodded. He was tired. Lerup was finished. Lucy was safe. The rest could wait.

Epilogue

Ben Clayton was just finishing his third helping of a very fine cooked breakfast when he heard a car draw up outside. He pushed his knife and fork together on the plate in front of him and went to the window to look out onto the long gravel drive of Harold Dunwood's country residence. He watched the chauffeur open the doors on a royal-blue Daimler Light Straight Eight. 'It's White,' he said, turning to Lucy. 'He's as good as his word, so far.' Lucy nodded and got to her feet to join him at the window. They heard the front door open and soon there was a sharp knock on the door of the dining room.

'Good morning,' said White, striding into the room without waiting for a response to his knock. 'Nice to see you both in such rude health, after all the excitement.' He swapped a pipe to his left hand, before he offered his right to Ben. His grip was paper dry, cold and very firm. 'Benjamin.' Grey eyes locked on to Ben's face. 'How has Mr Dunwood been treating you?'

'Very well, thank you.'

'I believe he will be joining us shortly. Lucy, you look well.'

'Thank you, Mr White,' replied Lucy.

'Is there any more news on Matthew or the policeman?' asked Ben.

'The doctors patched Matthew up last night. They

seem confident enough; he's a strong young man. But I'm afraid it looks like they will have to take the officer's arm off below the elbow. The rifle bullet smashed the bone up terribly ...' Lucy drew a quick breath and White turned to her. '... otherwise, he will be fine,' he continued.

'And Lerup?' asked Ben.

'Died of his injuries last night, without recovering consciousness – a bloody affair.'

Ben looked away, out of the window, to where the breeze was rattling rose bushes. This time, he had killed someone.

'Don't blame yourself,' White told him, 'if it wasn't for you he might well have escaped. And if we'd caught him alive he should have been taking a jump anyway, but with an HM prison rope around his neck.'

'It's not a ... comfortable feeling,' Ben replied.

'I know, I understand, but you must know that we're all very grateful for everything that you've done, a remarkable job.'

'Did you catch the gunman?' asked Lucy.

'Not yet,' replied White, 'but we think it was the leader of a communist group, and I'm pretty confident that we'll get him before he can scurry off to Russia.'

'So how on earth did Matt know about it?' asked Ben. A squirrel raced across the lawn.

'Poor misguided Matthew had got himself mixed up with some rather unpleasant people, throwing his hand in with these communists. They had somehow learned of Lerup's Nazi affiliations and intended to murder him. It seems that this was a step too far for Matthew, who stuck to his pacifist principles and decided to warn him.'

Ben exhaled noisily. He wondered how long this ache in his chest would last. He had no regrets, but he still couldn't shake this heavy feeling in his heart at what he'd had to do, the choices he'd had to make. 'So what will happen to him?' he asked, turning back to White.

'I will talk to him when he recovers, and we'll see if we

can't come to some accommodation. He's a good boy. He's my godson, you know. I'm sure he has plenty of useful information that we might exchange to overlook his misdemeanours. He's the right type and I'm confident he'll come back to us.'

The door opened, and Dunwood entered the room. 'Benjamin, my dear boy,' he said.

'It's good to see you again, sir,' he replied, shaking Dunwood's hand. 'I'm sorry we didn't get your engine parts to you on time.'

'Never mind that, you've been through the wringer, by all accounts; I'm just glad you made it home,' said Dunwood.

'Yes sir, we're very happy to be back. I don't believe you've met Lucy Kirk before.'

'I've heard all about you, young lady, and I'm very pleased to make your acquaintance,' said Dunwood, as Lucy greeted him with a wary smile and a little bow of the head. 'My wife has found you some proper clothes. Perhaps you gals can have some tea, while we chaps, er ...' Dunwood shot an encouraging look at Ben.

Ben glanced from Dunwood to White as he replied, 'Lucy should hear whatever we're going to discuss. There's not much she doesn't know about this affair.'

'Of course,' replied White.

'All right, well in that case, we'll get through the business and then May can join us,' said Dunwood. He ushered them all through to the drawing room. Ben and Lucy sat together on the sofa, with White and Dunwood taking the two armchairs opposite.

'The problem that we face,' started White, once everyone was settled, 'is that the only material evidence against Lerup was Stanley Arbethwaite's notebook, which was lost.'

'Why does that matter?' replied Ben. 'Didn't he kill your man, Derry?'

'He did, but we still need to make a solid case for his original arrest. His pro-Nazi friends will argue that the sniper confused things, and that Lerup acted in self-defence in the melee. We need to be entirely convincing about why we were there to arrest him in the first place, and to achieve that, we all need to be singing from the same song sheet. So far, we've managed to maintain a tight grip on what's gone out to the press, but it won't hold forever. Lerup has some powerful friends, and they will defend him stoutly in the absence of convincing evidence of his treason.'

'All right,' replied Ben, with a quick glance at Lucy.

'So we want you to tell the papers about your investigation into Stanley Arbethwaite's death, and your discovery of Lerup's blackmail. Perhaps you should suggest that Arbethwaite had been – heroically, with the defence of the country at heart – refusing to cooperate, and that Lerup then created the fatal accident to slow down the development of Supermarine's fighter ...'

'You want me to say that Lerup killed him?' said Ben.

'Yes,' drawled White, 'and then tried, with the help of his Nazi friends, to kill you to cover the whole thing up, leading to the tragic loss of Captain Emerton. It makes for a much simpler case, and will guarantee us the support of the man on the Clapham omnibus. Consequently, there will be little pressure for any sort of enquiry into the manner of Lerup's death. I'm sure that we can then overlook your role in that matter in the official report, avoiding any unpleasantness. And of course, your friend Stanley will come out of it looking rather better than he might otherwise.'

Ben was silent.

'But it was Anna ...' said Lucy.

'It's vital to my department,' continued White, 'that Annabelle's role in the affair, and her *involvement* with us, remain a secret. You have to understand that Annabelle did what she did for her country. It was not an easy decision, and it was never intended to lead to Arbethwaite's death. She's just as upset as you are. She was just doing her job, trying to keep the country safe.' White paused for a moment.

'She would have been here today to tell you all this, but I thought it prudent that we dealt with this situation without her.'

Ben remained quiet, looking out over White's shoulder, through the French windows and into the garden. The gale was building. So that was it, he thought, mission accomplished. Lerup was gone, no longer a threat – there were just some loose ends left, which they wanted him to tidy up. Anna was to be let off her part in Stanley's death, and allowed to return undercover. In exchange, Stanley got an honourable exit, and his own role in Lerup's demise would be swept under the carpet. But could he strike a bargain like that and watch the woman responsible for Stanley's death walk away scot-free?

'There are some other things that concern me about this business,' said Ben.

'Such as?' asked White, his voice strong over a rattle of rain on the window.

'The treatment of Lucy's father, Joe Kirk, and the other strikers; Lerup provoked them, knowing that it would deflect attention from the truth about Stanley – which Lucy's father was the first to recognise.'

'Should you agree to help us, Mr Kirk will be released without charge, and all record of the arrest expunged,' replied White. 'Lerup will be blamed for agitating the affair.'

'Benjamin,' cut in Dunwood, 'I will also reinstate all the strikers, including Lucy's father.' He glanced a little uncomfortably at her. 'I don't agree with his communist sympathies, but ...'

'He hasn't been a member of the party since my mother died,' said Lucy.

'No, well, indeed, and I've learned from Mr White here that Lerup led me down this path. I recognise now that he manipulated the strike for his own ends. I should have seen it and put a stop to it. But I didn't, and now the only way I can make amends is to set things back as they were before the strike started.'

'Even then, things aren't quite as they were,' said Ben. 'There's nothing that can be done for Stanley, but his widow is still in terrible financial trouble.'

'So this is what you're worried about, Benjamin – the debt that Mr Arbethwaite left his wife?' asked Dunwood.

'Yes,' he replied. 'I'm certain that Lerup pushed Stanley into debt in his efforts to manipulate blackmail. Now she stands to lose everything. And she's the most innocent party in all this.'

'Would it help you to see your way to helping us if I took care of those debts?' asked Dunwood, carefully.

'It would,' said Ben.

'Then consider it done,' said Dunwood, magnanimously, 'the man was in my service, after all.'

So, Dunwood wanted this deal to go through too, thought Ben. He wasn't surprised; Anna was very friendly with May Dunwood. They were powerful and wealthy protectors, which was good, because he wasn't quite finished. 'And Captain Emerton's widow?' he asked.

White and Dunwood exchanged glances, and this time it was White that said, 'Captain Emerton and the vessel were both lost in His Majesty's service, compensation will be paid in full to the widow.' White hesitated for a moment, and then added, 'So we're agreed?'

So we're agreed? He looked back at Lucy, who reached out and took his hand. She squeezed it encouragingly and smiled.

'Are we agreed?' repeated White.

'We are,' he said.

'We will expect you both to sign the Official Secrets Act,' White added. 'It will cover this entire affair.'

Ben and Lucy both nodded.

'Good,' said White. 'There's some work to do on your story, then we'll find a tame journalist, and after that I should leave the country for a couple of weeks if I were you, till the rest of the gutter-press hyenas lose interest.'

'I have a house in the South of France that you can use,' added Dunwood. 'It's beautiful at this time of year.'

'Thank you, sir.' Ben looked at Lucy. He could see that she was thinking the same thing – could they make it a honeymoon? Another thought. 'What about Spink?' he asked. 'And is there any word on Herr Rosenfeld?'

'I'm afraid that Herr Rosenfeld died in Nazi custody two days ago,' White intoned.

Ben lowered his gaze. It was as he had feared.

'I'm sorry. This is what we're up against. And we've spoken to Mr Spink; he knew that Lerup had paid Arbethwaite's debt, and he suspected there was an ulterior motive, but he says that that's all he knew. We have no reason to dispute that at this stage,' replied White, crossing his legs.

'Spink tried to frighten me off my investigation into Stanley,' said Ben.

'As well he might; there are some, shall we say, questionable aspects of Mr Spink's business that I'm sure he didn't want close scrutiny of – but he's not about to contradict our story, so long as no one is looking too closely at his affairs. And don't worry; we'll continue to keep an eye on him.'

'All right,' replied Ben, nodding.

'There's one final thing,' said White, glancing at Dunwood.

'Well, yes,' said Dunwood. 'Benjamin, you're well aware of my views on the possibility of war with Germany, so the political machinations that underlie this frightful business come as something of a shock to me. The fact that the Germans should be up to such a thing is obviously deeply concerning. And Anna had some story about U-boat engines ... but she doesn't know a piston from a spark plug, quite frankly. She said that you had the details and that they conclusively make the case for rearming.'

This was it, thought Ben, the final piece of their jigsaw falling into place. He had a sudden notion that White had somehow planned all of this – had he known of Rosenfeld's sympathies before he and Anna had even left England? He bridled, resentful at the idea of this monstrous manipulation. But even if it were true, he knew that this was still the right thing to do in the face of the German threat. He'd come too far to pull back now. Rosenfeld, Captain Emerton and Derry had all given their lives to get this information into the right hands. So he told Dunwood all the details that the former German air ace had supplied: submerged displacements, engines, their capacity and numbers.

At the end of it, Dunwood sat back in his chair, with a very grim expression. 'I can't tell you, Benjamin, how desperately sad this makes me. I really believed that Germany had some limited legitimate grievances, and that we should genuinely negotiate with them, and be prepared to compromise, until they were happy. A belief in which, I must say, Lerup was anxious to encourage me. I thought that Stalin and his Bolsheviks were more of a threat than the Nazis, but I was mistaken, and I see now that this man Hitler's ambition lies well beyond what's reasonable – we must accept that war is inevitable.' He shook his head, his ruddy complexion even more flushed than usual.

'We'll have to turn that postal plane of ours into a bomber as fast as we can go,' continued Dunwood, grimly. 'But the first thing we'll do is go and talk to Jimmy Bird at Supermarine, and you can tell him what you just told me and we'll make sure he's going full bore with that fighter. And then we must go and see Sopwith so he can get the Hurricane into production as fast as he can. We can't wait for the politicians on this one. Every month we lose could mean another twenty or thirty more planes on the aprons – as good as a whole damn squadron. If the balloon goes up in the next two or three years, it could make all the difference.'

Ben nodded. 'Yes sir.'

'Excellent, excellent – and as Lerup's treachery has

left me with no owner's representative, I was hoping you might take on the job. We'll keep you on at the factory, of course, vitally important to get on with that plane, but I'll make sure that Bartlett gives you enough time for sailing. What do you say?'

'I accept,' said Ben, but he could hardly believe it. He felt a little pressure from Lucy's hand. She was biting her lip, a suggestive cast to her gaze, and he guessed what she was thinking. He turned back to Dunwood. 'First thing, sir, I'd like you to take on Mr Kirk as the Captain – you won't find a better man for the job. And the second thing, I'd like Lucy here to join the professional crew – she's a remarkable sailor.' He heard Lucy gasp beside him, but he didn't take his eyes off Dunwood.

Dunwood returned his gaze, his face still grave – and for a moment Ben thought that he'd finally pushed for too much. But White was nodding approval, and Dunwood's expression slowly relaxed. 'My God, my boy, I do declare you'll go far,' said Dunwood, rising from the chair and offering his hand to Ben. 'Consider it done.'

Ben stood, a smile spreading across his face. He started to reach for Dunwood's hand but he never got there, as Lucy threw herself into his arms.

The End

Author's Note

Sir T.O.M. Sopwith's biography, *Pure Luck*, records that in February 1936, he sent Frank Murdoch to the M.A.N. factory in Augsburg. The German diesel manufacturer was to be responsible for the engines for Sopwith's new motor yacht, *Philante* (now the Norwegian Royal Yacht, *Norge*). While he was in Germany, Murdoch was astounded to see the extent of military production. When he reported the German preparations for war back to his boss, Sopwith called together the board of his aviation company, Hawker, and they agreed to commence production on one thousand Hurricane airframes. It was three months before there was any order forthcoming from the Air Ministry (one eventually arrived for six hundred planes in June 1936).

The planes started coming off the production line at the rate of about twenty a month, and with just six hundred Hurricanes and only three hundred Spitfires online with RAF squadrons at the start of the Battle of Britain, Sopwith's decision may well have crucially tipped the balance in the ensuing air war.

Acknowledgements

It took eight years to write this book and in that time many people provided support, encouragement, advice and information. I want to thank them all, but so much time has passed that I know this is now a very incomplete list. A special thank you to anyone who finds their name is missing.

My greatest thanks go to Anne Farmer and Frances Clarke, who both read this book more times than is healthy, and helped more than they will ever know to get it across the finish line. Mel Cain, Hilary Johnson, Georgina Hyde's book group and Tina Varkey all provided crucial advice at important moments. Richenda Todd did a great job of the editing and I have Neal Hock to thank for a scrupulous final proofread. But any remaining errors, omissions, misunderstandings (or changes to history in pursuit of the greater truth of dramatic tension) are all down to me.

And finally, I must also thank Marina Johnson for the loan of several books from the library of her late father, Peter – a well-known sailing author and editor. Those books made this one possible, just as Peter Johnson's encouragement pushed me to get my very first book into print. I have a lot to thank him for and this seems like a fine place to do it.

Mark Chisnell
Hamble, 2012

About the Author

Mark Chisnell has written three novels and nine non-fiction books. He is a former professional sportsman, and now also works as a broadcaster and journalist, writing for some of the world's leading magazines and newspapers, including Esquire and the Guardian. Mark's greatest achievement was probably hitch-hiking to Mt Everest base-camp in Tibet. In training shoes. Or maybe that was the stupidest.

Find Mark Chisnell online at:

www.markchisnell.com

Twitter: twitter.com/markchisnell

Facebook: www.facebook.com/mark.chisnell.writer

Goodreads: www.goodreads.com/markchisnell